BONE HORSES

pg. 41
July 24, 1959

camp

1.3 miles Coyote canyon

to spring

raven's nest

x#1 x#3 x#2

big red rocks

24"

3 skulls & scattered
bones 151 feet SSW
from the Arroyo Seco
sites.
    #1 appears to be
    from a newborn foal

jawbone separated from main skeleton
rib bones broken. this same bird showed up
again today. hot. afternoon rain

BONE HORSES

Lesley Poling-Kempes

A NOVEL

LA ALAMEDA PRESS :: ALBUQUERQUE

My deep felt gratitude to my friend and husband James Kempes who gracefully held me on course through years of drafts and revisions; to my children Chris and Mari who remind me every day to dream large; to my brother Charles Poling who read the novel with a professional eye and a loving heart; to my mother, Ann Reid Poling, and my father, David Poling, and their irrepressible, inexhaustible, and unconditional love and support of my creative musings since the day I was born; to Carolyn Barford whose deft hand and sumptuous imagination have once again given my story and its mythical place form and color; to my fabulous copyeditor and friend, Joyce Davidson, and her expertise and polish; to my friends and family, goddess-pals, guardian angels and hiking buddies who read early drafts of the novel: I am humbled by your optimism, good humor and unflagging enthusiasm. And a hearty salud to JB, Cirrelda and La Alameda Press, and to all indie publishers and the books you craft and birth.

Cover art & illustration: Carolyn Barford, mixed media

Library of Congress Cataloging-in-Publication Data
    Poling-Kempes, Lesley.
    Bone horses : a novel / Lesley Poling-Kempes.
       pages cm
    ISBN 978-1-888809-65-7 (alk. paper)
    1. Self-realization in women—Fiction. 2. Family secrets—Fiction.
    3. New Mexico--Fiction. I. Title.
    PS3566.O464B66 2013
    813'.54--dc23
                        2012048537

La Alameda Press
9636 Guadalupe Trail NW
Albuquerque, New Mexico 87114

www.laalamedapress.com

All of the characters and many of the towns, landmarks and geographical locations in this story are products of my imagination. The fictional story of the Coelophysis quarry near Agua Dulce is based in part on the actual and historic Coelophysis quarry discovered by Edwin H. Colbert and his crew at Ghost Ranch in 1947. I am indebted to Dr. Colbert's writings and conversations about that remarkable fossil find. Coelophysis is the New Mexico state fossil, and the Coelophysis quarry at Ghost Ranch has been a Natural Historic Site since 1976. I am also indebted to the field notes and stories given to me by Samuel Welles, a member of the U. C. Berkeley paleontological team that worked at the Canjilon Quarry near Ghost Ranch in 1934.

Know your own bone;
gnaw at it, bury it, unearth it,
and gnaw at it still . . .

T. S. ELIOT

{1}

Charlotte Lambert drove two blocks from the Santa Fe plaza to a small service station on the corner. Like everything else in the historic section of the New Mexico capital, the gas station belonged to another time. A faded and weathered hand-printed sign above the self-serve pumps instructed customers to "pay first." Charlotte turned off her car and walked to the booth.

"I'd like ten dollars on pump four," Charlotte said, sliding a ten-dollar bill through the little window. "And would you know which road goes to a town called Agua Dulce?"

"*Sí*, no roads go to Agua Dulce." The man picked up a fly swatter and held it in the air. "You can drive there, *tal vez*, but there's not much to the place. *Nada* for *turistas*."

"*Nada?*"

"Nothing." The attendant slapped the fly swatter down on the counter between them and flicked away the dead insect.

"I see. Do you have any maps?"

"I got lots of maps, but none of them shows how to get to Agua Dulce." The man pulled a map from a pile near the register and slid it across the counter to Charlotte. "It's the sort of place you get to by asking."

Charlotte returned to the red rental car parked by the gasoline island. She removed the pump and placed the nozzle into the car's gas tank. *Nada*. She was driving into the land of nothing. This is exactly what Charlotte had told Maddie Barford an hour ago: There's nothing to see, *nada* to visit, in Agua Dulce, New Mexico.

Charlotte and Maddie had come to Santa Fe from Scarsdale, New York to attend the fourth annual Conference for Private School Teachers. Today was the last day of the conference. For lunch Maddie had opted for Mexican food on the plaza with a group of PSTs from suburban Ohio. Charlotte had opted out of lunch saying she was not hungry and wanted a nap. "You're bored, Charlotte," Maddie said as they left the lecture room in the St. Francis Hotel just before noon. "I've seen it in your eyes all week."

"I'm not bored." Charlotte looked at Maddie. "Okay, I'm a little bored. Aren't you?"

"Yes. But I'm still having fun." Maddie followed Charlotte through the crowd in the hotel lobby to the foot of the staircase. "Don't take this person-ally, Char, but you've been almost no fun on this trip."

"Thanks." Charlotte turned and started up the stairs. Maddie grabbed her arm.

"Wait, Charlotte. You know I love you. But since we arrived in Santa Fe, it's like you're always preoccupied, out of the room somewhere."

"I'm just tired." Charlotte was tired. Tired of the lectures and the teach-ers, tired of Maddie's blunt and usually accurate insights. Tired of herself. "Maybe it's the altitude. We are seven thousand feet above sea level."

"Why don't you take the car somewhere this afternoon? Get out of Santa Fe and see the real New Mexico." Maddie released Charlotte's arm as she lift-ed a conspiratorial eyebrow. "You could go out to that town, you know, where your famous grandfather found those dinosaur bones way back when."

"Oh, no, it's too far," Charlotte said, stepping up the stairs. "I don't think I could find it. It's not even on maps, anymore."

"Oh, geez! Maps! Where's your sense of adventure?" Maddie sighed. "Char, aren't you just a little bit curious about that town, what was its name?"

"Agua Dulce? No, I'm not curious about Agua Dulce." Charlotte cleared her throat. "You're way off base with this one, Madeline."

"If I were this close to the place where my mother, well, died," Maddie said gently, "I'd go find it. Agua Dulce. Sweet Water. Pretty name. Maps or no maps, it's out there."

"Not necessarily," Charlotte said firmly. "Go eat, Maddie. I'll see you later."

The old pump clanged as the gasoline was metered out. Charlotte leaned into the sedan's side as she waited for her ten dollars to be dispensed. Mad-die was not way off base. In fact, Maddie had struck a major nerve and given words to the very thing that Charlotte had spent three days in New Mexico avoiding: that she was, indeed, a two-hour drive from *that* town—Agua Dulce—and the red desert where in 1959 her grandfather Albert Rose discovered the single most important fossil site of his career; the same red desert where Charlotte's mother Alicia Rose Lambert met a violent death in 1976.

"The place where your mother killed herself," Charlotte's father Leonard would say. Leonard Lambert had been dead six months now, but his opinions and theories about family events continued to ramble along at the periphery of Charlotte's thoughts. Leonard was always lightning-quick to stop and correct anyone's attempt to mitigate, dilute, diminish, or in any way modify the cold hard facts of the Lambert family tragedy: Alicia's suicide.

In June of 1959 Grandpa stayed somewhere here in Santa Fe en route to the Triassic desert badlands in northwestern New Mexico. Throughout the summer of '59 Grandpa Al and the twelve students in his Harvard field school came into Santa Fe once a month for supplies and to see a movie. Alicia was still in high school, but she had spent the summer in New Mexico, working alongside Dr. Al, as he was called, and his undergrads at the fossil site.

When Charlotte was a child, Grandpa frequently reminisced about Santa Fe, the charming Old World capital at the foot of the Sangre de Cristo Mountains. Grandpa was smitten by New Mexico, by the luminous landscape and atmosphere. In his scientific descriptions of the Coelophysis fossil quarry found on the desert near Agua Dulce the great Harvard paleontologist Albert Rose found time to wax poetic about the clarity of the sky, the quality of light. Charlotte had always wanted to see Grandpa's New Mexico, but not her mother's. And until thirty minutes ago and Maddie's blunt reminder, Charlotte had managed to keep her thoughts clear of Agua Dulce and the emotional shadowlands where twenty years ago Alicia spent her last dark hours.

Technically, both of Charlotte's parents had killed themselves: Alicia by leaping into the open, unforgiving space beyond a very high and very sheer desert cliff; Leonard by his passionate participation in a lifetime relationship with nicotine, the intensity of which would have appalled even the CEOs of the tobacco industry. Leonard's death to emphysema last January meant Charlotte was the last of the Lambert clan. There was no one else—Grandpa died in 1976, the same summer as his only child, Alicia. Grandma Ruth,

Alicia's stepmother, died six years ago in a retirement community on the west side of Boston. Leonard and Alicia each had no siblings, so Charlotte had no cousins. There were no brothers or sisters. No uncles or aunts. It was like living on the knife edge of extinction: unless Charlotte married and had children—and with the sudden dissolution of her engagement to Michael Norton, starting a family seemed like a long shot—when Charlotte died the entire Rose-Lambert species, like all those Triassic dinosaurs Grandpa spent a lifetime unearthing and reconstructing, would cease to exist.

Only Grandpa believed that Alicia's trip to New Mexico in July of 1976 had been about living, not dying. Right up to the last day of his life, Albert Rose insisted that Charlotte ignore what Leonard and Grandma Ruth said about her mother's last days. Over the telephone from his hospital bed Grandpa told Charlotte that he was *absolutely certain* Alicia went to New Mexico to embrace, not to end, her life. It was difficult to understand Grandpa—he was connected to oxygen, and his speech was slurred from the stroke—but he slowly and emphatically repeated the words into the telephone: "Alicia did not go to New Mexico to die."

Dr. Albert Rose died forty-eight hours later on August 10, 1976, four weeks to the day after Alicia. Charlotte was ten. Even before Alicia died here, Grandma Ruth disparaged all things New Mexican. When Charlotte was a child, any reference by Grandpa or Alicia to the state and its natural or cultural attributes elicited a disdainful expression from Grandma Ruth. Grandma's surly mind-set toward Agua Dulce and New Mexico was of little interest to Charlotte until that fateful summer when Charlotte was ten. After Alicia's disappearance, Grandma's relentless condemnation of everything and everyone New Mexican took on the dark, guilt-laden weight of unheeded prophecy.

Except to Grandpa. Up until the moment he died in Boston Memorial Hospital Grandpa defended the innate goodness and beauty of both Alicia and New Mexico.

Charlotte watched the numbers flip on the pump's chiming dial. It was entirely possible that Albert Rose had filled up the gas tank of his Willys Jeep at this very service station forty years ago. Grandpa was Charlotte's favorite person on earth—when he was living on the earth, and every day since he had departed. It had always been like that: they had a connection, Charlotte and her Grandpa, a bond that began before she had a name for him or him for her. Grandpa used to say that he knew who Charlotte was and how much he loved her even before she was born.

Charlotte replaced the gas pump, slid back into the car and unfolded the map over the steering wheel. According to Grandpa's publication about the Coelophysis quarry, Agua Dulce was on the high desert south of the Apache Reservation. Grandpa had shown Charlotte pictures of the canyons and rock formations—what he called the Triassic red badlands—where dinosaur fossils were frequently found. On the open map Charlotte's finger traced the highway north from Santa Fe and up the Rio Grande Valley to where the road split, straight north to Taos, or northwest to Dos Rios, New Mexico.

Most of what Charlotte knew about her mother's death she had read in the Dos Rios sheriff's report. There weren't a lot of details: the coroner concluded that Alicia R. Lambert had fallen from a 150-foot sandstone ledge and died of massive head and spinal injuries. At the time of death Alicia was dressed in her traveling clothes: shorts, a tee shirt, sandals. The Lamberts' red Volkswagen bug was parked a mile away at the very same campsite used in the 1950s by the Harvard field school. Alicia's wallet with three hundred dollars cash and a credit card was untouched in the glove compartment. There was no evidence that Alicia had built a campfire, or that she had unpacked any camping gear.

"Alicia's canvas field bag was not in the car," Grandma Ruth said when she and Leonard reviewed Alicia's suicide. "And there was not a single notebook. Alicia always had a field notebook with her. But not on that trip to New Mexico. Alicia was not prepared to do any research at the fossil quarry. And that flimsy little tent! What was she doing in the wilderness with a child's tent?!"

That flimsy child's tent belonged to Charlotte and was officially sanctioned by the Girl Scouts of America. Like her mother's body, the tent was never returned to New York. Alicia's body was cremated in Santa Fe and the ashes shipped to the Westchester Mausoleum several days later. Leonard sold the Volkswagen in Dos Rios rather than drive it back to New York. The tent and all of Alicia's belongings were donated to a Goodwill Leonard passed on his way back to the Albuquerque airport.

Charlotte folded up the map and flattened the creases with her fingernail. There was one more PST seminar this afternoon. This evening, all of the conferees would dress up in their vacation best and flock to the closing banquet. It was the same every year, whether they were in New York, Chicago, or the capital of New Mexico. The teachers would drink too much and dance and commiserate till after midnight. At breakfast tomorrow morning everyone would say good-byes through lingering hangovers. Charlotte and Maddie would catch the two-thirty flight from Albuquerque to LaGuardia, and be tucked safely back in their own beds tomorrow night.

This summer would be exactly like last summer. Only this summer Charlotte was single, having broken off her three-year engagement to Michael last December.

"You are the queen of the half commitment," Maddie told Charlotte last night before they fell asleep. "You volunteer at the animal shelter every other week, but you don't ever adopt a dog. You saddle soap that expensive English saddle you keep in your garage but don't take it anywhere near a horse. And you get engaged to wonderful men, but you never marry them."

Maddie claimed that Charlotte's cancellation of the wedding had nothing to do with her father's death, and everything to do with Charlotte's fear of love till death or worse do part and her distrust of everything that came with long-term intimacy, including the possibility of a less than happy ending.

"Listen, Char," Maddie said last night, pointing to the magazine she was reading, "this article is about you! No, really, wait, listen: you've had two engagements in six years, which makes you a player. You've jumped back in, even after failure. That's good. But according to this relationship expert, the odds are against a thirty-two-year-old woman having more than one additional opportunity for a marriage-bound relationship in the next five years."

Maddie read on in silence and then said, "You're not even promiscuous—that would raise your odds. Thirty-two years old, a schoolteacher in a suburban middle class community. Oh, Char, your numbers are not good." Maddie glared at Charlotte over her magazine. "You know, Michael was a good man. What are you waiting for, Prince freaking Charming?"

Charlotte was not waiting for Prince Charming. She just could not commit to Michael when she could not commit to herself.

The highway north out of Santa Fe climbed through the foothills of the Sangre de Cristos. Beautiful, luminous country. Charlotte began to relax. She could commit to this excursion. She could do this for Grandpa. She might not ever get to New Mexico again. It wasn't a monumental undertaking: just a few hours, a quick drive out into the countryside, a belated homage to Albert Rose and his scientific legacy on the New Mexican desert. Even if Charlotte never actually found the place once called Agua Dulce, or the fossil quarry that made Albert Rose famous, at least she would know she had tried.

Charlotte sighed and gripped the steering wheel. It didn't matter if Agua Dulce existed or not: Charlotte didn't need to find Agua Dulce. Charlotte just needed to prove to herself that she could navigate her own good path through life unfettered by the ghosts of the past.

{2}

Dorothea Durham stopped on the sidewalk midway between the hardware store and the corner and leaned into her cane. Thea was shaky and a bit tuckered out. She hadn't driven the Hudson from the ranch into Agua Dulce in years. Main Street was blazing hot this morning. It was June twentieth, nineteen-hundred-ninety something or another. Tomorrow was the first day of summer.

The traffic coming and going, stopping and starting, at the traffic light at Dos Hermanos and Main gave Thea something to measure the moments by. Thea didn't care about the exact hour of the day anymore, and she hadn't given much thought to the passing of years since she turned seventy-nine some uncounted number of them ago. But when her eyesight had begun to diminish, Thea's sense of time had become linked to a keen observation of the day-to-day nuances of the seasons. The here and now of the earth was the only sort of time-keeping Thea kept these days. She figured at her age, whatever it was, adhering to any sense of time was some kind of miracle.

Thea was just beginning to wonder how she would negotiate the street crossing when a long slender arm slid around her waist. "Nana Thea, don't you look like summer itself this fine morning!" Thea gazed up at the tall, lean form of her grandson, Jed Morley. "Walking to the post office?"

Thea held up Francis's envelopes and smiled. "I am, Jedidiah."

"Did you come in from the ranch with Francis?" Jed led Thea carefully off the curb and across the street. "Or did Uncle Barty drive you?"

Thea let Jed lead her to the far side of the street. "I thought you were spending the morning out at the drip tank."

"Just got back." Jed guided Thea up the curb and onto the sidewalk again. "Britches and I are headed out to the High Lonesome to meet Arthur. We've got to remove the old beam over the kitchen door. It rotted through where the tin roof pulled away."

Thea surveyed the shadows and forms in front of the post office. It was getting on to high noon, and the bright light made her eyes water, turning everything to yellow smudges. "Where *is* Britches?" Thea gestured at the street near them. Jed often left his horse tied to one of the meters.

"He's across the street by the drugstore. Near Gus."

Thea lifted her eyes and gazed to the far side of Main Street. Although she could not see the sorrel gelding, Leather Britches, Thea sensed the horse's large form at the bottom of the drugstore steps. Gus Treadle and the benched posse of Agua Dulce's retired lawmen would be seated in the shade of the drugstore's awning. When their official duties at the Dos Rios sheriff's office ended a decade ago, Gus and the boys had become Agua Dulce's unofficial greeters. The four met after breakfast each morning, and they kept abreast of the comings and goings of the Lágrimas Valley and environs from their bench at the entrance to the Mata Drugstore and Soda Fountain.

"Did Bartholomew bring you the bread I baked yesterday?"

"He did." Jed and Thea walked into the Agua Dulce Post Office. "If I can just keep the ravens away, your bread will keep me going for another day or so!"

Thea looked up at Jed's face. "Are you keeping a stone on the cooler lid?"

"I'm keeping three large stones on the lid. The ravens aren't getting into my food anymore, but they continue to go through everything else in my camp!"

"They're just looking out for you." Thea walked to the first wall of mailboxes, pulled her mailbox key from her purse and handed it to Jed. Jed opened the little door to box twenty-six and pulled out the mail stuffed into the narrow chute.

"You've got new catalogues and a few bills," Jed said as he closed the box door and walked over to his own mailbox. "Nana, who drove you in today and where are you meeting them?"

Thea dropped Francis's letters into the outgoing mail slot. "Well, actually, I drove myself into town today. Did you get mail? From your mother?"

"You drove the Hudson?" Jed turned to her, shocked. "What? Yes, I have a letter. No, it's not from my mother. You drove yourself to town? Does Francis know?"

"Francis knows." The bell on the post office door announced Francis's entry.

"Thea! Oh my!" Francis was a bit out of breath. "Jed, the Hudson is out back in the alley. Could you move it over behind the store?"

"Jed can just drive me home, Francis," Thea said.

"Can you drive the Hudson?" Francis was still breathing hard. He was in good shape for a man approaching eighty, but the arthritis in his knees made driving a vehicle, riding a horse, or jogging half a block a painful ordeal.

"Yes," Jed said after a small but perceptible beat. "Would you call Arthur and tell him I'll be an hour late? And tell Gus I'll be back for Britches in about half an hour."

"Okay." Francis turned to Thea. "I don't know what possessed you to drive yourself into town. I'm thankful no one was hurt. And all this nonsense about cremation." Francis glanced at Jed and then looked back to Thea. "A coffee tin for ashes?"

"I'm not possessed, and I'm too old to get hurt." Thea reached for Jed's arm. She was weary of explanations and questions, and everyone's worry and fuss about a whole lot of nothing. "I'll see you at home, Francis Durham. Let's go, Jed, I've got things to do."

〰〰〰〰〰〰〰〰〰〰

"Damn! I thought reverse was the grumpy gear!" Jed released the clutch and the truck leapt forward in the narrow alley. "How in blazes do you manage this old truck?!"

Thea hid her smile under the white hanky she used to wipe the perspiration from her upper lip. The truck reached the end of the alley, and after Jed coerced the truck's fifty-year-old transmission into second, drove up Dos Hermanos to the corner of Main. Mercifully, the streetlight was green and Jed cruised into a left turn without having to downshift. He successfully negotiated the third and final gear as the Hudson passed the drugstore where Britches stood tied to the hitching post near Francis and old Gus. Jed smiled and waved, knowing full well that Francis and all of Gus's posse knew it had been a few years—ten, to be exact—since Jedidiah Morley had driven the

20

Durhams' museum-quality Hudson. And all of them, deaf and not, could hear how Jed was doing a fair to poor job behind the wheel.

"Okay, so, Nana? You just got up this morning and decided to drive yourself into town?"

"Francis is very perplexed just now," Thea said, ignoring Jed's question. "I should have told him about wanting to be cremated instead of buried."

"What about the family plot in the cemetery?" Jed asked. "Why this sudden thing for cremation?"

Thea did not answer for a moment. Then, "Albert Rose. I had the nicest conversation with that great man Albert Rose."

"Dr. Rose, the paleontologist from back east?" Jed braked for a stray dog and cursed under his breath as he wrestled the clutch again. "He hasn't been to Agua Dulce in, what, almost half a century? I thought he was deceased."

Thea leaned over and placed her bony hand on Jed's forearm. "Last night I had the nicest dream about Albert Rose and his daughter, Alicia. I hadn't thought about Dr. Al for decades. But there he was with his students, smiling, dressed in his khakis and that wide-brimmed straw hat with the leather band. Dr. Al was sitting on a Thomas J. Webb Coffee tin. That tin was set down right in the ashes of the firepit out at the old field school campsite. Dr. Al tapped the tin with his pencil and said, 'Dorothea, you must find one of these.'"

"A very nice dream, but what does that have to do with—"

"I wanted to ask Dr. Al why he had returned to the Lágrimas after so many years, and from the dead, no less." Nana's eyes squinted at the horizon. "But then Dr. Al began talking to his students about the bones, about how their efforts to unearth the buried would bring to the light of day important clues about life long forgotten. Dr. Al's beautiful daughter Alicia was not with them. I asked Dr. Al where Alicia was and if they shared the same piece of heaven. But just then, just like that—" Thea snapped her bony fingers in the air between them "—I blinked and here I was again back down in old age."

Jed sighed. "A good dream, Nana."

"You must take care of Francis after I'm gone, Jedidiah." Thea's voice was fading with fatigue. "He will need to find a way to spend his last years without me."

"Of course I'll help him. We all will."

"And you must help me find one of those Webb coffee tins with the tight-fitting lid." Thea was looking Jed's direction again. "You and your Uncle Barty must go up into the barn and pull down the canvas tarps."

"The tarps? The ones we used to use for trail rides?"

"The very ones." Thea sat back, satisfied that Jed understood.

Jed drove past Old Skeeter McGee's retread tire shop. A sign said 'Open' but the place looked deserted. "Have you told Barty about all of this?" Jed figured his uncle could make better sense of Nana's dreams and plans than he could.

"I have. We spoke in the store this morning."

The Hudson reached the end of town. Jed held the old truck at what he guessed was about forty-five miles per hour—the speedometer had never worked, not in Jed's lifetime—because this last stretch of County Road 155 was hardly used and in terrible shape. People came out here for events at the baseball field near the abandoned schoolhouse, and to visit the War Memorial, which was a massive stone pile near the Lágrimas Valley Cemetery. North of the fenced cemetery were the crumbling walls of the old church. A new church had replaced the adobe chapel decades ago. Nowadays, the county road really just served the Durham Ranch that marked the end of civilization.

The open sand land rose like an ocean around the road. From here everything man made, owned, or claimed dissolved into a vast expanse of light and sky. The canyonlands rose into view, flat brown and featureless under the noon sun. Cutting into the sky to the south and west was the blue spine of the Agustina Mountains. Jed removed his Stetson, leaned his head out the open window, and let the dry June air blast his face.

"You feeling like you're going to have a fit?" Thea's hand reached across to Jed's arm.

"No, no, I'm fine," Jed lied. The old truck ran pretty clean, considering its age, and didn't burn oil or give off excessive engine fumes. But years of errand running for the hardware store had left a veil of industrial perfume in the seat fabric. Jed sensed the toxins the moment he slid behind the wheel. The open windows and moving air couldn't completely dilute the poison.

Before they even reached the cemetery, Jed's throat had begun to tighten, and his upper lip tingled, the first symptoms of an allergic reaction that could fade away as soon as he got out of the truck, or turn deadly serious if he did not. Jed pushed down on the accelerator.

"We're almost there." Jed pulled his head back into the cab. "Just another mile."

Without braking Jed steered the Hudson through the Durham gate onto the dirt road that headed west across the mesa to the ranch. Jed stuck his head back out the window and took gulping breaths of the hot dry air.

"Stop here, Jedidiah." Thea's fingers dug into his arm as the Hudson came to a skidding stop. Jed opened the door, slid from the seat and walked quickly into the sage by the road. His ears were ringing. The nearest epi-kit was in the saddlebag on Britches back in town. Thea kept an arsenal of the prepackaged epinephrine shots in her pantry, but there were two miles between Jed and those syringes.

Jed sat down on the sand beneath a juniper tree, removed his Stetson and placed his head between his knees. A few minutes later, Thea joined Jed on the warm ground and pressed a small bottle into his hand. Jed opened the bottle and sipped the familiar, bitter tincture of *raiz de indio*, skull cap and other roots made by Nana just for him.

"I've got one of your fancy shots, too." Thea lifted her left hand: in her palm was an unopened epi-kit. "I keep one in the Hudson's glove box."

Of course. Jed should have known that she was always looking out for him. "Thanks, Nana. I'll be okay now." Jed forced a smile.

"It's your grandmother, Conchata, you can thank. She won't let me leave the house without one of these newfangled gadgets."

Jed laughed and wiped the sweat from his upper lip. "But Conchata lets you leave the house and drive alone to town?"

Thea laughed and gently nudged Jed with her sharp elbow. Jed closed his eyes and listened to the cicadas that buzzed in the sage and saltbush surrounding the juniper tree. "How *did* you manage to drive into town?"

"Memory." Thea tapped her head with her index finger. "I looked into my memory and saw exactly where I was going."

"I'd like to develop that skill," Jed said.

"You're young yet, Jedidiah."

"I don't feel young." Jed pulled at a slender blade of gamma grass. "Every time I think I'm doing better, feeling stronger, moving away from the Great Collapse, I end up like this. Just a simple drive in an old truck, a few miles, and I'm toppled, shaking like a fool on the side of the road. Jesus, Nana, I'm twenty-eight going on seventy-eight."

"You've got lots of living to do yet. You're going to be a stronger man for all of this."

Jed rubbed his throbbing head. The skin on his wrists was tingling with what could still become itchy hives, but his throat had calmed down and his upper lip wasn't swelling. "I just want to be the man I was before I got sick."

At twenty-eight Jed should have been enjoying the prime of his life. Instead, he was living alone at an old cow camp on the southernmost boundary of the High Lonesome because his body could not tolerate the industrial-strength atmosphere of urban America. When Jed collapsed at a construction site last October, his friends and family thought he'd be back to his vigorous, over-achieving self in a few weeks. Instead, Jed got worse. Even after weeks of bed rest supervised by his mother, Bernadette, an experienced ICU nurse at Phoenix Presbyterian, Jed's system continued to deteriorate. When a specialist finally gave Jed's condition a dubious name with an irritatingly vague diagnosis—EIS, environmental illness syndrome—a desperate Bernadette called her brother Barty and asked if he could come and take Jed home to Agua Dulce.

Dennis Mata and Uncle Barty drove all night through a November snowstorm to bring Jed back to New Mexico. Jed moved in with the Durhams where everyone assumed that a month of Thea's homegrown food bolstered by Conchata's medicinal concoctions would cleanse Jed of the toxins that had infected his system. But by mid-February, it was sadly obvious that his immune system was going to require an indefinite stay in an environment completely untainted by modern America. Even the Durham's adobe house in the middle of nowhere contained potentially offensive products and objects. Thea and Francis removed everything and anything that might topple Jed's compromised system—store-bought detergents and cleaners, rags, rugs and pillows, kerosene lamps, scented candles. Jed never went near Uncle

Barty's house behind the service station and for months avoided downtown Agua Dulce. But even with so many precautions Jed was brought to his knees several times a week by breathing fits and giant hives.

On a sunny bright day in late February Jed had left the Durhams' house and moved out to the stone cow camp built by his grandfather. Dennis and Uncle Barty helped Jed erect a large canvas expedition tent. They designed a lean-to of logs to shelter his outdoor kitchen, and built a stone and canvas privy in a grove of juniper trees. The old corral and tack shed were mended and Leather Britches moved with Jed to the cow camp. Thus began Jed's new out-of-doors life on the red sand plateau one hundred feet above the Lágrimas River. After more than four months at the camp, Jed was feeling a bit better, although his immune system's balance was still volatile and unpredictable.

"I know it didn't go well in May with Beverly," Thea said after a long silence.

Jed looked out at the desert flattened by the noon sun. "I knew she wouldn't like it here. If I were living in Santa Fe, well, she'd like that. For a while. But Beverly McKibben isn't going to leave metropolitan Phoenix for a tent in the Lágrimas." Jed placed his hat back on his head. "I shouldn't have let her come to Agua Dulce. The strange sickness is bad enough, but having her see me here, living like an indigent cowboy, well . . . "

Jed reached into his rear pocket and pulled out the unopened letter. "Unless I get better and back to my life in Scottsdale, there just isn't enough love in the world to make Beverly feel comfortable in Agua Dulce. Ever. End of story."

Thea patted Jed's knee. "Well, time will tell about all that. Now, shall I drive us home?"

Jed eyed Thea. "All right. You drive. Slowly."

Thea's ability to drive had more to do with science and the path of least resistance than with the gifts of metaphysical sight. The deep ruts made in the mud of the ranch road during the spring rains functioned like inverted railroad ties that locked around the Hudson's tires and held it securely on the road. There was almost no steering involved.

The truck rolled to a gradual stop ten yards from the barn.

"I'll need to call for a ride back into town." Jed jumped out and helped Thea slide from the driver's seat.

"I suspect Francis will send someone out for you." Thea took Jed's arm and they walked up the porch steps. "Make yourself lunch, Jed. I think I'll take a little nap."

A white pickup truck roared into the yard and pulled up to a stop beside the Hudson.

"Yup, Francis sent Uncle Barty," Jed said.

Barty climbed from the cab and marched quickly across the dusty yard to the house. Little Bit, Thea's fourteen-year-old terrier, and the white rooster called George scurried across the sand. Barty waved his arms and shooed them out of his way.

"Everyone okay?" Barty reached Jed on the porch. Thea went on into the house.

"She's pretty tired," Jed said quietly. "But everyone's okay."

"What the hell is going on with Nana?" Barty asked in a hushed voice.

Jed opened the screen door and went into the house. Barty followed and poured himself a cup of cold coffee from the pot on the counter. "What was she thinking, driving to town?"

Jed shrugged. "Feeling frisky, I guess."

"I found her looking around the back of the store for those old coffee tins." Barty glanced down the hallway at Thea's bedroom door. "For her ashes."

"Yeah, so she said." Jed let Little Bit into the kitchen. George clucked about on the porch pecking at specks of dirt on the floorboards.

"Did she tell you it was because of some dream she had about that Harvard fossil hunter?" Barty studied the last gulp of coffee in the bottom of his cup. "And that she wants us to go up in the High Lonesome barn, pull down the old canvas tarps and the panniers that belonged to my father, and make sure everything is in good order? I haven't looked at that stuff in a decade! Why? Is she planning a camping trip to the mountains?"

Barty drained the coffee mug, rinsed it with tap water and set it in the sink. "You coming to town with me? You can sit in the back."

"Yeah, I left Britches out front of the drugstore."

"I saw him." Barty walked out of the kitchen and down the hall where he nearly collided with Thea as she emerged from her bedroom with a basket over her arm. "Nana, don't take this wrong, I'm glad you're home all right, no one was hurt, but I'd rather you call me for a ride into town instead of driving yourself, okay? Francis was just beside himself. You've got to think about him."

"I am thinking about him." Thea's cane tapped Barty's knee as she passed him in the narrow hall.

"And about those coffee tins you're wanting?" Barty followed Thea back into the kitchen. "There might still be one or two in the barn, in the storage closet off the old office."

Thea stopped in the middle of the kitchen. Little Bit sat down on the floor by her feet. Jed noticed Thea had changed into her garden boots.

"I thought you were going to nap," Jed said.

"Naps are for people with lots of time on their hands." Thea turned back to Barty. "Yes, those coffee containers are in the barn. Conchata says there are at least three under the shelf where you keep the paint thinner."

Thea opened the drawer at the end of the counter, pulled out cotton garden gloves and dropped them in the empty basket. "Barty, I'm a bit peeved with your mother just now. Conchata could have shared this piece of information earlier this morning and saved me that trip into town."

Thea turned and smiled at Jed. "But then I would have missed our little talk. And I so enjoyed our drive home together." Thea reached up and gently touched Jed's cheek. "Are you feeling better?"

"I'm fine." Jed looked at his uncle, who was frowning. "It wasn't anything much, just the old truck's fumes. Francis says they give him a headache, too."

"Where are the burros?" Barty stepped out onto the porch and surveyed the yard and the empty corral beyond. Jed followed. "How long they been missing?"

"They aren't missing, they're just out wandering." Thea stood between Jed and Barty.

"How long have the burros been *wandering*?" Barty asked.

"I don't know, since yesterday maybe."

Barty sighed and shook his head with disapproval. "They get into trouble. They're like teenagers. They need boundaries, a firm fence line."

"Teenagers need boundaries, but they don't need fences, Bartholomew."

Barty rubbed his eyes and then put on sunglasses. "If the burros aren't back by tonight, Jed and I will go out looking for them."

Thea grabbed the porch railing and slowly descended the stairs.

"How'd they get out this time?" Barty was studying the corral gate.

"Like they always get out," Thea said, exasperated. "Someone opened the gate."

Jed and Barty exchanged looks.

"And no, it wasn't me!" Thea walked around the side of the house toward the garden. "For heaven's sake, boys, I'm not strong enough to unlock that old latch. Conchata opened it."

Barty skipped down the stairs clearly frustrated and caught up to Thea. "I know that somehow you and my dead mother have been talking and laughing and gossiping since I was a boy. And I understand how angels and ghosts and long-ago friends *might* visit us in dreams from time to time. But they cannot, do not, unlock corral gates."

Thea's cloudy eyes gazed in Jed's direction. "Jed, didn't you say you saw the ravens open the latch of the army cooler out at the cow camp?"

Jed shrugged and smiled at his uncle. "I did."

"Exactly. Now get along, both of you." Thea followed the top of the wood fence with her hand until she found the low gate into the garden. "I have things to do."

{3}

It was three o'clock when Charlotte reached the junction for County Road 155. Driving from Santa Fe to Dos Rios had taken longer than Charlotte had anticipated, but she still had more than three hours before the banquet began. Plenty of time. She took a deep breath and turned the red sedan onto the narrow road south to Agua Dulce.

The green trees that marked the path of the Lágrimas River vanished to the east within a few miles of the junction. The vast desert was inhabited by scrawny cows that seemed rooted to the hard ground around stock tanks, and, every few miles, clusters of abandoned adobe houses. Charlotte passed several pickup trucks heading into Dos Rios, and one sedan came up quickly behind her, passed immediately, and disappeared into the distance. There were people out here, but Charlotte's sense of isolation escalated with each mile.

Charlotte considered turning back. But then she remembered Grandpa's stories about the fossil site, how of all the dozens of amazing places his work had taken him, the Coelophysis site near Agua Dulce was the place Grandpa thought about the most.

Forty miles south of Dos Rios, the highway angled around a large wedge of rocky outcroppings at the base of a red mesa and then straightened out due east. The road dropped down to the valley floor, and the river emerged, a glistening ribbon edged by bright green fields and clusters of trees. Beneath a canopy of mature cottonwoods was the B & B Service Station. Charlotte glanced at her gas gauge: three-quarters of a tank. Charlotte supposed that in the New Mexican outback it was just plain prudent to fill up whenever a gas station appeared in the heart of nowhere.

There was nothing indicative of Mobil affiliation, except a splendid winged horse—the iconic red Pegasus—sailing above the gasoline island. Charlotte pulled in and parked the car alongside two antique gas pumps—

bottle shaped with glass tops that made those near the Santa Fe plaza look downright modern.

The station's garage doors were wide open. A tractor was squeezed into the first stall, and a red Ford Mustang, circa 1967, was parked in the second. The wood fence between the station and the road was decorated with vintage metal signs and advertisements offering tire repair, oil change, carburetor flushing, Coca-Cola and cubed ice. The yard beside the station was filled with more antique gasoline pumps of all shapes and sizes. These pumps were no longer functional but were clustered together like a dated industrial sculpture garden along the side of the building.

Charlotte left the car and walked quickly across the hot gravel to the station, hoping to save some elderly attendant a trip out into the scalding sun. The office was empty. Charlotte removed her sunglasses and let her eyes adjust to the dim light. A cash register balanced on a narrow, metal counter. A small refrigerator hummed loudly against the rear wall. A calendar tacked to the fridge advertised the Mata Drug and Soda Fountain, "Home of the thickest malts in the Lágrimas."

A dropped tool clanged to the floor of the repair shop.

"Hello!" Charlotte called out. "Hello?"

Charlotte leaned into the open door to the repair shop. The garage was crowded with tools and vehicle parts, hoses, clamps, drums of oil, and plastic bottles of lubricating fluid. Chains and hooks hung from the ceiling. Charlotte dropped her eyes and located a man's legs clothed in grey overalls sticking out from under the tractor.

"Excuse me," she said loudly.

The legs slid out from under the tractor on a wheeled cart.

"I just wanted to buy a little gasoline," Charlotte said. "Do I pay first?"

"Well, no, you don't have to pay first." The mechanic stood up and walked over to the counter and wiped his hands on a rag. "I'll be right out."

Charlotte walked into the blazing sunshine. The mechanic followed. "How many gallons did you want?" he asked as he went ahead to the gasoline island.

"I don't need all that much. I just wasn't sure where the next gas station was."

He unhooked the pump. "Better to be safe than sorry. I'll just top it up."

He placed the nozzle into the sedan's gas tank and turned on the pump. He had chiseled cheekbones and broad shoulders, dark skin and shiny black hair. He was probably in his mid-fifties and, although stocky with middle-age, moved with a natural athleticism.

It took all of thirty seconds to top up the sedan's tank. Charlotte smiled apologetically. "I shouldn't have bothered you."

"No problem." The attendant looked over at Charlotte standing at the front end of the car. As his eyes focused on her for the first time, he startled and looked away, fumbling with the gas nozzle. Uncomfortable, Charlotte put on her sunglasses, opened the car door and dug about her purse for her wallet. When she reemerged from the car he was watching her. Charlotte handed him a ten-dollar bill.

"It took a dollar fifty," he said flatly. "I'll get your change."

The attendant walked back into the building. Charlotte followed. Inside the office, he opened the cash register and dug into the drawer for bills.

"I'm about out of ones. You'll have to take six quarters." He poured the quarters into her open palm and then handed her one five and two one-dollar bills. "Sorry."

"It's no problem, thank you. I'm sorry to have bothered you for so little gas." Charlotte stuffed the change into her pocket and exited the office.

"Miss, excuse me."

Charlotte stopped under the flying Pegasus and turned around. The attendent was in the shadow of the station doorway.

"If you don't mind my asking, what brought you to Agua Dulce?"

"Is this Agua Dulce?"

"A few miles up the road is downtown." His voice was almost friendly again.

Charlotte looked up at the winged horse on fire in the bright sun. "I heard that Agua Dulce was a real scenic place. I had a few hours, I wanted to see if it was real, was really, well, like everyone said it was: real scenic."

He stepped out of the doorway and into the sun. He nodded, but he knew she was lying.

"You want to drive to the far side of town," he said. "Out into the canyon country. About two or three miles out, that's the place you're looking for."

Charlotte stared at him. How could he know the place she was looking for?

"The painted sand lands, the stone spires, what they call the picture-postcard country. That's what most folks come looking for."

"Thanks." Charlotte climbed into the car, started the engine and steered the car back onto the two-laner. If her stricken face hadn't betrayed her extreme discomfort, her inability to speak complete sentences certainly had. *Real scenic. Like everyone said it was.* God! Charlotte's first-year composition students had a better command of the English language!

Charlotte looked in the rearview mirror: he watched her from under the flying horse, his dark eyes aimed like arrows at the back of the rented red sedan. *The picture-postcard country: what most folks come looking for.* He knew she wasn't most folks.

The road curved out of view of the station. Charlotte took a long breath to slow down her heart. It wasn't her fault. Even if that man did recognize some resemblance, even if he had known her mother, it wasn't Charlotte's fault.

At Leonard's funeral last winter, old friends of the family who had known Alicia told Charlotte that it was uncanny how much she resembled her mother. Uncanny. They said Charlotte was just as beautiful as Alicia was before that last winter, before Alicia's thick, brown, curly hair fell out during the chemo, before Alicia dropped twenty pounds and lost her curvaceous, Ruben-esque figure to the ravages of a bacterial infection that settled into her blood after the hysterectomy.

Charlotte took another deep breath and turned the air conditioner on high. Two miles beyond the B & B Service Station the two-lane highway became Main Street. A little sign welcomed visitors in Spanish and English to Agua Dulce, New Mexico, established in 1875. Population 4,244. Elevation 6,700 feet above sea level. Adobe houses in varying levels of renovation and disrepair lined the road. Wedged in between and alongside many of the traditional dwellings were single-wide trailers, flower gardens, woodpiles, and dog pens. People around Agua Dulce had a lot of vehicles, Charlotte noticed, and the sandy lots between residences harbored pickup trucks, horse and cattle trailers, Jeeps, and passenger cars. Cottonwood trees shaded the tin-roofed homes. Water sprinklers struggled to keep small patches of new summer grass growing under the relentless high-altitude sun. Children played kickball in an empty lot, and an elderly woman with a miniature dog on her lap watched the day pass from her lawn chair.

The homes gave way to businesses: there was an insurance office, dry cleaner, and hair salon across from an appliance store and steakhouse. The only residence on the block had a sign on the lawn, 'Mabel's Boardinghouse', and was a three-story frame building with a deep front porch and lace curtains across the tall front windows. Geraniums grew in pots on the steps.

The community of Agua Dulce extended two blocks on either side of Main Street. The universe of sand and sky began just over the back fences of the last row of houses. The red desert and the faraway blue mountains were visible at the end of every side street. Civilization claimed only a narrow strip of real estate within drinking distance of the river.

But it was enough. Agua Dulce was a real place. It wasn't bewitched or evil. It was just a little Spanish-Indio town on the northwest plateau of New Mexico. Charlotte began to relax. She had been such a self-absorbed adolescent with the gas-station attendant. She should have been more forthcoming, told the man about her mother and grandfather, how they had come here a long time ago. It was an old habit, withholding information, not acknowledging major chapters in the family story. But now Charlotte was in the town where Grandpa made paleontological history.

Surely people in Agua Dulce were familiar with Grandpa's work here in the late 1950s? Maybe not. A lot of time had passed. Even an event like the discovery of an entire quarry of dinosaurs, hailed as the single most significant fossil find in North America, eventually faded in the collective memory of a place. And then it was possible that the people of Agua Dulce had chosen to forget the Rose family's chapter in their community's story, what with Alicia's final contribution such a blight on the historical landscape.

The center of Agua Dulce was a traffic signal and four corners of false-fronted buildings. Charlotte waited out the red light behind a pickup truck overloaded with cows. Each side of Main Street was lined with angle-parked trucks and cars. A banner strung alongside the traffic light announced in red, white, and blue the annual Fourth of July parade and barbeque.

The First Bank of Agua Dulce occupied one corner. Across the street was the government-issue post office. The third corner of the business district was the end of a long, multi-windowed stuccoed building that looked like it had occupied this part of Agua Dulce since the town's creation. *Durham Hardware and Feed Supply* was painted across the front.

A brick department store extended down most of the block beside Charlotte's car. The faded, weathered but clearly legible sign proudly proclaimed *W.W. Woolworth's & Co.* The mannequins in the display windows were all sporting patriotic red, white, and blue cowgirl or cowboy outfits and holding sparklers in their inanimate hands.

On the last corner was the Mata Drugstore and Soda Fountain. A saddled, chestnut-colored horse was tied loosely by the reins to the wood railing of the front steps. The horse's bridle had silver buttons decorating the strap across its forelock and sported an impressively tooled western saddle. People walked out of the drugstore and down the steps without so much as a glance, as if a saddled quarter horse waiting on the sidewalk was an ordinary and unremarkable sight. Charlotte would be able to tell her American lit students that the Old West of Zane Grey and Owen Wister was, indeed, alive and well in New Mexico.

Four men well past retirement age sat on a wood bench near the horse, chewing toothpicks and watching the people and cars pass through the center of town. Charlotte wondered which of them had ridden in on that fine horse. The old men wore pressed shirts and big cowboy hats, and as Charlotte studied them, they turned their eyes and heads in unison to Charlotte's red sedan waiting at the light. They knew: a stranger had come into town. Maybe the gas-station guy had already wired ahead? Those old guys probably needed something to talk about.

Charlotte looked away and feigned interest in the other side of the street. Alicia must have given the old-timers back in 1976 something to talk about for a good long while. Maybe they still talked about her.

During the three days in July of 1976 that the sheriff's riders searched the desert for Alicia's body, Grandpa said he needed to go out to New Mexico. He even bought a plane ticket. Grandpa said he knew how to find his daughter. But Grandpa's physician said the altitude would kill him. Albert Rose had already suffered two strokes and could no longer participate in expeditions to fossil sites more than two thousand feet above sea level.

After Alicia was found in the boulders below the cliff, and Leonard returned from New Mexico with the sheriff's and coroner's reports, Grandpa insisted they needed more information and called the Dos Rios sheriff's department for more details about his daughter's death. Grandpa was an expert in tapophony, understanding the final moments of life through careful study of a skeleton's, or corpse's, death pose. Because someone in the office recognized Albert Rose's name, the sheriff himself spoke with Grandpa. During an hour-long phone call the sheriff explained how one of the riders had spotted Alicia's body when the high noon sun glanced off her watch. The rider climbed on foot into a rock field at the base of a sheer cliff where he found her body wedged between enormous boulders, her hand the only part visible above the jumbled stones. If not for the sun sparking on her watch, they might never have found Alicia.

"It was a miracle," Grandpa told Charlotte. "The size of that land . . . well, it was a miracle that rider found her at all."

The traffic light changed from red to green. Trucks, cars, and pedestrians began to move on Main Street. Charlotte followed the faded green pickup and its cargo of submissive cows into the intersection where the truck again came to a complete stop just short of the far corner. Whatever was holding up traffic had the rapt attention of the old timers and the handsome horse at the hitching post. Charlotte sighed and aimed the air-conditioning vent at her face.

If Grandpa had developed a theory about Alicia's last moments of life, he did not share it with Charlotte. Alicia's death always ended in the desert boulder field. Charlotte still wondered if it might have been easier if Alicia had simply vanished. Looking back at the Rose-Lambert clan's twenty-year avoidance of the whole topic, and the damage such long-term avoidance does to the avoidees, Charlotte had come to believe that a vanishing had to be easier on the family than a suicide. At least the family of a vanished loved one could hold out for, cling to, the possibility of a happier ending. Twenty years later, they could still believe their loved one was working her way home.

The truck carrying the cattle began to roll forward and Charlotte passed the old men on the bench. She smiled and looked at their tethered horse. He was a tall gelding with alert eyes and the friendly, self-composed posture common to well-treated horses. The sort of horse upon which riding happily into the sunset was an attainable, even frequent activity. Beyond the horse and the old-timers were the open doors of the drugstore. Ceiling fans whirled above the empty stools at the soda fountain counter. On it sat a large old-fashioned cash register and a display stand of postcards. A sign in the window said "MALTS."

Traffic stopped again. The parking space to Charlotte's right, directly in front of the horse, was vacant. Charlotte looked at the clock on the dashboard: almost four o'clock. She had skipped lunch and was out of water. She was both starved and thirsty. Charlotte turned the wheel and slid the car into the parking space and turned off the engine. She left the car and walked up to the parking meter. The horse watched her, as did the old-timers on the bench. Charlotte opened her purse and then remembered her pocket full of quarters.

"I have a *lot* of quarters," Charlotte said quietly to the horse. He blinked as Charlotte pulled coins from her khakis.

"*Buenos días,*" one of the old-timers called out.

The horse swung his head around to the steps. Charlotte looked up and her eyes locked onto a tall cowboy—dark and handsome and thin as a whip, dressed in weathered jeans and a tee shirt, his very tanned face partially hidden under a Stetson—descending the steps.

"Hey, Gus." The cowboy reached the bottom step and tilted his hat to Charlotte. "Hello."

The quarters slipped from Charlotte's hand like they were greased. They struck the pavement and bounced and rolled in ten directions. Quarters leapt across the sidewalk under the horse and skittered into the street under parked cars. One bounced like a marble against the wood of the drugstore's bottom step, circled back and came to a stop against the cowboy's dusty brown boot.

"Oh, gosh," Charlotte heard herself mutter.

"Goodness," one of the bench sitters, or all of them, said. "Here, let me help you, miss."

All four men struggled to unfold their old bodies and stand. The horse dropped his head and snuffled at the quarter near his left front hoof. Charlotte went after the quarters by the curb.

"Here you go," one old-timer said. His wrinkled curled hand appeared near Charlotte's. She took the quarter and looked up. He smiled and his face creased like tissue paper. "That's a lot of quarters you have there."

"It is," Charlotte mumbled, forcing a smile. Each of the four elderly men brought Charlotte a quarter and dropped it into her open hand. "Thank you! I'm so, well, what a clumsy thing to do!"

The old-timers returned to their bench. Charlotte wanted to sprint for the car but the cowboy was still retrieving quarters from the pavement beneath the horse. He finally straightened up and turned to Charlotte.

"Here," he said extending his arm. "There's a few more in the street—"

"—Thanks so much, that's okay." Charlotte took the coins from his hand, turned and walked back into the street. He watched her as she walked away. Charlotte could feel his eyes focus on her back. She felt the absence of his eyes, too, as he went to untie his horse from the railing. Charlotte really wanted to turn around and watch him gather up the reins, slide his boot into the stirrup, grab the saddle horn and swing a long leg effortlessly up and over that fine steed. Instead, Charlotte crawled about the undersides of the car reclaiming her precious quarters.

After the cowboy was back in the saddle, he and his horse remained on the sidewalk. He was waiting for Charlotte to finish her coin roundup and have a conversation. But Charlotte could not look at him. She was completely discombobulated and kept moving farther away until she was around back of the car, practically in traffic. The last stray quarter lay by the rear right tire. As Charlotte reached to retrieve it, the clip clop of the horse's hooves rang loudly on the pavement. Charlotte stood up. The cowboy and his horse ambled across Main, wove around a bakery delivery truck and disappeared down the street between the bank and the hardware store.

{4}

Charlotte thanked the men on the bench and climbed back into her car and started the engine. It was physically impossible to pull out of the angled parking space and drive out of town the way she came in, so Charlotte headed south on Main Street. Half a block from the traffic light the street choked down into a single lane where the Agua Dulce Water & Sanitation Department was fixing a broken water pipe.

Traffic began to move south again, and the activity of the business district was replaced by a pleasant shaded residential neighborhood. Charlotte looked for an unoccupied drive to turn around in, but being Saturday afternoon, every house had cars parked in and around it. Half a mile beyond, Agua Dulce and its cheerful if precarious civilization ended abruptly at a baseball field beside an abandoned school house, and what might have once been a small church and a cemetery. Beyond the cemetery, out where the sage began, was an enormous pile of stones. The top of the stone monolith was decorated with an American flag and a wooden cross. Agua Dulce, like most towns in New Mexico, didn't worry too much about the separation of church and state.

Charlotte slowed the car to turn around in the sandy parking lot behind home plate. Behind the abandoned school was the green shimmer of the trees that followed the river. Beyond the river the red Triassic desert undulated and wavered to the horizon. "About two or three miles out," the man at the station had said, "that's the place you're looking for."

Albert Rose's historic Triassic site was only a few minutes away. It was 4:16. Charlotte could still make it back to Santa Fe in time for the banquet if she turned around in the next ten minutes. Just a few more miles. She set the odometer back to zero and accelerated the sedan down the bumpy road.

The two-laner became a one-laner as the old highway cut deeper into serious wilderness. The only evidence of life was a raven that flew down and landed on a gatepost. Charlotte studied the gate: there was no name, no mailbox, just a dirt road that wove off across the hard ground and disappeared into the heat waves rising from the sand land to the west.

The topography of the Lágrimas desert was changing. The sand rose up to form perfect little hills marked by perfectly measured red and gold bands. Another mile and the landscape was only red—sand, rock, mesas, buttes and cliffs. This country was burned and hard. Charlotte smiled because she knew these red hills and striated spires: they were part of every fossil story Grandpa Al ever told.

Charlotte squinted at the landscape on each side of the decrepit road. Somewhere out there was Grandpa's beloved fossil site. Although his graduate students made pilgrimages to the famous quarry, Grandpa never returned. Even years before the quarry became ground zero in Alicia's tragic story, Grandpa exiled himself from this particular site. Grandma Ruth told Charlotte that Grandpa's work was finished in New Mexico, that there were more important Triassic sites in Europe and Africa, in the Antarctic. But Charlotte couldn't remember ever hearing Grandpa himself answer the question about why he never returned to Agua Dulce.

Until his heart began to skip and flutter, Grandpa traveled all over the world. Charlotte assumed he never returned to New Mexico because of the altitude, but he went into the Andes and all over Africa until he was in his mid-fifties. Why hadn't Grandpa visited the Lágrimas during all the years between 1959 when he and Alicia lived here for a summer and his first heart problems in the 1970s?

Charlotte glanced at the odometer. Four miles. The road was disintegrating into a hardly used wagon trail. Charlotte pulled the sedan over onto the sandy shoulder and stopped. She should at least stand upon Grandpa's beloved red desert.

Charlotte left the car and walked to the fence. Strands of dull barbed wire stretched straight into the infinity to Charlotte's left and right. The heat of this place where the earth was as large as the sky struck Charlotte's body like a wall. The inferno sucked the breath from her lungs and made the skin on her arms shiver and rise into goose bumps. She listened to the dull rhythmic sound of her blood pulsing through her head.

Red sandstone spires on the skyline swayed in the heat. The little green ribbon of the Lágrimas River had disappeared. The mountains seen on the horizon since leaving Dos Rios were close enough now to distinguish individual ridges and depressions in their massive sides. Their peaks touched the clouds that hovered like luminous islands above the earth.

Total silence pressed against Charlotte's ears. The intangible enormity of the desert and the vulnerability of her body triggered a current of fear through Charlotte's nervous system. Up and down changed places, and space expanded. She gripped the old splintered fence post for balance. The ground dropped away, or maybe she was rising? Charlotte could not find a fixed focal point. She closed her eyes and waited for the whirling to stop.

A flock of noisy, raucous jays flew over Charlotte. She opened her eyes and anchored her attention on the blue birds that landed in scruffy trees on the side of a small sand hill. Charlotte squinted into the red hot *nada*. What an unworldly, raw, lonely place to die! How many miles from the road did the sheriff's report say the body was found? Two? Three? There were several escarpments of sandstone cliffs visible to the southwest: was it one of those?

For twenty years Charlotte had carried in her head the facts found in the official sheriff's report; she could recite the two-page report verbatim. But now, out here where her mother's death was forever tethered to a physical place on the earth, where the shattered bones in her spine and neck could be attributed to the hard edges and solid surfaces found in a particular boulder field, where Alicia's midnight leap could finally be given three-dimensional context at a singular cliff that occupied a measured and identifiable location under the sky, Charlotte could not call to mind a single iota of pertinent data.

Charlotte sucked hard for oxygen in the hot air. This was what she was afraid of: the world of her mother's dementia. Leonard and Grandma Ruth had warned her: there are no safe trails into or out of Alicia's world. But this was Grandpa's world, too! Grandpa Al had made good trails, left his footprints on this land. But how could Charlotte separate the two, her mother's path to destruction from her grandfather's path to discovery?

Grandpa used to say that the truth was waiting to be found in the sand beneath her boots. But whose truth? And where did one begin to look for even partial truths in such an ocean of nothing? Charlotte had nothing and no one to help her. She didn't even know what questions to ask, or who to ask them of. Without Grandpa to guide her, she could stand directly upon his beloved quarry, gaze directly down at some valuable bone and never even know what she had found. The sad fact was if there was something out here of importance to Charlotte she didn't have the wit to recognize it.

The muscles in her throat were closing down. Could a person suffocate in such heat? Charlotte stared at her watch: the secondhand paused between the twelve and the one. Time had stopped. She tapped the watch face and after what seemed like an eternity the secondhand dragged itself through the thick atmosphere under the crystal to the next moment. Time was moving toward 5 p.m.

Charlotte walked back to the car and climbed in. She pulled a tissue from her purse, wiped her forehead and turned the key in the ignition. The engine paused and then started with a sputter. The temperature gauge on the dash was a little to the warm side but still within the safe zone. Charlotte switched the air conditioning to high and with both hands turned the steering wheel to the left. As the car wheels cut a semicircle across the rough asphalt and down onto the shoulder of the other side, a bird—a very large black raven— landed on the windshield.

"Hey! Hey, get off there!" Charlotte leaned forward over the steering wheel and waved at the bird. The raven's claws made clicking sounds on the glass as he scrambled for a foothold. "Go on!" She rapped a knuckle on the glass. The raven extended his surprisingly wide wings and flapped for balance. "Get off!"

The fence line on the other side was coming directly at the front fender. Charlotte grabbed the wheel and pulled hard to the left. The sudden direction change caused the raven to slide across the hood, but before he fell off the side of the car he opened his wings and effortlessly, elegantly, lifted into the air. The raven gracefully cleared the barbed wire fence and with a single flap of its wings, doubled its height and distance from the earth.

The car's recovery was not so graceful. It lurched awkwardly as it became airborne, and jerked down and slammed against the ground. The engine stalled but the air conditioner continued to roar. Charlotte switched off the fan, turned off the engine and looked out through the windshield. The raven floated into space and evaporated in between the earth and the sky.

"Oh, shoot!" Charlotte unbuckled the seatbelt and climbed gingerly from the car. The front end was listing up and to the right like a beached boat. Charlotte bent down and looked underneath; the front axle was high centered over a very large boulder. "Oh, shit!" she said loudly. "Shit. This is bad!"

Charlotte straightened up and looked up and down the road. No one. *Nada* and no one for miles. Even the noisy blue birds had vanished. Charlotte knelt down on her knees beside the car and studied the size of the boulder and the distance between the car's front right tire and the ground: both were forbidding. And now there was some kind of fluid leaking from the sedan's underside. "This isn't good," Charlotte said out loud. "This is not good."

Charlotte looked down the highway again. No rescue in sight. The four friendly old-timers had probably retired for the day, and Prince freaking Cowboy Charming and his splendid steed were miles away by now. Even the station attendant and his glass Pegasus had forgotten about her. No one knew she was out here; no one would come looking for her. There was nothing to do but walk back to Agua Dulce. It was only four miles, give or take a mile. Charlotte loved to walk. What would it take, an hour? She could do this. If she could avoid heatstroke, rattlesnakes, dehydration, and meddlesome ravens, there was really nothing to worry about.

It was remarkable, Charlotte thought as she retrieved her purse and hat from the car, now that she really was in trouble, the anxiety that had dogged her all afternoon had dissolved. She could swallow again, and her heart had settled into an oxygen-supplying pace.

Charlotte walked north on the highway with a long confident stride, grateful for her sturdy sneakers and light-colored slacks. The sun was still high to the northwest, but the heat of the day had noticeably lessened. Charlotte looked over her shoulder at the mountains. At least she couldn't get lost out here. Landmarks that large were hard to lose sight of.

The noisy blue birds returned and flew from bush to bush on both sides of the road. Behind her, the red sedan receded on the side of the highway. Charlotte had never felt so small, so insignificant. But out here everything was equally insignificant except the sky and the mountains. She had never been so far from people, from shelter or food, had never been so alone. She stopped and stared into the landscape on either side of the road. Behind her, the car had vanished. She ought to be terrified. But she wasn't.

After a brief rest, she began to walk again. This was nothing like being alone at her house in Scarsdale, or in Leonard's house in Briarcliff. Charlotte knew what *alone* was. She knew all about lonely, too. This was nothing like loneliness or aloneness. Being alone on the desert came with a peculiar but pleasant sense of connection.

After forty-five minutes Charlotte's stride slowed and shortened. As she became thirsty and fatigued she began to lose confidence in her stamina. Had she driven five miles out from Agua Dulce? Six? Where did she set the odometer? She could see nothing resembling buildings or even trees. The river was down in a canyon somewhere across the desert to her right, too far to walk to. She remembered the sign advertising malts on the drugstore's window. If she had not become the modern manifestation of Nervous Nellie when that cowboy appeared on the sidewalk she would have plunked a few quarters into the meter, walked into the drugstore and taken a stool at the soda fountain. One of those chivalrous old men, maybe even the tall cowboy himself, might have joined her for a chat and a cold malt. She could have avoided this mishap altogether.

Maddie would enjoy the details of this adventure. Later tonight, when Charlotte recounted her afternoon exploits, Maddie would tell Charlotte there was hope for her after all. But Maddie would also admonish her for shouting at a raven: "How many times does life land a wild bird on your windshield?"

The sun was razor sharp on Charlotte's arms and the side of her neck as it dropped down into the mountains. The Lágrimas desert was about to slide into dusk. Even a sun like this one was going to set, and this bright country was going to become dark. Very dark. Charlotte walked faster. She had to find help, find people, before nightfall.

Fifteen minutes later, Charlotte sat on a rock near the fence line. The mountains were navy blue, and the sand spires to the south had long, narrow shadow fingers beside them on the desert floor. The Lágrimas at sunset was a seductive sensuous summerland. Under such a sky, surrounded by a landscape whose size and colors were impossible to describe with words, a woman did not have to be delusional to feel as if she had left one life and stepped into another. Shed an old skin and found a new one. Out here it was easy to forget the mundane details of your life. Especially the unhappy ones.

Alicia miscarried in the fall of 1975. Charlotte didn't even know her mother was pregnant until after the fact. And the difficulties of the pregnancy were of secondary importance by that time because of the cancer and hysterectomy. Leonard told Charlotte that Alicia's surgery had successfully removed the diseased parts before they spread. But when Charlotte visited her mother in Westchester Memorial Hospital, it seemed the surgery had removed the healthy parts of Alicia along with the cancerous ones, and that her mother had lost more than an unborn child in the miscarriage.

Charlotte hugged her knees. She needed to get up and get going. But to where? The clouds were deep rose and purple and the boundaries and edges of the landscape faded with the last light. How was she going to walk when it was completely dark? Charlotte looked up the road. Far away, almost beyond the last grasp of her vision, Charlotte saw the outlines of animals standing on the road. Horses? Charlotte stood. The forms of the horses were fading. Charlotte began to jog towards them. If they were wild they would run; if they were tame, maybe they would help her.

Dusk turned the desert into a grey bowl. Charlotte kept her eyes on the horses. As she closed the distance between herself and the herd Charlotte saw that their ears were too big and their legs too short. These were not horses. She smiled. Tonight there would be no Prince Charming and no mythical flying steed carrying this schoolmarm back to safety. No, Charlotte's rescuers were five scruffy burros standing in the middle of the deserted road.

"Hello, fellows." Charlotte walked up to the first burro. "What are you doing out here?" The closest burro sniffed her palm and then looked back over his flank at the other four. "Are you lost?" The burros stared at her with glassy, round eyes. Charlotte smiled. "I guess we all know that I'm the lost one."

It was hard to distinguish their markings in the dim light, but two had a wide white stripe down the middle of their backs. A third was almost white with a gray mane and tail. The last two were probably brown.

"So, where's home?" The burros blinked and gazed off to the west. Charlotte gestured at the road ahead. "That way? Is there a ranch, people? Do you speak?"

Apparently some sort of signal was exchanged because all five burros turned around with the synchronicity of a drill team and began to march down the road toward Agua Dulce.

"Hey, don't forget me," Charlotte said, walking quickly to keep up. Even if they wandered like a lost tribe in the desert, up and down arroyos and across mesas all night long, she would rather be in the company of these burros than alone in the dark.

{5}

Holoman Farley pressed the cancer-chewed bulb of his nose into the warm pane of glass and squinted into the setting sun. From his stool beneath the third-floor dormer window he could keep an eye on the west. He scanned the horizon, watching for movement. There had not been a wild horse sighting near Agua Dulce in a decade or more, but every nerve in Farley's body sensed it: the return of the damned had begun.

Below in the alley behind Mabel's boardinghouse Earl Turnball parked his old sedan, climbed from the car and shuffled slowly across the yard. Farley dropped the binoculars and scowled down at Earl's bald head as it approached the porch steps. Earl had been out for a forbidden after-supper smoke on some side street in Agua Dulce. If Earl knew Farley was watching him from his third-story lookout, he pretended not to. Old fool. As if Farley gave a damn whether Earl Turnball dropped dead with emphysema.

Farley lifted the binoculars back to his watering eyes. It was all too easy to become complacent, to sit back and allow the undisciplined mind to drift into thoughts about inconsequential people like Earl. The devil used the elderly like that—decoys—so when evil began to rise again in those badlands, soldiers of the cross like Farley would be distracted. But Farley was not about to be distracted. Years of practice had taught Farley never to take his attention off the horizon; never leave a gate unlatched and never, ever, let a woman's body or words turn his head. Forget these commandments at your peril, Farley told himself each and every day, else the universe will flatten you; like Duende's devil-driven mustangs, the whole goddamned universe will run you down and trample you to dust.

This view of the desert from the third-story window was small but adequate. And it was cheap. No one else wanted this hot airless room. The low-ceilinged cell had two tiny windows: a dormer facing Main Street and the *llanos* beyond the river to the east, and a second dormer facing the badlands and the mountains to the west.

"If you want the room, it's yours," Mabel said with a cloying little curl of her smudged red lips. "I'll charge ya half of what the other boarders are paying downstairs."

That was three months ago. Farley did not want to move out of his Shasta permanently parked beside the Lágrimas landfill. But last winter his home of forty years had become uninhabitable. The trailer had always attracted distasteful roommates from the neighboring landfill: packrats, bees and a squatters' colony of mice inhabited the walls and ceiling of the aluminum hut. And centipedes as fat and long as horsewhips scurried across the metal sink and down the shower stall walls several times a week. Irritating and a damned nuisance, but Farley knew it was all part of the assignment: he was the Lord's sentry on the far western borderline, the crusader holding the sword at the gate to the Holy City.

In those last months, Farley fought to hold his own at the landfill. He tried to shoot the larger rodents with his shotgun, but only succeeded in blasting eight-inch-wide holes in the trailer's walls. And then one morning in early March a scorpion stung Farley on the toe after he carelessly slid his foot into an uninspected boot. His foot swelled until it was the size and color of a spoiled pumpkin. He couldn't walk into Agua Dulce and he couldn't drive his truck, neither. Not that he had a license, anymore. If not for the surprise appearance of his boss, Dos Rios County Waste Management officer Phil Griego, who stopped by the dump for an impromptu inspection, Farley might have died of gangrene.

In spite of all that was against him, Farley held on to his lookout at the landfill until the bitter end. It was the demon ravens that broke him. Those noisy meddling *brujas* masqueraded as birds and flocked by the dozens around the smoldering ashes of the dump. Phil Griego didn't believe Farley, but every afternoon those possessed robbers dropped blades from broken washing machines and launched shards of glass from busted televisions onto the roof of Farley's trailer. They placed upended nails in the sand beneath his truck tires and tucked burning newspapers and smoking mattress stuffing under the trailer's front steps. The ravens had one mission: destroy Holoman

Farley. Or at least maim and wound him enough to halt his half-century quest to eradicate the servants of Satan from the Valley of the Lágrimas.

It wasn't until today that Farley understood why he had had to move out of the trailer near the landfill and into Mabel's in Agua Dulce. It was all part of the Lord's plan, because if Farley had remained at his post on the desert he would have missed the red sedan's appearance on Main Street and the devil temptress's return.

Farley kept his Winchester wrapped in a flannel shirt in his footlocker. The footlocker was kept beside the three-legged stool under the western window. For hours at a time Farley sat on that stool, fingering the footlocker's latch while his eyes fingered the canyon country for a sign of ravens, women, witches, wild horses, and the seductive evil that possessed them all.

Mabel Duran said Farley was loco the way he was always talking about Apache *brujas* and bloodthirsty horses. Farley didn't care a hang what Mabel or anyone else around Agua Dulce thought of him. Never had. The people of Agua Dulce were just too stupid to see how infected they were by the venom that emanated from the scorched earth of this corner of northern New Mexico. Farley himself would have left this cursed valley years ago had it not been for the loss of that million-dollar race horse: as long as Duende was out in the canyonlands, Farley would remain in Agua Dulce. Until he killed that bewitched stallion, cut off the ears and strung them around his neck, Farley's holy mission would not be done.

Other men might be fooled by Duende's disappearance in a snowstorm, might believe the black Thoroughbred was dead these fifty years. Not Holoman Farley. Men like Dennis Mata and that son of a witch half-breed Bartholomew Bill claimed they saw the stallion leap from the cliff to his death in Dulce Canyon. But those men were blinded by the delusions spun by *brujas*, their wits dulled by the pleasures of the flesh and other indulgences pursued by possessed souls.

Dusk became darkness on the desert. Farley put the binoculars on the narrow strip of wood along the windowsill, stood and hobbled across the room. With a loud grunt, he stretched out on his narrow bed. He never climbed under the covers anymore, even in winter, but lay fully clothed under the old saddle blanket he'd slept with since he left his mother's home in Bluff,

Utah. Farley did remove his boots, but stuffed them with newspaper so the scorpions couldn't nest in them.

But Farley could not sleep. He left bed and shuffled across the floor to the footlocker. In his pants pocket was a small smooth key that opened the lock. He reached in and gripped the Winchester rifle. It was his father's, loaned to Farley in the spring of 1949 when he left Utah with the Thoroughbred stallion, Duende, bound for glory at the El Paso Downs.

Farley never saw El Paso and he never returned home triumphant from the track. Surely his mother wondered what had happened to him. Farley could never tell her how he had crossed into the land of evil; how he had lost Duende to a harem of wild mares; how Farley, just a kid, had to wrestle a skilled and beautiful *bruja* for his very soul. Farley never got to tell his Mormon mother how it was that he came to spend forty years defending himself against the stones thrown by the sinners of Agua Dulce, and warding off spells cast by an Apache witch. Farley could never tell his mother—and God knew how he had wanted to, had stayed awake nights thinking of the exact words that would clear his name in the family—how it wasn't his fault. The loss of that blue-blooded racehorse wasn't his fault.

Farley cleaned the Winchester's barrel and trigger with a piece of cotton. It was time to be very vigilant. He dug about the locker for the box of cartridges. Today, June 20, 1998, the witch whore everyone pretended was dead had returned to Agua Dulce.

Back in '76 when they brought her body out on horseback—he could see her boots, he recognized them—and loaded her into the ambulance, Farley had a suspicion. Over the years he'd become wise to the trickery of witches. Just look at Dorothea Durham: her skin was darker than any Indian's and it continued to darken, inhabited as she was by another supposedly dead witch, Conchata Lonewolf. Holoman Farley suspected it before, but today he was certain of it: you have to kill a *bruja* twice.

Farley never went back to Bluff on account of his brother-in-law's threats. When Curtis showed up in Agua Dulce with three thugs, Farley explained in plain English how the stallion had been seduced into the snowy wild by a herd of mustangs. Everyone around Agua Dulce knew about the wild horse harem that lived in the mountains in summer, the canyonlands in winter.

Thomas Bill had even caught a few. It wasn't Farley's fault there had been a blizzard, that the truck pulling the horse trailer had lost control and slid off the road, knocked him cold and released the black beauty stallion into the opaque white country, the home of the bewitched mares.

Curtis said Farley was the one who was bewitched, and if he ever saw Farley in the state of Utah he'd remove Farley's hands at the wrist and his testicles at the bone.

Farley's hands groped about the objects in the footlocker until his fingers pushed into leathery lumps. He did not pull the string out, but counted the shriveled coarse appendages with his fingers, whispering each number into the dark like a rosary. Twenty-four pairs. He remembered each and every one of those mustangs, how they looked, stupid and cornered, in the crosshairs of his Winchester. Indians counted coup. Farley counted horse ears. One more pair, Duende's, and he would be able to return home, the victorious son.

If only he could drive. After the gangrene in his foot Farley lost his license. A few days later, the sheriff took his truck and parked it in a fenced lot in Dos Rios. Farley would need a car. When the time came and God called upon him to eliminate the last vestiges of evil in the Lágrimas, Farley would take his knife and his gun, and somehow he would find a car. Farley's mother always said the Lord would provide.

The Lord could not, or would not, provide Farley with a stronger body. Ever since he'd moved into the boardinghouse on Main Street he'd been losing ground. Nearly every night Duende came from purgatory to haunt him. The old Thoroughbred stomped and snorted at the end of Farley's bed, pranced about in the half dark, his sleek black body young and powerful. Farley turned his face away, closed his eyes and feigned sleep, while Duende chewed on his feet, peeled away flesh, grazed bone with his enormous teeth. Some nights were so bad it felt like the horse was gnawing on the marrow of Farley's very soul.

Farley slammed the trunk lid closed, hobbled back to his bed and lay down. His skin was clammy and hot, his veins on fire.

"I seen you, Alicia Rose!" he croaked into the dark of the room. "Come back from the country of the dead just like the black-hearted ravens said you would."

{6}

The last light was absorbed by the mountains. To the east, two stars sparkled like perfect earrings above the shoulders of a mesa. A coyote howled and yipped from the direction of the river, but the burros gave it no heed. Charlotte kept a hand on the last burro's neck, and as it became more difficult to see the surface of the road, walked with her body pinned up against him. The desert air was cooling rapidly, and the burro's neck was warm and soft.

The burros veered in unison off the pavement of the old road and passed through an open gate. They walked into the west on a dirt road. The mountains to the southwest were outlined by stars that had emerged by the hundreds. By the thousands. Where was Agua Dulce? To their right, north? Charlotte was too tired and thirsty to care. Wherever the burros planned to spend the night Charlotte was going to spend the night, too.

The dark plateau ahead was lit by the faint but perceptible glow of an electric light. The burros' pace quickened, and Charlotte had to jog to stay alongside them. The road wound downhill and into a clearing edged by tall trees. The source of the light was mounted over a barn door. The burros did not turn for the barn but walked to a house where they stopped in an orderly line at the bottom of the porch steps. A small dog watched them approach from the top step. When the dog noticed Charlotte standing among the burros he turned his head to look at an elderly woman sitting in the porch rocking chair.

"Well, Egypt, you've been gone a good long while." The woman used the arms of the chair to stand. "All five of you home? Little Bit, are there five?"

The woman peered into the dark. Charlotte took a step away from the burros. The dog's eyes followed her. "Is there someone with you, Egypt?"

"Yes." Charlotte's voice cracked. She swallowed, cleared her parched throat and started again. "I'm sorry to intrude like this, but my car broke down, and I met the burros out on the highway . . ."

The woman gripped the railing and leaned into the night. She wore a nightgown with a fringed shawl wrapped around her very thin shoulders.

"Goodness, forgive me, my eyes are terrible these days." The woman moved along the railing to the steps and motioned at Charlotte with her cane. Charlotte stepped into the soft light.

"My goodness! I should have seen you coming." The woman lifted a gaunt hand to the house behind her. "Francis!" she called to the screen door. The dog began to wag his tail. "Oh, my, I think he's gone to bed. Francis! Come out here!"

The woman fumbled with her cane. "My eyes are terrible, my dear, but I should have seen you coming! Alicia Rose, I should have seen you coming!"

{7}

Barty Bill lay on his back staring at the ceiling of his bedroom. The digital clock on the bedside table clicked: one seventeen. Not quite the liver hour—3 a.m.—the time that people with liver problems, like his nephew, Jed Morley, were most likely to be tossing about their bedroll or walking out across the desert like a nocturnal animal. At least when Jed lay awake or wandered about in the dark of night, he was looking up into something grand: the open sky. If you had to be wide-eyed while the rest of the world slept, you may as well be staring wide-eyed at something good for your sleepless soul like a thousand stars.

Barty threw off the tangle of sheets. June was the hottest month of the year in the Lágrimas. Even so, the nights were cool. Yet even with the windows wide open to the *llanos* that dropped to the river, tonight Barty's bedroom was oppressive. Instead of stars and celestial wonders Barty was gazing at the nail heads and knotholes in the ceiling of his bedroom. He knew this night landscape well. When you build a house with your own hands the grooves and grain of each *viga* and lintel carry a sliver of your blood, sweat, and memory. Looking at the ceiling over his twin bed, even in the hazy dark, meant looking back at the winter afternoon in 1968 when Barty and Dennis Mata measured, sawed, and nailed the entire truckload of rough-sawn pine boards to the ponderosa *vigas* spanning the bedroom ceiling. It was a December day, bitter cold with a sun that came and went between the scurrying clouds of an approaching snowstorm. Like most days spent in the company of Barty's oldest friend, Dennis Jorge Mata, it was a good one.

Building with sun-dried adobe bricks, Lágrimas mud, and ponderosa pine logs hauled down from the Agustinas had always brought Barty the best kind of satisfaction. That's why he had agreed to let Jed rebuild the old house at the High Lonesome Ranch this past spring. Barty didn't care particularly if the old ranch house melted back into the mud of the Lágrimas. But when Jed saw the deterioration on the house's north side where the tin roof had peeled away and exposed the top of the adobe wall, he was critical of Barty's apathy.

"We could save the old house if we acted now," Jed told his Uncle Barty when they were out at the ranch last February working the horses. "But if we don't get up and replace that corrugated tin, when the summer monsoons come the water will turn that adobe house into adobe mud."

No one had lived at the High Lonesome house in thirty years. And Jed would probably never live in the house, even after it was renovated. Jed's immune system had gone loco in Phoenix last fall, and Barty's nephew had not spent more than five or six hours in an enclosed structure in eight months. The house itself had been vacant since Barty departed for Vietnam in 1965. When Barty returned from the war two years later he didn't move back to the ranch built by his parents. Barty told his sister, Bernadette, that he couldn't be living three miles out at the High Lonesome while managing a gas station down on the highway. Bernadette understood: she'd left the Lágrimas in 1963 and never looked back—went away to nursing school in Tempe, then married Raymond Morley, a Phoenix dentist.

In 1968 Barty bought the gas station and repair shop from Fred Yancy. Fred was retiring and moving into a new mobile-home community for senior citizens in Dos Rios. Within the year, Barty built the one-bedroom adobe house behind the station. Yancy had a pretty good-sized clientele, although Agua Dulce was hardly growing as a community. Barty had worked as Yancy's mechanic for two years after returning from Nam where he had earned his stripes as a helicopter mechanic. Helicopters and the mechanics who serviced them were not in high demand around the high plateau of northwestern New Mexico. But Barty knew his way around farm and ranch equipment and was especially knowledgeable about antiquated but functional vehicles like Francis Durham's Hudson truck. So with the money he'd saved from his years on the rodeo circuit and with a small loan from Francis and Thea, Barty bought what was soon called the B & B Service and Repair Station.

Within a few months Barty was working twelve-hour days as the most sought-after mechanic from Agua Dulce north to Orphan Gulch on the reservation and south to the old trading outpost at Deep Water. He had regular customers up in the county seat of Dos Rios and within the first year had acquired a dozen Santa Fe clients who paid him good money to drive sixty-five miles into the capital city to work on their vintage automobiles and Depression-era pickups.

Barty was a natural around engines and mechanical contraptions but he was downright gifted around horses. Maybe it was in his blood—Apache and Spanish on his mother's side, Scots and Welsh on his father's, horse people all—but Bartholomew Lonewolf Bill could read a horse's disposition, sense its breeding idiosyncrasies, determine its recent social history and pretty much ascertain its ancestral story in one good long uninterrupted glance. And horses knew it. Horses that were mean and hell bent on war with humans did their best to get away from Barty, and he was likewise agreeable to maintaining a distance. But horses with good hearts that had been abused, mistreated, overworked, underfed, and all around misunderstood sensed a comrade in him. Horses that avoided human interaction gradually allowed and eventually sought out his company, even though it meant bridled discipline and routine participation in ranch chores, roundups, Sunday rides into the mountains, rodeo parades, and other activities necessary for human-equine relationship building.

Thirty years had passed since Barty's decision to buy the station and set up his life in town. Barty used the barn and the corrals at High Lonesome for his horses, but he gave no thought to the old adobe house of Thomas and Conchata Bill that was steadily returning to the earth it was made from. And then late last fall, in November of 1997, Jed got sick and returned to the Lágrimas. After months of listless weakness Jed gradually began to recover some of his former stamina. When Jed began to pester his uncle about saving the High Lonesome ranch house from complete collapse, Dennis told Barty that Jed's concern was good and natural.

"It won't hurt you none," Dennis told Barty over a game of checkers a few weeks back. "You and me know, *compadre*, working the mud with the hands is salve for the soul, *verdad*?"

Verdad. So three weeks ago, Barty ordered and delivered building materials, and Jed went to work to rescue the ranch house that Barty's father, Thomas Bill, the North Carolina-born school teacher, built in 1930 for his half-Apache bride, Conchata Lonewolf. Barty and Bernadette were both born in that house. It was a joy-filled, blessed abode until 1950 when the winds of insurmountable sorrows swirled through the Lonewolf-Bill family. Thomas died in the summer of a gunshot wound to his chest. Conchata died of influenza two years later. Barty and Bernadette went to live with the Durhams at their ranch, and the house at High Lonesome was closed up.

The digits on the clock clicked. Barty turned his back to the clock's incessant accounting of what he already knew was going to be a sleepless night and stared through the window at the night sky over the northern horizon.

The station and repair shop brought Barty a good living, although Mobil debranded his business in 1987 because it didn't sell enough gasoline. The B & B Service Station was of so little concern to Mobil the corporate officials down in Albuquerque never bothered to drive up and retrieve their company horse. The red-glass effigy had come to be a landmark in the Lágrimas topography. The ultimate mustang, the last of its kind, Pegasus had flown untethered in the patch of sky over the old service island for close to forty years. Every other wild horse in the Lágrimas had been rounded up, shot or starved into extinction, but the Mobilgas stallion still eluded capture.

Barty turned on its electric heart for a few hours every Christmas, New Year's Eve, and Independence Day, and for anyone who came by the station on their birthday. And every few months, just because he could, Barty threw the switch and set that flying red horse on fire in the night sky for no reason and for nobody in particular.

Except for bouts of insomnia Barty had no complaints. His days passed in an even-flowing current of unremarkable, mostly predictable tasks. Midlife unrolled in a palatable, even monotonous rhythm. Excluding his nephew Jed's collapse in Scottsdale and his subsequent emergency return to Agua Dulce last November, nothing too big, burdensome or thought-and-worry provoking had come down Barty's path in decades. The ranch and the gas station inhabited a quiet and uneventful corner of the world where, excepting the expected fickleness of weather, farm machinery, and horses, the variety of concerns and emotions Barty wrangled in a given day remained within a familiar corral. Until today.

Today a woman with the face of an angel stepped into the B & B station, and the twenty-three-year understanding Barty had with the past—that the past stay put in the past—threw a shoe. This afternoon Barty looked into the face of a young woman and found the summer of 1959 looking back at him. Barty had seen plenty of beautiful women in his time—women with that same translucent skin, gray-flecked blue eyes, and hair so curly that no comb could coerce it into submission. Barty had been stopped in his tracks by women who reminded him of her, stared after them on the street, even followed one woman into a fancy department store in New York City before he was certain it was not her.

Today was different. This woman's appearance didn't just resemble individual aspects of Alicia Rose; this woman embodied her, had the light, quick-step walk of Alicia, bit her bottom lip when she was nervous, turned on her toes and stepped away as she tossed her curly head and glanced back to see who or what she might have forgotten. Or suddenly remembered.

She didn't say so, didn't act as if she had any more connection to Agua Dulce than the other tourists who pulled into the station for fuel and directions, admired the winged horse and inquired about his collection of vintage pumps and signs. But Barty knew: that young woman in the rented red sedan was either Alicia's ghost or her daughter.

She was at the gas station for only seven or eight minutes. But that brief blindsiding encounter was the reason Barty could not find his way into much-needed sleep. The young woman's appearance had unearthed a cache of memories Barty had worked long and hard to bury. And now all the sharp details of that terrible July day were stuck like shrapnel on the surface of his mind, as debilitating to Barty as the day he found Alicia's body. Barty was unable to stop the disinterring of images that had been methodically, deliberately allowed to blur and dissolve into oblivion years ago: Alicia's swollen lifeless face, her body burned and blistered, bruised, broken, and limp. So many times Barty wished he had never found her body at all, never seen the sun sparking off her watchband. Even if it meant no one ever knew what happened, it would have been easier to live with the memory of Alicia Rose as he had known her in 1959: seventeen and radiant with life.

Barty had never, not for a day, not in Vietnamese swamps hunting downed helicopters, not in Kansas when he lived the life of a reckless bachelor kicking about the rodeo circuit, never had he stopped thinking about Alicia.

Finding Alicia's body in the boulder field west of Dead Horse Canyon was the single worst moment of Barty's life. And he had survived two years in-country as a helicopter mechanic with a front-line medical unit, sat helplessly beside his father while he bled to death in the tall grass of a meadow high in the Agustinas and lost his unborn son in an automobile accident seventeen miles south of Dos Rios.

"Oh, Christ!" Barty sat up in his bed. Most people counted sheep when they couldn't sleep. Barty counted losses. Barty slid his bare feet into his boots and stood up. If sleep was going to come for him tonight it was not going to find him here.

Dressed in boxer shorts and cowboy boots Barty walked through the dark kitchen and out the back door to the shed where he kept tractor blades and old generators, broken pumps, saddles and camping gear. There was one bedroll stashed on the floor at the rear of the small room. Barty dragged the canvas bundle out and around to the east side of the house where the light from the station didn't shine. The bedroll weighed about as much as a man asleep, which is why no self-respecting cowboy ever carried one more than a few yards.

And what was Thea up to, anyway, asking him to pull out the bedrolls stored in the barn at the High Lonesome? There were probably six bedrolls out there, but no one had looked at them in a decade. Jed was using a bedroll out at the camp, but his was newer and belonged to Dennis Mata. The bedrolls that belonged to the Bill family were now little more than mice-eaten mattresses wrapped in brittle canvas. What was Thea thinking?

Barty hauled the bedroll fifteen yards from the house to a flat stretch of sand. The dark horizon of mountains was visible to the west. He untied the ropes and unrolled the canvas-encased mattress. Barty lay on top of the sheet. The cool air of the desert night seeped into the pores of his bare chest. Last March, when Jed moved out of the Durhams' house to the cow camp above the river, Barty had slept out under the stars with his nephew every night for two weeks. He told Jed it was because he missed sleeping out in the wild like when he was a young boy.

"I lived a summer under the open sky," Barty told Jed, "and it was the best home I ever had."

Barty didn't tell Jed that he met Alicia that summer. He didn't tell Jed that with Alicia by his side, or under his arm, or lying with her lithe body firmly against his torso, any stretch of sand or stone or sky was the precise center of paradise.

Barty scanned the Milky Way glazing a fifth of the sky above his bedroll. What exactly did that young woman know about her mother's summer in New Mexico? Albert Rose would have died when she was no more than ten or twelve years old. Her grandmother, Ruth, wouldn't have had many good things to say about Agua Dulce and its inhabitants. About Barty Bill.

A shooting star blazed across the sky and burned to dust beyond the horizon to the northwest. Barty eyed the black outline of the Agustinas. That young woman was probably here looking to put some sense into her mother's death. Barty closed his eyes. It would be easier to separate the dust of that shooting star from the dust of the desert than to find a satisfying conclusion about Alicia's demise.

"You're never going to feel good about what happened here," Barty should have told her when they stood in the hot sun by the pumps. "You're never going to understand how it happened or why, and you're never going to stop being angry, and sad. You are never going to stop blaming yourself and you're never, ever going to stop missing her."

Barty knew because he'd been trying to understand, trying to bring an end to the anger and sorrow, guilt and regret all these years, too.

In the summer of 1959 Alicia was a high school senior, innocent and trusting. Barty was twenty-two, estranged from his wife, grieving his dead child, self-pitying and bitter. Everything terrible that happened to Alicia, and to her father, Dr. Al, too, was Barty's fault.

Barty grunted and turned over on the bedroll. The bare skin on his back prickled with cold, but he did not slide into the covers.

He could have stopped things before they went too far, before he fell so much in love he began to forget that he was a sinner seducing a saint.

"Your sins have brought you here." Farley was waiting in his dented black pickup truck at the side of the highway when they brought Alicia's body out. "Your Father in heaven has been watching you," he mumbled when Barty rode past. "You have filled Him with shame, and even your dead *bruja* mama cannot save you and your dead whore from the fiery hell that awaits you both."

"Christ almighty!" Barty sat up on the bedroll. Jacobo Trujillo's tractor sat in the left bay of the garage awaiting installation of the alternator that had arrived via UPS this afternoon. And Barty needed to grease the axel on the rebuilt Mustang, tally up and pay the shop's gross receipts tax and order some kiln-dried roof joists for the High Lonesome roof renovation.

Barty refolded the tarp over the mattress, rolled up the bedroll and dragged it back into the shed. Still in his boxer shorts and boots, he walked through the side yard of defunct gasoline pumps to the station and unlocked the office door. He retrieved his overalls from the peg behind the lavatory door, pulled them on and switched on the fluorescent lights in the garage.

A man could never really say what was coming with weather, health, love or people. Even a good horse could develop a fearful preoccupation about something and spook at its own shadow. A beautiful woman—white, Spanish, Apache or in-between—could lose her balance and step from life without a sound. That's why Barty became a mechanic: there was a predictability to mechanical breakdown and a logical, usually linear path to recovery. Within the walls of the B & B Service Station was a roughly ordered universe. For brief moments, sometimes an hour or two, even a hollow-hearted man could believe in his ability to repair what was broken, to resurrect and restore to at least reasonable usefulness what has been dented, neglected, crushed, abused, warped, wounded or lost.

With both hands Barty lifted the alternator out of the box and set it on the counter. Maybe that's what that young woman was looking to do: unearth her lost faith in the inherent and reasonable goodness of the universe. It was a worthy mission, but just as sure as Barty knew an adjustable from a lug wrench, he knew she wasn't going to find anything resembling reason or goodness in the sands of the Lágrimas.

{8}

A rooster crowed. Charlotte sat up in bed and gazed into the sun streaming through the thin white curtain of a tall window. The rooster crowed again, only this time the cockadoodle ended without the do. Charlotte lay back down. Foggy with sleep, she wondered how flowers could grow from the ceiling. As her mind cleared she made sense of the drying bundles of tied flowers and leafy sprigs hanging upside down from the wood beams over the bed.

It took a few moments to organize her memories and images of last night: Charlotte was in a house on a ranch in the desert country somewhere between Agua Dulce and Nowhere, New Mexico. This house belonged to the Durham family and this bedroom with a four-poster bed draped with a hand-stitched quilt belonged to Bernadette Lonewolf Bill, the grown daughter of Dorothea, the elderly woman who last night greeted Charlotte like she had known her all her life. Dorothea led Charlotte to this bedroom as if she had been expecting her. As if Charlotte—or Alicia—had come and gone from this house many times before.

"It's all prepared," Thea said, grasping Charlotte's elbow as they walked into the dark room. "You know where the bathroom is. The window is open to the night air, but there's an extra quilt in the closet if you need it."

Although Bernadette left for college some thirty years ago, her bedroom was kept exactly the way Bernadette liked it as a teenage girl. The rocking chair had pink and white hand-pieced pillows that matched the bed coverlet, and handmade dolls and rag-stuffed animals were crowded on a small bench under the window. The only obviously contemporary object in Bernadette's bedroom was a small television set. Francis Durham, Thea's affable soft-spoken husband, told Charlotte that on a clear day the old TV was able to catch fifty percent of the signal sent out by the PBS station down in Albuquerque. Before climbing into bed last night, Charlotte turned on the little set and fiddled with its antenna, but the only picture reaching Agua Dulce from the outside world was carried within fuzzy silver snow.

Charlotte slid from the high bed and walked barefoot to the window. The faded blue sill was crowded with small black and white stones someone had arranged in a long line. On the other side of the wavering pane was a garden with hummingbirds buzzing in and around yellow and red columbines. Morning-glory vines with the first blue blossoms of the summer climbed across the lower half of the window, and dozens of paper-thin pink flowers bloomed in a low hedge along the fence. Charlotte was surprised to see so many flowers and so much color in a desert garden.

The window had a view of the far end of the barn and part of the corral. A cottonwood tree with a rope swing dangling from a branch shaded the corral where the five burros stood along the railing. Their ears and eyes were aimed directly at Charlotte's window.

Charlotte slipped into Bernadette's polka-dot bathrobe and opened the bedroom door. The house was quiet. Not wanting to wake her elderly hosts, Charlotte walked on tiptoes down the hallway to the little bathroom. After a shower under a trickle of water that went hot and cold in unpredictable spurts, she put on her stiff but dry underwear she had hand-washed in the sink last night. She pulled on her wrinkled khaki pants and her not so white shirt. The desert sand had stained her socks a terra cotta color, so she slipped into her sneakers without them.

Charlotte had a travel toothbrush in her purse but no toothpaste. Last night Thea had told her to look for and use whatever she needed, so Charlotte opened the carved pine door of the cupboard and looked for toothpaste. The shelves held dozens of apothecary bottles with hand-scribbled labels—mullein and coltsfoot cough syrup, *yerba mansa* and astragalus root tonic—and little opaque white jars with comfrey and calendula salve. She removed the lid of one and inhaled: the thick, clear contents smelled like peppermint tea.

The cabinet also had store-bought items—aspirin, deodorant, witch hazel, lanolin, petroleum jelly, and toothpaste. The tube of toothpaste was relatively new, but the faded labels and dated containers of some of the other toiletries suggested they were more than a decade old.

Charlotte stood before the open window and towel-dried her hair. Without setting gel and a hairdryer, her hair would be unmanageable and fly in fifty tangled directions from her head. She buttoned up and tucked her shirt into her rumpled khakis and stepped away from the tiny tin-framed mirror over the sink. She looked like a desert vagabond. But somehow it just didn't matter. Even after spending the night in a strange house where at least one of the elderly inhabitants mistook her for her dead mother, she felt rested and inexplicably composed.

Charlotte fussed once more with the incorrigible curls above her right eye and then left the bathroom. The house smelled like bacon, laundered cotton, and the potpourri created by the fresh and drying flowers. So much for waking her elderly hosts. Evidently, they had been quiet for Charlotte. It was only 6:30 but Francis and Thea had been up for a while.

"The burros brought her here," Thea said over the sizzling bacon.

"I just don't want you letting them out like that, Thea," Francis said. "They get into trouble . . . well, good morning, Charlotte!"

"Come in, come in!" Thea waved her cane at Charlotte. Thea was dressed in a baggy pair of pants and a denim shirt with a glass brooch pinned on the collar. Her white hair was tucked carefully into a knot at the base of her thin brown neck. "Francis, you'd best get out to the barn and feed those burros so we can get on with breakfast!"

"Right back!" Francis slipped out the door and stiffly negotiated the porch steps. The scruffy little terrier Charlotte had met last night remained at the door looking in through the screen.

"This looks wonderful," Charlotte said. The square table was set with old blue and white china on a white linen tablecloth. "You shouldn't have gone to so much trouble."

"My dear, I've fed Francis two eggs, toast and one slice of bacon on this china every morning for sixty-five years."

Thea's right hand slid along the edge of the linoleum counter until she found the stove's enamel edge. After pulling a pot holder from her apron pocket, she groped for and grasped the handle of the cast iron frying pan. Nearly blind, she overcame her handicap with practiced agility.

"What can I do, Mrs. Durham?" Charlotte asked.

"First off, you call me Nana or Thea like everyone else in the family." Thea stopped and looked into the sun coming in the window over the sink. "Why don't you feed Bit and George?" Thea pointed at the pantry. "You'll find a sack of dog food on the left side. Give a half scoop to Bit and a half thimbleful to George. Bit's food needs some water; his teeth, you know, are about gone. Their bowls are out on the porch."

Charlotte found the sack in the pantry and measured out the dog food.

"Who's George?" Charlotte asked as she opened the screen door and stepped out onto the porch where Bit hopped about in half circles.

"George is Bit's ears."

Charlotte poured the dog food into the blue plastic bowl by the door and placed a few pieces in the identical bowl beside it.

"Bit's ears?" Charlotte scooped a cup of water from the water bucket near the door and added it to the food in the first bowl.

"Bit is deaf," Thea said through the screen. "Except for the cicadas in summer, Bit's is a silent world."

Charlotte's legs were suddenly enveloped in a flutter of white feathers, and something sharp pricked her big toe through the top of her sneaker.

"Ouch!" Charlotte leapt across the porch. "Oh gosh!"

"He pecked your foot, didn't he?" Thea said on the other side of the screen door. "That would be George. He wants you to know that he knows you're here. He's Bit's best friend. George listens for both of them."

Charlotte watched the white rooster move to the bowl beside Bit. George seemed more interested in rearranging the food than eating it, dexterously picking up the individual morsels with his beak and then dropping them onto the porch floor beside Bit's bowl. Little Bit ignored the rooster and ate his own food with great care and attention, lifting his head to a level position while he slowly and deliberately chewed each small mouthful.

"I didn't know roosters and dogs could be friends."

"Oh, my, yes, best of friends." Thea opened the door and leaned out. "Except for the way he herds the hens into the coop at dusk, I'm not sure George knows he's a rooster. Of course, if a coyote is anywhere around—any sort of danger for the hens, for Bit, for me, even—that little feathered friend will create the loudest racket you can imagine. Conchata says that George is a German shepherd wrongly birthed into a rooster's body."

In the corner of the porch an old crockpot sat on the floor. There was no top on the pot and whatever was cooking gave off a powerfully unpleasant smell.

"What are you slow cooking in this crock pot?"

"Oh . . . " Thea squinted down at the porch floor. "Well, yes, that's my arthritis formula. Tell me, dear, does it need some more water."

Charlotte held her breath and leaned over the pot. She exhaled and stood up. "It looks kind of low . . . should I add more?"

"Yes." Thea filled a measuring cup at the sink and handed it out the door to Charlotte.

"It smells terrible," Charlotte said as she took the cup. "What's in this pot?"

"Chaparral—that's what smells so bad—flowers and stems, and some yucca root. No bark, it causes cramping."

"How long does it cook like this? And then what do you do with it?"

"It cooks on low without a top for five days—two more to go, and then we'll strain it through cheesecloth."

"And then what?"

Thea raised one eyebrow and gazed at Charlotte. Thea's eyes, unlike most of the Native American and Spanish folks Charlotte had seen in New Mexico, were ice blue.

"We store it in a dark jar in the pantry. Come in here, I have some."

In the narrow pantry Thea held up a jar half-filled with amber-colored liquid.

"How do you use it?"

"I take ten drops in hot water twice a day."

"And it helps?"

Thea set the jar down on the pantry shelf.

"Of course it helps."

"How did you learn about this?" Charlotte looked around at the pantry shelves. There were a dozen more jars

"Conchata."

"Are the bundles of flowers hanging all over the house for Conchata's medicines?"

"Yes, her *remedios*, teas and tinctures. Come late summer you can't walk ten feet up the road toward the holding pond or out across the *llanos* before she's telling you to stop and gather something."

"Ra-may-dee-os? Are they old recipes?"

"Remedies, yes, very old, my dear. Some are Indian, some are Spanish. Would you take the cream out of the fridge and place it on the table?"

Charlotte found a white china pitcher with a chipped lip in the fridge and placed it on the table beside a small glass vase filled with the same pink flowers she'd seen from her window. Grandma Ruth set a formal table for Sunday brunch, but her china and silver always made Charlotte nervous and self-conscious. Dorothea's table of mismatched and chipped plates and cups made Charlotte feel welcomed: welcomed and at home.

"Are you Spanish or Indian, Thea?" Charlotte asked. "Or both?"

"Neither. I was born in Oklahoma. My folks were Sooners, immigrants from Poland who came to America for a new life."

Charlotte looked at Thea standing at the sink. "You've very suntanned."

Thea shrugged. "Live here long enough and the sun of Agua Dulce gets into your blood."

Charlotte looked out the screen door and across the packed dirt yard to the corral. She could see the furry tips of the burros' ears. Francis was pouring feed from a can into their trough and the burros began to jockey for position beside him.

"Do the burros go out walking every evening?"

"If they could! They're supposed to stay in the corral or in the upper pasture, but every so often they get this wanderlust, find an open gate and out they go!" She waved her hand through the air. "I have my suspicions as to who helps them get out," Thea said, shaking her head and pointing a finger out the window at the sky. "Gates don't just open themselves."

"No, I guess they don't," Charlotte said, deciding not to ask exactly who or what let the burros out. She was just grateful they'd been out on the old road when she needed them last night. "But they always come back, don't they?"

"Once they wandered about the valley for five days. There are mountain lions, coyotes and out at the Agua Dulce landfill . . . well, there are people who would harm them if they found them beyond the ranch boundaries. I made Francis and Dennis and Bartholomew drive up every canyon to the west and then the whole of the river from here down towards the *cuchilla*. Not a sign of em. Not even Conchata knew where they were. They walked in at dusk on the fifth day. Of course, I could hardly scold them."

"Why?"

"Because they brought George back with them, of course!"

"The rooster?"

"Yes. I don't know where he came from, but I knew why he was here."

"Why?"

"The same reason you're here."

Charlotte paused before asking the obvious and expected question. Conversations with Thea, she was learning, did not always follow a logical path.

"Why am I here?" Charlotte finally asked.

"Because this story needs you to be here."

Charlotte looked at her feet on the wood plank floor. Since last night and their introduction on the back porch, all of Charlotte's conversations with Thea Durham had come back to this fatalistic supposition. Thea was absolutely unwavering in her belief that the prescient universe of comings and goings, of sunups and sunsets, of accidents and so-called wrong turns had steered Charlotte to the Durham doorstep. Charlotte did not accept Thea's quasi-paranormal evaluation of her arrival last night. Charlotte was, after all, an eyewitness to her own foolish undoing.

"I need to make arrangements to get back into Santa Fe this morning."

Thea turned and glared across the kitchen at Charlotte. "You just got here."

"I need to call the rental car people and let them know the car is out on the desert. I need to tell someone to come out here."

"Of course," Thea said. "You know where the phone is."

Charlotte had called Maddie at the hotel last night and explained about the car breaking down, and the burros, and the miles of walking to the Durham ranch. Maddie's first question was *how* exactly did Charlotte plan to make it to the Albuquerque airport by two o'clock? Maddie's second question was *why* exactly Charlotte would bother to make their plane at all?

"See, this is what I was talking about, Char," Maddie said. "You don't even recognize something wonderful when it falls into your lap. People pay good money to play cowgirl in the New Mexican outback."

It *was* beautiful here. The idea of staying on a day or two was tempting. But Charlotte didn't even know these people, although they clearly remembered her mother and grandfather.

Charlotte called the rental car office on the kitchen telephone and explained what had happened and where she was, and that she needed to get to the Albuquerque airport by two o'clock today.

"You can't possibly go today!" Thea said loudly across the kitchen.

Charlotte watched Thea serve fried eggs and bacon strips onto the three blue and white plates while the rental car woman located Agua Dulce.

"They'll call back in a little while," Charlotte said as she placed the receiver back onto the wall-mounted telephone. "They're going to send someone to retrieve me and tow the car."

Thea turned around. "You can't leave today! What about the Fourth of July? That's just a week off. You love the parade, and the picnic and fireworks at the cemetery and the card game at Bartholomew's afterwards."

Charlotte's stomach tightened. Thea was mistaking her for her mother again.

"Conchata says you really must stay longer if we're to sort things out. You have something—" Thea stared at the ceiling, frowning, "—something that's yours, but something you need to share before you leave."

"I don't know what Conchata means by that," Charlotte said.

"Well, exactly! I don't know what she means, either."

George the rooster strutted and clucked on the porch. He stopped and lifted his head and let out a loud crow that dissolved into a descending gurgle. It was the same erratic call that had woken Charlotte this morning. Little Bit, oblivious to his friend's comical song, peered through the screen at Charlotte.

"How long has Little Bit been deaf?"

"Years, I suppose." Thea handed Charlotte two plates with eggs. She set them on the table. "Little Bit acted the same. He just became difficult to round up, even at mealtimes."

"When did he and George hook up?"

"Two summers ago. Bit was wandering along the *acequia* and I heard this great commotion just about dusk. Francis ran out and found George flapping and squawking at a rattlesnake. That old snake was buzzing away, trying to warn Little Bit to stay clear. But Bit didn't hear and was just about on top of the rattler. From then on, George began to follow Bit. And Bit began to watch George."

Francis walked slowly across the sandy yard toward the house, whistling.

"You and I have so much to talk about," Thea said. "You must have many questions about the years between now and then. And you'll want to see Dennis and the Mata brothers. And Bartholomew, of course."

Thea sighed loudly and shook her head. "I daresay Bartholomew will want to see you, although he won't say so."

"I don't know, Thea, if I can stay that long. As I told you last night, I was at this conference in Santa Fe and I have a plane reservation for this afternoon. I'm traveling with my friend, Maddie, and this visit was really an accident."

"You drink coffee, don't you?" Thea looked Charlotte's direction.

"Yes."

Thea turned off the burner, pulled the pot holder from her pocket and removed the top of the kettle of boiling water. From a canister on the counter, Thea scooped seven heaping spoonfuls of ground coffee directly into the boiling water.

"I know you like it strong, just like the boys." Thea's glassy eyes had a mischievous twinkle. "Do you ever make coffee this way?"

"No," Charlotte answered slowly.

"But you remember how, don't you?"

"Yes."

Grandpa Al used to make her mother this kind of coffee on Saturday mornings in Cambridge while Grandma Ruth was still asleep. Grandma didn't like the gritty coffee made the "chuck-wagon way" and claimed the grounds floated like sand in her cup and became caught in her teeth. But Grandpa showed Charlotte how the coffee grounds actually drifted to the bottom of the pot when he threw in the cold water just before pouring.

"It's simple science," Grandpa would say. "The cold water settles to the bottom and drags the coffee grounds with it."

Grandpa and Alicia would sit at the kitchen table and sip their camp-style coffee black, smiling across the table at one another. Charlotte used to smile with them, although she sensed that her mother and grandfather were sharing the memory of a secret faraway place that did not, could not, include her.

Thea filled a small glass jelly jar with cold tap water and tossed the water into the brewing coffee in the kettle.

"Cowboy coffee," Thea said. "Folks around here still think it beats what you get from those fancy machines."

Until this very moment and Thea's naming of it Charlotte assumed *cowboy coffee* was something Grandpa had made up. It had never occurred to Charlotte that it was the way real cowboys made coffee. But then, until yesterday and her encounter with the boot-chap-Stetson-sporting gentleman and his fine-looking gelding in front of the drugstore, Charlotte couldn't have said with any conviction that there was such a thing as real cowboys on real horses still roaming the Southwest.

{9}

Francis opened the screen door and entered the kitchen. His face was flushed with exertion and sun. Little Bit came in with Francis but George remained out in the yard pecking at something in the sand beneath an old green truck parked near the corral.

"We were just sitting down," Thea said to Francis's back as he washed his hands. "I was about to send Miss Rose to find you because I couldn't see you."

"You can't never see me, Thea." Francis winked over his shoulder at Charlotte as he dried his hands.

"Don't make fun of me, Mr. Durham," Thea hooked her cane over the edge of the table. Francis pulled out a chair and helped Thea sit down. "I see more than most."

Francis pushed in Charlotte's chair after she sat down and then took his own seat. After a moment of silence Thea and Francis picked up their forks and began to eat. Charlotte did the same. She was starving: she had missed lunch yesterday and although Thea had given her egg salad on thick slices of homemade bread and fruit before bed, Charlotte's stomach felt like a hollow gourd.

Charlotte reached for her juice just as Thea lay a hand on her wrist.

"I know you think I'm forgetting, but I'm not."

Francis eyed Thea across the vase of little pink flowers.

"I know you are not Alicia. You are her daughter, Charlotte Lambert." Thea released Charlotte's wrist and looked at Francis. Francis spooned preserves onto his toast.

"Oh, it's all right," Charlotte said. "Everyone who knew her says I look a lot like her."

"Yes," Thea said. "And just now, carrying the plates like that, the morning sun catching your hair . . ."

Thea reached out and touched the tip of a curl near Charlotte's ear. "I'm certain we sat like this, Alicia and I, on another June morning." Thea picked up her fork and picked at her egg. "Through my eyes, the present, this time just now, and the present of the past, look about the same. Only the faces from the past are clearer."

"Little Bit has taken a liking to you," Francis motioned at the old dog settling down for a nap beside Charlotte's chair leg.

Charlotte reached down and stroked one of Bit's soft deaf ears. "He's very sweet."

Francis poured coffee from his cup into his saucer and after adding a drop of cream lifted the saucer to his lips and sipped loudly.

"Don't mind him," Thea said as she handed the plate with toast across the table to Charlotte. "Mr. Durham likes his coffee lukewarm. Do you have a dog of your own?"

"No, I don't have any pets."

"No pets?" Thea's jaw dropped. "You seem to get along right fine with animals—the burros let you walk alongside them and they can be just the most unsociable lot. Old Egypt has nipped at more than one person who placed a hand on his back. And George only pecked your foot once. Why, every first Tuesday of the month when Jerry Graber comes to read the electric meter, George trips him up so badly Jerry swats at him with his clipboard. Feathers fly! There are some people George will not let near the house."

"I do work as a volunteer at the humane society, walking dogs every other Saturday," Charlotte said.

"You haven't fallen in love with some lonely hound and brought him home?"

"Well, no."

"And you said you live alone?" Thea leaned on one elbow and peered at Charlotte.

"I own a small house a few blocks from the school where I teach."

"How old are you, Charlotte?" Thea asked.

"I'm thirty-two."

"Never married?"

Francis cleared his throat but Thea ignored him.

"No, I've never been married," Charlotte said with jovial conviction. "I just haven't, well, the timing has not been good."

"Oh, love never cares about good timing. But why haven't you adopted?" Thea asked.

"Adopted?" Charlotte swallowed.

"A dog." Thea spread a thin smear of jam across her toast.

"Dogs are a lot of responsibility," Charlotte said. "I'm at school all day and I like to go away on weekends. It just seems like too big of a commitment. I really couldn't give a dog what it needs."

Thea stared at the toast in her hand. The kitchen was silent except for Francis's coffee sipping and Little Bit's gentle snoring near Charlotte's foot.

Thea set the toast back down onto her plate. "You haven't done well since your mother and grandfather died, have you?"

Charlotte flushed and looked down at Little Bit.

"Charlotte, what about that rental car?" Francis asked quickly. "We could tow it; Barty has a truck with a gadget for that."

Charlotte looked across the table at Francis. His eyes were so kind.

"I called the rental people," she said. "They're sending a tow truck this morning."

Francis nodded. "What other arrangements do you need to make? You said you have a plane today?"

"She can't catch a plane today," Thea stated loudly. "She can't *leave* today."

Charlotte looked from Francis to Thea and back to Francis.

"I have a ticket for a two o'clock flight to New York this afternoon. All of my things are at a hotel in Santa Fe. My friend, Maddie, will check out of the hotel with my suitcases later this morning and meet me at the airport."

"We're three hours from Albuquerque," Thea said. "Francis can't drive you. He's too slow and long drives put him to sleep. And his manager, Ralph, can't leave the store on a Sunday."

Francis smiled sympathetically at Charlotte. "There are plenty of people to drive you. If you left here before nine, weekend traffic through Santa Fe permitting, you *might* make it. Got things to do back home?"

"Actually, I'm on summer break now," Charlotte said. "But, yes, I have plans."

"Oh for heaven's sake, Francis, she can't leave today!" Thea slapped the table with her hand. "Why, Conchata would give me no peace for a month!"

"You are welcome to stay here as long as you like," Francis said calmly. "But we certainly understand you have a plane to catch today."

Charlotte was feeling increasingly confused about what she had to do today and why: the more she thought about catching a plane to New York the more out of sorts she felt. And then the way Thea reacted, it seemed Charlotte's actions were putting people she hadn't even met, especially Thea's friend, Conchata, out of sorts, too.

"Where does Conchata live?" Charlotte asked. Maybe if Charlotte met Conchata she could depart New Mexico in peace. "In Agua Dulce?"

Francis looked at Thea and waited for her to answer.

"Sometimes." Thea sipped her coffee. "She's a trifle hard to pin down."

"Why will she be so upset if I leave today?"

"Well, that's a long story. She's Bartholomew and Bernadette's mother, you see, and Bartholomew, well, he . . ."

"You both have a daughter named Bernadette?" Charlotte took another piece of toast from the basket.

"No, we have the same daughter named Bernadette," Thea said.

Francis sighed. "You'd have to stay here all summer to understand this family's tree."

"Your family, in many ways," Thea said to Charlotte as she picked up a piece of bacon. "And you *should* stay here all summer. All summer. And learn about your family. You have a lot of catching up."

Charlotte glanced at her watch. Seven o'clock. She had to make a decision soon.

"What do you teach back in New York?" Francis asked.

"I'm an advanced placement English teacher at a private girl's school."

"Well, there now!" Thea said. "You can teach English here!"

"There isn't a school here anymore, Thea," Francis said matter-of-factly.

Thea waved her hand in the air between herself and Francis as if shooing away his words.

"And what of your father, what's his name, Leonard?" Thea leaned closer to Charlotte.

Charlotte swallowed a bite of toast and cleared her throat. "Leonard died of lung cancer this past winter."

"I'm so sorry," Thea said, frowning. "I'm so sorry. Who do you have now? Are you in love?"

"Thea, let the girl eat!" Francis said.

"It's okay," Charlotte said, trying to sound as if it were okay. "No, I'm not in love."

"And no dog," Thea said, clucking her tongue and shaking her head.

Charlotte stared at the bright yellow yoke bleeding from the egg plucked from George's hen house. Charlotte had no one because she loved no one. And no one loved her. Not even a dog or a rooster. How *had* she come to be so alone and loveless?

"So, why do you have to catch that plane this afternoon?" Thea continued. "If you don't have a dog or a boyfriend or family, anyone waiting for you back in New York, there's really no hurry. You can stay here. That bed will be empty until Bernadette comes in August for Jed's thirtieth birthday."

"You're so kind, but I have a lot of projects waiting, a lot of things I need to get home for." Except for bringing in the mail accumulating in her mailbox, Charlotte couldn't remember what those waiting projects and lots of things might be precisely. But she was certainly doing a fine job pretending like she knew. "I couldn't impose; you don't even know me."

This time it was Francis who leaned over the plate of toast and vase of pink flowers to Charlotte. "Alicia Rose's daughter, and the good Dr. Albert Rose's granddaughter, could never impose on us."

Charlotte focused on her plate of food and waited for the sad, little-girl-left-behind feeling in her chest to subside. It took a few minutes of earnest attention to her eggs, bacon and toast before Charlotte regained her composure.

"Did you know them well, my mother and my grandfather?"

"No one really *knew* Alicia," Thea said softly. "She was a beautiful mystery, your mother."

"Now your grandfather, Albert, I knew very well," Francis said. "We played many a game of cards and horseshoes. Dr. Al had a great capacity for making people feel comfortable, equal, even if they never set foot in a college. We used to sit out on the porch for hours, talking about fossils, geology, about lumber, crops, birds, about the changes in weather, too. He was interested in everything, everything. I used to think your grandfather would buy a piece of land in the Lágrimas, build a little adobe *casa* so that he could return whenever he wanted."

"Why didn't he?" Grandpa Al had never mentioned such a plan to Charlotte.

Francis's fingers smoothed the tablecloth around his plate. "Oh, just the unforeseen turns in the road. Dr. Al's journey angled away from here, I guess."

"You see, that's exactly what I'm talking about," Thea said. "Charlotte's road took a hard turn and brought her to this doorstep, to this kitchen where we said good-by to Dr. Al. You remember, Francis, how Albert stood right there, his straw hat in his hand. Ruth and Alicia waited out in the Jeep. Alicia wasn't feeling well—she had the stomach flu that last week in camp. Ruth blamed Albert, said he let his daughter just run wild all summer and now she was paying for it. I gave Dr. Al a thermos of coffee brewed with canela bark and told him it would ease Alicia's nausea. But our farewell was hurried and many a word went unsaid. I just knew, I *knew* that morning I'd never see him again."

"Thea—" Francis began.

"—Sometimes it takes years to finish what was begun," Thea said. "All those unspoken words waiting to be found like misplaced letters."

Francis stood up and carried his plate to the sink. He turned on the tap and squirted dish soap into the water. Charlotte gazed into the kitchen. This place felt known, familiar. What of hers was waiting to be found? Charlotte's focus shifted from Francis at the sink to the translucent middle space between them. Grandpa Al stood in the center of the room where the sun illuminated his white short-sleeved cotton shirt. He held his frayed "diggers" hat in one hand and a blue and white china cup in the other. Grandpa looked across the filaments of morning light at Charlotte and smiled in that way that told her just how much he loved her.

Tears welled up in Charlotte's eyes and she reached down and touched Little Bit's head. Francis washed dishes. Thea rearranged her eggs with her fork and took bites that would not satisfy a bird. Charlotte wiped the tears away and sat back up. Thea was lost in her own thoughts, her slender fingers tapping the handle of her coffee cup. Charlotte wanted to say that she wasn't so loveless after all. Grandpa loved her. Charlotte had allowed his love to slip out of sight, out of reach. But it was here, waiting for her in the Durham kitchen.

"Charlotte, you decide what you want to do today," Francis said as he dried his hands on a towel. "I'll help you get to wherever you need to be, Santa Fe or Albuquerque. But you are most welcome to stay in our home as long as you like." Francis left the kitchen.

"More coffee?" Thea pushed her chair away from the table.

"Please, let me get it." Charlotte stood and retrieved the coffee pot. "Why did he leave in such a hurry?" Charlotte asked, as she poured coffee into each cup.

"Francis always leaves in a hurry."

"No, Grandpa, why did he leave Agua Dulce in such a hurry?"

"Because of Ruth." Thea made a clucking sound with her tongue again. "Your grandmother only came for a brief visit late in the summer. Ruth didn't like the desert, the fossil site, the town. She said the summer out here on the far side of uncivilized had ruined Alicia."

"Grandma Rose did not like to camp," Charlotte said. "And she always worried about germs and infections. She had tuberculosis as a child, so I guess you can't blame her for being cautious. Do you know where the fossil site was?"

"Well, *I* couldn't find it anymore. Bartholomew knows where the old site is but pretends like he doesn't. Dennis could take you out there."

Francis returned to the kitchen and retrieved his cap from the pantry.

"Francis, she wants to see the fossil site."

Francis studied Charlotte's reaction to Thea's declaration.

"I could take another plane tomorrow or the next day," Charlotte said. "I could stay for just a day or so longer."

"Oh, that's wonderful!" Thea said, holding her wrinkled brown hands to her heart.

"Okay." Francis was smiling, too. "I'll talk with Dennis about your grandfather's site when I see him this morning."

A gleaming green pickup truck with *Durham Hardware* printed on the side door circled around the sandy yard between the house and the barn and stopped at the bottom of the porch stairs.

"That's my ride, ladies." Francis walked to the screen door and out onto the porch. Little Bit scrambled to his feet and followed Francis outside. He adjusted his cap and walked carefully down the porch steps to the waiting truck. A young man waved through the truck window.

"That's Ralph," Thea said, waving back. "He takes very good care of my Francis. But I do wish he would go back to Albuquerque and finish college."

"Do they always work Sunday?"

"Yes. The ranchers are always working Sundays, and Francis decided he had to stay open to accommodate them. But he loves the store. It's where he wants to be."

Thea stood at the sink. Charlotte cleared the table. A day or two stop-over, what could it hurt? It wasn't like she was about to do something rash or irresponsible, quit her job and vanish into the horizon.

"Oh, this will be wonderful!" Thea slid the last dishes into the sink of soapy water. "There's the upper box canyon of the ranch to see, and then the fossil site, of course, and you'll be wanting to have a Mata malt."

"At the drugstore?" Charlotte cleared the coffee cups. "On Main Street?"

"Of course." Thea washed and rinsed the dishes and handed them to Charlotte to dry. "Why, Dennis used to make you a double chocolate malt each and every time you came into the store with Dr. Al."

Charlotte said nothing. Her stomach didn't even react this time. Thea was old enough to have earned the right to remember whatever she wanted about the present of the past or the present of the present.

"I just don't know why I didn't see you coming." Thea stopped soaping a plate and looked directly up into Charlotte's face. "Last month, or was it the month before? I dreamed about a child lost in the canyonlands. I looked for him all night in that dream. I could hear a small voice carried on the wind, but I never saw him. A boy. I had Francis read every page of the Dos Rios and Santa Fe newspapers every day for two weeks. I even called Martin Abrams, the sheriff. But no one knew anything about him. Even Conchata was of no help. I could not sleep. I really felt we needed to go looking for a lost child."

Charlotte said nothing. Did Thea believe she was the lost child of her dream?

Thea's hands felt about the soapy water for a submerged plate or cup. "My vision is not good you know." Thea pulled the last plate from the sudsy water, dipped it into the clear rinse water and handed it to Charlotte.

"Conchata can be very difficult to understand. She can just go on and on and she throws Apache and Spanish and English all together into a garbled word stew. Honestly, it can make a person half mad."

Charlotte dried the plate and placed it onto the stack in the cupboard.

"I'll change into a dress and then we'll go into town." Thea removed her cotton apron and hung it behind the pantry door. "Did you find everything you needed in the bathroom?"

"Yes, thank you."

Thea took her cane from the chair and then stopped and turned around by the phone on the wall.

"You know, we could put your clothes into my new Maytag and they'd be clean by noon. You can go through Bernadette's closet and find something to wear this morning. What do you think?"

Charlotte looked down at her rumpled trousers. "I guess that's the thing to do. Thanks. And could we wait for the rental car people to call back before we go out?"

"Of course. We'll go when you're ready." Thea looked at the telephone. "I could call Bartholomew to come and drive us into town." Thea considered this for a moment. "No, you can drive us. Bartholomew can be so stubborn and moody. Conchata says he has always been his own worst enemy."

Thea left the kitchen but stopped in the hall and looked back at Charlotte. "Conchata's pretty certain it was *mariola* tea. The thermos I gave Albert that morning: she insists it wasn't coffee brewed with canela bark, but was cold *mariola* tea."

Thea went on down the hall. Charlotte dried the remaining cup and then hung the dish towel over the oven handle. She walked to the middle of the kitchen and stood under the bundles of roots, herbs, and flowers drying from the pine beams of the ceiling. She hoped she wasn't making a mistake by staying on at the Durhams' for another day or so. What did Grandma Ruth call it? The far side of uncivilized.

Little Bit was asleep on the porch. In the open yard beyond the house George strutted, his every move scrutinized by the burros that watched from the corral. Except for the soft ticking of the clock in the living room at the far end of the house, and the erratic buzz of the hummingbirds in the garden, it was absolutely quiet. At the very least, the far side of uncivilized was a peaceful and undemanding place.

{10}

Mabel rang the breakfast bell. Farley began his slow descent of the three flights of steep stairs. When he reached the small dining room the three other boarders—old crones and geezers, all of them, two foolish men and one foolish woman—were seated at the breakfast table. Farley never said hello, although they all persisted in greeting him every morning, every noon, every evening, as if they were important in his world. They were not. Mabel Duran was important because she provided meals and enabled Farley to live here. But that was all Farley needed from people, and all he wanted.

"Good morning, Holoman Farley," someone said. "How'd ya sleep?"

Farley said nothing. They all knew damned well he had hardly slept, same as always. Except for Earl who had regular and continuous ear infections they had all heard the commotion last night. Every one of them in the boardinghouse had lay unmoving in their beds and listened to the witch horse crashing about Farley's room, had heard Duende's great jaws lock down around Farley's legs and splinter apart more tendon and bone.

Before sitting down at Mabel's yellowed-lace-covered table, Farley turned to the room at large and said loudly, "I saw her. You're thinking I didn't, but I saw her. Yesterday. She thought I wouldn't be looking, wouldn't be paying attention after all these years, but I saw her."

"Sit down, Farley, and eat your pancakes," Mabel said as she poured coffee into a porcelain white cup and handed it to Earl.

"What's that?" Earl asked the table. "Who'd he see?"

Farley looked at Mabel serving coffee at the far end of the table and for just an instant between blinks of his eyes he saw Alicia Rose. It was an old game. Duende played it, too, made all the black horses, even the small, underfed burros of the Lágrimas, look like registered Thoroughbreds.

"I told you before, Farley, if you go on about the evil spirits in my house you're out." Mabel paused by Farley with the coffee pot held in the air between them. "And your only option after here is the state old folks' home in Santa Fe where they'll lock you up for crazy. So sit down and eat."

Farley sucked on his butter-plastered pancakes and slurped black coffee. The boarders talked about the weather and about Agua Dulce's upcoming Independence Day parade. Farley placed his mind back on the problem—the return of that evil woman—and commended himself for years of devoted watchfulness.

"Who's going to the post office this morning?" Farley said through half-gummed food.

Everyone knew Farley was looking for a ride. No one said a word.

"I'd like to go along."

Everyone at the table continued to eat as if they had not heard Farley. Farley looked from face to face until his eyes found Earl Turnball.

"I'll take ya, Farley," Earl said softly across the table. "But you can't make any trouble. None of that swearing at the ladies and cursing the birds. And you can't go in the drugstore with me—I have to get my eardrops prescription filled. After the post office you can sit in the Falcon and keep your disrespect-ful hands and words to yourself."

"Shit," Farley spit into his coffee cup. He pictured Earl slipping on the stairs and his neck snapping like a dry stick at the bottom.

"What was that?" Mabel asked from her perch at the end of the table.

Women were always doing that—pretending not to hear and then not to understand when all along they know a man's desires precisely. It was them that placed all that lust in a man's groin, made him a fumbling fool, half mad with need.

"I'll be leaving at ten," Earl said as he stood up and wiped his lips with a napkin. "You be around back at the alley, Farley, and no binoculars. Nice breakfast, Mabel. Those pancakes fill me every time."

Farley stood up so quickly that his fork clanged to the floor near his shoe. He couldn't take his binoculars to the post office but he could take his knife. He could hide it down in the crotch of his pants where everyone thought he was numb and shriveled. He'd show them Holoman Farley was still a man to be reckoned with.

"Pick up the fork, Farley," Mabel said, rolling her eyes over the rim of her coffee cup. "And leave my linen napkin on the table. I found five of them in your room last week."

Farley shuffled slowly, painfully up the three flights of stairs to his room. One of these days, he would show this godforsaken town that he knew exactly what he was doing. One day, the people of Agua Dulce would thank him for his relentless pursuit of the evil ones of the Lágrimas. And that day wasn't far off. Very soon, sooner than they knew, Farley was going to cut and string the ears of that bewitched horse, Duende, and twice murder that milk-skinned, Apache-loving temptress, Alicia Rose.

{11}

I told everyone the truth: Charlotte Lambert left the hotel after lunch and disappeared into the New Mexican outback." Maddie was jubilant. "You were the talk of this morning's departure breakfast. *You*, Charlotte! The woman who never *ever* deviates from the lesson plan! And now you're missing your plane home to go and see your grandfather's fossil site? Far-fucking-out!"

"Maddie, I didn't deviate from the plan. I ran over a boulder." Charlotte stood in the pantry at the end of the phone cord hoping that Thea in her bedroom could not hear this conversation. "The plan is this: I'll fly home noon on Wednesday. I tried to get on the Tuesday nonstop, but it's booked. I'll come on Wednesday."

Maddie snorted. "And where's the car?"

"Out on the old road. They're sending a tow truck for it this morning and I'm mailing them the keys."

"Of course." Maddie said. "You've taken care of everything. I'll leave your bags at the front desk. But really, Char, don't hurry back! I'll go by your house, take in the mail and newspaper. I'll even water your lawn every few days all summer."

"Three days, Maddie. I'll be back Wednesday night."

"Charlotte, for once, just *once* in your life why don't you let yourself get swept away by something? Anything! Horses, burros, a sandstorm, *something*!"

"I'll call you when I get in on Wednesday," Charlotte said. "Say goodbye to Patricia and everyone else for me, okay?"

Thea's new Maytag was an impressive state-of-the-art machine tucked into the hall closet. Charlotte loaded her few articles of clothing into the washing machine and when Thea still had not emerged from her bedroom, she left the house and wandered about the corrals. Bit and George marched in a procession behind Charlotte until she approached the vicinity of the hen coop. As Charlotte neared the chickens pecking about the barnyard, George broke into a run and raced ahead into the feathery crowd, clucking and fluttering his wings. An antique Hudson truck was parked near the side of the barn. Its green paint was chipped and scratched but its body was remarkably rust free. Block letters on the door said *Durham Hardware est. 1947*. The Hudson was obviously the predecessor to the new green truck that came for Francis this morning.

Although it was cool under the cottonwood tree, the unshaded yard was already hot. Little Bit ambled along a path close to the cooler side of the barn. George wandered under the corral fence and through the legs of the burros where he pecked at minuscule specks of grain in the dirt. From the corral's top railing Charlotte watched two of the burros drag an overturned water trough across the sand with their teeth.

Charlotte looked back at the house. It was almost nine o'clock. Thea had gone to change into her "good dress" almost an hour ago. Maybe she had fallen asleep, or had simply forgotten about their plan to go into Agua Dulce and have a malt? Charlotte climbed down from the fence. Just then, George scurried under the corral gate and straight across the yard to the house. Little Bit was dozing under the old truck but somehow the deaf dog intuited George's frenzied departure, scrambled to his little feet and left the shade under the Hudson to follow George at a stiff but vigorous lope. The two reached the bottom of the porch stairs just as Thea appeared at the kitchen door.

"We're off!" Thea called out the door. Thea had changed into a flowered shirtwaist and a newer pair of orthopedic walking shoes. At the truck Thea handed Charlotte a ring of keys. "Open the tailgate for Bit." Thea pointed her cane at the rear end of the Hudson. "If George tries to jump in, shoo him out."

"We're taking this truck?"

"Yes, the sedan needs a new water hose or meter or some such thing."

Thea opened the passenger door, climbed onto the seat and arranged her dress neatly across her thin knees. Charlotte positioned herself behind the remarkably large steering wheel, closed the door and found the ignition on the dash.

"Pump the gas a few times before you turn the ignition," Thea instructed Charlotte.

After vigorous pumping on the gas pedal, Charlotte turned the key in the ignition. The engine turned over effortlessly.

"How old is this pickup truck?" Charlotte adjusted the narrow rearview mirror. "It must be a collector's item."

"Francis bought this Hudson in 1947, the year he bought the hardware store from Enoch Strand." Thea was looking at Charlotte's hand hovering over the column-mounted gear shift. "It's a three speed."

"What?"

"There are three forward gears," Thea said.

"Oh, of course," Charlotte depressed the clutch, pushed the gear stick and heard a grinding sound under the truck. Thea leaned over, placed her bony hand on top of Charlotte's and pushed the stick firmly into first gear.

After yesterday's mishap in the rented car, Charlotte was feeling self-conscious about her driving skills. But the old truck was actually easy to drive and after finding second gear without Thea's help, Charlotte aimed the Hudson onto the road she had walked in on with the burros last night. The truck crested the mesa above the house and Charlotte shifted successfully into third. Little Bit flitted back and forth across the rearview mirror as he happily raced from one side of the truck bed to the other.

From the mesa top, the world of the Lágrimas opened in four directions. Even through her sunglasses, the brightness of the sky and the intensity of the colors of the earth caused Charlotte's eyes to squint into slits.

"Isn't it a glorious day!" Thea wore sunglasses and faced straight ahead, her hands folded on her lap. "My yes, a good day to go to town."

"Yes," Charlotte said, smiling with Thea. The ranch road was very rutted, and Charlotte had to concentrate to keep the truck's tires out of the deep grooves.

"Maybe it's the bareness of the land, the unfettered view, but around Agua Dulce there's very little privacy." Thea tilted her head Charlotte's direction. "People here try to pretend they don't notice a stranger, aren't interested in you, but they're really hoping you'll look their direction. Dr. Al looked at everyone. He remembered everyone's name. And everyone remembered his name, even after he'd been gone years."

Charlotte slowed the truck as it reached the open gate where the ranch road reached the pavement of CR 155. Agua Dulce was to the left, north of the ranch. To the right and south about five miles was the disabled rental car.

"My grandfather loved people." Charlotte released the clutch, gave the engine some gas and eased the Hudson onto the highway. "His students would return years after they'd graduated. They'd come into his lab at Harvard and he'd fix them coffee—that cowboy way—and they'd sit down at those big fossil-covered lab tables and tell him all about their work, their families. I was amazed by how many students Grandpa had taught. And yes, he *never* forgot a name. I used to be just a little bit jealous of them, of the hours and days in the field they'd shared with him, the places they'd seen together."

"I first met them at the store," Thea said. "A day to remember. Dr. Al came in first thing one morning, just after we'd opened, dressed in those tan pants, a list of supplies on a notepad in his hand, a smile on his face. Alicia was dressed in baggy jeans with the cuffs rolled up, all the rage at the time, you know, a man's denim shirt belted at the waist. Her white skin just glowed with the first glaze of summer. The men in the store, even my Francis, why, they stopped breathing, all of them, when they saw Alicia standing there beside her father in the sun of the doorway. She did that. She took a man's breath away. But you know I don't believe she was ever really aware of it. It wasn't what interested her. Her attention was always somewhere else, someplace far away. Of course, everyone wanted to go to that place with her."

Charlotte knew all about her mother's daydreaming. Alicia's inability to remain focused on the matter at hand was legendary: she would place Leonard's shirts into the washer, remember them days later and pull them out molded and ruined; and the kitchen kettle was replaced at least once every few months because Alicia would put water on to boil, forget to put the whistler down, and return and find the kettle empty and disfigured on the stove burner. Alicia's lack of attention to everyday life caused Grandma Ruth to seethe with frustration.

"Dr. Al was brilliant but he never made others feel inferior. People around here had never known a man of science and learning like that. Of course there was Thomas Bill, Conchata's husband, a college man from North Carolina. He was quieter, more reserved than your grandfather. Thomas left the university before he finished his degree. They would have enjoyed one another, don't you think? But Thomas died years before your grandfather came to the Lágrimas."

"Did Conchata come from North Carolina, too?" Charlotte studied the bluffs and buttes that lifted off the desert to her left. She had passed all of this yesterday, but seeing the landscape from behind the steering wheel of the Hudson with Thea chatting away beside her about Grandpa like he was here just yesterday made the huge earth of the Lágrimas friendly and welcoming.

"Oh, no. Conchata came from a mountain village on the far side of the reservation. Conchata's mother was Apache, her father Spanish. How much fuel do we have?"

Thea pointed at the dashboard in front of Charlotte. Charlotte glanced down at the dash where the needle of the circular gas gage bobbed between empty and half full. The speedometer needle did not move at all, but remained permanently pointed at the large zero. "Maybe a quarter tank?"

"Enough. We might go by and visit Bartholomew later. I tried to call him this morning, to tell him you were back. But he gets out early with the horses—he's always up with the lark, if he goes to bed at all. First thing every morning, he'll go see Jed. They're renovating the old ranch house. Have you ever laid adobe?"

"Laid adobe?"

"Adobe brick. All of the buildings around here, at least the old ones, are made of adobe brick and mud."

"They don't have adobe brick back east."

"No, I suppose not, but they should." Thea tapped her chest bone with her knuckles. "Adobe is very good for the heart."

Buildings rose into view on the red horizon, and to the right the green trees that edged the Lágrimas River lifted into the landscape.

"Tell me, is the school coming up on the right?" Thea pointed at the first brown structure. "Thomas Bill built that school."

"I thought there wasn't a school in Agua Dulce."

"There's a school *building*, but there is no school. No teachers. No books. They bus the children into Dos Rios."

"But why? It's so far."

"The Apaches have their own school up in Dulce. The Dos Rios school board says there aren't enough children in Agua Dulce for a public school. And since Agua Dulce is not part of the reservation, the children have to be bussed into the consolidated public school in Dos Rios."

"Aren't there Apache people in Agua Dulce?"

"Yes. But the Apaches here don't get the benefits of reservation living. They're living with a foot in two worlds, and both worlds are claimed by a third world that for the most part hasn't any idea what the world of the Lágrimas is about."

"It's probably a better school in Dos Rios," Charlotte said. "The consolidated districts usually have more teachers and equipment."

"Fiddlesticks! The children have to sit on the bus for an hour and fifteen minutes each way. Last winter, two were injured when the bus slid off the road into the arroyo at Dead Man's Curve the week before Christmas."

"Oh, how terrible!" Charlotte looked at the little adobe school surrounded by sand and cactus. A chain-link fence enclosed a swing set, wood seesaws and a tall slide. The front gate was opened and cars were parked in a neat row along the side of the building.

"Some of the local parents won't let their children return to school in Dos Rios," Thea added after a moment. "They won't get any education at all."

"Isn't that illegal?"

"They'll home-school the children." Thea clucked her tongue in disapproval. "I was home-schooled in Enid, Oklahoma and went on to college. Nothing wrong with that. But some of these parents can't read or write themselves!"

"Who uses the building? There are a lot of cars parked here."

"The Agua Dulce Fourth of July committee must be meeting this morning."

Charlotte studied the crooked crosses and haphazard rows of stone markers inside the fenced graveyard. "And what is the rock pile out beyond the baseball field?"

"That's the marker for the Lágrimas miracle."

"What miracle was that?" Charlotte slowed the Hudson so she could study the stone hill. It had a wide base and narrowed as it rose some twenty feet above the desert floor.

Thea turned to Charlotte across the cab. "Surely you remember? The six horses came for the Bataan boys who died in the Philippines. You never saw them alive but you found their skeletons in the canyons."

"The boys' skeletons?"

"The horse skeletons. The bone horses that you sketched in your notebook!"

Charlotte pressed down on the accelerator and steered the Hudson down the middle of the road. It was time to get to Agua Dulce and move Thea back into the present. Charlotte would ask Francis later about the Bataan brothers and their stone monument. Francis could tell her the story without placing Charlotte within it.

They reached a small but charming adobe church. Charlotte had missed the cross-shaped, pitched-roofed chapel with the bell tower when she drove past here yesterday.

"Is this church still used?"

"It is. There are many Spanish Catholics in this valley," Thea said. "I was raised Protestant back in Enid. Spanish Catholics, God bless them, they tend to overdo the casket and burial thing. They take final rites to a place even the dead find morbidly depressing. When Conchata died, her younger brother, Devon, spent a small fortune on her casket. It weighed far too much." Thea paused while she leaned into the space between them. "You can see what I mean about a foot in two worlds. After the funeral Mass at the church, for the Apache part of the ceremony, to free Conchata's spirit from the bondage of the earth, the Lonewolfs had to carry Conchata across moving water. The Lágrimas was frozen, which might account for Conchata having one foot here and one foot on the other side. If Thomas had been alive when his wife died, being that Protestants don't go for a lot of ceremony, he would never have tolerated Devon carrying Conchata's body about the valley in that flamboyant casket. Conchata was sorely disappointed with Devon, but she forgave him, that's her nature. She even came to be amused by the whole fiasco surrounding her leave taking."

Thea drew in a large breath and sighed. "I'm going to be cremated."

The Hudson drifted to a standstill in the middle of the road.

"Conchata's dead?" Charlotte rapidly reviewed the various conversations in the last twelve hours that had included Conchata, looking to understand why she had assumed that Conchata was a member of the living. "This is the same Conchata you and Francis were talking about at breakfast?"

"Bernadette and Bartholomew's mother, Conchata."

"I thought she was, well, you have all those herbs and flowers for her remedies . . ."

"Well, certainly." Thea stared vacantly out the front windshield. "Francis thinks it's because of that extravagant red-velvet-lined casket that I have decided to be cremated. But it's not. Conchata has had nothing to do with this decision. In fact, the only person who has had anything to do with my decision is Dr. Al."

"Grandpa?"

"Yes, Dr. Al was sitting on the coffee can in the center of the firepit—there was no fire, of course, just ashes from fires that burned out decades ago piled around his boots—that got me to looking for a container with a good tight lid. One that can be carried by horseback up into the mountains. Was your grandfather cremated?"

"Oh, gosh." The Hudson was threatening to stall. Charlotte depressed the clutch and fumbled with the gearshift until it slipped into a lower gear and the truck pitched forwards. "Yes, Grandpa was cremated."

Downtown Agua Dulce was a busy hive of pickup trucks, cars and pedestrians all of whom recognized the Durham Hardware Hudson and waved at the truck as they drove by. From the rear bed Little Bit wagged his tail at every vehicle and person on Main Street. Like yesterday, the four kindly old-timers were sitting on the bench at the bottom of the Mata Drugstore steps, but there was no horse tied to the railing.

"You can park on the street," Thea said, motioning out her window. "Or we can go around the corner to the alley behind the store."

"Here's a space," Charlotte swung the truck into the last spot before the corner. "Right in front of the post office."

Charlotte turned off the Hudson and rubbed her hands. They were sore and sweaty from gripping the narrow steering wheel.

"Ironic, isn't it?" Thea asked.

"What's that?" Charlotte was still mulling over her colossal confusion about Conchata Lonewolf Bill.

"Ashes. Dr. Al, a bone lover, became ashes. And what of Alicia's bones?"

"What?" Charlotte looked at Thea.

"Was your mother's body buried?" Thea looked straight ahead at the post office.

"No. She was cremated."

Thea opened her door. "Like her father, Alicia loved bones. Used to drag bones back from the desert. Said she'd return one day and retrieve them."

"The dinosaur bones?" Charlotte asked.

Thea slid her legs out of the cab and lowered her feet to the pavement.

"No, horse bones. Surely your mother told you about the bone horses?"

"No, I don't remember any stories about bone horses. I only heard them talk about the Coelophysis bones found at the quarry."

Thea shifted her torso back around and faced Charlotte.

"Goodness. Alicia was hurting more than I understood."

Thea climbed from the truck cab and closed the door behind her. Charlotte pulled the key from the ignition and left the truck. Of course Alicia was hurting more than everyone understood. Didn't her desperate and dramatic last act on the desert make that fact perfectly clear?

{12}

"Will Little Bit wait here in the truck?" Charlotte rubbed Little Bit between the ears.

"He'll wait for hours, even days." Thea tapped her cane against the parking meter. "Bit can't hear you calling, but if you ever need to find him, just go back to where you last saw him. Little Bit is nothing if not patient."

Charlotte joined Thea on the sidewalk.

"A dime." Thea pressed the coin into Charlotte's palm. "For the meter."

Charlotte dropped the dime in the slot. Thea slid her arm around Charlotte's.

"They're watching us, aren't they?" Thea said.

"Who?" Charlotte looked across the street in the direction of Thea's pointing cane.

"Gus and the boys." Thea waved her cane at the elderly cowboys on the bench before the drugstore. Gus and the boys held up their hands and stiffly but energetically waved back. "You've given them more to chaw about in the last five minutes than they've had in five years."

"Gus and the boys," Charlotte smiled and waved. "They're very sweet."

Inside the post office Thea directed Charlotte to the first wall. "Box twenty-six." Thea pulled a key from her purse and handed it to Charlotte.

Charlotte scanned the numbered doors, found twenty-six and slid the key into the lock. Inside were several letters and a thick rolled pile of magazines and mail order catalogues. Thea took the small pile from Charlotte.

"The thing is, if Alicia didn't tell you about the bone horses, I'm thinking there's a whole lot more your mother and your grandfather didn't tell you."

Charlotte placed the key in Thea's open hand. Thea dropped it back into her purse and snapped it closed.

"They must have had their reasons," Charlotte said. Didn't they say that what you don't know can't hurt you? What Charlotte did know hurt plenty.

"The car rental agency said just mail the keys." Charlotte dropped the key and fob with the return address into the mail slot.

A woman in her forties wearing white short-shorts and a red tank top and far too much make-up for a Saturday morning anywhere except perhaps Times Square stepped into the lobby. She had a small child in tow.

"Good morning, Violeta!" Thea bent over and looked into the face of the beautiful girl who laughed into her tiny hands.

Thea stood up. "And hello, Rosa, how is everything?" Thea's glassy eyes scanned the space around Rosa's head.

"Like it always is." Rosa's sullen, blue-shadowed eyes studied Charlotte inch by inch from her dusty sneakers, up the cuffed Levi's, over the white T-shirt, and finally to the frizzy tips of her brown hair. Rosa gave off a dull, disapproving energy that collided with the liveliness of the little girl who sparkled beside her. "What do you expect with a son-in-law in prison? And you know my Agapita? They've switched her back to the early shift and she's off to Dos Rios *before* sunup. She only makes minimum wage and she does more work than her supervisor who drives a new Chevy."

"Agapita needs to enroll at the Community College," Thea said matter-of-factly. "She needs an education, Rosa, to get a better job."

Thea looked away from Rosa, whose expression had deteriorated from disagreeable to fuming, and smiled down at Violeta. "Are you starting kindergarten this fall, Violeta?"

"No *Híjita* of mine is getting on that bus!" Rosa said loudly, snatching Violeta's hand.

Thea tapped her cane on the linoleum floor and took Charlotte's arm. "This is Charlotte Lambert, Rosa. Charlotte is a schoolteacher in New York. She's visiting us for a few days."

Rosa shrugged.

"Violeta, you come and visit me," Thea said to the small girl with shining eyes. "We'll make some lemon bread again for you to take to your daddy, okay?"

Little Bit wagged his tail when Thea and Charlotte emerged from the post office.

"Pour some water from this bottle into Bit's dish there," Thea said, reaching into the truck cab and pulling out a canteen. "It's terrifically hot."

Charlotte filled the bowl and Bit lapped up water immediately.

"Violeta's father, Lucho Varela, is my grandson's oldest friend."

"Why is he in prison?"

"Because he hit and killed a pedestrian in Dos Rios last winter. He was drunk. Driving *very* drunk. And now his daughter is sentenced to life in the prison of Rosa Tomé's trailer."

Thea stopped and looked up at Charlotte. "They are ignorant people, may God bless them. They have no education, only bitterness and blame. And no humor, the Tomé's. No laughter. It's a miracle that child smiles."

Thea walked to the corner ahead of Charlotte. "This part of Main Street will be crowded with people on the Fourth of July. You'll want to get here early. Unless you're thinking of riding in the parade?"

"That's almost a week off," Charlotte stated. "I have to go home before that."

"You don't have to do anything," Thea said without looking up. "And you are home. You've just forgotten what home looks like."

Several ranchers in big hats stood just inside the door of the Durham store.

"Chester, Bobby J., Gonzalo, *buenos días.*" Thea lifted her cane in greeting. Each man tipped his hat as Thea steered Charlotte inside. The window ledge behind the cash register was home to a hedge of potted geraniums and Thea stopped and poked a finger into the soil of the closest plant.

"They need water," she said over her shoulder to the clerk by the register. "Are you feeding them that fertilizer, Roberto?"

Roberto did not answer, but stooped over, picked up a watering can under the counter and jogged to the side of the store.

Thea left the bundle of catalogues on the front counter and, with her cane tapping the lower level of shelves and her arm still hooked firmly through Charlotte's, proceeded into the store. Dorothea's pace quickened considerably. She knew every aisle and post, each uneven floor board and the precise location of the wood display cases and metal cabinets. Charlotte glanced at bins of nails and screws and washers, electrical and plumbing parts and supplies, shelves of rubber boots, shovels and slickers. Along the back wall were fishing poles, coils of wire and fencing, and sacks of chicken scratch and rabbit feed.

At the rear of the store heavy wood doors with iron hinges and handles opened to the supply yard. Francis and another man were bent over a pallet of cement bags. Francis and another man were bent over a pallet of cement bags.

"Francis!" Thea called into the open sunlight.

Francis and the other man straightened up and turned around. The other man was the gas station attendant.

"I was just telling Barty about last night," Francis said, squinting at Thea from under his cap. "And Barty was just telling me that he already met Miss Charlotte."

"Already met?" Thea looked at Charlotte and then at Barty.

"At the station yesterday," Barty said as he readjusted his cowboy hat. "She came into the station and bought gas."

"Yes, that was me." Charlotte said. Barty stood with his hands on his hips. He didn't look as fierce as yesterday, but his expressionless face still made Charlotte uncomfortable.

"And you didn't call me, Bartholomew?" Thea was as astonished as she was annoyed.

Barty shrugged and studied the pallet of cement bags.

"I was just telling Barty about the burros and all," Francis continued. "How Charlotte just walked in out of the dark."

"Well, evidently Bartholomew did not introduce himself." Thea took Charlotte by the arm and walked across the yard to the men. "Charlotte, I want you to meet Bartholomew Bill. Bartholomew, this is Charlotte Lambert, Alicia Rose's daughter."

"Hello," Charlotte extended her hand. Barty did the same and they quickly grasped and released hands.

"Bartholomew is like the bone horses," Thea said.

Francis, Bartholomew, and Charlotte all looked at Thea.

"What are you talking about, Dorothea?" Francis asked.

"Alicia never told her daughter about the bone horses, about her drawings, her notebook, the names and stories. I figure there's probably a whole lot Alicia did not tell her daughter."

"Francis, did a delivery of peat moss come in yesterday?" Ralph called across the yard from the doorway.

"Back here." Francis walked off with Ralph.

"I've got to load this cement and take it out to the ranch." Barty turned on his boot heel and went to the truck parked near the pallet of stacked bags.

"How's Jed today?" Thea called after him.

"About like always, I reckon." Barty slung a bag from the pallet up into the truck. "He won't come over to the ranch till I finish with the cement."

"Taking his tea?"

"I reckon so."

"We're going over to Dennis's for a malt." Thea spoke to Barty's back as he lifted a second bag from the ground into the truck. "I've invited Charlotte to stay as long as she likes."

"Which won't be very long," Charlotte added quickly. "I've got to get back home."

"Bartholomew?" Thea waited until he turned around and faced her. "Conchata says Charlotte has something that belongs to you."

Barty's dark green eyes shifted to Charlotte.

"What?" Charlotte shook her head. "I don't think so . . . "

Barty bent down and reached for another bag of cement.

"Thea, I don't know what you're talking about," Charlotte said quietly. And Conchata is dead, so what does she know?

Barty closed the truck gate and wiped his forehead with his sleeve.

"Well, if Miss Lambert has something of mine I reckon she'll give it to me in her own good time." Barty repositioned his cowboy hat over his thick hair. "And my mother's been known to skewer the facts a tad. I'm off to the ranch. Call if you need something, Nana."

"You'll be joining us for supper tonight?"

"Tonight? I don't know; there's a horse needing some attention down in the *bosque*—"

"—Of course you'll come." Thea directed Charlotte back into the store. "Bartholomew's not so tough as he pretends. He's just afraid of you is all."

"Of me?" Barty couldn't be half as afraid of Charlotte as she was of him. "Why?"

"Because you might say something or do something that cuts through that tough hide of his and makes him remember something he pretends to have forgotten." Thea patted Charlotte's arm. "Now, let's get our malts, shall we?"

Gus and the rangers tipped their hats as Thea and Charlotte strolled up to the drugstore. "Good morning, boys," Thea said. "Her name is Charlotte Rose Lambert and she'll be visiting for a while. Looks just like her mother, doesn't she?"

Thea entered the Mata Drugstore and Soda Fountain with the same proprietary attitude she had over at the Durham Hardware store. Wide ceiling fans whirred above the narrow aisles where people browsed the shelves for medicines, toiletries, and drugstore sundries. The pharmacy was at the rear of the store. The pharmacist, a tiny, fine-boned man with silver-streaked black hair, waved to Thea.

"I'll be right there," he called out. "Have a seat, Thea."

Thea and Charlotte slid onto the swiveling stools at the polished wood counter. Seated to Thea's right were two young girls spinning around and around on their stools. Before them on the counter were thick pink malts in tall frosted glasses. Every few spins, the girls stopped and sucked on their malts through straws.

Thea tilted her head toward them. "You're the Begay sisters, aren't you?"

The girls smiled and leaned forward to stare at Charlotte through long black bangs.

"Is your mother here today?"

They pointed at a short round woman in a bright calico dress standing in the aisle. The pharmacist appeared at the counter before Thea and Charlotte.

"I'm sorry to keep you waiting." His round brown eyes took in Charlotte's face. "*Díos mío*, you certainly are your mother's daughter."

The pharmacist extended his hand across the counter. "I'm Dennis Mata and you would be Charlotte Rose." Dennis held Charlotte's hand between both of his. "I was very fond of your mother. I never thought I'd see her beautiful face again. What a special day!"

"Thank you." Charlotte smiled. Dennis Mata seemed to like her face as much as Barty Bill disliked it. "Actually I'm Charlotte Rose *Lambert*."

"Of course! What can I get you? I already know what Thea wants as she's ordered the same double chocolate malt for thirty years. God help us if there is ever again a chocolate shortage in the Lágrimas!"

"There was a chocolate shortage?" Charlotte asked.

"Oh, *sí*, rationing of everything here back in the forties. When there are shortages *en los Estados Unidos* Agua Dulce's supplies are the first to be cut. Goes back to the frontier army days, when they were chasing Cochise and Geronimo and their warriors all over this country. The people of the Lágrimas would not help the U.S. cavalry. *Los federales* never quite trusted the people of the Lágrimas, half Spanish, half wild *indios*. We don't even trust ourselves!"

"He's pulling your leg, dear," Thea said, placing a hand on Charlotte's arm. "Geronimo was here but never Cochise. Do you see today's flavors on the blackboard?"

After reading over the two columns of ice cream flavors, which included at least two—mesquite toffee and chokecherry cheesecake—that were most likely not found anywhere else in the lower forty-eight, Charlotte decided to go with the historically proven favorite and ordered a double chocolate. Dennis made the malts himself. Because Dennis was very short, he stepped up and down on a raised platform built behind the counter as he mixed malts and served customers.

"I worked with your *abuelo*," Dennis said, scooping ice cream from a metal barrel pulled from the freezer. "*Sí*, every day for a month I helped him move rock and debris. Very hot that summer. I was a teenager. Dr. Al worked like a common laborer and he never complained."

Dennis placed the tall, cold glasses before Thea and Charlotte. "Now, pardon me, ladies, Earl needs his prescription refilled. Sometimes I think he drinks it by the dropper-full!"

Thea, Charlotte, and the Begay sisters enjoyed their malts in silence. It was the richest, thickest chocolate Charlotte had ever tasted. She turned to say so to Thea but stopped: Thea's eyes were closed and her thin body was supported by the counter where her upper torso was balanced on her elbows.

One slender, tanned and finely lined hand held the long spoon beside her malt glass.

Charlotte stared into the deep-brown malt before her and listened to the sounds of the drugstore around her. Three women chatted in Spanish by the front door. The Begay sisters giggled and whispered nonsense to one another. The freezer of ice cream hummed and a car without a muffler rumbled through the traffic light on Main Street. Nothing extraordinary; nothing to write home about. Yet something remarkable was unfolding in the small perfect universe of the Mata drugstore.

Thea began to spoon at her malt, awake again.

"Grandpa loved this place, didn't he?" Charlotte asked her.

"Yes, he did," Thea said between spoonfuls. "He certainly did."

The Begay sisters finished their malts and resumed their stool spinning, looking at Thea and Charlotte every few turns.

"This is Charlotte," Thea said to them. "She's a teacher from New York."

They kept spinning, only slower.

"What do you do all summer?" Charlotte asked the closest sister.

"We take care of mama's goats."

The sisters' mother walked up to Thea and rested a hand on her shoulder.

"Hello, Susannah." Thea said. "I want you to meet my friend, Charlotte." Thea turned and faced Susannah. "She's thinking about starting a school."

Susannah was athletic and sturdy. She smiled at Charlotte. "Starting a school?"

"No, actually—" Charlotte began.

"—A fine idea, but be warned, there's no money." Susannah said. "And the school board won't let you use the old school building. However, if you do begin a school, please tell me how I can help. There would be others, too, who would help you in whatever way was necessary."

Susannah turned to Thea. "Where would they meet? The library?"

"I hadn't thought of the library." Thea grabbed Charlotte's hand and squeezed it.

"Keep me updated," Susannah said. "It's so nice to meet you, Charlotte. Come girls."

"Thea, I couldn't start a school," Charlotte said as the girls walked away with their mother. "I wouldn't know where to begin. I don't even live here."

"You're here now." Thea scraped the bottom of her glass with her spoon. "Now, I need to find Francis's toothpaste; what teeth he has are very sensitive."

Thea slid from the stool and, following her hand along the side of the counter, went to the far wall where Dennis took her by the arm and led her to the toothpaste.

Near the front register Charlotte looked over a rack of picture postcards of Dos Rios and the Lágrimas River Valley, and of the badlands near Agua Dulce and the ubiquitous Agustina Mountains. To Charlotte's disappointment there were no photographs of Geronimo, wild horses or cowboys. Charlotte chose a postcard of the badlands with the blue line of the mountains in the distance and another card with a picture of the highway through Dos Rios with a flock of very fat sheep blocking traffic. When Charlotte returned to her somewhere-else life in New York and shared the details of this corner of New Mexico with her American lit students, she was going to need pictorial evidence to prove she was not making the whole place up.

Charlotte bent down to look at tiny baskets kept in a glass case under the front windows. The brown grass baskets were exquisitely crafted. A small card explained that *jicarilla* meant little basket; the grass baskets in the case were made by members of the Jicarilla Apache tribe.

Shoes with astonishingly thick rubber soles shuffled across the wood floor into Charlotte's peripheral vision. Afraid that the person had not noticed her kneeling down by the cabinet, Charlotte stood up and was face to face with the ugliest man she had ever seen. His skin was blistered and blotchy, burned and raw. He had almost no hair, and although Charlotte looked into them for only a second, she was certain his eyes were yellow.

Charlotte stepped back and smiled, trying to hide her shock at his appearance. When the man did not return her smile, Charlotte looked away. Thea was still talking to Dennis at the rear of the drugstore.

"Witch whore," the man mumbled.

"Excuse me?" Charlotte reluctantly looked back at the shriveled man.

"Witch whore." He took a step toward Charlotte causing her to move back against the counter. "I've waited a long time."

"Farley!" Dennis walked the length of the store in two seconds flat. "Holoman Farley!"

Dennis placed his short sturdy frame between Charlotte and the man. "Charlotte, why don't you go and help Thea."

Charlotte eased past Dennis and walked quickly to the rear of the store.

"Did Dennis say Farley?" Thea was squinting and frowning. "Is Farley here?"

"I guess so." Charlotte took a deep breath. Her heart was racing.

"Did you talk with Farley?" Thea continued to peer at the front of the store where Dennis was escorting the ugly man out the open doors.

"It's my fault, Miss Thea." Earl, the man needing the eardrops, walked up to Thea and Charlotte. "I never should have brought him along. Every time it's like this: every time I tell Farley to stay in the car and he doesn't. I'm so sorry. He's such a nuisance."

"Earl, it's not your fault." Thea took Charlotte's arm. "Is he gone?"

"Yes," Charlotte said.

"Dennis took him back to my car," Earl said. "I'll drive him home. I'm so sorry."

Earl spoke briefly to Dennis at the door and then walked down the steps to the street.

"I hope you won't let Farley scare you off," Dennis said when he returned.

"I'm okay," Charlotte said with false cheerfulness. Her heart was pounding like she'd had a close encounter with a moving train.

"Farley is a very nasty resident of Agua Dulce," Dennis said, looking back at the front doors. "You just forget about him. Everyone does."

"Charlotte hopes to see her grandfather's fossil site," Thea said, fanning her face with a letter produced from her purse. "I told her you would be the one to take her out there."

"Of course. We can take the Jeep." Dennis walked them to the front door.

"I don't want to impose," Charlotte said.

"No problem. I've needed an excuse to get out there for years. And my grandson Javier loves dinosaurs. We'll make a day of it!"

Thea took Charlotte's arm again. "Dennis, charge our malts to my account."

"These are my treat." Dennis stayed with Thea and Charlotte until they were on the sidewalk. Like Charlotte, he scanned the cars parked along the street. Little Bit wagged and hopped about the rear of the Hudson but the ugly Farley man was not to be seen.

"Dennis, did you see that rascal Farley?" Gus wobbled to his feet and tipped his hat at Thea and Charlotte. "He oughtn't be allowed in your store. He's a criminal!"

"I know, Gus," Dennis said. "He just appeared so quickly!"

"He can be invisible," Thea said icily. "Farley's been known to sneak up on Conchata."

Charlotte shivered. Dennis noticed her discomfort and placed his hand reassuringly on her shoulder. "He's just a nasty old man. You forget him. I'll plan our fossil excursion, okay?"

Dennis went back into the store. Gus remained beside Charlotte. They were the same height and he looked Charlotte squarely in the eyes: "You give me a call if Farley bothers you. Treadle. I'm listed under Gus Treadle. Day or night, me and the boys will come right over."

{13}

Charlotte drove the Hudson south out of town. Thea fell asleep against the truck door. Charlotte was exhausted, too. One moment Agua Dulce was a picture-postcard perfect Old West town of friendly folks and simple pleasures—Thea, Dennis, Francis, Gus, the Begay sisters and Susannah all made Charlotte feel like she belonged here, or could. But then standing in the shadows were fearsome, confusing people—Rosa, Farley, perhaps even Barty Bill—who made the Lágrimas Valley someplace Charlotte did not want to linger in too long.

Thea stirred when the truck rattled over the cattle guard and onto the ranch road. "Of course he's still dangerous," Thea mumbled in her sleep.

It was high noon. The sky was cloudless and so terribly, gloriously blue Charlotte could not look at it, even through sunglasses. What was she doing here? She was here for the fossil site. For Grandpa and the people and places he knew, the earth he walked and slept and worked upon. Charlotte would stand upon Grandpa's fossil site and then go home.

A horse and rider emerged on the road ahead. The rider pulled up the horse and waited for the Hudson to reach them. When the truck was twenty feet from the pair Charlotte brought the truck to a stop. The dust cleared from the air and Charlotte saw it was the horse and rider from the drugstore sidewalk.

The cowboy leaned down from the saddle and looked in the window. "Morning."

"Good morning. I'm Charlotte. I came in last night."

"The burros found her, Jed." Thea straightened up and smoothed her dress.

The cowboy was named Jed and he studied Charlotte in a friendly unconcerned way. Maybe he didn't recognize her, didn't realize she was the same woman who scrambled on her knees about the sidewalk after a handful of quarters.

"This is Charlotte," Thea continued, "Charlotte Lambert. Now I suppose *you're* going to tell me that *you've* already met."

Jed shifted forward in the saddle and leaned his elbow on the saddle horn. "I can't say as we've *met*."

"No, we haven't," Charlotte said. "We have not met."

"I'm Thea's grandson, Jed Morley." Jed tipped his hat. "Pleased to meet you."

"Likewise." Charlotte involuntarily touched her hair as if it were a hat. Likewise?

"How long are you visiting?" Jed asked.

"Charlotte's going to start a school here in the fall," Thea said before Charlotte could answer.

"No, I am *not* starting a school!" Charlotte said, glaring at Thea. Thea curled up her lips and said nothing. "I'm sorry, Thea, I know you mean well," Charlotte said, embarrassed. "But you've got to stop telling people that I'm starting a school. I'm just visiting for a few days."

Jed was amused. "Where are you from, Charlotte?"

"New York. Scarsdale."

Jed lifted an eyebrow. "Westchester County. How'd you come to be found by the burros?"

"Her grandfather was Dr. Albert Rose," Thea said. "The paleontologist from Harvard."

Jed stared at Charlotte a long moment. "Of course, the famous Coelophysis quarry."

"Why don't you come back and have lunch with us?" Thea asked.

"Not today, Nana. I have to finish work at the Delgados'." Jed pulled up the reins and the horse stepped away from the truck. "It's been a pleasure meeting you."

"The pleasure's all mine." Charlotte bit down on her lower lip before she offered up another dime western one-liner.

"Come for supper," Thea called across Charlotte. "Bartholomew's coming."

"I'll see." Jed reached out and touched Little Bit's head as he rode past the back of the truck. Charlotte put the truck in gear and drove slowly down the road. Horse and rider receded back into the dust swirling across the rearview mirror.

"Those are his mother's jeans and shirt," Thea said glancing at Charlotte's borrowed clothes.

"These are Jed's mother's clothes?" Charlotte asked. "Oh, gosh."

"Stop here." Thea pointed to the side of the road. "Tell me, the sweet clover—I can smell it—it's blooming, isn't it?"

"What does it look like?" Charlotte stopped the truck. "Small yellow flowers on long, sort of bushy stems?"

"That's it." Thea opened her door and slid from the truck. "We need to gather some."

Charlotte turned off the engine and climbed from the cab.

"Here!" Thea waved her cane across the tops of the tall bushes of willowy yellow flowers. "I need several bunches. Go to the glove compartment and bring the snippers."

Charlotte retrieved a pair of pruning shears from the glove box.

"I want you to cut a bunch about this big." Thea held her hands a foot apart. "From several plants, not just one."

Charlotte chose a large bush and knelt down.

"Thank the plant," Thea said.

"Thank the plant?"

"Yes, you are being given something: say thank you."

It seemed foolish, but Charlotte thanked the plant and every other plant she took cuttings from. After she had gathered a fat bunch of the long-stemmed clover from several patches along the road, she carried it to Thea ,who had returned to sit in the truck.

"Is this enough?"

Thea's face opened into a smile as her hands brushed over the tops of the clover. "That will be fine. Just fine. Put it here in the cab with us so it doesn't blow away."

"What will you use the clover for?" Charlotte started the truck and continued down the road. The roof of the barn and then the windmill near the adobe house were now visible.

"*Alfalfon* sweetens the air, but I'll use this for the linen chest. It keeps away the moths."

"How did you learn about all of these plants?"

"Conchata." Thea angled her head and looked at Charlotte. She had removed her sunglasses and her ice-blue eyes gleamed like tiny stars in the dark brown of her face.

"You must have been very close friends," Charlotte said.

"We still are, my dear."

George was waiting by the barn and opened his wings and strutted up to the parked truck as Little Bit scrambled out. They both escorted Thea to the house. Charlotte picked up the clover, the pile of magazines and letters, and the paper bag with Francis's toothpaste. She caught up with the trio at the bottom of the porch steps.

"You can tell the time by it." Thea motioned with her cane at the rocking chair gently moving back and forth. "Always at high noon, this is the chair. Everyone comes for a sit on the hickory rocking chair." Thea grabbed the railing and slowly moved up the steps. "I don't believe it's Conchata. Maybe you can tell me who has come to visit?"

Thea looked over her shoulder at Charlotte.

"I don't know what you mean, Thea." Charlotte stood on the porch. George pecked at the floor near the empty dog dish.

"My eyes are terrible these days," Thea said wearily. "You must tell me who's waiting in the chair."

Charlotte reached over and touched the rocker's arm. The chair ceased moving. "There's no one here."

Thea sighed, opened the screen door and went into the kitchen. Charlotte withdrew her hand from the empty chair. The chair began to rock again in the breeze that was undetectable to Charlotte or the windmill across the yard by the barn. Charlotte went into the kitchen and set the bundle of mail and the bag on the counter. She placed the sweet-smelling yellow clover on the table and looked at the slim fading body of Thea.

"You saw him this morning, surely," Thea said. "It's been years, oh my, many years, and I can hardly see anymore. But today I saw Albert Rose in my kitchen."

Thea went to the pantry and returned with a pair of scissors and a ball of twine. "Conchata was just saying that we only see who we love to remember." Thea began to cut the long clover stems. "You know who waits for you in the rocking chair."

"I'm sorry, but I really do not." Charlotte tied the twine around the clover. Thea watched for a moment and then snipped at the clover stems again. When all the plants were the same length, Thea brushed the snippings into her palm and tossed them into the trash basket under the sink. She returned to the table and took Charlotte by the arm.

"If you opened your heart to your mother, Charlotte, I imagine you might see her again, too."

⁕⁕⁕⁕⁕⁕⁕⁕⁕⁕⁕⁕⁕⁕⁕⁕

No one came for Sunday supper. Thea was irritated with the boys, but Francis said Jed had a heap of work out at the High Lonesome and Barty was working on Chester's tractor tonight so Chester would be able to turn over his field in the morning.

"But this was a special occasion," Thea said. Francis, Charlotte, and Thea sat on the porch sipping some herbal tea concoction of hops, passion flower, and chamomile that Conchata guaranteed would make everyone sleep deep and dream well. "You'd think the boys could make an effort for Charlotte Rose."

Charlotte was both disappointed and relieved that Jed and Barty had not come for dinner. It was clear that Barty had no desire to get to know Charlotte, and that was just fine. And although Jed was polite and accommodating, Charlotte was in Agua Dulce for just one more day, two at most, depending on the airlines, and then it was back to her real life in New York. She'd never see these people again, anyway.

Conchata's after-dinner tea made Francis, Thea and Charlotte so sleepy they all departed the porch chairs before nine o'clock. Charlotte went to the bedroom to change into a pair of Bernadette's cotton pajamas. As she walked down the hall to the bathroom she overheard Thea and Francis talking in the kitchen.

"We discussed this all before," Francis said wearily. "We have those plots in the cemetery. If you want to be cremated, well, I'll honor your wish. But I'm not putting your ashes into an old Thomas Webb Coffee can."

"It's not about the coffee can," Thea said. "It's about taking the ashes where they need to go. And those coffee tins fit perfectly into the panniers, now don't they?"

"But Thea, I can't climb on a horse anymore!"

Charlotte closed the bathroom door before she heard Thea's response.

{14}

Before the first light grazed the cliffs west of the ranch house, Charlotte looked out the bedroom window at the dark garden. She was standing in black, soft piles of feathers from which she pulled a letter. Even with the envelope held close to her eyes Charlotte could not read the writing. Who was this letter for? The paper disintegrated into ash and floated down into the piles of black feathers.

"You left me handfuls of ashes," Charlotte whispered to the garden.

Charlotte opened her eyes and wiped her face with the back of her hand. The sky to the east was flushed with rosy dawn. From somewhere near the barn George greeted the day with a full-bodied atonal cockadoodle-do. Handfuls of ashes. Just a dream. Thea's talk about death and ashes, the visit to the post office, the raven on the windshield, who wouldn't dream about black feathers and lost letters and handfuls of ashes?

After the standard breakfast of bacon, toast, eggs, and a pot of cowboy coffee, Francis and Charlotte went out to the shed at the rear of the house and retrieved a metal cooler. Charlotte and Thea packed food and beverages into the deep box—bags of nuts and dried fruit, jerked meat, cheese, and a loaf of bread. Francis filled several thermoses with tea and lemonade and four canteens of water. Before they closed the lid, Thea added a tiny flask of whiskey—"in case it rains." It seemed like a colossal amount of food and drink for two adults and one child, Javier, Dennis's grandson, but Francis said it was always best to go over-prepared into the desert.

"Beautiful and dangerous, the canyon country," Francis said as he latched down the lid. "You go into that country same as people did a hundred years ago: hoping for the best, prepared for the worst. You'll have to stop for ice at the drugstore. Remind Dennis."

"Or go by Bartholomew's," Thea added from the kitchen where she was tying flower tops into cotton bags to soak in a pot. "He has an ice machine at the station and he just might change his stubborn mind and go along. Bartholomew loves a day in the desert with Dennis."

"Barty's not gonna go." Francis smiled at Charlotte. "Best to just leave him be, Thea."

At eight sharp Dennis and his Javier arrived in an old yellow Jeep with a canvas roof. "My youngest son's youngest son has never seen the dinosaur quarry," Dennis said as he helped Charlotte into the front seat of the doorless Jeep. "Javier, this is Miss Charlotte. Her grandfather was the scientist who found the dinosaurs!"

Javier had dark eyes and an eager, pleasant face. "Did your Grandpa see the dinosaurs?"

Charlotte laughed. "No, my Grandpa just found their bones."

When they reached the end of the ranch road and Dennis turned the Jeep south onto the cracked pavement of the old highway, Charlotte squinted ahead for the crippled sedan. Thankfully, her disabled rental car had been towed back into Santa Fe. Charlotte glanced at the spot but said nothing when the Jeep passed the boulder that Charlotte had attempted to drive over.

"We're looking for a wire gate," Dennis pointed at the fence line to the right. "There was never a real entrance to the quarry, just a cut in the fence. We used bailing wire and cedar posts for a gate."

Javier held onto the back of his grandfather's seat and leaned his head in close to Dennis's neck. Except for the low windshield there were no windows and no doors. The canvas top shaded the front seats, but riding in the Jeep was like sitting in a wind tunnel.

Dennis spotted the break in the fence line and steered the Jeep up a sandy shoulder to the gate. Charlotte climbed out and did exactly what Dennis instructed—unwrapped and unhooked the various lengths of wire holding one post to the next. Dennis drove into the desert at a slow, steady pace. When they crossed deep sand the Jeep lurched and fishtailed, and Javier gripped Charlotte's seatback with his arms. Charlotte looked back: the asphalt road had vanished and the Jeep's tracks were hardly more than soft impressions on the desert floor. They approached buttes and formations that from a distance looked to be just small mounds and knobs. Up close, the stone monoliths' mass and size were astonishing. The Agustina Mountains were directly ahead, and the horizon to the west followed the topography of sharp ridges and sloping peaks.

"None of this has changed." Dennis lifted his hand to the landscape. "This was what Dr. Al saw. He watched for the beginning of this arroyo." Dennis steered around a cactus the size of a small tree, and the Jeep slid down a moderately steep hill to the bottom of the arroyo. "Now, we look for the break in the rock scree and drive out of the *arroyo* and head south. There, by that sand hill, do you see it? Pointed stone, with a hip on one side? On the desert you learn to mark your way with these small but *muy importante* landmarks."

"What if the landmarks change?" Charlotte asked. And how did her mother drive across this sand and stone in a Volkswagen?

"This land changes slowly." The Jeep ascended a long slope. When it crested the sandy hill, a landscape of deep, burned red opened before them. "We always consider the long view. The mesa that looks like a broken spear to the west, the line of that low mountain that seems to have shrugged its shoulders? The quarry is marked by the red hill to the left of the yellow cliff with the flat face. This was the road of Dr. Al and his fossil site. You don't find it unless it is shown to you."

Dennis drove to a juniper tree and parked the Jeep in a small canopy of shade.

"Take yourself a canteen, Charlotte. *Y usted*, Javier."

Charlotte and Javier scrambled to keep up with Dennis as he strode up the steep red hill. Halfway to the top Dennis stopped and stood with his hands on his narrow hips. Javier ran past his grandfather up the slide to a rocky escarpment. Charlotte caught up with Dennis. She was breathing hard. Dennis was hardly winded.

"Altitude," Dennis said, smiling. His hand swept the air over the slope before them. "We are standing on the bones. Javier!"

Javier bounded across the hill and landed on his knees near his grandfather.

Charlotte knelt down and dug her fingers into the hot sand. "There are still fossils here. Grandpa's team didn't take them all."

Javier used his hand like a sieve, scooping the sand and shaking it through his fingers.

"The bones are still here, but they were re-buried," Dennis knelt beside Charlotte and Javier. "Dr. Al said there were more than a thousand bones buried in this hillside. It spooked the locals, such a bone yard! But to your grandfather these bones were gold! I thought he would come back the next summer. I was ready, I loved working the backhoe for Dr. Al. Others came over the years, but your grandfather, no, he did not return."

"I saw the fossils in his lab at Harvard." Charlotte sat on the sand beside Javier. "There was a large plaster block from the Agua Dulce quarry under excavation."

Charlotte stood up and turned around on the hillside. "Grandpa used to say, 'Imagine a place where the earth is as bright and large as the sky: that's where the bones call home.'"

"Why did they bury the bones?" Javier eyed the sand below his knees.

"To protect them," Charlotte and Dennis both answered.

Dennis smiled at Charlotte. "Dr. Al said that the next generation of fossil hunters would have their questions."

Dennis leaned over to his grandson frowning at the hill holding the dinosaurs captive. "*Preguntas*, Javier, Dr. Al did not know to ask. So he left bones in the earth so the bone hunters of the future could return and ask new questions. You, *m'jito*, could be one of those scientists."

Charlotte wandered sideways along the slope, picking up grey and white fragments from the surface. She tongue-tested them the way Grandpa had taught her: a fossil stuck to the tongue, a stone did not.

"Javier, come here," Charlotte called.

Javier took leaping steps across the sand. "Did you find a dinosaur?!"

"No, but I'll show you how to know when you have found a fossil. Take this little grey stone—it could be a fossil, a fossil looks just like a stone. Touch it to your tongue. If it sticks and pulls just a little, it's a fossil."

Javier was soon tongue-testing every stone, rock, pebble, and chunk of wood on the hillside. Dennis watched from the shade of a juniper tree. Charlotte walked to the top of the hill.

"Where was the camp?" Charlotte called down to Dennis.

Dennis stood up. "Come, I'll show you the summer home of your *abuelo*."

Dennis took Javier's hand and they walked down the hill, past the Jeep, and on around the far side of the yellow cliff to the west of the quarry.

"The field camp was here, on the little flat of sand surrounded by the junipers. The trees gave shade and wind protection for the tents."

"Are there bones here too, Papa?" Javier leaned into the shade made by Dennis's body.

"No, Javier. This is where the fossil hunters lived."

As they walked into the shade of the juniper grove, Charlotte stopped to take in the view from the field camp. It was a good view, a good place. The trees were mature and thick, and the hard level sand would make an excellent surface for a season of camping. The landscape to the south and west was clean and wide all the way to the mountains.

"It's just as I imagined it," Charlotte said. A summer home that Grandpa and his field school students hated to leave. Did those young men and women still reminisce about that summer, tell their children and grandchildren about this faraway desert home, how it felt at high noon, at dusk? How could they not compare every place they ever called home to this camp site?

Alicia pined for this place. For summerland. On cold, dreary afternoons in New York she recalled her summer days in these canyonlands. She told Charlotte that she and Grandpa belonged to summerland, and summerland belonged to them.

"They had tables made of planks set on sawhorses under the junipers here." Dennis walked to the base of a large grouping of trees. "The tables were always covered with fossils and notebooks, pencil stubs and water canteens."

Charlotte walked over to Dennis and Javier, who munched on an apple and slid to the ground by his grandfather's boots.

"There was a pine board nailed above the wash tub sink." Dennis smiled and held his hands between two high branches. "Carved into the wood was, 'No Fossils. No Jam.' Isn't that just like your grandfather?"

Charlotte laughed. "Grandpa loved to joke and play."

"But everyone had jam, every day!" Dennis winked at Charlotte as he walked past her. Javier remained seated in the shade. "Come, let's find the camp firepit."

Charlotte followed Dennis out into the open sun.

"These stones mark the old camp fire." Dennis dropped down and dug into the sand in the center of the stones. To Charlotte's astonishment, he pulled up chunks of charcoal and handfuls of ash. "This is where they had their morning and evening cook fire."

Charlotte sat down on one of the rocks now half buried in sand.

"They cooked all their meals over an open flame, and then roasted marshmallows until the fire died down. I stayed out here a few nights that summer, slept on the ground with the students. Dr. Al did that, too. The fire died out and then all eyes went up, *todos arriba*, to the stars." Dennis lifted his arms. "Living between the bones in the earth and the stars in the heavens, that was a summer to remember, *verdad?*"

"*Verdad*," Charlotte repeated.

They had lunch beneath the largest juniper tree near the quarry. Dennis recounted how Dr. Al did not excavate the fossils here, but dug under tangled groups of dinosaurs and then encased the Coelophysis skeletons in massive plaster casts reinforced with juniper limbs. There were seven blocks pulled from the hillside quarry the summer of 1959, each weighing at least a ton. Dennis's tractor transported each and every block across the canyonlands to the county road, where they were loaded onto flatbed trucks. The fossil blocks were shipped all over the country, to every major paleontology institution in the United States.

Charlotte had heard about the difficulty of excavating the bones, the discussions about which skeletons would be saved, which had to be broken apart. The quarry was actually a mass burial caused by some catastrophe—a flood or avalanche. Over the years, Grandpa had visited the quarry's blocks under excavation at various universities. The Coelophysis skeletons were like his children. Grandpa had photo albums and drawers of files and notes about all of the bones—where they went to be prepared and exhibited, their size, and maps of each and every skeleton's position in the block. Grandpa was planning to write a book about the Agua Dulce quarry and the herd of Coelophysis that apparently died in one momentous calamity.

"I visited the skeleton the students named Celie," Charlotte told Dennis. "Celie was on permanent display at the Museum of Natural History in New York. My mother took me to the exhibit one winter afternoon. She explained how each skeleton's death-pose held valuable information about its life. And its death. Grandpa was a pioneer in the science of tapophony."

Charlotte ate her peanut butter and jam sandwich. She had been only six or seven, Javier's age, when she visited the museum in New York. Until just now, she had not thought about that afternoon.

"Dennis, do you remember my mother talking about the horse skeletons she found out on the desert?" Charlotte sipped at her canteen. "Thea said something about bone horses, about Alicia having a notebook of them."

"Hm, yes, of course I remember. The horse bones were everywhere that summer. The government men had been here the year before, the drought, you know. They came to remove the wild horses. They shot them down where they found them all over the country. Your mother would draw the horse skeletons. She had a notebook that she carried always."

Dennis sat back against the juniper tree. Javier had fallen asleep with his head on his grandfather's lap.

"Was that okay with my grandfather?"

"Dr. Al said Alicia had a gift," Dennis said, "and that one day she could become a fine restoration artist."

"So Grandpa didn't mind that my mother spent time drawing horse skeletons?"

"Alicia gave them names. She gave the wild horses their place in history. And wasn't that what Dr. Al did with his dinosaurs?"

{15}

Thea was asleep on the sofa in the living room when Charlotte returned mid-afternoon. Charlotte went quietly into her own room and lay down on the bed. She was asleep instantly. Voices from the corral woke her in the late afternoon. Francis and Barty were discussing the flat tire on the wheelbarrow, Francis saying he could use the hand pump to fill it and Barty saying the tire had to be replaced.

Charlotte climbed into a clean pair of Bernadette's Levi's, found another T-shirt in the bureau and pulled on her shoes.

"You had quite a nap!" Thea said when Charlotte entered the kitchen. "I thought of waking you, but you looked so peaceful."

"You came in and I didn't wake?" Charlotte was a light sleeper. At home she woke when the morning newspaper landed on the driveway at dawn.

"You're going to be sunburned on your shoulders. I have a salve." Thea went to the pantry and came out with an opaque white jar filled with a thick sticky substance. "Rub this on your skin where you're raw and burned."

Charlotte took the jar and read the label: *canaigre* root & prickly pear salve.

"Please set the table for four." Thea said. "Bartholomew is here."

Charlotte placed the jar on the counter and opened the dish cabinet. As she pulled out and set the dishes, she told herself Barty would not ruin her last evening with the Durhams. Dennis said Barty's grumpy moods were his way of keeping people at arm's length. Charlotte was happy to stay two arms' lengths from Barty Bill.

"Francis asked Jed to come." Thea opened a drawer and pulled out four cloth napkins and gave them to Charlotte. "But Jed's not feeling much like socializing tonight."

Charlotte placed a folded napkin by each fork. Translation: Jed wasn't feeling like socializing with that silly city girl who came in out of nowhere and moved into his mother's bedroom.

Francis and Barty were on the porch talking about someone's new filly and someone else's alfalfa field. Thea fussed over a chile stew at the stove, talking in a half whisper to either herself or her invisible companion, Conchata. Charlotte placed the plates and bowls onto the table. In the past two days the chips, crazing, and color imperfections of Thea's ancient Blue Willow ware had become more familiar than Charlotte's own Waterford china, which in comparison seemed impersonally perfect and characterless.

Thea reached a hand into the deep pocket of her apron and pulled out a small paper bag. She studied it a moment before walking to the porch door.

"Bartholomew! Peggy Barton brought me *yerba de sangre* from Santa Fe. For Jed. I'll place it here on the counter."

"Right, Nana," Barty answered from the porch.

Suppertime at the Durhams' was markedly different with Barty at the table. Francis asked Charlotte polite questions about her day with Dennis at the old quarry, and Thea attempted to draw Barty into the conversation by asking him about Dr. Al's summer camp. Barty's answers were so vague and cryptic, Charlotte began to wonder if he had really known Grandpa and the fossil diggers at all.

"I wasn't at the quarry every day the way Dennis was," Barty said, glancing at Charlotte. "Dennis can tell you lots more about the whole operation and what the newspapers said about the discovery. All I did was help Dennis load the blocks onto those semis brought out from Albuquerque at the end of the summer."

Barty was up clearing the table before Charlotte finished her last spoonful of stew. Francis frowned at Barty's abrupt departure from the table but said nothing.

"Bartholomew," Thea said quietly, "there's pie."

Barty sat back down, his pressing appointment with a horse or a tractor or the far side of town momentarily postponed by homemade apple pie. Charlotte pulled the pie from the oven warmer and placed it on a trivet on the table. Thea sliced eight pieces and served four of them onto the blue and white dessert plates.

"I know you saw Alicia's notebook," Thea said to Barty as he took a plate of pie. "You took her all the way out to that waterhole you called the Spring of the Seven Trees. Twelve skeletons were out there. You told me Alicia sketched and named each of those horses."

Barty set the plate on the table before him and picked up his fork. "I showed Alicia the skeletons by the spring. She drew them all in her notebook. I don't remember their names." Barty looked at Thea. "It was almost forty years ago."

They ate pie in silence. When Francis finished his slice he set down his fork, wiped his mouth with his napkin and cleared his throat. "If I remember correctly, Alicia found the first horse skeleton about a mile from camp. Dr. Al said she was quite taken by the bleached bones, such a different sort than the fossils coming out of the sand at the quarry."

"That notebook caused quite an argument between Dr. Al and Ruth Rose," Thea said. "Ruth just couldn't understand why Dr. Al let Alicia spend the whole summer hunting and sketching horse skeletons and running like a wild girl about the canyonlands day and night. When Ruth came in August there was quite a scene out at the camp, I'm told. Quite a scene."

Barty took his plate to the sink and retrieved his cowboy hat from a peg behind the pantry door. "Right fine supper, Nana," he said, positioning his hat on his head. "Francis, I'll take the wheelbarrow with me and get it back to you tomorrow."

"All right then." Francis carried empty plates to the sink of soapy water.

"I'd like to understand one thing before all is said and done," Thea said, staring at the table before her. "What did Alicia and Dr. Al do with that bone horse notebook?"

"You know, it's all so long ago, I figure it just don't matter." Barty pushed open the screen door and held it ajar with his boot. "Not much good in digging up the past. It just don't matter what happened."

"Really?" Charlotte turned in her chair. "All my life I've been told it didn't matter what happened. My father, my grandmother, everyone said it was all so long ago, it just doesn't matter." Charlotte stood up and faced Barty across the kitchen. "Well, it matters to me! It has *always* mattered to me!"

Charlotte clumsily sat down. Little Bit remained asleep by her chair, oblivious to her outburst. After what felt to be the longest moment of Charlotte's life, Barty cleared his throat.

"I didn't mean to insult you, Charlotte. I apologize." Barty stepped onto the porch, gently closed the screen door and vanished into the dark yard. A moment later, his truck started up out by the barn. Headlights blazed briefly across the kitchen before Barty and his truck drove up the road. When the low drone of the truck was replaced by the steady song of the crickets, Charlotte went to the sink and began to wash dishes.

"Damn it!" Thea said from the pantry where she was scooping food for Little Bit and George, "Bartholomew forgot the *yerba sangre* for Jed."

"I'll take it out first thing in the morning," Francis said. He wiped the rinsed dishes and put them away in the cupboard. Charlotte felt she should explain to Francis, to Thea, why she had yelled at Barty. It really had nothing at all to do with Barty, about what he said or didn't say. Barty's choice of words just happened to be the same words that Leonard and Grandma Ruth repeated like a mantra after Alicia and Grandpa died: it doesn't matter, the past; it's all so long ago.

Charlotte drained the dishwater and wiped her hands on the towel Francis handed her.

"Why don't you walk up to the reservoir with me," Francis said. "I have to check one of the irrigation gates."

The irrigation pond was on the plateau above the ranch house. It was a ten-minute walk at the slow pace Francis and Little Bit favored. George strutted along some twenty feet behind all of them, racing from one side of the road to the other, pecking at minutiae in the dirt and weeds.

The reservoir was situated at the base of peach-colored cliffs where a stream emerged from a narrow canyon. Francis explained how the stream that filled the pond was fed by a spring that seeped year-round from the stone walls of a box canyon. Charlotte could see into the deep canyon carved by the stream where the green canopy of trees caught sundown as the sun lit the eastern ledges of the cliffs.

Francis knelt down beside a cement-lined channel and peered through a wire screen at the water running below. There were leaves and sticks caught in the filter. Francis opened the screen, pulled out the leaves and debris with his hands, and reset the screen.

The cliffs were luminous. The clouds were exactly the same hue, and the irrigation pond reflected the peach, watermelon, and rose of the sky. The flycatchers skimming the surface of the water for insects became light catchers in the incandescent glow.

Francis, Charlotte, George, and Little Bit ambled back the way they had come. The sun dropped into tomorrow on the far side of the western mountains and the air shifted. The heat of the day was swept away and replaced by the fresh sage-scented air of the high desert evening.

"I didn't mean to sound so angry at Barty," Charlotte said when they reached the curve in the road and began to descend from the plateau down to the little valley of the ranch house. "I just needed to say that it has mattered to me what happened to my mother all those years ago. But I didn't need to get so angry at Barty."

"Barty, of all people, knows nothing is so long ago it don't matter."

Francis stopped and whistled for Little Bit and George who had wandered into the sage. When they reemerged, the dog and rooster continued to walk the line between the road's edge and the bushes. The dusk light made the cottonwood trees and the sage indigo blue. Two ravens sailed overhead bound for the cliffs, their wings cutting the air with synchronized precision.

"You go ahead and ask the questions," Francis continued. "I'm not saying you'll get the answers. I'm just saying you have a right to ask the questions."

"Questions—*preguntas*," Charlotte said. "But what questions do I have the right to ask?"

Francis looked at Charlotte. His hands were hooked over the top of his denim overalls.

"Bartholomew was the rider who found your mother's body," Francis said without emotion or apology. "You might want to ask him a question or two about that."

Charlotte lay in bed staring into the dark room. Tomorrow was her last day in Agua Dulce. Wednesday she would get on a plane for New York, for home. She'd been gone just six days.

"Ask questions about the questions." That's what Grandpa would say.

Preguntas: Why did Grandma Ruth dislike, no, despise, *loathe*, a place as beautiful as Agua Dulce? And why was Thea so interested in Alicia's notebook? And what *did* Alicia do with her notebook from the summer of 1959? It should have been with Grandpa's field notes and files. Did Grandma or Leonard throw the notebook away after Alicia and Grandpa died?

It was after midnight. Charlotte had yet to fall asleep. Except for the ticking of the old clock in the front room, the house was silent.

One last *pregunta* escorted Charlotte into sleep: Did she really want to know the answers to her questions?

{16}

Barefoot, in her pajamas and robe, Charlotte stood beside Thea at the stove waiting for the water to boil. Today Charlotte was going to make the breakfast coffee.

"Thea, if it's still okay with you and Francis, I'd like to cancel my flight home tomorrow and stay for another week."

"Why of course it's still okay!" Thea said as she pushed the bacon strips around the frying pan in a spattering herd.

The kettle whistled. Charlotte turned off the burner and measured and tossed the coffee into the boiling water. The course grounds congealed into a black foamy layer on top of the water. Charlotte stared into the brewing sludge. It looked like bubbling mud but smelled like the cowboy-worthy java it would soon be.

Francis entered the kitchen with the newspaper. He smiled at Charlotte standing proudly over the brewing coffee.

"Francis, Charlotte has decided to stay!" Thea said. "Isn't that wonderful!"

"Well, that's just grand. Just grand."

"I need to get my suitcases from the hotel in Santa Fe," Charlotte said, still staring into the coffee sludge. "Is there someone who could loan me a car, or who is going into Santa Fe and could go by the hotel and pick up my luggage?"

Francis set the newspaper on the counter. "You could go and get our little sedan from Barty. Or I can ask around the store this morning, see who's going into town."

Francis tapped the paper's front-page headline. "Seems the Dos Rios sheriff found a child suffocated in a car trunk."

Thea gasped and closed her eyes. After a moment, she opened them again. "It's not our boy. Conchata says it's not our child. But what a tragedy for that family."

After breakfast Francis, Thea and Charlotte sat on the porch chairs. Thea reached over and grabbed Charlotte's knee. "I need you to take the *yerba sangre* out to Jed this morning."

"Are you comfortable driving the Hudson?" Francis stood up as the truck with Ralph behind the wheel descended the mesa.

"Yes," Charlotte answered. "I'm okay with the Hudson."

Ralph pulled the truck up and stopped near the porch steps.

"Well, then, take the Hudson," Francis said as he secured his cap on his head. "I'll find someone to retrieve your suitcases."

⁂

It was a testament to Thomas Bill's building skills that the sixty-year-old house at High Lonesome was standing at all. The L-shaped structure had a foundation of river cobbles and dirt, and the adobe bricks were mortared together with mud. Nowadays adobe structures followed strict state building codes: secured to rebar and concrete stem walls sunk no less than eighteen inches into the ground, the adobe bricks were stabilized with asphalt, as was the mud mortar. And the walls were secured together with a poured concrete bond beam. Modern adobe buildings contained almost as much concrete and aggregate as they did clay, dirt and straw. Around Santa Fe most contractors had stopped using adobe bricks altogether and framed adobe-looking houses with wood. Hot in the summer and cold in the winter, the stick houses, as Jed called them, didn't function anywhere near as well as adobe.

Thomas Bill did not have access to those materials in 1940, and so he built the Bills' adobe in the traditional way. Adobe, even the old-fashioned, asphalt-free variety, was just about indestructible unless it came into pro-longed contact with water. Barty was out here today trenching and pouring concrete under his parents' house because the rain had found a way through the ripped tin roof and leaked into the adobe.

Barty's shovel struck stone.

"Arthur!" Barty had to yell to be heard over the grinding of the cement mixer and the roar of the generator. "Add more water to that mix! Too dry!"

Arthur saw Barty waving at the water bucket.

"Yeah, man!" Arthur grinned and poured water into the revolving mouth of the cement mixer. "Now it looks good!"

Barty sighed. He'd known Arthur Varela since the day he was born in the Dos Rios hospital more than twenty years ago. Barty had coached Arthur in high school before Arthur ripped out his left knee and had to quit the love of his young life, football. The illegal hit that blew out Arthur's knee seemed to have blown out his good sense, too: Arthur dropped out of Dos Rios High School his senior year and now, at twenty-one, was well on his way to a life of driving, drifting, and drinking.

"Turn it off." Barty gestured at the mixer. Arthur switched off the generator. "Fill up the wheelbarrow."

Arthur pushed the unwieldy load of wet, sloppy cement to the north wall of the house. He was strong and agile, his movements quick and confident. He still had the body of a high school athlete, but Arthur did not in any way resemble a student. Nowadays Arthur wore the clothes favored by his Dos Rios gangster buddies—muscle shirts, baggy jeans hung low on his hips, a bandanna tied around his buzz-cut scalp. His left forearm sported a tattoo of a puma gripping a dagger between its teeth.

"Stop here!" Barty pointed at the first trench at the northeast corner. "We'll begin filling here."

Arthur parked the wheelbarrow with a grunt. Together they shoveled the wet cement into the tunnel dug earlier under the eroding wall. Jed would rebuild the failing walls, and replace the damaged adobes, once there was a better foundation. But Jed couldn't be around the wet cement and wouldn't return to the site until the new foundation was completely cured.

"Pack it down," Barty said, scooping another shovelful and tossing it into the cobbles alongside the new trench. "It's going to be weight bearing."

Arthur grunted and kept shoveling. It was only mid-morning, but it was very hot and very dry. They moved on to the next trench, filling and packing down the cement. Arthur returned to the mixer and, in the roar of the generator and portable mixer, made up another load of cement. Barty scraped the sides of the wheelbarrow. After emptying the last scoop into the third trench he stood the shovel against the wall, removed his gloves, and leaned into the shade alongside the house.

Barty squinted out at the southern *llanos* where the three mares stood under the lone cottonwood tree near the water tank—two bays and a pinto that had become friends. The two sisters were once good saddle horses. Barty and Jed still took the elderly mares out for easy jaunts along the river. Unlike the pinto, they were sociable girls and liked the company of people. Yesterday when Barty and Jed were prepping the trenches, the sister mares had walked right in through the front door of the house and stood around like two old women, nudging and gossiping while they nibbled at the straw sticking out of the mud walls.

"Arthur, how's that cement?"

" *Uno momento!*"

Barty leaned a shoulder into the shaded wall and slapped his gloves against his thigh. No use getting worked up. Arthur was doing the best he could. Or so Barty kept telling himself.

"The hardest student is my most important student," his father used to say. "I'm only succeeding if he or she is making progress."

Barty didn't appreciate his father at the time, but Barty had never met a teacher who could hold a candle to Thomas Bill's enthusiasm for teaching.

The cement mixer stopped with a grumbling clunk. "It's pretty much like mostly done." Arthur called out.

"Pretty much like mostly done," Barty repeated as he walked over to Arthur. " *Díos mío!* Speak Spanish if you're going to butcher the *Inglés* so completely!"

"Oh, *sí*!" Arthur laughed.

"Are you going to retake the GED test?" Barty shoveled while Arthur readjusted his bandanna around his concentration camp haircut.

"Nah, *porque* it's way too hard, man! I've already failed it pretty damned badly once already. I don't need no diploma. I earned six grand last year working at the ice plant in Dos Rios."

Barty motioned at Arthur to move the wheelbarrow closer to the wall. "What happened to that job?"

"Nothin' happened. I got tired of it."

"You're dripping cement. Watch your tilt. You worked for that Finley man, didn't you, the owner?"

"Yeah, man. He was the worstest boss I ever seen!"

Barty watched Arthur retrieve his pants that had begun to slide down his hips. "A belt would help," Barty suggested.

But Arthur needed a good deal more than a belt. He needed a whole new wardrobe and a second chance at the last five years of his life. "Ike Finley is a difficult person, I'll grant ya that, Arthur. But the world is full of tough bosses, and without an education, you're gonna spend a lot of years working for them."

Barty knew Ike Finley because of horses. Barty wasn't working horses the way he used to, but he had agreed to take on Finley's pinto last winter. The mare had suffered some sort of abuse from Ike's son-in-law long before the horse was moved to Finley's corral. Ike said the pinto had been kept in a stall the size of an outhouse at his daughter's place for over a year, and the only contact the mare had with humans was with teenagers who tossed firecrackers into the stall. By the time Barty took the horse from Ike's and brought her to the High Lonesome, the pinto was pathologically afraid of people and about dead from malnutrition. The mare now received a bucket of grain laced with Nana's nerve-toning oat tincture twice a day, eating alone out by the water tank. The other horses including the two sisters were fed in the corral.

"If you had your GED and then went to the tech vocational school or even UNM, you could get much better work, Arthur."

"I can't pass that test." Arthur was shoveling the cement into the third trench. Barty began to shovel, too.

"Did you study for the last one?"

"Nah. I don't know how to study for it. I do okay with the math—I'm pretty good at those numbers—but I can't get past the English." Arthur looked up at Barty. "You know, coach, I butcher the *Inglés* on paper too!" Arthur laughed and shook his head. Barty smiled in spite of himself.

"I thought the library had tutors, a reading program all summer, Inez and them."

"*No sé.* Maybe. None of them does the GED stuff."

"They might if you asked." Barty ran the back of his shovel over the wet cement, smoothing it down into the trench, and packing it around the exposed cobbles. Little bits of straw stuck out of the wall. Barty pulled at one and the straw broke in his fingers. Harvested some sixty years ago, that piece of straw was dried and mixed into the adobe bricks laid out in the sun on the field south of the house. Two thousand of them. Conchata's brothers and cousins helped lay the adobes into walls. Barty's uncles, the Lonewolf brothers, used to joke about the summer they worked with the new school teacher Thomas Bill, who passed the day telling stories about the low green mountains surrounding his North Carolina and who insisted that even Apache warriors like his new brothers-in-law needed to learn to read.

Conchata's brother, Victor, went off to Utah and worked for years in the coal mines. After a brush with lung disease, Victor returned to New Mexico and worked a summer with Thomas Bill. Barty remembered his father sitting on the new porch every evening with Uncle Victor, reading. That fall when he was twenty-four, Victor enrolled at the university in Albuquerque. Four years later, Victor was making a good living as a CPA in Dos Rios.

Victor Lonewolf's story was exceptional around the Lágrimas. Those who went away rarely returned. War or better jobs took them from Agua Dulce and Dos Rios. But not Uncle Victor. He brought his education home. He was generous, too, and did Thomas Bill's tax returns gratis for the remainder of his life. Uncle Victor said it was because of Thomas's relentless campaign to teach him to read that he trumped the hand of poverty.

"It wouldn't be that hard to find a tutor, Arthur."

Arthur moved the wheelbarrow to the fourth trench. "The test's only three weeks from now. I got other plans."

"What if I found someone to work with you?"

"Nah, I don't need it."

"I know someone who could help you study." Barty listened to himself. Who the hell did he know who could help Arthur? Jed? His hands were full. Dennis's sister, Felicia? She was a retired teacher but at sixty-eight she'd have no patience with Arthur's arrogant pride and cavalier disrespect for everyone and everything, especially himself.

"Who?" Arthur looked up over his shovel.

"I'm working on it."

A dust cloud billowed into the air behind a vehicle approaching from the north. Barty squinted to detect a defining color through the fine red haze.

Dark green. Hudson green. Either Thea was out illegally driving again, or she'd sent someone over in the truck.

The Hudson pulled in by the barn and stopped. Barty removed his gloves and adjusted the hat on his sweaty head. Barty hoped it was Thea behind the wheel, despite the danger to life and limb, to herself and everyone else on the road. But he knew before she even opened the door and climbed from the cab that it was Alicia's daughter.

Arthur stood up and stared at the curly-haired woman. She was wearing a pair of Bernadette's Levi's and she still looked startlingly like her mother.

"Who's that?" Arthur motioned at Charlotte with his chin.

Barty bent down and inspected the new tire on the wheelbarrow. "A friend of the Durhams." Barty squinted back at Charlotte. She waved. Barty and Arthur each lifted a hand.

"What she want?"

"I don't know." Barty stood up. "Keep shoveling before that load dries."

Charlotte seemed cemented in place beside the Hudson, so Barty walked over to the barn. He was still embarrassed about last night, about saying it was all so long ago it didn't matter. Jesus, couldn't everyone see in his eyes how much it mattered?

"I'm sorry to bother you," Charlotte said when Barty reached her. "Thea sent me over with some *yerba* for Jed." She looked at Arthur shoveling the wet concrete. "Thea thought Jed was working here this morning." Charlotte held out the bag.

"*Yerba de sangre.*" Barty took the bag and peered inside. "I forgot it last night."

She had on sunglasses but Barty knew what her eyes were saying: he'd forgotten the *yerba* last night because he was so busy being thoughtless and rude.

"Jed's not here today. He's out at his camp." Barty gestured to the tire tracks wavering into the *llanos* southeast of the house. "I'll get it to him by mid-afternoon. We have a few more loads to pour before I can leave here."

Charlotte nodded. Just like her mother, she waited, listened intently, let a person talk and talk and talk while she gathered in what she needed to know before reentering the conversation.

"Thea said it was important that Jed make this up before noon." Charlotte pointed at the bag in Barty's hand. "She told me this three times."

Barty laughed. "Thea can be like that. I suppose you could drive out there right now. The Hudson would make it." Barty looked down at her sneakers. "You'll have to park and leave the truck, walk the last half mile. You can't drive up to the cow camp."

"I'm a pretty good walker," Charlotte said. "Remember, the burros?"

Barty studied her face. There were differences: She had a mole near her right eye—tiny, lovely, like a brown tear. And her chin was more pointed than her mother's, with a small cleft. But the hair and the dimples, the way her head tilted as she completed a sentence.

"You walked a pretty far piece that night."

"I did, but it was nothing, really."

"Okay, you're gonna take the road there." Barty pointed to the left of the house. "It's just two ruts from here on. In another mile and a half the ruts end at a row of stones. That's where you park. From there you follow a cow path that veers off to the east toward the river. You won't see the river; it's down in a canyon. But you'll smell it. Might hear it, too."

Barty turned back to Charlotte. "You can't get lost. Jed's camp is on the last ridge before the plateau drops to the *bosque*. First you come to a stone corral where he keeps Leather Britches—that's his horse. If Jed's not there, just leave the bag inside the tent. But be sure to tie up the flaps again." Barty pointed to the sky. "'Cause of the ravens." Barty handed the paper bag with the *yerba de sangre* back to Charlotte.

"Okay. Thanks." Charlotte walked around the front of the Hudson, opened the door and climbed into the cab. She started the engine with too much gas, ground through several gears until she found first, and finally steered the old truck around Barty.

Barty lifted his hand and she slowed the truck. "If you're not back by supper we'll come looking for you."

Charlotte seemed startled by Barty's comment. He meant to reassure her. But as she drove away he realized how she might have missed his attempt at humor. And Charlotte could hardly be amused. Her mother's disappearance on the desert had proven lethal.

"Oh, geez." Barty shook his head as he walked back toward the house. Arthur had stopped the mixer and lit a cigarette. He looked like an ex-convict or a heroin pusher from the Dos Rios barrio. Barty could only imagine what a suburbanite like Alicia's daughter thought about two half-breeds spending their day trying to patch together an adobe ruin in the middle of nowhere. It wasn't called High Lonesome for nothing.

"Who's that?" Arthur exhaled into the air over his head. "Jed's woman?"

"No, she's not Jed's woman. She's visiting from New York, staying at the Durhams'." Barty picked up his shovel and began to smooth the concrete in the fourth trench. Arthur sucked at his cigarette. His eyes followed the slow but steady progress of the Hudson across the *llano*.

"What's her name?"

"Charlotte."

"Charlotte what?" Arthur exhaled through pursed lips, still watching the truck.

"Charlotte Lambert." Barty straightened up and frowned at Arthur.

"Why'd she stop?" Arthur pushed the cigarette in the sand and was about to toss the stub when he saw Barty watching him. He slid the butt into his pocket. "She likes horses, *no*?"

"I don't know if she likes horses." Barty looked over at the windmill. Charlotte had stopped the Hudson beside the water tank and the two bay mares had ambled over for a chat. The pinto watched from a safe distance under the tree, afraid of a stranger, of attention, of a change in the routine. Charlotte's hand came out of the window and stroked one of the old sisters' forelocks.

"What's she doin' here?" Arthur asked. "Looking to buy a horse?"

"I don't know, Arthur! I never met her before Saturday."

"Okay, coach, *Jesu Cristo*!" Arthur shoveled concrete. Barty watched Charlotte. She stayed with the horses longer than most. Arthur looked up again. "Your crazy mares like her; she must be a horsey person for real, *que no*, coach?"

The mares did like her, else they would have turned away and moseyed back to their private horse land under the cottonwood tree.

"She's a school teacher. If she heard your language, Arthur, she'd plug up her ears or put a sock in your mouth, for real, *que no*?"

"She's the person you're thinking could tutor me for the GED, s i?" Arthur straightened up, shaded his sunglasses with his hand and watched the Hudson inching over the bumpy road to Jed's. "I'd learn to study with her, man! *No problema!*"

"Arthur, you treat that woman with respect, do you understand?"

"I understand, coach." Arthur looked hurt. "I don't mean no harm."

"I didn't say she was the one who could tutor you." Barty tipped the wheelbarrow and Arthur scraped the last of the mix.

"But she could, huh?"

Barty realized Arthur was actually thinking about preparing for the test. "She probably could, Arthur."

"Would ya ask her for me?" Arthur stopped scraping and waited for Barty to answer.

Barty didn't want to ask her, but he wanted to help Arthur. "I'll think about it."

{17}

Arthur roared off toward Agua Dulce in the gunmetal grey Honda Civic Barty had rebuilt in exchange for Arthur's help around the ranch and service station. Barty was glad to be alone again. He opened the corral and waited for the mares to come in for shade, then walked inside the office, retrieved his lunch box and sat down on a bale of hay.

It was noon. Charlotte should be heading back out from Jed's in about fifteen or twenty minutes. Barty could hide in the barn when she drove by. Or he could act like an adult and go out and flag her down, ask how Jed was doing, ask her if she was staying around for the next week, and if so, would she tutor a former high school football star who'd become derailed by misfortune and disappointment and all the frustrations that attached themselves to children from poor, uneducated families?

Through the barn door to the east Barty watched the horses coming up from the river. His large quarter horse Dolly trotted ahead of Noches, the older mare that followed at a walk, reluctant to leave the cool of the *bosque* trees. They moved into the shade by the water tank where the other horses stood.

Why would Charlotte say yes? She was leaving, what, in a day? She'd say no. She wasn't staying long enough to tutor Arthur. She was on vacation. She didn't have any experience with students like Arthur. Barty chewed his sandwich and swigged iced tea from a thermos. He would ask Charlotte, she'd say no, and he'd have at least made an effort. But then who would tutor Arthur?

The low hum of the Hudson's Super Six engine rolled in from the desert. Barty stood up and brushed the hay dust from his jeans, put on his Stetson, and walked to the side door near the tack room. He had promised Thea he would look for those coffee cans in the cabinet where they kept paint and linseed oil. And she wanted the laces replaced on the panniers. Last he saw them, the leather straps were kept with the tools out by the feed bins. Barty stared into the dusty office pretending to apply himself to Thea's requests. But all Barty could think about was the approaching Hudson.

The Hudson's engine dropped into a smooth idle. Barty left the office and walked to the open doors of the barn. Charlotte had stopped to talk with the two sisters again. She left the truck and walked over to where the horses stood in the shade under the cottonwood tree. Charlotte was feeding them something, apples? Where did she get apples? After giving each an apple, Charlotte walked in the direction of the pinto that stood at the far side of the water tank, muscles tensed, ready to bolt. Barty could see it in the mare's posture even from a distance. The pinto was an attractive horse, but Charlotte was about to learn her beauty hid a debilitating handicap: fear of human contact.

Charlotte stopped in the open sun between the tree and the water tank. She must have picked up the mare's 'stay away or I'll run' body language. Charlotte's body language was actually very good; she kept her arms against her torso and didn't face the mare head on. Barty couldn't see her face, but he imagined she was talking to the pinto. The horse's shoulders and head were angled away from Charlotte, but her ears were aimed directly at the human intruder. The two sisters were listening, too. Barty figured one more step in the pinto's direction, and the horse would bolt. Not far. Just to the other side of the water tank, maybe into the *llano* beyond the cottonwood tree. But Charlotte did not take another step. Instead, she placed the apple on the ground, turned and walked back to the Hudson.

Maybe Charlotte was a horse person. Alicia had been a horse person, although she rarely had climbed on a horse and ridden unless Barty had invited her to ride with him on some errand around Agua Dulce or the ranch. But Alicia had known horses; Alicia had asked him to name every part of a horse's body, inside and out. Barty didn't always know the name of each part, but he had told Alicia what he did know. Dr. Al had known more than Barty about the relationship and placement of the two hundred and ten bones in a horse's body. By summer's end Alicia's field notebook was filled with sketches of dozens of horse skeletons—sun-bleached skulls and wind-and-time-scoured pelvises, detailed drawings of individual sacrum, tarsal, tibia, patella and carpal bones, of gleaming white scapulae and vertebrae. The bone horse notebook was a work of art. Alicia transformed the massacre of all those wild horses into something beautiful.

The Hudson moved toward the barn. Where was Alicia's notebook? Barty moved back into the shadow of the doorway. Alicia had drawn the parts of the human body, too, in that notebook. Not just bones. Muscle and flesh. Curve and bend. Male and female. Lovers. Alicia was a magnificent artist. Dr. Al said she could become a fine replicator, bring life to species that had never been seen. She had a precise hand and an eye for detail, and also the kind of imagination that gave two-million-year-gone dinosaurs three-dimensional form. In the hand of Alicia Rose science and art merged.

In Alicia's field notebook love and art merged, too. The lusty, devouring plein-air relationship of Barty and Alicia was captured in exquisitely rendered pencil drawings. Barty saw the drawings only once when the pages of the notebook were blown open on the ground beside him. The sketches were perfect, dexterous and beautiful, intimate and scandalous. Barty was haunted by the power of Alicia's drawings—haunted by the power that could be unleashed by those drawings should the notebook fall into the wrong hands.

The Hudson rounded the road past the ranch house but did not slow and stop when it reached Barty's pickup parked near the corral. The curly-haired driver steered the old vehicle past the barn and down the road, and Barty did not step out until the Hudson was a speck of green on the High Lonesome *llano*.

Barty drove slowly back to the gas station. He'd call her this afternoon. He'd ask her about tutoring Arthur as soon as he unloaded the wheelbarrow and empty cement bags at the station. Barty reached the county road and sat staring at the black asphalt melting in the desert heat. This time Conchata had it wrong. It was Barty who had something of Charlotte's: in the drawer of his bedside table was the field watch Alicia was wearing when she died. Charlotte's father had left it at the sheriff's office. Gus had brought it to Barty. But like Alicia, the wrist-watch did not and would not ever belong to him. It was time to let her go.

{18}

Thea had explained to Charlotte how Jed lived in a cow camp on the bluffs overlooking the Lágrimas, but her description didn't prepare Charlotte for Jed's actual home. As Charlotte walked the horse trail the last half mile to the camp, she vacillated between wanting Jed to be at home, and praying he was not. Jed had no telephone, of course, so he wasn't expecting Charlotte or anyone else. Thea said it was okay to drop in on Jed; he was used to it.

According to Thea, Jed lived out on the edge of the High Lonesome Ranch because he needed a lot of fresh air. Jed had overdosed on some sort of insecticide or lawn fertilizer back in Phoenix. Even so, Charlotte figured that anyone who chose such a remote, edge-of-the-known-world camp for a home wanted one thing: privacy. She hated to invade it, and wondered what the protocol was for unannounced visits to a recluse at his desert hermitage.

It was Jed's horse Leather Britches that greeted Charlotte at the cow camp. Britches was grazing on the short grasses that grew in the juniper grove and watched Charlotte approach. When she was thirty feet from the camp, he lifted his head and nickered. Not a fearful sound; not an alarm. Just a greeting that defined the boundaries of the gelding's home turf, and also informed Jed that someone was here.

Jed appeared in the trees behind Britches. He wore his cowboy hat, jeans and an unbuttoned and very faded denim shirt. His bare chest was the color of cedar. He held a wet bandanna in one hand.

"Hello, Charlotte." Jed's green eyes flickered over a friendly but quizzical smile. "Thea must have sent you."

Charlotte held up the paper bag. Britches swung his head around and knocked it from her hands to the ground. Charlotte laughed and bent down to retrieve the bag.

"Britches!" Jed waved his arm at the horse. "Where are your manners! Go on!"

Jed took the bag and peered inside. "*Yerba sangre.*" He smiled and motioned for Charlotte to follow him. "A bitter tea that cleanses the liver. You can never have too much *yerba sangre* in your camp."

They walked into a clearing where there was a firepit, and a table and two chairs near a large juniper. Jed gestured for Charlotte to take a seat.

"I don't keep a lot of ice, but I have bottled juice in the cooler."

"Thank you." Charlotte sat down. The wood table was rough from age and weather, so the top was covered with a cotton tablecloth. A hurricane lantern surrounded by small, black stones sat in the center. Several bandannas were folded and placed in a pile on the table.

Jed removed a stone from the top of a metal cooler on the ground and pulled out two dripping-wet bottles of juice. He set them on the table.

"Ravens," he said as he closed the cooler and replaced the stone on the lid. "They're the most determined birds!"

Charlotte took a long drink of the cool cranberry juice. "I haven't decided if I like ravens or not. Their intelligence is almost scary."

Jed sat down on the chair across the table from Charlotte. "And they're so interested in us humans. What's that about?"

Jed took a long drink and set the bottle down on the table.

"This is quite a place you have out here." Charlotte looked around at the neat and well-appointed camp. The tent was impressive, fit for a safari. The outdoor kitchen utilized every crook and elbow of the cedar branches that embraced it on three sides. The stone firepit was fitted with a large grill and had two flat-topped boulders placed on either side, making natural counters for food prep and plate warming. Charlotte could not hear the river, but she detected the unmistakable scent of water.

"The river's over there," Jed said, motioning behind the tent. "There's a path down the cliff. It's steep but safe."

"How long have you been out here?"

Jed took a gulp of juice and wiped his lips with the back of his hand. "Since February. It was pretty cold. I don't know which is harder to live with: the snow and wind of March or the intense heat of June."

"You grew up here in Agua Dulce?"

Jed stood and walked over to the tent and pulled down the flap that served as the door across the opening. He secured the canvas with several ties.

"Actually, I grew up in Tempe, Arizona. I love the wilderness, but I'm a city boy." Jed looked at Charlotte. "I'm assuming Thea told you how I came to be here. I have difficulties with enclosed places. Physically, not psychologically. I seem to need a lot of open space." He opened his arms to the camp surrounding them. "So here I am."

Jed sat back down on the chair across the table from Charlotte. "I have what they call chemical sensitivities, environmental illness. I collapsed in Phoenix eight months ago and moved to Agua Dulce before Christmas. I thought I'd be back at work by now."

"I've heard of people having reactions, but not so severe as yours. What work do you do?"

"I own a construction company in Scottsdale."

No wonder this cowboy was so genteel: he was an urban entrepreneur slumming it for a few seasons as a man of the land. And Charlotte thought he was doing it very well. "There are people who would pay good money to live in the New Mexican outback for a week or a month."

Jed eyed Charlotte over his juice bottle; he didn't believe her.

"No, really! This is very exotic! My grandfather spent summers living in wild places. When I was a child he sent me postcards from little towns near his remote camps—in Canada, Wyoming, two summers in Zimbabwe, one summer in Antarctica. He was studying fossils. My grandmother used to say he was really just a man playing like a boy in the summer dirt. I thought his life was wonderful."

"Your grandfather was the paleontologist they called Dr. Al, right? He was here in the Lágrimas in what, the late 1950s?" Jed's hands rearranged the black river stones in the center of the table. His fingers were slender and graceful, like a woman's, and he handled the stones like rare gems as he placed them into a geometric design on the table. "Your grandfather is legendary around here. Even my Uncle Barty speaks of him with a kind of awe." Jed lifted his eyes and smiled at Charlotte. "And that's saying a lot."

Jed's hands continued to move the smooth black stones on the white cloth, but his eyes were on Charlotte. A heat wave rippled down her neck and spine.

"Grandpa had a fossil field camp out here. I visited the quarry yesterday with Dennis Mata. It was more beautiful than anyone had ever described it to be."

"I was there years ago." Jed's eyes moved across Charlotte's flushed face. "You look a little hot. It's cooler down by the river. Do you want to walk down the cliff, or do you have somewhere you need to be?"

"I don't have any place I need to be." Charlotte pushed the damp bandanna into her neck. "I've decided to stay a few more days."

"Are you a bone digger?" Jed stood up and walked to the tent. Charlotte followed.

"No. I don't know much about fossils. I teach high school."

Jed turned around but kept walking. "I guess Thea already told me that. Is she still trying to get you to start a school?"

"She is kind of relentless."

Charlotte followed Jed down the steep but well-maintained trail that angled and hairpinned down the cliff. The Lágrimas River was high and the current splashed and roared around the boulders that had broken from the stone walls and landed in the river. When Charlotte reached the river's edge she settled down onto a wide, flat rock and took off her shoes. She placed her feet in the cold water. Jed removed his sandals and stood in the mud along the edge of the river.

"This is spectacular," Charlotte said, gazing skyward. The canopy made by the cottonwood trees splintered the sun into manageable streaks of light and heat. The *bosque* was verdant with tangled thickets of scrub oaks and tall, feathery grasses. Some kind of purple flower made a carpet between the elms and cottonwoods. "It's so green down here."

"There's nothing not to like, as my uncle says." Jed walked along the riverbank, his bare feet sucking and sliding around in the brown mud. He studied the shallow water along the shore and when he saw a stone that interested him, bent down and pulled it from the river. After drying it with the tail of his shirt, he slid the stone into his pocket. Charlotte looked about her; there were smooth gray stones everywhere in the shallow water, but she did not see any of the black ones Jed had collected for his tabletop display.

"You think you might be living out here for a while yet?"

Jed picked up one of the flat gray stones and skimmed it out across the top of the river. The current swallowed it immediately.

"Could be."

Charlotte picked up a stone and threw it into the water. It made a loud thunk before it sunk into the river. "How deep is it out there, in the middle?"

"Maybe eight feet, ten. We had a lot of snow last winter and the snow-pack in the mountains is still melting. Come late July, the flow will be cut by half."

"What do people with chemical sensitivities do if they don't have a family ranch or know how to live in the wilderness?"

"They suffer. They live the best they can in whatever dwelling they can find with the fewest irritants. I heard of a Minnesota woman who moved her bed onto a porch. Slept out there through the winter. Another guy camped in his son's tree house in suburban Bakersfield. I think he's still living there. So I'm what they call lucky. I get all this."

"You probably don't see it this way," Charlotte said, "but there's something very admirable about leaving it all behind—the routine, the career, the pursuit. Most people couldn't do it, even if they wanted to."

"Out here you live with the rhythm of the natural world." Jed walked into the river until the water soaked his jeans up to his knees. The current was strong and he leaned upstream to keep his balance. "You give up everything you thought was fundamental to your sense of well-being and you become someone very different. Without the forty-hour-plus work week, and the so-cializing and schmoozing and shopping and daily maintenance that is the norm for urban living, you learn how to do a lot of nothing. Can't say if that's admirable, though."

"You and your uncle are rebuilding the ranch house? And you'll move there?"

"We are. Don't know if I can live there." Jed walked back to shore, sat down on one of the rocks, and brushed the wet sand from his feet. "I'm meeting a friend at one. We should get going."

Charlotte followed Jed back up the steep trail. He seemed unaffected by the heat and the strenuous ascent and kept turning back to check Charlotte's progress. Charlotte's thighs burned when she reached the last steps to the rim, and her heart pounded like it could break a rib as she gulped for oxygen.

When they reached camp, Britches was standing in the trees by the kitchen, dozing. Jed handed Charlotte a bottle of water pulled from the cooler. "Would you like something to eat before you head out?"

"I told Thea I'd be back for lunch." Charlotte chugged the water. "I'm fine."

Jed walked into the trees and took Britches by the halter and led him toward the stone corral. "I'm gonna saddle up Britches. If you wait a few minutes, I can give you a ride back to the truck. Those stiff Levi's of my mom's are just the worst sort of thing for hiking in this heat."

While waiting for the light to change on Main, Charlotte studied the old Woolworth's across the street. Through the fiesta-dressed mannequins she could see the interior of the department store. Someone was looking through the window, peering through the lacy frills of the skirt hems directly at the Hudson stopped in traffic. Charlotte squinted and leaned into the steering wheel trying to get a better look at the person, but he or she immediately withdrew into the store.

Charlotte rubbed her arms now prickled with goose flesh. Gus and his troop of retired rangers were not on the bench by the drugstore. Too hot, Charlotte supposed, even for hardened lawmen. After three days in the Lágrimas, Charlotte was learning about the colorful variety of people who called this community home. During their ride on Britches from the camp to the Hudson, Jed told Charlotte how there really wasn't a dominant culture here: the Lágrimas had been settled over the last century by Jicarilla Apaches who had left the reservation for jobs in Dos Rios, by Hispanics who had moved out of Santa Fe looking for farm and ranch country, and by Anglos who had come in with the federal WPA soil conservation and education projects of the 1930s. After World War II, Agua Dulceños began to commute to cash jobs in

Dos Rios and even Santa Fe. There was a substantial exodus of residents from the valley in the 1960s and 70s. Those who stayed had to eke out a living with a small business that somehow filled a niche, like the Matas' drugstore, the Durhams' hardware, or the B & B Service Station.

Although the population was a wide mix of Hispanic, Apache, Anglo, and a combination of all three, Agua Dulce became a community because everyone was equally de-tribalized. Everyone had left their home country, whether it was over the mountains, across the continent, or on the far side of the globe, and started a new life in the Lágrimas Valley. And everyone struggled to make a go of it.

"Drought, world war, and depression are great equalizers," Jed said over his shoulder to Charlotte seated behind him on Leather Britches. "There's some racial tension here, but it's not the dominant theme. People in Agua Dulce have shared too many of the same calamities to waste a lot of energy in us-versus-them arguments."

They rode all of ten glorious minutes on Leather Britches, but those minutes were like a whole season of good feelings to Charlotte: the pleasurable rhythm of a horse's walk, the smell of warm fur and hot dust, the creaking of a leather saddle as it absorbed and accommodated the movements of horse and riders. Charlotte hadn't realized how much she missed horses until she was around them again.

The signal changed from red to green. Charlotte fumbled with the gearshift, pressed down on the gas, and let the clutch pop into the bottom of her sneaker. The Hudson stalled.

"Oh, Charlotte," she said as she pushed the clutch back down and restarted the engine, "don't be so easily seduced by a man and his horse."

Even Maddie, ever the optimistic romantic, would warn Charlotte away from this one. It was one thing to be swept away for a day or two by an unavailable Prince Charming. But a cowboy who handled river stones like precious pearls, and made living with nothing out beyond the reach of time look like paradise-found was a dangerous association to court even in the imagination.

{19}

Barty held the telephone receiver to his ear and walked out the office door. The Durhams' phone rang once, twice. He eyed the flying red horse. This year for the Fourth of July, like every year since Barty bought the station, the red horse would blaze across the holiday sky in direct defiance of the Mobil Oil lawyers who had, in three different legal missives over the past ten years, forbidden such display of their company icon at the unaffiliated, officially de-branded B & B Service and Repair Station. Thankfully, Mobil had larger financial and legal worries to manage in other more potentially profitable parts of the world. The issues surrounding the unlawful lighting of the flying horse at the service station in Agua Dulce never proceeded beyond occasional verbal harassment via telephone from a junior attorney in Houston.

The phone at Thea's rang six times and still no one answered. Fine, Barty thought, it wasn't meant to happen.

"Hello, Durham residence." It was Charlotte. Barty spun around on his boot heel and walked back into the office.

"Yes, hello, this is Barty." He cleared his throat. "How long are you staying at the Durhams'?"

Charlotte hesitated before answering. "I don't know. I haven't made my return reservation."

"The reason I'm asking is that I know a young man, Arthur, Arthur Varela, he was out at the ranch with me today. He needs to pass the GED in three weeks up at the Dos Rios High School. If someone doesn't help him with his English, and I think his science, too, he's going to fail. And if he fails, he's not going to try again."

Charlotte was silent at the other end of the phone. Barty returned to the doorway, shading his eyes with his hand. At this time of day in early summer the angle and brightness of the sun illuminated the flying red horse from the outside in.

"I was wondering if you would tutor him for a couple of weeks." In an effort to sound friendlier Barty heard himself using the voice he had developed for timid horses. "You could meet in the library. Inez opens it every day in the summer. It's air-conditioned."

"I've never seen the GED," Charlotte said, after a pause. "I've never tutored a student for something like that."

Barty leaned his shoulder into the wall. "You'd be a helluva lot better than anyone else around here. Some help right now for Arthur could mean the difference between a good life and a difficult one. My father used to say that the most difficult student was the most important."

Barty winced. He hated it when people implied it was his moral responsibility to solve someone else's problem. Lord knows, he'd been serving himself first for half a century. He backtracked. "You know, this really isn't your problem."

A pickup truck driven by Ned Saunders drifted into the gas station and came to a stop by the pumps. Ned turned off his engine when he left the road because he still believed there was gas rationing, and nothing Barty or anyone else said could convince Ned that the war was over.

"I have a customer." Barty waved at Ned and walked back into the office to hang up the phone. "I shouldn't have asked you to take on someone like Arthur. I'm sorry, Charlotte."

"I'll do it."

"What?" Barty watched Ned through the office window. He was climbing from the cab.

"I'd like to do this. You said it was just three weeks until the test?"

"Yes, three weeks. But just a week or so of tutoring would really help him." Barty could hear her breathing. Or maybe it was his breathing. What was he doing? Three weeks? He was encouraging her to prolong her visit for three weeks. "I have to get off the phone. Ned is getting out of his truck and he shouldn't handle a gasoline pump. I'll call you later."

Barty hung up the phone and walked out to Ned. Ned's truck was parked at a reasonable if not typical distance from the pumps, closer to the cactus garden than the gasoline island.

"How much, Ned? A few bucks worth?"

"You got it!" Ned smiled broadly. He had absolutely no teeth left in his old gums.

Barty unhooked the pump and opened the truck's gas cap. He had to pull the nozzle to the end of its hose to reach the truck, but he managed. The gas flowed and the pump bell clanged with each quarter gallon.

"What ya been doing, Bartholomew?" Ned talked real loud. "How many horses ya got nowadays?"

"I'm not keeping a lot of horses, Ned. I only have the seven just now. And Jed's Leather Britches, of course."

"Ah, ya know, I always said to my Suzie, may she rest in peace, Bartholomew isn't a teacher like his father was, but he's doing the same work—guiding those less fortunate horses to a better life in this world. Ain't that true?"

"Why, thank you, Ned, I never saw it that way." Barty put the nozzle back on the pump. Ned was already holding out two dollars, his allotted ration of gas.

"Yessiree, some folks thought you were nothing like your dad, especially those years you was moving from town to town. Remember? You was lost for a while, doing bit work on the reservation, you know, after you lost your unborn, your Benjamin in that accident, after Kitty left, before you enlisted. And then the rodeos, trying to kill yourself on bulls and all. But I always seen the way you were with the mares, and I seen Thomas Bill take a troubled kid under his wing and ease them forwards just exactly the same."

Ned started the truck engine, pulled out of the station and vanished around the curve in the slow-motion driving style favored by the elderly. The trance of late-afternoon early summer returned to the B & B's corner of the world. Cicadas buzzed and a meadowlark sang its heart out on top of the fence post across the road.

Now, why was he so anxious? He'd called and asked Alicia's daughter to stay in Agua Dulce. Practically insisted she stay in Agua Dulce. Good lord, what had he done that for? Barty remained a few more minutes by the gas pumps. Above him, the sun pierced the horse's glass heart just like the lyrical song of the lark pierced Barty's stone heart. Barty had *done that*—asked Charlotte to stay and tutor Arthur—because it was exactly what Thomas Bill would have done. Barty couldn't claim that he'd been privy to his mother's messages from the great beyond all these years. But today he could say with certainty that as sure as he could hear the song of that lark, he'd heard and heeded the song of his father.

{20}

Scavengers and trespassers had invaded the landfill since Farley's last visit to his Airstream six weeks ago. He could see their tracks in the sand. Farley would report them to Philip Griego and the solid-waste authorities in Dos Rios as soon as he was back at Mabel's where there was a public telephone. This particular county landfill had been closed down being that it was full up. The state inspector said it was worse than full up—it was harboring some nasty toxins, too. No more burning was allowed out here. Griego was going to bring in a dozer and push dirt over the whole smoldering pit.

Closing the landfill to the public was just fine with Farley; it meant nobody would be out here poking around his trailer, tampering with his treasures. And Farley had treasures: sewed into the seams of the mattress, stuffed between the panels of the trailer's plastic-and-aluminum wall, tucked in rolled envelopes in the defunct gas line, and slid between the corrugated roof and the scrap-wood sides of the outhouse. Treasures found in the refuse people heaved from the back of pickup trucks and then piled and pushed down the sides of the landfill.

In the castoff and thrown away, in the buried, Farley scavenged and disinterred what people wanted to forget, to hide. There was, finally, no hiding from the Lord. Farley had developed a system over the years: from twenty feet he could eyeball trash bags and know which held waste and useless debris, and which bags held clues to personal or community secrets. Legal and financial statements, desk calendars and notepads were his most precious finds. Personal letters were paper gold, and Farley kept that collection tied in plastic food bags in the old stove's air vent.

It didn't even matter that Farley could not read the evidence he had gathered against Agua Dulce's sinners. The sins leaked through the ink on the pages, stung the flesh of his fingertips as he ran his hands across the words.

Living at Mabel's had greatly hampered Farley's ability to keep an eye on and a hand in what came to the landfill. Today was only Farley's second visit to his old home in four months. It took persistent bartering, badgering, and blunt threats to get Earl to hand over the keys to his Falcon. Farley relied on Earl's cigarette addiction to wrangle use of the vehicle for a few hours. Earl's doctor forbade him to touch even a filtered smoke to his lips again for as long as he lived, which couldn't be much longer, as Farley saw it. Farley made sure he always had a pack or two of Marlboros tucked in the trunk in his room. And when he needed the use of a car, Farley tempted Earl with his tobacco stash.

Right now Earl was sitting under a tree behind the backstop at the baseball field on the south end of Agua Dulce sucking on as many cigarettes as he could with those old lungs. Maybe today Earl would smoke himself dead under that tree. Maybe after they buried Earl they'd forget about Earl's car and Farley could hide it somewhere and use it as he needed.

The day of reckoning was here. Everyone with any sense of good and evil, justice and punishment could smell it in the air, feel it throbbing deep down against their groin. Farley could feel it; he felt it so bad he had about stopped sleeping. Just lay awake on his bed thinking of everything to be done. Sitting in the dark whispering aloud his lists of tasks, naming the obstacles, naming the enemies that would try and stand between Farley and the promise of paradise about to rise from the ashes.

God, it was hot! Farley shuffled from the Falcon across the barren sand to the Airstream door. He fumbled with the key until the sticky lock sprang free. Farley swung open the door and backed away from the trailer. That's when he noticed someone had been out here in a truck with wide, bald tires. They left a track around the Airstream and then drove over to the far side of the pit where they set fire to whatever they had thrown into the hole. Farley surveyed the scraps of rags and food wrappers in the newest pile; nothing caught his eye.

Farley turned his head to the west, to the fence line and the boundary between his territory and the evil country. His heart jerked sideways in his chest, pulling at the artery that kept him alive. It wasn't what he was seeing in the landscape that caused Farley's internal organs to spasm: it was what he saw in his mind's eye. The drawings. The pictures. The confession that made Farley's crusade inevitable, unavoidable, ordained by God Himself.

Farley slid his gaze along the barbed wire to the south until the rusted strands disappeared in the branches of a cedar. An old cedar, with a gnarled and twisted trunk three feet across. His heart knocked out against his chest bones again, and his knees began to throb. Farley lurched across the sand to the cedar. He hadn't dug under that tree in, what, seven or eight months?

Farley fell onto his knees and pulled at the rocks piled to the back side, pushing away a low branch that served as camouflage. Farley pushed and rolled the rocks aside, and heaved himself belly down on the sand while he dug down into the hot earth with his fingers. Finally, his fingernails scratched across metal and he clawed at the top of the tin can.

A ruckus began near the trailer. Farley hoisted himself up on his elbows and hunched forward like a toad. He could hear the ravens but he could not see them. Kraking and croaking. Glass shattered. Farley grasped the cedar branch and tried to stand. The branch snapped and he fell down onto one of the rocks, bruising his hip. The commotion of the ravens intensified. Farley forced his eyes to open and focus: the ravens were inside the Airstream. Five of them, six, seven. They finished their mayhem and flew like a cloud of locusts out the trailer door and directly at Farley under the cedar tree. They carried scraps of fabric and paper in their beaks. Farley struggled to stand and grabbed at the ravens as they flew over the fence and into the purgatory on the other side. Farley dropped to his knees and shoved the sand and stones back over the tin can. He flung himself over the burial and rolled over and looked up through the tangled maze of branches. Two hard black eyes glared down at him. Farley buried his head in his hands. How could he fight such an enemy? The raven made a gurgling, mocking sound deep in her throat, then pushed off into the air with a force that rocked the tree. She flew into the west—the home of Duende, the home of the undead.

Farley shuffled back to the trailer. He did not look inside, did not want to know what black magic the ravens had unfurled. He closed the trailer door, locked it, and walked to the Falcon. The smoldering fire in the pit had showered the car with ash and Farley could hardly breathe to start the engine. Farley was prepared for this. This was exactly as it was meant to be. He had always known that the fire that would destroy Alicia Rose would most likely consume him, reduce him to ashes, too.

{21}

"Charlotte!" Thea called from the other side of the house. Charlotte tucked wayward curls under the Durham Feed baseball cap and went to the kitchen.

"We're going to the west pasture to see if the *malva* is thick enough to cut." Thea wore a wide-brimmed straw hat and baggy trousers. Actually everything, even panty hose, bagged on Thea's body. Thea, like Charlotte, wore one of Francis's long-sleeved denim shirts.

Ralph Garcia was going to Santa Fe today and would retrieve Charlotte's suitcases from the St. Francis Hotel. Charlotte was feeling reluctant to give up her borrowed clothing and hand-me-downs. After four days in Bernadette's jeans and T-shirts, Francis's hats and denim shirts, and Thea's gloves and bandannas, Charlotte felt like she belonged in New Mexico.

"We'll need bags like the ones we used yesterday when we picked the clover."

"I remember." Charlotte retrieved a stack of paper grocery bags from a shelf in the pantry. Plant hunting and picking occupied most of yesterday. It seemed every grass, bush, nut, root, twig, and weed that grew upon or under the sandy soil of the Lágrimas had some medicinal value. It was impossible to walk ten feet from the house or barn without Thea stopping to pick, pinch, pluck, cut, or peel a piece of some plant or shrub.

The flower garden was more than a source of visual and aromatic pleasure. Even the showy cutting flowers had some medicinal purpose. Last evening Charlotte picked nasturtium leaves and blossoms for the supper salad, and infused yarrow tops in the evening tea. The purple coneflowers would be harvested for throat tonic when they matured; the stems and leaves of the hollyhocks that would be taller than the burros by mid-July would be tied into bundles and dried for next winter's annual outbreak of sore throats amongst the Lágrimas *viejos*.

"Gus has tonsillitis every January," Thea said. "I can't look at the red and pink hollyhocks without seeing Gus's red and pink throat!"

Thea insisted that Charlotte learn to identify the herbs and plants used in Conchata's medicines and teas. To that end, last night on the porch Thea brought out a thick notebook stuffed with plant specimens, roots, leaves, and scraps of bark. Loose pieces of yellowed paper fell from the dried pages that were covered top to bottom, margin to margin with notes, drawings, and maps. The bulging cardboard journal—a school composition notebook Conchata bought in Santa Fe in the 1940s—was held together with rubber bands and kept in a drawer in the pantry.

Thea and Charlotte had to finish the plant picking by lunch today because at one o'clock Charlotte was meeting Arthur Varela at the Agua Dulce Public Library. Charlotte had replayed the phone conversation with Barty over and over in her head trying to figure out why she had so quickly agreed to help this young man pass the graduate equivalencey degree test. Every time she reviewed that conversation and Barty's asking if Charlotte would tutor, *yes* continued to be just about the most surprising and unexpected response she could have given. Charlotte wondered if she would have agreed to help Arthur if she had not just spent an hour at the cow camp, sat under the old cottonwoods with her bare feet in the river, and ridden horseback slow and easy across the desert with the tall, narrow, summer-sage-scented Jed Morley.

Thea bent down and studied the crockpot on the porch. "We'll strain this chaparral when we return."

The Hudson was parked by the barn. Little Bit and George—the rooster was allowed to come along on ranch errands—were already in the truck bed. Charlotte walked first to the corral and greeted the burros Paco and Old Egypt. When she turned for the truck, Thea was already in the cab and was positioning herself behind the steering wheel.

"Charlotte, would you close the truck gate for Bit and George?"

Charlotte went to the rear of the Hudson and closed and latched the tailgate.

"Did you bring the second pair of cutters?"

"Yes." Charlotte opened the passenger door and held up the small snippers she'd grabbed from the pantry counter. "Thea, shouldn't I drive?"

Thea started the truck and gave the engine a slow rev. "Climb in, Miss Rose."

"I thought Francis didn't like you to drive anymore."

Thea's spindly leg slowly let out the clutch. "Just off the ranch, my dear."

With both hands tightly grasped around the steering wheel, Thea directed the truck toward the far side of the barn. Charlotte braced herself for the collision that seemed inevitable between the Hudson's front fender and the barn's east wall. But at the last possible moment, Thea veered the truck to the left and miraculously avoided a head-on with the barn.

Thea's line of sight was through the middle of the steering wheel, and she leaned forward as she drove the truck on the road to the irrigation reservoir. This was the road that Charlotte had walked with Francis three evenings in a row. It had deep ruts that could twist an ankle, and those trenches became the tracks that held the Hudson's tires on course. As they approached the narrow bridge over the *acequia*, Charlotte's hands gripped the edge of the seat below her knees. But, again, Thea's driving abilities defied her lack of visual ones: she centered the truck and passed safely over the rickety planks. On the other side, the Hudson lurched as the tires struggled to find alignment in the road ruts, pitching Bit and George from one side of the truck bed to the other. After a final neck-wrenching snap the truck locked down into the eroded grooves like a train onto its rails.

Thea grinned, pleased with herself. "I've lost George over the truck side a time or two."

The road passed several draws of straggly grasses and tamarisk bushes, and dipped down and back up narrow *arroyos* shaded by old cottonwoods and elm trees. When they reached the irrigation pond, Charlotte leaned out the window and looked at the lush cattails and grasses that grew along the little reservoir's shore.

"Do you find some of Conchata's plants here?"

"*Yerba mansa* grows here—that's why the cattails moved in."

"*Yerba mansa*." Charlotte repeated the words with a vibrating "r" and quick "s."

"Lizard tail, swamp root," Thea said. "Come August, we'll make a tincture for those stubborn bronchial infections that come around Thanksgiving."

The road descended into a stand of cottonwood trees. Francis and Charlotte had not walked beyond this point. Thea pointed at the cliffs. "You follow that to the stream. Up in that narrow canyon, about a mile, you come to the spring head. The water is squeezed from stone in the box canyon."

"How can that be?"

"It just is."

Ravens hovered in the air just above the cliff tops. Charlotte watched their playful sky dance, then turned to Thea. "Why are there so many ravens?"

"They stay here all their lives." Thea's eyes shifted into the direction of the cliffs to the north. "Their children remain, and bring in their mates, and then their children remain. They know a good home when they've found one. A place where water seeps from stone, well, what could be finer than that?"

They followed the road out of the trees and up a hill. When the truck crested the ridge, the Agustina Mountains and the wide red-and-gold desert of buttes and spires emerged before them. Like every other day, the sky over the Lágrimas was a profound blue.

The road dwindled to a dusty trail and ended beside an unmoving windmill and an aluminum water tank. Thea let the truck drift to a stop in the sand near the barbed-wire fence.

"This is the end of the ranch," Thea climbed from the truck. "Don't forget your hat."

Charlotte opened the tailgate and George fluttered out. Charlotte picked up Bit and placed him gently on the ground.

"What are we looking to pick out here?" Charlotte tucked the bags under her arm and followed Thea to the water tank. George strutted past with a great show of feather-fluffed self-importance. Bit walked straight to the shade at the base of the tank and sat down.

"You'll want to walk carefully around this," Thea tapped her cane against the aluminum tank. "Favorite place for rattlesnakes. Moist and cool."

Charlotte nervously surveyed the ground near her sneakers.

"Just in the shade, my dear. Snakes can't tolerate the sun at this hour."

"What are we looking for, Thea?" Charlotte asked again. "There's not much out here that I can see." Thea wasn't even looking at the ground, but was staring into the distance. "Thea?"

"We're looking for all kinds of things. Of course, most of what we need is up there." Thea pointed at the indigo-blue form of the mountains. "Everything changed when the horses left. Folks forgot the high country."

Charlotte walked along the fence looking at the ground. There was a low, thick bush with bell-shaped white flowers. Charlotte hoped she wasn't going to have to collect those white flowers, as there were only two clumps anywhere near the tank.

"Is it the white flowers?" Charlotte called out. "Shall I pick these small white flowers?"

"Jimson weed? Why, no, they would make us all loco!"

Thea looked briefly at Charlotte and returned her attention to the Agustinas. "I can count my days from here."

Charlotte gave up trying to locate the object of this morning's expedition and rejoined Thea at the fence. "Count your days from here to where?"

Thea pointed the tip of her cane into the landscape of red-and-gold vastness before them. "I've been dreaming about the high country. I haven't seen it in years. Neither has Bartholomew. But he dreams of it, too."

"Shouldn't we gather what it is you came to find?" Charlotte asked.

"We will. It's back on the road at the foot of the hill."

"We passed it?"

"Would you drive, dear?"

Thea slid into the truck and closed the door. Charlotte helped Bit and George back into the truck bed and closed the tailgate.

"Did she ever forgive him?" Thea asked Charlotte as she slid behind the wheel.

"Who? Did who forgive whom?"

"Your grandmother, Ruth. Did she ever forgive Dr. Al?"

"I didn't know that Grandpa needed forgiveness."

Charlotte did know that Grandma Ruth was more often annoyed with Grandpa than she was pleased. But Charlotte thought that was how all married people interacted. There was always a battle simmering in the Lambert house. Alicia and Leonard lived on the edge of a war zone for years. The last year was the worst, especially after the hysterectomy. When Alicia finally began to recover her physical health, Leonard began to work later and later into the evenings. Charlotte never saw her parents together except when they were arguing or stone silent.

No wonder Charlotte didn't marry Michael or Douglas five years before him; who wanted to live combat alert for the rest of their lives? Francis and Thea Durham were actually the first married couple Charlotte had known who genuinely enjoyed each other's company.

Charlotte steered the truck around the water tank. Thea turned to Charlotte: "Ruth's very last words to Francis were that she would never forgive Albert for bringing his daughter to this god-forsaken place. Stop where the *arroyo* crosses the road."

Thea pointed to a grassy area where bushes and small trees grew in a cluster. Charlotte stopped the truck. "What happened to my mother that was so unforgivable to my grandmother?"

"Love happened. I don't believe it was that Alicia fell in love that upset Ruth Rose so much. It was that Alicia fell in love with a half Apache. In those days, good white girls didn't fall in love with Indians. Now, tell me if the clover is yellow."

Thea was talking about Barty Bill. Charlotte stared out the window but saw nothing resembling yellow clover. She saw her mother looking into the face of Barty. Only his face wasn't guarded and tight with age and disappointment. Charlotte saw Barty's face as Alicia had known it when he was a young man in his prime. Or was that Jed's face?

Charlotte shivered. "The clover is yellow?"

"Yes, the sweet yellow clover."

Charlotte turned off the truck and climbed out. Thea remained in the truck cab with her head against the door, ready for sleep. George and Little Bit followed Charlotte along the *arroyo* bottom where the clover grew in clusters of willowy bushes. Of course Ruth Rose would not want her stepdaughter to fall in love with an Apache cowboy. Ruth was born and raised in Boston, a card-carrying Daughter of the American Revolution whose ancestors believed in the inherent superiority of Anglo-Saxon America. Ruth Cabot herself had broken several Brahmin rules when she married a widowed professor with a young daughter. No, someone like Barty Bill, the half-breed son of an expatriated Confederate and his marginally Christian Jicarilla squaw, would simply not do for Ruth Rose's Harvard-bound stepchild.

Charlotte thanked and then gathered armfuls of the long-stemmed sweet yellow clover. But why was Grandma Ruth still so angry about New Mexico after so many years? Had Alicia kept in contact with Barty? Maybe they had an ongoing affair. Did Albert know? Leonard? Leonard was angry with Alicia after the miscarriage and cancer, as if it were somehow her choice to be so sick. And when she took off for New Mexico, Leonard told Grandma Ruth he didn't know if he wanted Alicia to return. Ever.

Was Barty with Alicia the night she died? Maybe they argued and Alicia, desperate and hurt, climbed that cliff and jumped. Even if Alicia had not premeditated her suicide, her story still came to the same dead end. Love could make such fools of people. Was there a remedy in Conchata's book of native cures that could heal love sickness? Charlotte would look tonight.

Charlotte carried the bundles of sweet clover to the truck and gently stuffed them into the paper bags. Grandpa never returned to the New Mexico fossil site. Was it because of Alicia and Barty? Even if Albert accepted his daughter's love for Barty Bill when she was a teenager, surely he was disappointed when Alicia returned to re-kindle that love as an adult woman with a husband and child. After Alicia's death, Grandpa's pain and guilt must have collided with his affection and love for his daughter, and become an emotional quandary that fatally wounded an already weak heart.

After Little Bit and George were loaded back in the truck bed Charlotte quietly climbed into the Hudson's cab and started the engine. Thea did not wake, but snored softly into her arm against the window.

No wonder Barty avoided Charlotte. Charlotte avoided Barty for the same reasons: guilt, shame, anger, loss. Charlotte and Barty were the worst sort of kindred spirits. As the recipients of Alicia's deepest love, they were both irrevocably injured by her final melodrama.

Charlotte would stay fourteen days and tutor Arthur Varela through the GED. And then she would return to New York and go on with her life—*her* life that had absolutely nothing to do with her mother's life. Thea was wrong: the story ended here.

{22}

The low rambling adobe building that housed the Agua Dulce Public Library was located on a shaded lane two blocks west of Main Street. The flat-roofed structure also accommodated the office of the local State Farm Insurance agent, Mr. Pedro Jaramillo. Pedro was the grandnephew of Dr. Phillip Jaramillo, whose last will and testament stipulated that half of the old Jaramillo residence become the Agua Dulce Public Library, and the other half be deeded to his sister's only son, Pedro.

The Agua Dulce Public Library was not, as Barty had claimed, air-conditioned. But with three-foot-thick adobe walls insulating the industrious efforts of an ancient swamp cooler, the library's three reading rooms, office, and lavatory were at least ten degrees cooler than downtown Agua Dulce.

Today was Charlotte's third meeting with Arthur Varela. Charlotte had used the library's ponderously slow internet connection to download information about the national high school test. After taking one of the trial exams herself, Charlotte was familiar with the academic requirements. However, after her first session with Arthur two days ago, Charlotte was certain that only a miracle could get Arthur through the English grammar and literature section of the test.

Arthur could perform complex math in his head, and had an impressive ability to memorize; he knew every state capital, could spout out the year and significance of just about every important event in U.S. history, and knew the order of more compounds on the periodic table than Charlotte. But Arthur had the reading skills of an underachieving sixth grader.

After Thea and Francis retired for bed last evening Charlotte sat out on the rocking chair on the porch wondering how to help Arthur. She had initially hoped that his struggle to read was just his reluctance to sit in a library chair, crack open a study guide, and be corrected by a total stranger. But at the end of their second session Charlotte had to face the truth that had nagged her since their first session: Arthur lacked fundamental reading skills. How he had made it into high school without some teacher in his first eight or nine years of public education verbalizing this blatant shortcoming was both a mystery and an outrage to Charlotte.

Arthur worked mornings with Jed out at the High Lonesome ranch house. They quit work for a few hours at lunch each day and returned when the heat broke in the late afternoon. Charlotte and Arthur met during the two-hour lunch. Around the Lágrimas midday was not a time to try and do anything; except for the drugstore prescription counter, the air-conditioned lobby of the First Bank of Agua Dulce, and the rear office at the Durham Hardware, where Ralph caught up on the books while Francis caught a nap on a cot, all of Agua Dulce shut down for siesta. Even the post office locked its door until two o'clock. Men, women, children, dogs, cats, horses, lizards, and snakes slunk off to some retreat in the deep shade. Even the ravens vanished.

Arthur was giving up a much deserved nap to meet Charlotte each day at the library. And thus far, Arthur had not complained. Today, like every day, Arthur arrived promptly at one. Through the small window in the main room of the little library, Charlotte watched Arthur park his Honda with the fancy chrome hubcaps on the shady side of the street behind the Hudson. As he emerged from the low-slung car he pulled off his muscle shirt and replaced it with a clean, modest T-shirt. He slipped the bandanna from his head and walked into the library.

"*Buenos tardes, señoritas,*" Arthur said as he entered the library. Inez Hoover, the librarian, raised an eyebrow over her reading glasses, then returned to her cataloguing.

"Good afternoon, Arthur." Charlotte motioned at the chair beside her. Arthur dropped down onto it. "We're going to try something different today. The GED workbook isn't helping. Actually, the workbook isn't going to help at all until you learn to read."

Arthur let out a disgusted howl. "No! I can read!"

"Well, you can read a little, but you need to read a lot." Charlotte pointed to three paperbacks she had culled from the teen-fiction section in the rear room. "I want you to choose one of these and read it aloud to me."

"No way!" Arthur scowled at the books spread on the table. "These are for kids!"

"They're for teens. Open one. You're going to read aloud to me."

Arthur fingered the edges of the three paperbacks. "I don't like any of these!"

"Choose one, or I will."

After a loud sigh he opened the sports novel. His rough, tanned fingers fumbled to find the first page.

"Go ahead. Begin." Charlotte sat back in her chair. Arthur began to read in an almost inaudible voice. He stumbled over every word with two syllables, and stopped completely when he reached a word that could not be easily sounded out. He quit before the end of the first paragraph, frustrated and humiliated.

"Shit! I hate to read!" Arthur slammed the paperback onto the table. Inez frowned at him over her glasses.

Charlotte pulled her chair closer to Arthur so she could talk to him privately. "Okay, you hate to read. Of course you hate to read—it's difficult for you."

Arthur sank his head into his hand and leaned away from Charlotte and the pile of books.

"I bet your fancy *gringas* back in New York aren't *estupido* like me!"

"You're not stupid, Arthur! I've seen how easily you do the math. You can become as good a reader as anyone, but you're going to have to work at it and you've got to start *now*."

He snorted loudly. "It's too late for me. This is a waste!"

"It's never too late to become a good reader. This is not a waste, test or no test!"

Arthur eyed Charlotte over his bent arm. She couldn't figure out if he was a nice guy with a dangerous attitude or a dangerous guy pretending to be nice.

"I want you to read and to stop if you don't know a word and we'll sound it out together."

The door opened and Susannah Begay and her two daughters walked into the library. Susannah smiled and her daughters gazed shyly at Charlotte through their long bangs. They went back to the children's room without making a sound.

Arthur straightened up and looked around the main room. Three other children had come in and were coloring on tablets at another table. They were listening to Charlotte and Arthur's exchange, but pretending like they were not. Charlotte knew that Arthur was well known and a little bit feared by the Agua Dulce young people. His three years as Dos Rios High School's star running back still carried considerable social weight in the Lágrimas.

"We can sit in the back room if that's easier for you," Charlotte said quietly.

"This is okay." Arthur glanced at the children and then at Inez, who pretended to be absorbed in the card file.

Charlotte leaned in near Arthur's ear. "No more swearing, okay?"

He opened the book again. "Okay."

Arthur began to read. He still hesitated with two syllable words, but with Charlotte's help worked them out phonetically. The children coloring at the next table stopped whispering to one another. In the children's room, Susannah's daughters had moved their little chairs over to the door. All of the children in the library were listening to Arthur read the story.

After a slow, frustrating half hour, Arthur managed to read ten pages.

"This is hard, *no?*" Arthur laughed, but he was not joking.

"You've done very well." Charlotte surveyed the room. The Begay girls had joined the three children at the next table, and Susannah sat with two other parents in chairs near the magazine rack. A teenager and her mother who had come in to use the internet had swiveled their chairs around to face Arthur. Even Inez had put away her box of filing cards and taken off her reading glasses.

"I like baseball," the oldest boy said to Arthur. "I want to be a major league player when I grow up. Could you read some more?"

Arthur cocked his mouth into a self-conscious smile. "Nah. Maybe Miss Charlotte will read to us, *no?*"

Inez began to re-shelve books at the far side of the front room. "They have story hour every Tuesday and Thursday," she said over her shoulder. "They just love to be read to."

Charlotte opened the book, found Arthur's last sentence and began to read. She read poetry to her students in Scarsdale, but she hadn't read a story aloud to children since she worked as a classroom aid her last year of college. The story was actually pretty good—it included a gifted but troubled athlete, a jealous and disgruntled teammate, and a gruff but loving coach. Charlotte glanced up at the room around her: everyone, adults and children alike, even Arthur and Inez, had settled down into that safe interior place called story land.

"You read real good, Miss Charlotte," Arthur said when she closed the book fifteen minutes later.

"You'll read like that, too, but you'll have to keep at it every day."

"Will you read some more tomorrow?" It was the little boy who wanted to be a ball player. His mother waited for him by the front door.

"Arthur?" Charlotte deferred to Arthur in the chair beside her.

"Me? Nah, I'm too slow."

"I'll make you a deal: I'll read aloud after you read aloud," Charlotte said. "And you must read on your own at home tonight. From one of these other books."

Arthur stared at the paperbacks on the table.

"Romance or mystery," Charlotte said, "your choice."

"Geez!" Arthur stood up as he grabbed the mystery. "What if I don't know a word?"

"Sound it out. If that doesn't work, write it down and we'll review it tomorrow."

Arthur looked at the children staring at him, suddenly embarrassed by his poor reading skills. He scribbled on the card pulled from the back of the book and placed in on Inez's desk, stuck the paperback into the rear pocket of his baggy jeans, and pulled out a shiny chain of keys from his front pocket.

"I gotta go work." Arthur opened the library door. The heat of the summer afternoon rushed into the library. "Oh, Charlotte, I almost forgot! Jed said you're welcome to, you know, come out and help. *Any* time. It's pretty damned hard work, but you're not a woman who runs from a challenge, *no?*"

Arthur lifted one eyebrow over a rakish smile and left the library. Inez, the parents, and the children all directed their attention to Charlotte. She ignored their curious stares and gathered up the books and papers on the table before her.

Susannah and her girls walked over to Charlotte.

"I think that was just lovely," Susannah said, joining Charlotte at the table. Susannah wore another brightly patterned calico skirt that accentuated her round hips. Several strands of turquoise decorated her plain white blouse. "I wish Arthur's niece Violeta could have been here! Perhaps I'll go by and see if she could come to the library with my girls tomorrow."

{23}

"Pull those leads tight, Arthur!" Jed called across the small mountain of sand between them. "I want this wall straight."

"Only *gringos* use these speed leads, *sabes*?" Arthur pulled the string taut and secured it around the batter board marking the far end of the wall. "Used to be it didn't matter none if adobe walls were straight, *que no*?"

Jed eyed the yellow line. He wanted the speed lead to be strong enough to take the bumps and pulls inevitable during adobe laying.

"*Que no*, Arthur. But the wall will be stronger if it's straight." And besides, Jed wanted to say, I'm not *gringo*, *sabe*? Although Jed was too brown to be white in the Anglo world, he was too white to be brown in the indio-español world.

Jed walked the circumference of the trenches that would become the foundation of the new room he was adding onto the south end of the ranch house. The interior footprint was fifteen by twenty-five, large enough to accommodate one person comfortably through the winter. Jed hoped to move into the renovated ranch house by late fall, before the snow flew. This addition would be heated entirely by a passive solar trombe unit boosted with direct sunlight from the oversized windows along the south side. Even if Jed could not adequately heat the rest of the old house, he could at least live comfortably through the winter in this one large room. It had to be more civilized than the safari tent. Jed planned to have the solar panel set up and connected by late July. He would then be able to cook indoors on a small hotplate, and in the evenings he'd have honest to goodness electric light to read by. When the new solar room was completed, Jed's life was going to be downright luxurious.

"Let's get this sand and dirt shoveled back around the footings, and then we can move across the middle." Jed grabbed a shovel and began to move the mountain of dirt dug from the trenches out of the center of the open air room.

"Yesterday, I told her you wanted her," Arthur said as he wound string around a spool.

"Wanted her who?" Jed eyed Arthur from the far end of the addition. Arthur was six years Jed's and Lucho's junior, but Arthur's development seemed to have stalled out in his third year of high school. He continued to relate to Jed and everyone else as if they were all teenagers. Jed had nothing in common with Arthur socially, but Arthur was an excellent worker when he put his mind to it. And he was Lucho's only brother. With Lucho Varela in prison, Jed felt a certain amount of big brother responsibility for Arthur.

"The teacher, Charlotte." Arthur flashed his big smile beneath his bandanna and sunglasses. "She's teaching me to read, bro."

"You don't know how to read?" Jed stopped shoveling and looked at Arthur. "How'd you get so far without reading? You're kidding, right?"

"Nah, it's true. I just faked it, bro." Arthur placed the spool of string near the wheelbarrow and picked up a shovel. "I pretended good, huh? Even to myself."

"Geez, Arthur, no wonder you dropped out of school!" Jed tamped the earth around the new concrete trenches Uncle Barty and Arthur had poured three days ago. "Will you still take the GED in a few weeks?"

"Probably not. Maybe fall. Anyways, I told her you wanted her to come out. Teacher teacher—that's what the children call her at the library."

"I already told Charlotte she's welcome to come out."

"She's pretty, *que no*? Educated city girl. The way you like 'em, huh?"

"Stop now, Arthur."

Uncle Barty's pickup pulled round the barn and parked by the corral. Barty waved at Jed and then disappeared into the barn. He emerged a moment later with work gloves and an old baseball cap instead of his Stetson, ready to lay adobes.

"That mud in the mortar pit should be ready to go, Arthur." Barty walked the circumference of the addition's footprint inspecting the new footings. "Francis sent a new hose. It's in the truck bed. Hook it up to the pump at the corral over there. Let's move! This day is going to be a hot one!"

Arthur stuck his shovel upright in a mound of sand and took off at a jog for Barty's truck.

"Why are you so hard on Arthur?" Jed used an old broom with short, stumpy bristles to sweep the sand and loose debris from the top of the footings. "He's a good worker. He's here every morning by seven."

Barty watched Arthur fit the new hose onto the pump head near the corral.

"Because he's walking down a slippery road. He's got a foot on both sides of the line, and he doesn't get it."

"Yeah, I know, he hangs with a rough gang, but he's—."

"—He's drinking and he's probably smoking, and that rough gang he spends weekends with in Dos Rios does worse, too. Arthur has got to get his GED and get back into school."

Arthur finished attaching the hose and walked back toward Jed and Barty, unrolling the hose behind him on the sand.

"Uncle, it could take him a while longer to get his GED," Jed said in a low voice. "He told me this morning that his problem is, well, Arthur just can't read."

"What?" Barty frowned at Arthur. "No way!"

"Charlotte is basically teaching him to read."

"Jesus!" Barty muttered.

The mud mortar for the adobes was mixed in a pit made at the base of the little hill of fine-grained dirt and sand kept near the construction site. Arthur filled the pit with water. Jed helped him knock the mortar sand down into the puddle. They kept adding dirt and water until the mix was a thick substance that would glue the adobes into rows.

"I told Barty about the GED," Jed said to Arthur. "How you're working on the reading first."

"Yeah, man, bummer, huh!" Arthur glanced at Barty who was checking the strength of the speed leads. "But, it's not too bad, *que no?*"

Jed eyed Barty.

"Arthur, you're lucky to have someone help you. Don't forget that." Barty took a hoe and pushed around the mortar in the pit, checking for rocks and dry clumps. "What I'd like to know is why didn't you say something years ago? You could have told me you couldn't read."

"No way, coach! You're the reason my teachers kept passing me, no? So I could play football!" Arthur wasn't jesting anymore. "For the glory of the Dos Rios High School Cougars!"

Jed studied his uncle's face: Barty was lost in thought. Jed said nothing, as he had learned years ago to leave Barty alone with his thoughts, lost or not.

Jed, Barty, and Arthur laid three courses of adobe by 10:30 and stopped for break. They sat in the barn on hay bales sucking at oranges and sipping iced saffron tea Thea had sent out. Just as they finished their break the Durham Hudson appeared on the horizon. Jed leaned out the door and watched the old truck pull in near the barn. Charlotte emerged wearing a pair of his mother's old overalls.

"We're in here, Charlotte," Jed said, walking out of the barn. "Just taking a break. Are you going to help us this morning?"

"Well, I thought I could at least watch," Charlotte adjusted a baseball cap on her head. "I don't know how useful I can be. I've never done anything like this."

"Good morning, Charlotte." Barty tipped his cap and walked past Charlotte.

"Teacher teacher!" Arthur said with a wide grin. "You're gonna be the student this morning, *verdad*?!"

"You're going to need some gloves," Jed said. "Adobe is real tough on skin."

Jed grabbed a pair of work gloves from the seat of Barty's truck—he always carried extra pairs—and handed them to Charlotte. "We won't work you too hard."

Jed caught Charlotte's eye. She smiled but looked away. Charlotte was preoccupied, or nervous, or both. She watched Arthur and Barty walking back to the adobe pile. It wasn't Arthur: Charlotte and Arthur had found their own terms; they were becoming friends. No, Jed sensed that Charlotte's ambivalence about coming out here had to do with his uncle.

Barty and Arthur began to lay the fourth row, plunking and positioning each adobe in the layer of mortar Jed had laid and leveled on top of the previous row. Barty and Arthur laid adobes quickly along the line set by the speed lead. Jed needed the wheelbarrow filled with mortar to keep up with them. He showed Charlotte how to knock the dirt down into the water pit and mix it into a smooth thick sludge with the hoe.

"Keep drinking water, Charlotte." Jed found one of the canteens in the shade beside one of the pallets of adobes. "Rule is, drink *before* you're thirsty."

Charlotte took the canteen, unscrewed the top and took a long drink.

"Thanks. I'll remember that." Charlotte's cheeks were flushed with exertion and her dark curls had unfurled around the bottom of the baseball cap. Mortar from the pit had slopped onto the front of her overalls and dried on her forearms and under her chin. Even her sunglasses were smudged with mud.

"Arthur told me about his reading, or his *not* reading. I think it's extraordinarily nice of you to stay and work with him."

Charlotte dragged the hoe through the sludge in the pit. "I've never taught reading. It's good for me to remember the fundamentals. I've been spoiled: I teach students who have had the best of everything. The biggest emotional challenge of their lives comes when they find out whether or not they have been accepted into an Ivy League school."

"Where'd you go to college?" Jed was aware that Barty and Arthur had stopped talking and were listening to their conversation.

"Bryn Mawr in Pennsylvania. You?"

"Stanford."

Charlotte stopped hoeing and looked at Jed. "Really."

"I don't look like I'd belong at Stanford?" Jed wiped his forehead with his denim sleeve.

"I didn't mean it that way." Charlotte was embarrassed. "But you fit here. I mean you seem to be so at home in this environment."

"More mortar!" Barty called from the far wall.

Jed began to shovel the new load into the wheelbarrow. Charlotte stood back from the pit and squinted at Arthur and Barty. Arthur had removed his shirt and Barty was working in his T-shirt now. Jed hoisted the filled wheelbarrow, pushed it around the perimeter of the low walls and parked it by Barty.

"We'll quit at noon today," Jed said.

Barty's gaze shifted from Jed to Charlotte, who was drinking from the canteen. "We'll do another row all the way around."

Jed straightened up and looked down the row. Arthur was cutting an adobe brick to fit into the corner. "We'll quit at high noon. Charlotte and Arthur have work to do at the library at one o'clock, remember?"

Barty scooped a trowel of mortar, plopped it on the wall, and leveled the mud. "I didn't know about Arthur," Barty said in a low voice. "If I'd known he couldn't read I would have done something years ago."

"Well, you can do something now." Jed shoveled more mortar onto the top of the adobe bricks. "We'll quit at noon."

{24}

At twelve-thirty Charlotte parked the Hudson in the shade of the old cottonwood tree in front of the library, walked the three blocks to the drugstore, and ordered her daily double chocolate malt. It was heaven, that tall, cold glass of creamy, sugary, rich chocolate. The drugstore was always empty at this hour—even Gus and his boys obeyed the siesta curfew and ambled home for a nap—and Dennis and Charlotte had gentle conversations about the weather, or the postcard display, or the story behind the ice cream flavor-of-the-day. After half an hour on the soda fountain stool, Charlotte was refreshed and ready for a tutorial session with Arthur at the library.

Arthur's punctuality was admirable, and his determination to improve his reading skills intensified with each day's session. If he was tired, he did not show it. Today would be their sixth meeting and Arthur was already twice the reader he was when Charlotte began to tutor him a week ago.

Yesterday Arthur had read aloud to the children for a full hour. The afternoon story circle had expanded to a core group of nine little people. Five were young boys who worshipped Arthur, and came as much to be around him as to hear the story. Their admiration for Arthur Varela began with his Honda's rear spoiler and chrome mirrors that the boys inspected each day before entering the library. The pre-teen boys copied Arthur's wardrobe—baggy pants, muscle shirt, and a bandanna tied around the head. Like Arthur, they removed the head apparel when they came inside. It baffled Charlotte, Arthur's tough guy exterior. He was actually quite a gentleman underneath the ghetto walk and gangster clothing. And a very tender and accommodating side emerged when he read aloud to the children seated around the library table.

Inez was unlocking the library when Charlotte reached the Hudson parked before it on the street. Inez loved her job—she told Charlotte it was all she ever wanted, to be the librarian in Agua Dulce. Inez had gone to a library science school in Texas and had returned to replace the retiring librarian, her Aunt Criselda. Charlotte thought it enviable, Inez's knowing what she wanted to do in life and where she wanted to do it.

Charlotte waved to Inez and opened the cab door of the Hudson. Her forearms and shoulders ached from hours of mixing mortar, and lifting and setting adobes. But Thea was right: adobe laying was good for the heart. After a morning of work with Jed, Arthur, and Barty out at the High Lonesome Charlotte felt useful and deeply contented. And not just because she liked being around Jed. The part of Charlotte's heart that was quickened by this new sense of gratification was not tethered to her attraction to Jed, or to the growing ease of their conversations and the playfulness of their interactions. Working with adobe and mud was therapy, pure and simple. There was a rhythm to the work, and everyone on the site was part of the team that shared just one goal: building the walls one row of adobe bricks at a time.

Jed's canteen sat on the Hudson's front seat and Charlotte pulled it out and took a long drink of tepid water. It occurred to her that she had not given a lot of thought to much of anything beyond Agua Dulce in the last few days. She moved happily from the Durhams' house to the High Lonesome, to the drugstore and the library, day after day. In Agua Dulce Charlotte's physical, intellectual, and emotional life was directed by whatever or whoever was at hand. The world beyond the boundaries of the Lágrimas horizon was gradually ceasing to exist.

A white sedan pulled up and parked on the street in front of the Hudson. Charlotte put the cap back on the canteen, scooped up books from the truck seat, and closed the cab door. The door of the white sedan opened and Rosa Tomé, clad in her signature shorts and wedged heels, slid from the driver's seat. She glared at Charlotte and then reached back and pulled Violeta from the rear seat. Arthur emerged from the passenger's side, grinning ear to ear as he lifted a hand to Charlotte.

"Teacher teacher!" he called over the top of the car. "I came with my niece!"

Sixteen children showed up for Arthur Varela's story hour. Many brought coloring books and crayons and industriously worked while they listened. Others dragged their chairs to the table to sit as close as possible to him. In spite of the disapproving scowl from her grandmother Rosa, little Violeta claimed the chair directly beside her Uncle Arthur. Charlotte abandoned her usual place at Arthur's right side and sat in a chair by Inez's desk, figuring if he had trouble with a word he'd signal her.

But Arthur did not have trouble; the rapt attention and obvious adoration of the children seemed to give him confidence. He just forged forward, shamelessly pushing his mouth around words he wasn't sure of, bumping through syllables with playful aplomb, reading the story with drama and feeling. Maybe it was because it involved an athlete's relationship with a gruff but caring coach, a very big baseball championship, and a college scholarship on the line, but Arthur read the story like it was his own. And by the second hour of the sixth day and the turning of the last page and Arthur's dramatic declaration of *the end*, that book *was* his own.

Inez and Charlotte exchanged looks when he closed the book on the table before him.

"Well, I guess we better get out some more books!" Inez left her desk and headed straight for the shelf of teen paperbacks.

Parents who had been waiting in the library for the past half hour were anxious to get their children and be on their way. But the children didn't move. They remained clustered around Arthur, asking him questions about the story, about baseball, about his tattoo. Finally, Rosa left her place by the magazine rack, where she had pawed through fashion magazines during the story hour, and walked into the circle of children.

"Time to go," she said as she lifted Violeta up by the arms. "Arthur, you can catch a ride back to your Honda, *que no?*"

"I could bring Violeta with me," Arthur said, standing up. Violeta's face brightened. "I'll take care of her. We can walk to the trailer from here."

"No, she's been here long enough already."

Arthur's face tightened. "It's only a ten-minute walk, Rosa. We could get a malt at the drugstore! What do ya think, Violeta?'

Violeta nodded enthusiastically as she pulled her wrist from Rosa's grasp and began to walk back through the children to Arthur. Rosa reached over the boys between her and Violeta and clamped her hand down on Violeta's head. Her grip stopped the five-year-old in her tracks.

"*Vamanos* now." Rosa pulled Violeta up against her plump thigh and walked her to the door. Two of the waiting parents stepped aside to let them pass. Rosa frowned at them and said loudly, "Her father's a bum."

Arthur's eyes remained glued on Rosa as she pushed Violeta through the door and outside. Charlotte thought he was going to go after them, but he did not. Everyone in the library watched him. No one said a word.

"Excuse me." A humiliated Arthur extracted himself from the tangle of children clustered around him and walked into the lavatory in the back of the library.

Charlotte looked over the books Inez had pulled from the teen shelf. "Arthur will begin a new story tomorrow," she said to the children with as much enthusiasm as she could muster. "One-thirty. We'll see you then."

The parents began to claim their children and depart. Charlotte glanced back at the restroom door, but Arthur did not reemerge to say his usual good-byes.

༄༅༅༅༅༅༅༅༅༅༅༅༅༅

Charlotte gave Arthur a ride through town and out the county road to the B & B station where his car was parked. Arthur said Coach Barty and Jed had lunched at Jed's camp and were taking a quick swim in the river before returning to work.

"You should join them, teacher, in the river. *Very* nice place to spend an afternoon."

Charlotte ignored Arthur's suggestive tone of voice. He had been ill-tempered and rude since they left the library.

"You know about Jed's fiancee?" Arthur said flatly. "Beverly something. Very fancy lady."

Charlotte let this information sink down into her belly but did not allow her shock and disappointment to reach her face.

"Arthur, you have a lot of influence with the children around here. Do you know you're a role model?"

"Too much influence, if you ask Rosa Tomé!" His arm hung out the window and his hand slapped the exterior of the Hudson. "Bums! Rosa thinks the Varela brothers are bums! She's the reason Lucho drank himself into jail. Rosa should be in prison, not Lucho!"

"You have every right to be angry and insulted by Rosa Tomé." Charlotte looked at Arthur. "But you know Violeta is your biggest fan."

"No! She thinks I'm a slacker. That's what she hears!"

"She was so proud of you today. Violeta told every child who came into the library that you were her daddy's brother. Her *tio*."

"People used to say Lucho was the smart Varela."

"You're plenty smart, Arthur. Look how quickly you've improved your reading." Arthur looked across the seat at Charlotte. "The children respect you. You'd make a good teacher."

"Teacher *teacher*?" Arthur scoffed. "Me? Nah!"

"You, yes."

As they approached the B & B station the flying red horse leapt into view in the hot sky. Charlotte turned the truck into the station and drove around back of the shop. The grey Honda was parked under the massive old tree that grew between the station and Barty's house.

Arthur secured the bandanna around his hand. "So you think like maybe I'll get through the GED?"

"Yes, I do. Maybe not till next fall or winter."

Arthur closed the door and leaned back in through the open window. He tapped a small snake tattoo on the underside of his left forearm. "Lucho has one just like this. Rosa says I'm just like Lucho: nowhere to go but down. She won't never let Violeta be with me."

"So prove her wrong," Charlotte said, resisting the impulse to correct his double negative. "And someday you can be Violeta's teacher-teacher!"

Arthur guffawed and pushed himself up and away from the truck. "We'll see, Charlotte. But don't go holding your breath or nothing. See you *mañana*."

"*Mañana*, Arthur."

Charlotte watched Arthur swagger across the sandy yard to his car where he removed his shirt before climbing in. He started the engine and roared away in the Honda down the dirt road to the High Lonesome. Charlotte sighed loudly. What if Rosa was right and he had nowhere to go but down? What a terrible thought!

A dip in the cold water of the Lágrimas River was very tempting. And so what if Jed had a fiancee? They were just friends, and Charlotte would be gone soon, anyway. But Barty was out there, too. Charlotte stared up the ranch road at the dust cloud created by Arthur's car. Thus far, she and Barty had managed to avoid any real conversation. It was like they had an unspoken agreement to keep the unspeakable unspoken.

She took in a long, deep breath of the dry air: she was holding her breath a lot these days. Not because she was waiting for something to happen, but because she was hoping for something not to happen.

The traffic signal at Main and Dos Hermanos turned red and Charlotte stopped the Hudson near the corner. It was still siesta, and Gus and his boys had not yet returned to the bench by the drugstore. Charlotte pressed her forehead into her hands on the steering wheel; she was so tired she could fall asleep right here in the Hudson. The light changed and Charlotte passed through downtown and out into the open country toward the Durhams'. Who was she kidding? The unspoken agreement was not between Charlotte and Barty. It was between Charlotte and herself—the self that had dutifully placed her head in the family tar pit decades ago. And what Charlotte was hoping would not happen had already happened years ago between her mother and this very place.

{25}

"What day is today?" Charlotte asked no one in particular in the Durham kitchen. "I really should call home. There might be some important messages."

In mid-June, before Charlotte departed for the conference in Santa Fe, her father's attorney, Richard Boudreau, had informed her there would be papers to sign upon her return from New Mexico. Charlotte's return was now ten days overdue; Mr. Boudreau's office was probably wondering if Leonard Lambert's only child and sole recipient of his estate was interested in claiming her inheritance.

"You, Charlotte, have a team of shoulds pulling your wagon." Thea followed her tapping cane through the pantry doorway into the kitchen. "Time to set those horses free."

"Today is Wednesday the first." Francis emerged from the hall dressed in his daily uniform of overalls and plaid shirt. "Feel free to use the phone anytime you need it."

The Durham Hardware truck pulled up and stopped at the bottom of the porch steps. Ralph emerged and carried Charlotte's suitcase up the steps and into the kitchen.

"Good morning, Mrs. Durham, Charlotte." Ralph removed his cap. "I'm sorry it took so long for me to get into Santa Fe and retrieve your suitcase." Ralph lifted the bag. "Where would you like this?"

"She's staying in Bernadette's room." Francis sat down at the table and helped himself to another pancake.

"Thank you, Ralph." Charlotte stared blankly at the familiar Samsonite suitcase. "But wasn't there a carry-on bag, too?"

"This is all they gave me at the front desk." Ralph frowned. "I'm sorry. I didn't know there were two or I would have asked."

"It's not your fault," Charlotte said quickly, smiling as she took the bag from Ralph. "I'll take this to my room."

Charlotte carried the heavy suitcase down the hall to Bernadette's room and set it at the end of the bed. What she really needed was her carry-on with her toiletries and shampoo. Charlotte studied the bag and raised her eyes to her image in the mirror: baggy jeans, T-shirt, her hair a web of curls. Except for her shampoo and curl-taming conditioner, she had everything she needed. And wanted. Whatever was in the suitcase could stay in the suitcase. Charlotte opened the closet door, pushed the black Samsonite under the hanging shirts, and closed the door.

Back in the kitchen Thea had talked Ralph into having a cup of coffee. Charlotte joined everyone at the breakfast table.

"Last year, if I remember correctly, it was you who was disgruntled, Dorothea," Francis said. "You didn't like the Suazos' heavy hand with the silk sunflowers from the five-and-dime in Santa Fe."

Thea sniffed and dragged a piece of pancake through her maple syrup. "July is *not* the season for sunflowers, real *or* plastic."

Ralph smiled. Francis looked at Charlotte. "People decorate and beautify the baseball field and cemetery a few days ahead of the Fourth of July. Families like to place flowers on the graves, string banners across Main Street, put flags and streamers on just about everything. But Thea doesn't care for the plastic flowers."

"The dead don't much care for the fake flowers," Thea said. "Conchata doesn't like the way those plastic ones have no real color or smell."

"They certainly do have color," Francis said. "But they are a bit flat in the smell department. Even among the living." Francis winked across the table at Charlotte. Ralph laughed and drained his coffee cup.

Charlotte went to the stove, retrieved the coffee kettle, and brought it to the table. She poured Ralph and herself another cup. The making of the 6 a.m. pot of coffee was now entrusted to Charlotte. It was her favorite morning chore. She also fed and watered the burros, threw out the chicken scratch, and pulled weeds and watered the garden before the sun became too hot.

"You might find a stone or two today for the memorial," Thea said, lifting her hand and waving at the window behind her. "Out there, when you go walking."

"Thea's talking about the war memorial by the cemetery," Francis explained. "Sunup on the fourth folks bring a stone and place it on the memorial. It's a way of remembering those not here anymore."

"It's a way of remembering a miracle," Thea said.

"What was the miracle?" Charlotte asked. "The Bataan boys and the horses?"

Francis leaned closer to Charlotte. "They were *wild* horses and they never ever came close to men. In fact, they were invisible. Until that day when we were burying the six boys killed on Bataan. The boys were captured by the Japanese and died during the Bataan Death March in the Philippines during World War II. It's in all the history books. When the boys' bodies were finally brought home to be buried, the horses came to honor them. Six mustangs. Walked right in close and stood until the graveside service was over. Then those wild horses turned and walked back into the desert they came from."

"The boys were killed on Bataan," Thea said, wiping her lips with her napkin. "But they were taken directly to heaven on the backs of those splendid horses."

"And so the stone monument . . . ." Charlotte was trying to understand the connection.

"It began as six individual stone piles over each of the graves," Ralph said. "But then so many people heard about the horses, they started coming to see the graves, and they brought stones to remember the boys, or to remember one of their own boys lost in war. Over fifty years the six piles over the six graves became one monument."

Francis nodded. "People bring stones from all over the state, the country, even from Asia and Europe."

The four of them sipped coffee in silence. It was a comfortable sort of silence that Charlotte had become accustomed to around the Durham kitchen table. After several minutes Thea put down her fork and looked across the vase of petunias at Francis.

"Bartholomew says the canvas panniers out in the High Lonesome barn are in good condition excepting for their straps. I'm sure you can order those."

"Not sure what company still outfits those," Francis said after a reflective pause. "But I'll do some calling. Slim down in Corrales might know. He used to work with all the packers."

Thea turned to Ralph. "You look up the number for Francis. It's in the ledger book in the top drawer in the office." Thea closed her eyes. "Conchata says it won't be listed under Slim's Saddles; it will be under Maurice Buckingham."

Thea opened her eyes. "He's retired now, Slim is, but he's still living there in his house next to the old saddle shop."

"I'll look him up this morning," Ralph said.

Thea fingered the handle of her coffee cup. "I've been meaning to ask Bartholomew which horse he's thinking of putting Charlotte on."

Francis raised his eyes to Charlotte and then turned to Thea. "You mean for the parade on the Fourth?"

"Oh well, that too. I suppose that's the horse Conchata is talking about."

Thea pushed her chair from the table and reached for her cane. Ralph was up and at her elbow before she stood, but Thea waved him away. "For heaven's sake, Ralph, sit down and finish your coffee! I'm old and blind, but I'm not helpless."

Ralph returned to his chair and shrugged good-naturedly at Charlotte. "You riding in the parade?"

"This is the first I've heard of riding in a parade. I haven't ridden a horse in years."

"But she loves to ride horses," Thea said from the pantry where she was rummaging around the shelves. "Charlotte gave up horses when her mother died."

Ralph and Francis both looked at Charlotte.

"I just outgrew horses," she stammered. She looked into Francis's kind eyes. "You know how it is. But I was once a very competent rider."

Ralph and Francis said their goodbyes and departed for town. Thea sat alone at the table lost in thought or, more likely, in conversation with her pal, Conchata.

Charlotte rinsed her dishes in the sink and mulled days and dates: July tenth, Alicia's D-Day, was nine days away. Did the coroner's report place Alicia's death on the day she was found or the day they guessed she had jumped? Or did death actually begin with the first notion of suicide, and was the death pose a posture the deceased actually began to assume hours, even days or weeks, before the life-taking event?

Charlotte drained the sink and dried her hands. She would call the airline this morning and make a reservation for a flight home on July eighth. It would mean she'd cut short Arthur's tutoring. But a plane to New York by the eighth would guarantee that this urban cowgirl got the heck out of Dodge before July, tenth when the showdown between the lethal past and the fragile present opened fire.

⫫⫫⫫⫫⫫⫫⫫⫫⫫⫫⫫⫫

Charlotte took the morning off from work at the High Lonesome because Jed, Barty, and Arthur had headed out for another load of mortar sand. Even though they were surrounded by sand, Jed explained that it wasn't the right sand for adobes. Jed and Barty had a special source in an *arroyo* north of the ranch where they retrieved sand as they needed it.

After the chickens were fed and the burros watered, Charlotte did not pick up the telephone and call the airline. Instead she put on her hat and walked out of the house and up the ranch road with Little Bit and George. They ambled all the way up to the irrigation pond that reflected the morning sky like blue glass. Little Bit stood in the shallow water and sniffed the air, while the cliff swallows skimmed the surface for flies and gnats. George inspected the sandy shoreline a few feet from Bit's side.

The path along the stream bed of the Little Stream of the Gypsum was in the bottom of a deep canyon where trees, grasses, and bushes grew. The water splashed and tumbled down the rocks into small sand-bottomed pools

180

and bees buzzed around blossoms and feathery flowers that probably had medicinal properties. Charlotte would have to ask Thea or consult Conchata's massive notebook of *remedios*. Ancient ponderosa pine trees towered over even the oldest cottonwood trees where birds fluttered and called. The path crossed the stream several times, and Charlotte leapt from stone to stone across the clear water, leaving her own footprints in the mud alongside deer and raccoon prints.

The box canyon where water seeped from the stone walls was completely shaded by the cliffs and the trees that grew around the natural pool filled by the spring. The top lip of the stone overhung the canyon and so the grassy amphitheater resembled a cave. Little Bit was slow today and Charlotte sat down on a flat slab of rock and waited for the old dog and his feathered bodyguard to catch up. The oozing water gathered and became a stream that trickled and danced down tumbled rocks and boulders that had crashed from the upper canyon walls eons ago, perhaps bumped by the shoulder of some dinosaur.

Lying on the bottom of the clear stream was a grey oblong stone that shivered in the current. Charlotte reached down and picked up the stone. It was cold and smooth, and as it dried it became silvery. With the stone in her hand Charlotte lay on her back and looked up at the blue band of sky held between the canyon lips. Except for the half-hour she'd spent on the river with Jed, this was the first time in nearly two weeks that Charlotte's body had been surrounded by green, engulfed by a world fed and nurtured by water.

Little Bit and George finally reached Charlotte in the canyon. George stayed on a sandy mound above the little pond. Bit nuzzled Charlotte, lapped at the water, and moved to a cool place under the trees where he quickly fell asleep. Charlotte put the silver stone in her pocket, removed her shoes and socks, and with her feet numbed by the cool stream, lay back on the boulder and covered her face with her hat. The bubbling, babbling clunking sounds of the stream pulsed in her head and carried Charlotte down under the glistening canyon.

"We begin with what is on the surface."

Grandpa leaned over the lab work table, but Charlotte was too small to see what he saw. He smiled as he reached into the plaster and rock and pulled at something caught in the debris. Finally, Grandpa lifted a watch from the rubble.

"This is what we know." The watch dangled in the air between them. Grandpa handed it to Charlotte. "Now you ask: how do we find what we don't know we've lost?"

Charlotte opened her eyes. The sun had cleared the top of the canyon walls and the pond was no longer in the shade. Charlotte sat up. Little Bit was still sleeping. George was tucked under a brambly bush nearby. Charlotte removed her feet from the stream and placed them on the warm rock to dry. She tucked her hair back into the cap and looked at her wrist watch. Almost noon. As she stared at the watch face the dream returned: Grandpa in his lab. Grandpa handed Charlotte a watch.

Charlotte pulled on her socks and shoes. George fluffed and fussed over Little Bit until the dog woke. Charlotte was reluctant to leave the wonderful canyon and the water world it harbored, but she had to meet Arthur at 1:30. And she did look forward to meeting Arthur at the library.

Charlotte and her fur-and-feather entourage emerged into the hot brightness beyond the canyon and walked around the reservoir. Charlotte stopped to study the red-and-gold sandstone cliffs above the irrigation pond. She remembered the silver stone and pulled it from her pocket and turned it over in her palm. Grandpa Al was a scientist. Dr. Albert Rose, chairman of vertebrate paleontology, did not accept a truth without first reviewing all evidence and examining every piece of available information. In 1976 Grandpa told Charlotte that he *knew absolutely* that Alicia had not gone to New Mexico to die. He would not have come to this conclusion about Alicia recklessly. Grandpa must have had some piece of information, some sliver of irrefutable evidence that allowed his belief in his daughter's good intentions to remain undeterred, even after her bizarre death.

Why hadn't Grandpa shared this piece of information with Charlotte during their walk home across Cambridge after the memorial service, or that night after supper when they sat on the front porch in the summer dusk watching the neighbor children play kickball in the street? Why didn't Grandpa whisper what he absolutely knew into the telephone when he lay dying in Massachusetts General Hospital? Surely he knew he was dying, recognized his own death-pose asserting itself in his bones, moving into the tissue of his muscles, dimming his vision and quieting his thoughts.

And what had happened to the bone horse notebook everyone talked about? Last February after her father died, Charlotte sorted through every box in the attic of the Briarcliff house prior to its sale. She had personally reviewed everything of Leonard's, both at home and at his office at General Electronics. She found nothing belonging to her mother or her grandpa. Charlotte had seen the inventory of Grandpa's gifts to Harvard after Grandma Ruth died in 1986: the files and photographs, fossils and artifacts given to the Museum of Natural History. There were four cardboard transfer files labeled, "New Mexico, 1959." Charlotte had studied every file folder, every catalogued item and inventory list but there was nothing about a field notebook of bone horses, and nothing at all attributed to Alicia Rose Lambert.

Alicia and Grandpa had spoken on the telephone almost every day. After the miscarriage and hysterectomy they often talked on the phone late at night. Leonard usually went to bed early, but Alicia frequently stayed up after midnight. She would call her father on the phone in the downstairs hall and if Charlotte's bedroom door at the top of the stairs was left open, she could hear Alicia's end of their conversations.

"I wanted it to be my choice," Alicia said into the phone one night in late December of 1975. "But you're right, Dad, it wasn't that I was planning on having more children. I just wanted it to be my choice. *My* choice."

There was a long silence on Alicia's end of the conversation. "I was so young," Alicia said finally. "You're not to blame. You did what you believed was best for me. And I wanted to believe that you and Ruth were right, that it was best to make a swift and clean end of it and go on with my life. I didn't know how it would be, how I would feel after all these years."

Alicia never finished college. During her senior year at Harvard she traded in her notebooks and pencils for diapers and grocery lists. Whatever Alicia had fallen in love with in Agua Dulce—Barty Bill or those bone horses, or some exhilarating sense of herself as an emerging woman—was snuffed out when she married Leonard, when she became Charlotte's mother less than twelve months later.

Charlotte held the silver stone in her closed hand as she walked back to the ranch house. In the kitchen Charlotte eyed the telephone on the wall. Making an airline reservation didn't seem so important now. Whatever had prompted her earlier anxiety about staying on in Agua Dulce had evaporated. Jed called it the Agua Dulce trance, this sudden inability to place oneself and one's life into context with the people and activities of the contemporary world. No, she could make a plane reservation another day. And besides, if Charlotte fled Agua Dulce because of the approaching anniversary of her mother's death, then once again the losses and regrets of her mother's story, and the shoulds and should nots of the Rose-Lambert clan, would take hold of the reins to Charlotte's life.

Charlotte went to her room and placed the smooth, silver-grey stone on the bureau. She would remain in Agua Dulce another two weeks because that's what she told Barty she would do and that was what she wanted to do. She wasn't in New Mexico because she was escaping something, hiding out or lost in a trance. And Jed? He had a fiancee. Good. It would be easier to be friends. And friendship was what Charlotte needed about as much as anything she could think of except maybe love.

{26}

When Barty returned at noon from the sand-gathering expedition he found Thea and her cane knocking about the interior of the storage shed behind the gas station

"What are ya doing, Nana?" Barty stood in the doorway and let his eyes adjust.

Thea steadied herself by grabbing onto the handle of the generator stored in the small shed. Her other hand rested on the bedroll Barty had pulled out a week ago. "There's one good bedroll here. There must be others."

"That's one of the new ones. Remember? Dennis ordered in tarps and pads for four new bedrolls when the Matas had that family reunion up in Colorado four years ago."

Thea smiled. "Conchata said there were good bedrolls but she forgot to say who they belonged to!" Thea walked to Barty in the doorway and took his arm. "Tell Dennis you'll be needing to use two of them. Now, there are three sets of twin sheets in my linen closet. And air out the wool blankets on the clothesline."

Barty said nothing. Maybe if he just went along with the high country camping trip in the mountains fantasy Nana was planning she wouldn't notice how it never actually happened.

"I brought some *cascara sagrada* leaves for you. I left them in your kitchen."

"I'm not having problems just now." Last winter Barty had struggled with occasional constipation, and the *cascara sagrada* and ginger root tea had been greatly appreciated. "But thanks for thinking of me."

"I'm always thinking about you. Did you look about the barn for those old coffee tins?"

"I did. But they're long gone."

Thea sighed, completely defeated.

"About the coffee can." Barty took off his hat. It was fiercely hot in the shed. "Are you forgetting about the family plots at the cemetery?"

"Well, I haven't forgotten, certainly. And this isn't my idea, you understand. It's your mother's. And Dr. Al's."

"Now you've lost me."

"Oh, I know." Thea was very fatigued. Barty took her by the arm and led her out the open door. "It doesn't matter just now. But I will be needing a coffee can or a similar container with a very tight fitting lid for my ashes."

"You seem to be planning your death like it's a potluck supper!"

"Look at me, Bartholomew. I'm disappearing."

Thea *was* shrinking, her body so thin she seemed to be evaporating inside her dress.

"Most people don't put their ashes into coffee cans. Why are you doing this?"

"Because I want it to be easy for Francis. Because it's the thing to do. Because I'll have everyone's attention for at least a few days."

Barty leaned into the door frame and sighed. "You have my attention right now. What can I do?"

"I want you to promise me that you'll do it my way, whatever that way might be, to the smallest detail."

"Okay, I suppose."

"You must promise."

"I promise. I'll do it your way. Can you tell me now what that might be?"

"No. I'm not sure myself."

Barty stepped back outside. Thea followed him.

"How'd you get here? Ralph drive you over?"

"No, Bartholomew, that beautiful child, Charlotte, drove me over on her way to the library. You'll have to drive me home."

"Be my pleasure." Barty closed and locked the shed door and replaced the key under a flagstone to the left of the stoop. "Let's go over to the house. I need some lunch. It was hot as Hades out shoveling that sand this morning."

Thea took his arm and they walked together across the sandy yard to the house. "You have a bit of trouble around her, don't you?" Thea asked.

"No."

"Yes, you do. Conchata says Charlotte's not going to leave Agua Dulce until everyone knows everyone and this family's tiresome tradition of blaming and regretting has ended."

Barty opened the door and guided Thea into the dim, cool kitchen.

"You have things that belong to her, Bartholomew."

"I thought you said she had something for me?"

"Yes, well...." Thea tapped her crooked index finger against her head. "Things up here. And in here." Thea placed her hand against his heart.

"Alicia and I were children," Barty said, taking Thea's hand from his chest. "And it ended badly. Let it rest."

"Conchata says it never ended at all, and she certainly won't let *me* rest until everyone knows everything."

Barty went to the fridge and pulled out a bottle of root beer, Thea's favorite. "It did end, at least to those among the living, on July 10, 1976. Can I make you a sandwich?"

He popped off the bottle top and handed the root beer to Thea seated at the table.

"Yes, thank you." Thea took tiny sips from the soda bottle. "I can't remember you saying her name aloud. Funny how names have so much power over us."

"No reason to say her name aloud."

"Piff!" Thea waved her hand at him. "It's the same with Benjamin: you said his name when you named him but I don't believe I've heard you say it since."

"He was already gone when we named him. There was no one to call by that name."

"Benjamin Bill. It was a good thing, seeing him, naming him in the hospital morgue. Do you still take stones to the roadside marker?"

Barty pulled out the mayonnaise and cold cuts from the fridge, and unwrapped a loaf of Thea's bread. "Haven't stopped there in a while. Years I reckon."

"I hardly know what year it is anymore. I think when you are out of time you finally don't worry about it anymore." Thea stared at the wall above

Barty's head. He kept glancing at her while he made the sandwiches, but she seemed to have left the room. Finally she shifted her petite body on the chair and smoothed her dress with her thin hands. "Conchata says Benjamin is very much with us. He very much wants to be here amongst us, to have time with his father."

"Well, I'm getting older every day. I reckon he'll have time with me soon enough." Barty wanted to tell Nana that he and Benjamin had been out of time since before they met, since Benjamin died in Kitty's womb when Kitty's car crashed into the mesa that night of the terrible ice storm. But he said nothing as he placed the sandwiches on plates and set them on the table.

"Francis told Charlotte that you were the one who found Alicia's body." Thea picked up half of her sandwich, took a bite that would satisfy a mouse and set it on the plate again.

"Everyone knows that. She might as well, too." Barty took a root beer for himself from the fridge and sat down across the table from Thea. "It was all in the sheriff's report."

Barty had read the report—made a special trip into Santa Fe late that summer just to put nagging questions to rest. But there was nothing in the report but the raw facts. The questions remained: why was Alicia up on that ledge in the dark, in the pouring rain with her rain slicker left in her car? She knew better, or used to. And why hadn't she told him, or Thea or Francis, or Dennis that she was coming to Agua Dulce? And when she came into the hardware store that afternoon, why didn't she leave some kind of message? Buford Salazar talked with her, told Alicia when the Durhams would return from a relative's funeral in Enid, Oklahoma. And then Alicia left town. The first law of the desert was you tell someone where you're camping. Maybe Ruth Rose was right and a despondent and mentally unstable Alicia came to the Lágrimas in July of 1976 to end her life.

"Not all." Thea picked up breadcrumbs from the plate with the tip of her index finger. "It wasn't all in the sheriff's report."

Barty went on eating his sandwich. Thea leaned toward him across the table.

"You have plenty to tell."

"It's all in the report."

"Not about how Alicia knew better than to camp without letting someone know, and then how her rain slicker was left in the car."

He stopped chewing. He really wished Nana wouldn't do that—read his mind, or seem to. Maybe it was Conchata he was having this conversation with. He swallowed his food and took a sip of root beer. Two mothers standing on either side of the great divide were both a blessing and a curse. Barty could only imagine what Nana and Conchata would be like when they were at long last reunited, best friends in the good country on the other side.

{27}

Jed splashed cool water from the canteen onto his face and stood naked and shivering, his gaze to the southwest. Planets and stars clung to the last of the night and the three-quarter moon cast a golden shimmer onto the tips of the mountains and the sides of faraway buttes. First light leaked into the ink blue sky. Dawn couldn't come soon enough today, July Fourth. It was always a challenge to sleep under such a bright moon, but last night's insomnia wasn't really about the moonlight. Jed had been lying awake since four a.m. wrestling with too many conflicting feelings to count, name or sort.

Jed returned to the tent that was lit by diffuse moonlight and dressed in jeans, T-shirt and socks. He sat down on the cot he had not slept upon in a week and pulled on his boots. How could he be home and feel homeless? How could he, a man so recently jilted by his fiancee, fan the first smoldering embers of interest and desire for a complete stranger? Not only did he not deserve a relationship with this woman—a romantic liaison upon the heels of a breakup assumed the questionable and distasteful attributes of what was universally known as rebound—but Jed had nothing whatever to give her.

Dawn came and the sky turned pink and yellow. The moon became a transparent orb and faded into the hot light of the approaching sun. The fire popped and cracked in the stone-lined pit and Jed placed the water kettle to one side of the grill. He liked to have the eggs frying and the coffee black and ready to pour when Uncle Barty walked into camp.

The flames dropped down to hot embers and Jed slid the frying pan onto the grill. The eggs hit the pan with a loud hiss. There was just enough room on the grill to lay four pieces of thick bread to toast. Britches nickered from the juniper grove and Jed looked up as his uncle walked out of the trees.

"You must have some of that Indian blood, Uncle, because you are as silent as a ghost!" Jed stood and lifted his spatula in greeting.

Barty laughed as he grabbed a tin cup from the branch over the wash tub. "Ah! You're a pampered city boy! A hobbled burro with a cow bell could sneak up on you. Sleep well?"

"Just fine," Jed lied, flipping the eggs. "Why aren't you at the memorial ceremony at the cemetery, it being Independence Day and all?"

"I'm all out of stones," Barty said. "Coffee ready?"

"Yip." Jed tossed Barty the bandanna he used for a pot holder. "How's everyone at the ranch?"

"Same as yesterday—two self-absorbed, witless boys bossed about by the ladies club of five mares, including that silly pinto I wish someone would take off my hands."

"It was your idea to work with those reservation geldings," Jed said, handing his uncle a plate with eggs and toast. "They're just young and rambunctious. As for the pinto, she's a *pinto*. Always a bit loco those horses, yes?"

"Yes." Barty carried his plate and coffee to the table and sat down on one of the chairs. "The first time I laid eyes on her I knew that mare couldn't be rehabilitated."

"There's always a chance you can bring a horse like that along." Jed joined Barty at the table. "I've never seen you just give up on a horse."

"Oh hell, I'm older. I don't have the patience to figure out the pinto's point of departure—where she first went sideways. She's afraid of everything. Movement. Stillness. Sound. Silence. People. Animals. She'd be fine out here."

"Hey, there's movement here. And people and animals, too. But you can put that pinto out with us if you think that would help her. Me and Britches don't mind a little company."

"A little company?" Barty tore off a piece of toast and dragged it through egg yolk on his plate. "Sometimes it's better just not to get involved."

The sun broke onto the peaks of the mountains and slid down their sides to the desert floor. Barty motioned with his fork at the western canyonlands where the spires and buttes stood razor sharp beside their own shadows. "Damn! I like the way a summer day arrives out here!"

"You liked living here, huh?"

"I did." Barty scooped up the last of his egg with a piece of toast and wiped his mouth with a bandanna. "Though I hardly knew it at the time."

"What is it you're not saying this morning?" Jed left the table with his plate and cup.

Barty studied Jed for a moment. "I know you're lonely, the future is kind of murky, and you're probably feeling kind of vulnerable since things with Beverly are, well, not going forward just now."

"Never going forward." Jed took the kettle off the fire and poured the hot but not boiling water into the pan. He soaped his dishes in a mild yucca root detergent that Dennis ordered in from some natural cleaning products company in Albuquerque. Thea said Conchata thought it was just wonderful that folks were using the soap her grandmother used to make.

"You never know." Barty joined Jed by the fire. He slid his plate into the soapy water and poured the last of the coffee into his cup. "You're getting stronger every day. You two might still work it out."

"It's not just me being here." Jed washed the tin cups and placed them into a second pan where Barty rinsed them. "You know, things came up, differences between us, before all of this began to happen."

"I suppose."

"I know mom told you how she felt about Beverly years ago." Jed looked up at his uncle drying the dishes with a towel. "Mom wasn't surprised that Beverly had trouble with my collapse and then the illness. She hasn't said so, but mom is relieved the engagement is off."

"Oh, Bernadette is the most amenable person I know. She'd come to like Beverly, you know that."

"Well, it doesn't matter anymore." Jed stood up and looked his uncle in the eye. "And it wasn't just Beverly's reaction to my getting sick that threw me a curve. It was her reaction to Agua Dulce when she was here last month."

"But you have your problems with Agua Dulce, too, Jed."

"Yeah, but mine are founded on experience and Beverly's were founded on appearance. This is where half of my ancestors are from. This part of the world just doesn't exist in cosmopolitan America. It's all part of a myth, a pretend kind of place people visit to get away from it all. No one ever *stays*.

Beverly couldn't stay here. And we never even got to the part in the family story about my grandmother being a high-profile *bruja*, for Christ's sake."

Barty hung the cups back on the tree branch and placed the plates on a plank shelf. Jed went back into the tent, retrieved his hat and sunglasses, then closed and secured the tent flaps behind him. Barty closed up the cooler.

"Ravens, remember?" Jed motioned at the stones sitting on the ground beside the cooler. Barty smirked and plunked the heavy rocks onto the cooler lid.

Britches was standing near the table, ready to remind Jed that it was time for breakfast. Barty walked up to Britches and rubbed the tall gelding between the ears.

"So, you're okay about Beverly breaking off the engagement?"

"Yes. No. My pride is hurting. We were together for four years. And she didn't have to tell me in a Dear John letter. She could have brought it up over the phone at least."

"Except you're almost never near a phone."

"You're making excuses for her, why? I'm pretty certain you had cool-to-lukewarm feelings for Beverly McDermott."

Jed and Barty walked with Britches through the juniper grove to the corral.

"I'm not making excuses for Beverly," Barty said, pushing aside a tree branch. "I'm just trying to see it from all sides."

Jed opened the shed where the tack and feed were kept, scooped oats into a small bucket, and, with Britches bumping his shoulder, walked to the trough inside the corral.

"Impatient, this one," Jed said as Britches pushed past him to the food. "But I like a horse that goes after what he wants."

"Like you, Jedidiah?" Barty said as he pulled Jed's saddle out of the shed and hoisted it onto the stone wall of the corral.

Jed studied his uncle. "This is what you've been not saying all morning, isn't it?"

"What?" Barty returned to the shed and came out with a curry comb.

"Charlotte. This is all really about Charlotte Lambert, isn't it?"

"No."

"She's a smart, attractive woman who happens to be in Agua Dulce for a little while. And frankly, I need some friends my own age."

Barty brushed Britches with quick, hard strokes. Britches had finished eating and stood waiting to be saddled.

"Friends are good," Barty said as he smoothed the blanket across Britches's back. "I know it's lonely out here—"

"—I'm lonely but I'm not looking for convenient comfort. I wouldn't do that to such a nice woman. I wouldn't do that to *any* woman."

"I know that. But sometimes a woman can look so fine, and be so welcoming, well, good judgment just rides right out of your camp. You know there's nothing worse than letting a woman down. Especially if you really care for her."

"I'll do my best to remember that." Jed swung the hand-tooled saddle, a gift from Barty for his fifteenth birthday, onto Britches's back. He ducked and reached for the strap under Britches's belly. "We'd better get going if we're going to make fools of ourselves in the parade this morning."

Barty looked at his wristwatch. "Yup. I need to get back to the High Lonesome and saddle up Noches. Charlotte's gonna ride him in the parade."

"I heard. Nice of you to let her ride a bit while she's here."

"She's only been riding Noches around the east pasture. Charlotte was a good rider once. Rode in those fancy English events they have back East. You see it in the way she sits, the way she handles Noches. She'd probably play polo if you asked her."

Jed laughed. "Maybe I will. Ask her."

Jed led Britches out of the stone corral. Barty followed alongside.

"That silly pinto has taken a liking to her." Barty stood back while Jed mounted Britches and adjusted himself in the saddle. "I've seen it before."

"Seen what before?"

"Seen a horse and a human with similar handicaps gravitate to one another."

Jed adjusted the reins and looked down at his uncle. "I don't follow you."

Barty shrugged. "The pinto was so deeply mistreated way back when she can't hardly take a step without expecting the world to clobber her again. Charlotte seems to navigate the same way: so cautious and wary she's always off balance."

Jed shook his head, not understanding. "What happened to Charlotte? Who mistreated her?"

Barty adjusted his hat and walked ahead of Britches. Jed and Britches rode up alongside him. "Uncle Barty, who or what mistreated her?"

"Me." Barty stopped and looked up at Jed. "Me and her mother. Years before Charlotte was even born, things occurred that caused whole families grief and harm."

{28}

Holoman Farley never attended the Lágrimas Valley's Independence Day festivities. The parade through downtown Agua Dulce and the picnic and fireworks out by the cemetery were just another excuse for the locals to indulge themselves in food, drink, and the sins of the flesh. And the pagan ritual at the cemetery at sunrise for the so-called war heroes: half breeds all! Those boys' souls were carried off to purgatory on the backs of Satan's horses, and there weren't enough stones in the Lágrimas to bury the sins of their families.

Farley had his own Independence Day tradition: back when he could walk for miles at a good clip, Farley would pack up his Winchester and cartridges and head out into the desert. He'd set up way back on the national forest land where no one could hear or see him, and then take out prairie dogs, jackrabbits, and piñon jays. Before 1950 and the mustang massacre, Farley used to shoot at the horses, too. Once in a while he'd get close enough to the wild herd to hit one. The mustangs were difficult to sneak up on until the government professionals came in and showed those devil mares they were not wanted on this earth.

At 6 a.m. Farley sat at Mabel's breakfast table dressed and ready for the day. He listened to Mabel making biscuits and coffee in the kitchen. Just like July Fourth, 1959, today Farley was going to make an exception to his pious avoidance of Agua Dulce's holiday festivities. This morning he was going to stand in the crowd on Main Street and pretend to watch the parade. And later this afternoon, just like in July of 1959, Farley was going to find himself a lookout in the scrub oak that grew behind the abandoned school, watch the picnic on the baseball field, and wait for her. She'd become complacent, distracted, all the men at the picnic unable to keep their eyes and hands off of her. It would get dark and everyone's eyes but Farley's would lift to the sky and watch the fireworks. She'd let down her guard, feel protected among her admirers, forget how the wicked cannot find refuge anywhere, even under the cover of darkness. It was all part of the perfection of the Lord's plan.

She'd forgotten how Farley had been chosen all those years ago to cleanse the contaminated souls of the Lágrimas. The veil of vanity, the pleasures of the flesh had removed her memory. He recognized Satan's slave that day in the drugstore, the dull eyes and blank stare of the possessed. She almost fooled him, she looked so innocent!

Farley squeezed his eyes shut and covered his ears. Mabel was singing. The smell of coffee and eggs, the sun of morning catching the vase of flowers on the table, summer bees in the hollyhocks, mother, home. Farley's heart pushed a plug of old emotion up into his throat. Emotion he could not be swayed by, not today! No, home would be his after his mission was completed. Home was heaven, home was where the sinful could not wander free, home was where everyone who had hurt him, scorned and rejected him, was dirt dead with no names and no faces. No bones and no bodies. No life, not even in memories.

Earl shuffled into the dining room. "What are you doing up so early? Did you go to the war memorial at sunup?"

"The parade." Farley opened his eyes. "I'm going to the parade."

"Good morning, Earl!" Mabel called from the kitchen.

"Morning, Miss Mabel." Earl pulled out his chair at the far end of the table and sat down. He studied Farley for a moment. "You don't go to parades."

"You don't know what I do and don't do, so button it up."

Mabel stood in the doorway. Farley didn't look at her, but he knew she was frowning and that her ugly face was wrinkled up like an old peach.

"You don't have to talk like that, Farley," the old peach said. "Maybe if folks knew exactly what it is you do and don't do with your time they'd like you more."

"It's none of anyone's business what I do. I don't give a damn if people like me. They're just distraction."

Mabel grunted disapproval, exchanged a look with Earl, and went back into the kitchen. Earl stared straight ahead.

Farley cleared his throat and wiped his runny eyes with his napkin. "You going to the picnic?"

Earl turned his head and peered down the table. "Don't even ask, Farley. I ain't giving you a ride anywhere anytime ever again."

Farley picked up his fork and tapped it on the table. Fine, he would walk. Or he would find someone with a need to give him a ride—a need for tobacco or alcohol or cash. Better if Earl didn't know anyway. Not that it would matter afterwards what people knew. After she was dead he would rise above this stinking cesspool and step onto the throne and take his rightful place by his Lord. Farley was holding his own ticket home, bought with blood, sweat, tears, and what felt to be a thousand years of suffering and patience.

{29}

Each year the participants in Agua Dulce's Fourth of July parade gathered at nine o'clock at Barty's service station. When Charlotte drove up in the Hudson the usually empty yard was crammed with parked cars and trucks and trailers. Horses and riders were everywhere. National rodeo champion Cody Tsosie was signing autographs by the gas pumps under the flying horse, and Barty and Jed were helping a group of teenagers hook their float to the rear of a decorated pickup truck. Jed waved at Charlotte and pointed at the cottonwood tree at the far side of the repair shop: Noches, Britches, and Barty's muscular quarter horse Dolly stood calmly watching the spectacle.

"I'll be right there," Jed called across the crowd.

Charlotte hoped that Jed would notice that she was *not* wearing his mother's clothes. Charlotte had taken Thea's advice and gone into Woolworth's yesterday afternoon to buy some new apparel. For the parade she sported a pair of new Levi's that actually fit her hips and waist and did not have to be cuffed. Charlotte also wore a new plaid cowgirl shirt with pearl buttons and a fancy leather belt that the salesgirl, a locally respected barrel racer, assured Charlotte was all the rage with the rodeo crowd.

Charlotte walked through the pickup trucks decorated with red, white, and blue streamers and paper flowers, and past the fire engine and the six members of the Lágrimas Volunteer Fire Department. The fire chief, a large-boned, booming-voiced Anglo named Grant Strickland, had his four children seated on the top rail of the ladder truck.

Gus Treadle and the members of the Dos Rios sheriff's posse, active and retired, were seated on their horses and waiting in parade formation.

"Charlotte!" Gus called when she walked out of the crowd. "Well, then, don't you look ready for a parade!"

Gus and the boys were all dressed in starched white shirts with red badges sewn on the sleeves. They wore turquoise-embellished bolo ties and spotless white hats. Stiff, new dark blue Levi's were secured to their hips with belts boasting the largest silver buckles Charlotte had ever seen. And each of Gus's guys carried a flag.

"Hello, Gus! Don't you fellows look dandy!"

"I see Noches over there," Gus said, nodding at the sorrel mare standing alongside Britches. "You go and get yourself ready, and if there's anything you need, you just ask. Okay?"

"I appreciate that, Gus. I've never ridden in a parade and I'm a bit nervous." Actually Charlotte was more than a bit nervous. She walked over to the cottonwood tree and, after saying hello to Britches and Dolly, stood before Noches and rubbed her soft nose.

"Good morning, beautiful," Charlotte said. Noches blinked her eyes and bobbed her head a few times. "I'm counting on you to show me how to do this."

Britches nickered as he watched Jed approach. Like every other man in the vicinity of the service station, Jed was dressed in stiff new Levi's, a starched shirt, and a spotless cowboy hat. Even his boots were shiny.

"You might want to climb into that fancy saddle, and let me adjust those stirrups." Jed removed Noches's reins from the fence, turned the mare around and led her out into the open space between the rear of the station and Barty's house. "I'll give you a leg up."

Charlotte walked to Jed and Noches. "I'm feeling kind of nervous. Just like before a horse show when I was young."

Jed smiled. "Barty says you're a very accomplished horsewoman. And he doesn't often use the word accomplished. If it makes you feel better, I'm a tad nervous, too. And everyone over there with the possible exception of Uncle Barty and Gus is jittery. But it just wouldn't be a Fourth of July parade if there wasn't a mishap of some sort. See the 4 H'-ers and their livestock processional? You can be sure there'll be an unscheduled ruckus around that group."

Charlotte laughed as Jed boosted her onto Noches and adjusted her stirrups.

"They have the 4-H go first so that when those animals make a break for it—usually downtown somewhere between the hardware and the drugstore—they don't spook the horses. I've seen it many times: Main Street a pandemonium of people and panicked animals. How's that?"

Charlotte slid her boots into each stirrup and adjusted her legs and torso. "Perfect."

Jed patted Charlotte's knee and then stepped back to look at her. "Yup, just perfect."

"This is a great saddle," Charlotte said, blushing. "And I trust Noches to stay calm."

"Nothing spooks Noches." Jed walked to Britches and then swung up into the saddle with one fluid movement. "You'll be fine."

Gus Treadle and his flag-bearing boys were positioning themselves alongside Cody Tsosie in front of the fire truck now loaded with volunteers in firefighters' suits and helmets. Ponies and horses and their riders were all taking positions behind the decorated pickup trucks. Barty emerged from the back of the gas station and paused in his tracks for just an instant when he saw Jed and Charlotte on Britches and Noches. Charlotte leaned over and fussed with her stirrup, although her leg and foot were perfectly comfortable. Perfect. Just perfect. That's what Jed said. So why did she feel so very imperfect in the eyes of Barty Bill?

Barty reached Dolly and, with less grace than Jed but with equal athleticism, swung up onto the tall, sturdy quarter horse.

"Morning, Charlotte," Barty said as he tipped the front of his hat. "How's that saddle work for you?"

"It's perfect," she said. Jed and Britches had walked ahead a few paces but Jed turned around in his saddle and smiled back at Charlotte. She smiled, too. "Everything's just perfect."

꧁꧂꧁꧂꧁꧂꧁꧂꧁꧂꧁꧂꧁꧂

After the parade Charlotte took a cool shower and dressed in one of Bernadette's pleated cotton skirts and a bright blue peasant shirt. Barefoot, she left the bedroom and found Francis out on the porch spit shining her boots. Francis himself was dressed in a new creased pair of Levi's and a red shirt with a silver bolo tie. Even his hair, what little there was of it, was pressed into place.

"Don't you look fine," Francis said as he set down the boot. He pulled a silk bandanna from his pocket and held it out to Charlotte. "You've got to wear a silk on the Fourth."

Charlotte felt overdressed for a picnic and fireworks display until she stepped onto the baseball field beside the cemetery and looked over the crowd: women of all ages swirled about in calico skirts, flouncy shirts, and fancy stitched cowboy boots, their chests laden with strands of turquoise, coral, and shell necklaces, their wrists wrapped in thick silver bracelets. Everyone brought platters, baskets, coolers, and casserole dishes of food and placed them on long tables set up along the baseline between third and home plate. If folks suspected Dorothea Durham's salads and cakes were laced with healing roots, body-balancing flowers, and system-cleansing twigs it did not inhibit their appetite for them. Thea's bowls and platters were among the first to be emptied of their contents.

Charlotte herself finished the buffet line with a paper plate so over-weighted with food it threatened to fold in half. Even Jed, who never seemed to have much interest in food, carried an unwieldy plate away from the buffet tables and leaned against a tree and ate with uncharacteristic gusto.

Since her horseback appearance in the parade between Jed and Barty, and behind Gus Treadle and his retired posse, Charlotte's status in the valley had been elevated from stranger to visitor. She was still an outsider but no longer a foreigner, and people greeted her by name and initiated conversation.

Gus's family, which included his two younger brothers from Dos Rios, widowers like himself, and his son, Gus, Jr., his wife and two kids from Santa Fe, set up their picnic camp on the baseball field several yards from the Durhams'.

"We always jostle for that spot closest to the home team dugout because of the shade," Gus told Charlotte, pointing at the huge cottonwood tree behind the bleachers. "We got here ten minutes too late this year, so we'll have to settle for the shade under this little elm. Now, Charlotte, you tell me if the Durhams don't treat you right. There's plenty of blanket space here with the Treadle tribe, and we even got an extra lawn chair."

"That's a kind offer, Gus," Charlotte said. "And thank you for helping me through the parade today. I really enjoyed it all, although I'm a bit sore tonight."

She patted her tender thigh muscles.

"You were a right fine pretty addition to our parade," Gus said. "And the way you jumped off Noches and grabbed that toddler who wandered into the street after the fire truck, well, I'd be proud to have you on my team. All the boys and me thought you ought to plan on being here next year. That's how traditions get started around Agua Dulce: something good gets repeated until we can't remember doing without it."

"I'll remember that," Charlotte said. Jed was listening to their conversation from his perch against the cottonwood trunk. "But who knows where I'll be a year from now?"

Charlotte stood in line for lemonade that was being served by the tankful from the tailgate of a pickup truck parked at the far side of the food tables. A hand tapped her on the shoulder. She turned around and faced Earl Turnball.

"Good evening, Charlotte," Earl said, bowing his mostly bald head. "You look lovely in that skirt. Are you enjoying our picnic?"

"Oh, I am," Charlotte said. "The food is wonderful!"

"It is. But I can't say as the fireworks will be much to remember."

The line stepped forward. Charlotte filled her cup with lemonade from the spigot and stepped aside so Earl could do the same.

"You know, I've never been one to get all that excited about fireworks," Charlotte said. She sipped her lemonade and scanned the field. Jed had left his place against the tree. "I think this is just about the nicest Fourth I've ever celebrated."

Earl's arthritic hands struggled to hold the cup and simultaneously operate the cooler's spigot.

"Here, Earl." Charlotte reached for the spigot handle. "Let me turn this for you."

Earl's face grimaced with aggravation. "I'm just not as agile as I used to be."

Charlotte walked with Earl back through the crowd on the infield. The sun was finally lower than the trees and most blankets and chairs were in full shade now. Earl led Charlotte to a group of elderly men and women who shared a folding card table covered with a lacy white tablecloth.

"This is Mabel Duran," Earl said, sweeping his hand to the blue-haired matron seated on the lawn chair at the head of the table. "Mabel, Charlotte Rose Lambert. And these are my housemates, Gerald Mondragon and Selena Chacon-Smith."

Earl leaned close to Charlotte. "Of course, we didn't bring old Farley."

"Who?" But then she remembered: the yellow-eyed troll from the drugstore. "Oh, *him.*"

"You would be the same Rose as Dr. Rose?" Mabel peered up at Charlotte through thick, butterfly-shaped glasses. Pearls hung loosely around Mabel's thick neck and pink rouge defined the apples of her cheeks. "My mother, may she rest in peace in the third row, left, of the cemetery gate, offered those bone diggers rooms, but they didn't want to live in town." Mabel turned to her tablemates. "I was newly engaged to Leroy that summer, working at the bottling company up in Dos Rios. I never met Dr. Rose, but my mother thought it was scandalous the way those college kids had to live out on the desert."

Mabel looked at Charlotte. "Dr. Rose insisted they loved it. And I'm told he was the sort of man that made you believe what he said to be true."

"And what he said *was* true." Earl glanced up at Charlotte, worried that she might be offended by Mabel's critical assessment of Grandpa's choice of summer accommodations. "Your mother told me so herself. Living in the fossil camp was the best home she'd ever known. That's what Alicia Rose told me: the best home she'd ever known."

"I reckon that's why she came back," Selena said as she dabbed her narrow lips with a cloth napkin. "Looking to find what she once had. Of course it don't work that way."

Charlotte's eyes moved from face to face around the little table. "No, I suppose not."

"And we'll never know because, well, *because.*" Mabel lifted her eyebrows at Selena.

"Because it don't involve you," Gerald stated loudly. He was methodically working his way through a wedge of chocolate cake the size of an adobe brick.

"There might have been an answer in that note that got lost," Mabel said, raising her finger and tapping her cheek as if her memory was accessed through her mouth. "You know, Earl, the note you saw Alicia Rose tuck under the cash register?"

"What note?" Charlotte asked.

"I don't know if it was a *note*. Could have been a sales receipt or someone's grocery list," Earl stated flatly, obviously uncomfortable.

Earl turned around and with his back to his nosy housemates, spoke in a lowered voice to Charlotte. "I was in the store buying turpentine that day in 1976. I saw your mother at the front counter. Recognized her in an instant. No doubt that it was Alicia Rose. She slid something under the cash register. Don't know that it even belonged to her. Just a small piece of yellow paper, looked like a note. When I paid for my turpentine I saw the paper sticking out of the corner of the register. Whatever it was got lost or misplaced, or was found by whoever it was meant for. No one else saw it but me. I told the sheriff about it."

Charlotte looked down at her hand locked around the plastic cup of lemonade.

"But she did tell me it was the best home she'd ever known," Earl said softly. "I know that for sure."

Charlotte walked across the baseball infield, weaving around blankets and chairs and people. So what if there was a note from her mother to someone? But why hadn't Leonard or Grandpa mentioned that Alicia had stopped at the hardware store, possibly to see the Durhams, and had perhaps left a note before heading out to the quarry? Was this why Grandpa insisted she had not come to New Mexico to die? It didn't seem like particularly strong evidence. Not to a scientist like Grandpa.

Through the maze of people milling about in the glinting, golden late-afternoon sun, Charlotte's eye caught the clean white of Jed's cotton shirt. He was standing by the visiting team's dugout with four women of various ages pressed in around him. The valley women were circling the wagons around their prodigal son. Charlotte changed her route and navigated a path across the field to the Durhams that did not take her near Jed's encampment.

Alicia said it was the best home she ever knew. Just a campsite on a piece of sand below a red cliff under a wide sky. And wasn't home about a connection between one's heart and a place and its people? Did Alicia lose her heart in Agua Dulce?

Charlotte stopped beside Francis, who was eating a dripping slice of watermelon.

"And where would Bartholomew be?" Thea asked Dennis. Dennis and Javier were also slurping their way through a watermelon wedge. "I suppose he has some horse to move, cow to water, car to start, *something* to justify being the last person in the valley to come to the picnic?!"

"He always gets here." Dennis wiped his mouth with a paper napkin. "He'll get here."

"You know, for years he and Bernadette were the first on the field with Conchata, and then with me and Francis." Thea was squinting at the crowd. Charlotte wondered how many faces Thea could recognize, or if she depended on clothing colors and hat sizes to provide identification clues. "And even after Bernadette left for school, she'd come back for the Fourth and get Bartholomew to come with her. But then there were years Bartholomew wouldn't come at all—had a horse auction to attend, or someone's backhoe needed an emergency repair, so he stayed at the station and watched the fireworks from his garage. Now Bartholomew just comes late."

"But Barty loves the Fourth of July." Jed strode up beside Charlotte. "You know each year he risks fines, maybe even jail time, when he flips the switch and ignites that flying horse. If that's not the re-enactment of the Declaration of Independence I don't know what is!"

Dennis laughed as he tossed his melon rind into a plastic trash bag hung at the end of one of the tables. "Those Mobil people think Agua Dulce dried up and blew away decades ago!"

Javier stood near Charlotte's elbow and tugged at the sleeve of her peasant shirt. His cheeks were the color of the watermelon he had just finished. "I've been licking a lot of stones but no dinosaurs!"

Charlotte laughed. "I know it can be *very* frustrating. Maybe we can go out and look again on the desert for fossils, okay?"

"My man!" Arthur strode up and slapped a hand on Jed's shoulder. He sized up Charlotte from head to foot. "Teacher *teacher*! Very nice!"

Arthur took a deep bow. Jed stepped back and surveyed him. "Where've you been? I looked for you at the soda fountain. I said I'd buy you a cold one after the parade."

Arthur fidgeted with the bandanna tied around his scalp as he took in the families and folks on the field. "I had to go into Dos Rios last night. Got late so I stayed over with my *compadres.*"

Arthur would not look directly at either Charlotte or Jed. He was dressed in clean jeans and a T-shirt, but wore his dark sunglasses and gangster head gear.

"Did you look at the workbook I gave you?" Charlotte asked him. "Those worksheets I downloaded from the internet?"

"Nah, no time." Arthur turned his back to Jed and Charlotte and faced the field of picnickers. "Is Violeta here?"

Jed studied Arthur with obvious disapproval. "She's here with her grandmother and the Tomé clan. Over there by the cemetery entrance. They came late."

Arthur walked into the crowd. Jed went after him and placed his hand on Arthur's arm. Arthur stopped and looked up at Jed, frowning, almost angry.

" *Que pasa?!*"

"We're working tomorrow," Jed said. "First light."

Arthur shrugged Jed's hand from his arm. "Maybe, boss man. Depends how late tonight is, *verdad?*" Arthur glanced back at Charlotte. "Might be a night to remember."

"I'll be there first light, Arthur." Jed stepped back. "You can come or not."

"It's Sunday. I need some time off." Arthur turned around and stood square to Jed. "The adobes aren't going anywhere." Arthur looked at Charlotte. "You said we aren't meeting tomorrow cause you're going into Santa Fe, right teacher?"

Charlotte nodded in agreement. "Yes. I'm going to Santa Fe."

Arthur shifted his gaze back to Jed. "See, even Charlotte is taking Sunday off. I gotta find Violeta."

Arthur walked through the crowd to the Tomé clan by the cemetery. Even from a distance it was obvious that with the exception of Violeta, who jumped up into his open arms, Rosa and her family were not delighted to see Arthur.

"What kind of friends does Arthur have in Dos Rios?" Charlotte asked Jed.

"The wrong kind. The kind that make him forget everything he's working toward." Jed watched Arthur hoist Violeta onto his shoulders. "The kind of friends who tell him he's the loser the Tomés believe him to be and then help him to live down to that ideal."

Dennis and Francis were pouring coffee from a thermos. Thea sat back in her lawn chair and closed her eyes. She mumbled something to herself, or to Conchata, and then took a deep breath and slipped into a nap. Charlotte and Jed stood facing the baseball field. Arthur walked about with Violeta perched high on his shoulders, his hands holding her hands as he spun around and around. Rosa Tomé glared at them, but did not interfere with their game.

"Arthur is walking the fence right now." Jed looked down at Charlotte. "He could jump to one side and land on his feet, make something of his life. Or he could fall off the other side and end up in prison like his brother."

"I shouldn't have told Arthur we would skip meeting tomorrow."

"No, it's okay. Arthur need a few days off. We all do."

{30}

The warm summer dusk claimed the baseball field and everyone gathered up their picnic areas and retrieved sweaters and flashlights from their cars and trucks. Chairs and blankets were rearranged to face the outfield where Grant Strickland was barking orders at the fire department volunteers. They set up three small platforms to launch the fireworks and moved the water truck onto the field where it was parked within easy hosing of the platforms.

Dennis, Frances, and Jed began to make wagers as to what this year's selection of fireworks would include. There were some obvious favorites from past years; Dennis and Francis reminisced about several especially outstanding failures that had malfunctioned at blastoff and exploded into the trees or grazed the roofs of vehicles before fizzling out safely in the desert beyond the old church and school. Jed was in Scottsdale last year, and the year before that, too, but Dennis assured him there were some surprises even for city slickers in the Agua Dulce Fire Department's arsenal of fireworks.

"There's Uncle Barty." Jed gestured at the crowd behind them. Charlotte looked past Jed and saw Barty's white truck on the far side of the cemetery. Barty climbed from the cab, positioned his hat on his head, and walked around the cemetery and into the crowd. He was respectably handsome for a man pushing sixty. In his youth he must have been quite the ladies' man, Charlotte thought. Like his nephew.

"You'll want to see the red horse tonight," Jed said to Charlotte. He was watching Barty, who had stopped to talk with a man who was pointing at the rear tire of his car. "You haven't really experienced the Agua Dulce Independence Day celebration until you've witnessed the miraculous if unauthorized resurrection of old Pegasus. Excuse me."

Jed walked quickly around the families clustered on blankets on the ground. Charlotte followed his white shirt as he faded into the edge of the field and intercepted his uncle. Jed and Barty spoke briefly near the visiting team's dugout and then Jed walked on alone into the ebbing darkness at the far side of the old school. Barty made his way to the Durhams. Thea recognized the familiar outline of Barty and lifted her cane to greet him.

"Bartholomew! You made it!"

Barty stopped beside Thea's lawn chair and placed his hand on her shoulder. He nodded cordially at Charlotte.

"Where's Jed gone to?" Thea squinted into the dusky crowd surrounding them.

"To check on Britches. He's thinking he'll watch from the other side of the school. I'll go and keep him company." Barty turned to Dennis who stood with his arm around Earlene. "I'll catch you and your pocket change later back at the station."

Dennis guffawed. "Enjoy your full pockets while you have 'em, cause you're going down like the Shanghai Rockets tonight—in flames, *compadre!*" Dennis looked at Charlotte. "We play poker. Under that infernal red horse. Between us, Barty here hasn't recovered from his losses last year. He's out for revenge."

Barty frowned. "I don't remember losing a dime. I do, however, remember feeling sorry for Earlene, what with you gambling away all her rainy day money, so I let you win a few!"

Dennis shook his head. "After the fireworks me and Ralph and Francis'll help you recover your memory!"

Thea make a tsk-ing sound. "They'll stay up half the night and then wonder tomorrow why they can't drag themselves from their beds to do chores! Boys will be boys. And men will act like boys on the Fourth."

"Yes, well, I'll see you all later." Barty tipped his hat at the women and then turned on his heel and walked back into the crowd. Thea stabbed her cane in the dirt beside her chair. Francis rested his hand on her arm.

"He's right. Jed needs company."

"Barty isn't the company Jed needs just now."

The fireworks began with a fizzling, sizzling streamer of red that exploded in the night sky over roofs of the old school and church. The spectators crowded together in the baseball field, the crosses and markers and bouquets of flowers standing in rows within the cemetery fence, and the stone monolith out on the desert beyond, momentarily bathed in brilliant light. And just as quickly, all slipped back into the summer night's soft darkness. Charlotte looked over at the schoolhouse. She could easily walk over and find Jed. They had spent the entire day together, and it felt odd now with Jed gone. But Barty was with Jed. Charlotte and Barty had come to an understanding of sorts, and she no longer felt like Barty disliked her. But she still wasn't entirely comfortable around him. Or he around her.

With a bullhorn and an industrial-sized flashlight, Grant Strickland coordinated all of the volunteer firefighters so that they set off three rockets at the same time. The rockets shot skyward and opened into sprays of red, white, and blue flowers that bloomed over the desert south of the baseball field. The spectators applauded as two more equally dazzling rockets arced over the field and split into silver streamers. As these fizzled into the black sky gigantic fountains of fire were ignited on each of the three platforms.

"A crowd favorite," Francis said over the noise to Charlotte. "They look like they might whirl out of control into the kids down front there, but they never do."

"What's the Fourth of July without a little danger?" Dennis said.

A final rocket was launched high into the sky. It paused in the black. The crowd on the field held its collective breath and then the rocket exploded like a meteor directly overhead, crackling and sparkling into a raucous fanfare. Red, white and blue sparks rained down over the Agua Dulce baseball field and dissolved into harmless ash before reaching the spectators. Charlotte heard herself exhaling and laughing with everyone around her.

"That was the best dang show they've ever put together," Francis said as he and Ralph began to fold up blankets and chairs. "Just for you, Charlotte! Best ever!"

"Now where'd Barty go to?" Dennis peered into the dark near the school. "I hope he reminds Jed about the card game."

"Jed doesn't like cards," Thea said. She was standing with her arm hooked through Earlene's. "I don't remember Jed playing cards."

"Oh, Thea, Jed plays cards all the time," Francis said. "I see Britches's profile over there by the swing set. Jed's still here."

"You can play cards with the boys," Thea said to Charlotte.

"Yes, you come, Charlotte," Dennis added. He and Javier hoisted the cooler between them and headed for their truck.

"I'm not much for poker." Charlotte carried Thea's folding chair across the field behind Ralph, who had the Durhams' cooler. She kept an eye on Britches near the old playground. She couldn't see Jed, but he was somewhere near his horse. When they reached the truck the headlights of parked and departing vehicles made it impossible for Charlotte to see beyond the glare. She wanted to at least say good night to Jed, but in the chaos of moving cars and people it was impossible to locate him.

Ralph climbed into the Durhams' big truck and started the engine. Thea lingered at the side with her hand on Charlotte's arm.

"Let's go." Francis held out his hand to help Thea into the cab. Just then Barty walked into the headlights.

"Jed's gonna ride Britches over to my place. He says to say good night to everyone. The exhaust fumes are pretty bad."

"He should be sipping that tonic," Thea said. "I wonder if he brought it along. Charlotte! I want you to take this bottle . . . ."

Thea leaned into the car and fumbled about the glove box.

"Oh, Thea, I'm sure he has some," Francis said. "Jed will be fine."

"I'll take it," Barty said. "I'll give it to him at the station."

Thea ignored them both. "Here, Charlotte." Thea extracted her thin body from the large cab of the truck, took Charlotte's hand and placed a small bottle in her palm. "You go and catch Jed. You tell him to take four drops every fifteen minutes for the next hour. Go, quickly! Before he rides out."

Charlotte looked at Barty and then at Francis.

"We'll wait for ya here," Francis said. Barty shrugged and nodded.

Charlotte jogged around the cars and trucks jostling for exit position in the impossibly crowded parking lot. She went around the front side of the old church and then across more sand to the front steps of the school. Britches was no longer there. Charlotte peered into the darkness beyond the deserted building. Finally her eyes found the vague outline of a horse and rider walking into the desert. Charlotte ran around the wire fence and cut across the school yard. There were no swings attached to the old swing set, but someone was moving in and out of the dangling chains. She stopped by the broken seesaws, breathing hard from her quick jog.

"Hello?" Charlotte peered into the dark at the person. "I'm trying to catch up with—"

"—Witch whore."

Charlotte stumbled back into the legs of the seesaw.

"I been watching you." Farley's lips smacked. "We been here before, witch, remember? Devil got your tongue?"

Farley lunged through the chains. Charlotte turned to run but her boot heel caught the cement footing and she crashed into the metal bar.

"Stay away from me." She gripped the rail for balance. "Don't come any closer."

"Your hell ravens can't find you now." Farley shuffled around the end of the swing set. Light from the headlights of departing vehicles brushed across the dull film of his eyes. Charlotte glanced over her shoulder but she was too far away for anyone to see or hear her. "But I found you."

Charlotte's heart was racing. Why couldn't she move, turn and run? Call out?

"Stop!" Charlotte held out Thea's tincture bottle. "Stay away from me!"

Farley's eyes fixated on the bottle thrust in the air between them. His body flinched like it had been stabbed. There was something dangling from his neck, a string of dried fruit, or leather pieces. He grabbed the necklace and lunged again at Charlotte. Charlotte grabbed the hem of her full skirt, hoisted it to her thighs and with a quick hop was on the other side of the seesaw.

"Nowhere to run!" Farley's voice was shaking, his mouth spitting words through the shriveled objects on the necklace. "I told you before, Apache whore—you can't run from your damnation!"

Charlotte bent down and scooped up a handful of gravel and sand and hurled it at Farley. It struck him in the face, and he careened backward.

"Charlotte?" a voice called out from the darkness. "Charlotte!"

Farley shrank into the black night as the large dark form that was Britches and Jed rode up to the swing set. Charlotte scanned the schoolyard but Farley had vanished.

"Charlotte?" Jed dismounted and pushed aside the broken chains to reach Charlotte. "Who were you talking to? What are you doing here?"

"Oh, God, it was that awful man!" Charlotte held the tincture bottle against her chest. Her hand shook and her voice cracked. "The one from the drugstore."

Jed looked around the schoolyard and then took Charlotte by the shoulders.

"The drugstore? What happened?" Jed's face was only a few inches from Charlotte's. He smelled like saddle leather and sage. His hands were firm and warm on her shoulders. She began to relax.

"Everyone says he's crazy," she said softly. "He was right here."

Jed walked around the yard and peered into the dark. "He's gone."

He walked back to Charlotte standing against Britches.

"Are you sure?" Charlotte squinted all around the yard.

Jed motioned to Britches. "Britches would be agitated if someone was hiding out in the dark."

Charlotte reached up and stroked the horse's soft neck. "Why did that old man come after me?"

"I don't know. He's one weird guy." The last cars and trucks were pulling onto the highway and headlights swept across the schoolyard. "You can file a complaint with the sheriff. Maybe they'll put him away this time. Barty swears Farley murdered his father but was never charged because of inept law enforcement. But that was half a century ago. They might lock him up now."

Charlotte shivered. "I don't want to file a complaint. My family doesn't need to take up any more of the Dos Rios sheriff's time. I'll be gone in a week, anyway."

"Why are you over here?" Jed looked back at the departing vehicles. "Where's Francis?"

Charlotte remembered the bottle of tincture and uncurled her hand. "Thea wanted you to have this. She sent me."

Jed took the bottle and held it up in the dark between them. "Licorice and dandelion tincture: I must have ten of these in my saddlebag." Jed looked from the bottle to Charlotte. "What does Thea think I do, sip it on the rocks?"

"She said take ten drops every—"

"—fifteen minutes." Jed smiled. "Let's get out of here."

Slices of conversations and the sound of car doors echoed across the sand to the school yard. Jed turned to listen to something. Charlotte heard it, too: Arthur's voice.

"You're a control freak, Rosa!" Arthur was very angry. "You're the god-damned reason Lucho is in prison!"

More angry words were exchanged in Spanish. A door slammed and an engine started with a roar. Tires screeched and Arthur's Honda swerved around the last cars merging onto the county road and sped up the highway towards Agua Dulce.

"I hope he doesn't do something really stupid tonight." Jed said.

The last truck departed the parking lot near the cemetery and drove north to town. Silence dropped onto the schoolyard and the desert surrounding it. Charlotte realized that Francis's truck was no longer parked near the field.

"They just left me," Charlotte said incredulously. "I can't believe they just left me!"

"Who? Oh, Thea and Francis. I can." Jed slid the reins over Britches's head and turned back to Charlotte. "That would be just like Thea."

"Leaving me here?"

"Leaving you here with me." Jed walked around to Britches's left side, slid his boot into the stirrup, and climbed into the saddle. He quickly pulled his boot from the stirrup and reached out his hand to Charlotte. "Use the stirrup. Grab the rear of the saddle and I'll pull you up behind me."

"What are we doing?"

"We're riding Britches back to the Durham ranch."

"Okay." With her right hand Charlotte grabbed the back rim of the saddle where a jacket was rolled up and tied. Jed's hand took her left hand as she slipped her boot into the stirrup. "I haven't ridden in a flouncy skirt before."

"First time for everything." Jed leaned away as Charlotte hoisted herself up, over and onto Britches's hindquarters.

"This is your mother's skirt," Charlotte said as she positioned herself behind Jed and smoothed the skirt over her bare legs.

Jed nodded. "Always liked that skirt."

{31}

Instead of paralleling the county road south to the Durham ranch, Jed reined Britches into the open desert north of the church and school. The night sky was enormous, and seemed to expand in size with each step Britches took into the landscape. Stars and planets laced the black ocean above their heads and the earth began to feel very small. A three-quarter moon glowed in the southwestern sky.

"I didn't know so many stars and planets were visible to the naked eye," Charlotte said. "I almost never notice the moon or think about the night sky in New York."

"I lost sense of the sky in Phoenix," Jed said. "At least at night."

"We're heading north. Isn't the Durham ranch to the southwest?"

"Very good." Jed spoke over his shoulder. "Really. You have a great sense of direction. We're heading north to a nice view of Barty's flying horse. You *have* to see the flying red horse on the Fourth of July."

"Aren't you expected at a game of cards tonight?"

"Oh, maybe later. The game lasts till tomorrow morning."

Britches had a gentle, swaying gait and Charlotte's stiff, sore body relaxed into the horse's rhythm. "I think this is just about the nicest way to travel. I don't know why everyone around here doesn't ride horses from place to place."

"Because horseback means you're not going all that far," Jed answered. "And wherever you're going, it's going to take you longer to get there."

Charlotte smiled into Jed's neck. His black, wavy hair was caught under the collar of his shirt. In the infinitesimal bits of light drifting down from the stars she could just make out the line of his jaw and chin. She dropped her head back and looked up into the sky. There was no vocabulary for this landscape or for the way she felt. Charlotte was intoxicated by space.

Britches reached the summit of a long incline and Jed reined him to a stop. They had been ascending a narrow, solitary mesa that stood like an island above the desert floor. Below them to the right was the Lágrimas Valley marked by the feathery dark forms of the trees that hugged the river. Behind and to the left were the lights of Agua Dulce, the stoplight at Main and Los Hermanos changing just now from red to green. The headlights of vehicles traveling south on the country road spotlighted the buttes and sand hills that edged the highway north of town. To the faraway west, beyond the orderly rows of street lamps and porch lights, the Agustinas made a bridge between the dense earth of the desert and the twinkling starscape of the universe.

"It's beautiful up here," Charlotte whispered.

"It is." Jed turned to Charlotte in the dark behind him. "You getting cold?"

"A little. I left my sweater in Francis's truck."

"You can use the jacket tied up under the saddle."

"I'm okay."

Jed reached back and took her hand and placed it around his waist.

"We'll both be warmer."

Charlotte wrapped her other arm around Jed's torso and shifted her legs until she was against his back. He was very thin and she clasped her hands loosely together over his belt buckle. She was warm immediately. Warm and flushed.

Jed reined Britches to the right and they angled across the dark mesa to the northeast. The moon was to their right and cast their soft, moving shadow on the ground to their left. The dark ribbon of the Lágrimas River was far below them.

"See it?" Jed pointed into the dark. "Over there. The flying horse."

Britches stopped and Jed shifted to one side so that Charlotte could see past him. As if she could miss it! The red horse was the brightest light for miles, and seemed to be leaping from trees into the sky over the gas station.

"Wow!" Charlotte exhaled. "It's magnificent!"

"Every Fourth. Uncle Barty lights it on New Year's Eve, too. He'll leave the horse on all night. He'll complain that the glare keeps him up, but Barty loves that flying horse."

"Why does anyone care if he lights that horse?"

Jed leaned forward in the saddle and shifted his weight. "The B & B station was officially disowned by Mobil almost fifteen years ago. No one ever came for the sign. Mobil should be grateful that Uncle Barty's cared for and maintained that antique all these years. Dennis says they should declare the station a historic landmark. What with all those old pumps and signs he's collected, the place could be a museum!"

"He's a regular outlaw, your uncle." Charlotte gazed down at the glass horse galloping into space. "Did you go to the war memorial this morning?"

"I didn't." Jed leaned into the saddle horn and continued to gaze over Britches's head at the desert. "It's a nice tradition, though."

"This community has a lot of legends about horses. The mustangs that were shot down, and then the wild horses and the war heroes; horses seem to be a lot more than just horses here."

Jed nudged Britches toward the far side of the narrow mesa top. Charlotte felt Jed's chest expand with a long inhalation of the cool night air, and gradually deflate as he exhaled. Britches reached the edge of the mesa, and dark space opened before them. How Britches could see was a mystery to Charlotte, but the horse stepped off the ledge of flat ground and without stumbling or sliding climbed down the steep slope of sand and pebbly stones. Charlotte's eyes held on to the flying red horse until it vanished into the mesa line.

"Do you think it really happened?" Charlotte leaned into Jed's back for warmth.

"The mustang massacre? Yes. I remember coming across horse skeletons out there in the canyonlands years after it happened."

"No, I mean the horses they say came in during the burial of those six soldiers. Do you think that really happened? Six wild horses just appeared?"

Britches reached the bottom of the slope and followed a shadowed narrow wash that wound to the left before straightening out onto the moonlit plateau. Jed didn't seem to be guiding Britches at all.

"I think it really did happen," Jed finally answered. "Six mustangs, they say, stood in a line while they said last rites over six soldiers killed on Bataan. The boys were from ranching families in the Lágrimas sent to train at Fort

Bliss. They were part of the 515 Coast Artillery, an elite group of anti-aircraft gunners who went to the Philippines with General MacArthur. They were the first U.S. regiment to engage in combat with the Japanese in the Pacific. More than half of them never came home."

Britches wove around large rocks that looked like crouching people in the shadows. Charlotte shivered as she remembered Farley coming out of the dark in the playground.

"The Agua Dulce boys survived the Japanese assault, but died as prisoners of war in the spring of '42 during the Bataan Death March."

"Their bodies were returned to Agua Dulce and buried in July?"

"Yes. For months no one knew where they were or what happened. It was a terrible time, families hoping their boys were still alive, were POWs. They suffered terrible deaths: dysentery, malaria, starvation."

"So years later when the mustangs were shot down by the government, those six horses that came into the cemetery were most likely killed, too."

"The Lágrimas ranchers depended on that wild herd for their own horses—they'd go out and try to catch a few each spring and domesticate them. That's when Barty learned so much about horses. He was very good with the mustangs when he was young."

"And he still keeps a few horses around."

"Not if he can help it," Jed said. "But he can't say no, either, so he always has a handful of horses that need some kind of special care. And they get it."

Charlotte thought about the pinto living on the edge of the trees by the High Lonesome windmill, one foot poised, ready for flight. Fight or flight, weren't those the options? Charlotte had always chosen flight, physically, emotionally, mentally. That was why she understood the pinto: Charlotte couldn't run as fast as that horse, but she could distance herself from a spooky or unpleasant situation with lightning speed just by removing her attention, shutting down her emotions, and walking away. Charlotte could cut something or someone from her mind and heart completely. And where did she learn that? Leonard? Grandma Ruth? Her mother?

"I heard your uncle tell Dennis Mata that the pinto was the most dog-gone lost horse he'd ever dealt with."

"Maybe so. I think Barty isn't giving the pinto the attention she needs."

Charlotte leaned close to Jed's right shoulder. He smelled clean—no detergents, no deodorant, just night-on-skin clean. "Why not?"

"He's afraid he'll fail her."

Charlotte shivered. The night air was chilly and her legs and arms prickled into goose bumps. Jed reached back and began to untie the jacket tucked against the saddle.

"Why don't you put on this jacket."

Charlotte took the canvas jacket and pulled it on. "Wasn't there a death march of native people here in the Southwest?"

"Several. The Long Walk of the Navajos and the Mescalero Apaches in the 1860s, plus forcible removal of scores of other tribes off their lands by U.S. soldiers. History has an ugly way of repeating itself."

Britches wove through a grove of cottonwood trees. A barbed-wire fence separated them from the backyards of houses on the edge of town. They were coming into Agua Dulce from the east.

"Here's a little fact from the historical record: the regiment from New Mexico, the 515?" Jed spoke over his shoulder. "Before the war they were a regiment of Indian and Spanish horse soldiers. They were retrained at Fort Bliss, gave up horses and rifles for bunkers and anti-aircraft guns."

"So when the mustangs appeared during their burial . . ." Charlotte stopped talking.

"The stuff of legends," Jed said after a moment. "It doesn't even matter if it really happened. The story—both the good and the bad—is part of the community psyche."

Crickets chirped in the sage and a coyote yipped from the direction of the river. Music and voices from televisions drifted out of open windows as they passed homes. Britches's ears flickered back and forth taking in the noises of the night around them.

They reached the east end of a narrow residential street. Britches's hooves made musical sounds as they struck the pavement. Two blocks more and they crossed Main Street.

"Ghost town tonight," Jed commented as they wove around a parked car and onto a sandy lot. "The men are playing cards and shooting the bull at Barty's, and the women are sharing leftovers and gossip at the Matas'."

"And we're the lucky ones riding between the worlds," Charlotte said softly.

Britches followed the pavement of a narrow side street until it ended at the well-lit yard of a welding shop. Jed reined him around a wire fence past several trash bins and then into the darkness beyond. They were back on the open desert. Charlotte looked at the houses that marked the west edge of town. Alone, a few weeks ago, she would have been nervous heading away from those lights, from cars and paved streets, telephones and civilization. Tonight with Jed and Britches, she felt there was not another place on the planet she would rather be. If her watch stopped now and she never moved beyond this moment, Charlotte would feel she was the luckiest woman who had ever lived in this world or any other.

From this side of Agua Dulce the wall of the Agustina Mountains dominated the horizon almost as much as the sky. Jed said it was about three miles to the Durhams' if they took the old highway. But they were following an old cow trail along the national forest boundary that would cut the distance by a third. Charlotte wanted to say she was in no hurry, but Jed had a card game to attend, and they couldn't ride around in the desert all night anyway, could they?

"The Egyptians used to fill a tomb with everything the dead would need in the afterlife," Jed said after several minutes of silence. "The Apache people kept it much simpler; all you need is a good horse to cross safely to the other side. When my grandmother Conchata died, her brother Lewis set a mare loose up in the mountains there." Jed pointed into the black mass rising off the moon-shadowy desertscape directly in front of Britches.

"I'd like to think that a horse will come and carry me to the other side," Charlotte said, gazing over Jed's shoulder at the dark form of the Agustinas. "But I don't like to think of that horse abandoned up in the mountains. Do your relatives still do that when someone dies?"

"If they do, they don't talk about it. My mother says without the wild herd a horse can't survive out there. They'll try and work their way back home."

Charlotte pressed her cheek into Jed's shoulder blade and studied the line of the mountains defined by the stars and ridges and slopes and galaxies. It wasn't difficult to imagine a horse stepping from the terra firma of the night earth into the terra extraordinaire of the heavens twinkling just a breath away.

"Uncle Barty never told me himself, but Dennis says that when Barty and Kitty's baby Benjamin died in that car accident, Barty took his best colt and his favorite mare up into the mountains and set them free."

"Why both the mare and the colt?"

"Well, the colt couldn't make it without the mare. And the mare wouldn't make it without the colt, either. I suppose it was sort of metaphorical: Barty knew losing the baby had killed a part of Kitty. He lost her, too. They divorced."

"How old was their baby when he died?"

"Benjamin hadn't been born yet," Jed said quietly. "He was within a month of his birth."

"Oh, God. How terrible for them."

"After he turned the mare and colt loose in the mountains, Uncle Barty cut himself loose, too. Lived a summer alone on the desert. Francis and my mother were real worried about him, thought he might do himself harm. But Thea said that Conchata—you know how they *talk*—said not to worry. Barty was okay. Or would be." Jed paused. Charlotte felt him take another deep breath. "He spent a spring and summer in the same High Lonesome cow camp I'm living in."

"How long ago was that?"

Jed thought a moment and then turned his head over his shoulder. His face was only inches from hers. "That would've been the summer of 1959. I remember because Benjamin Bill's gravestone says he died in January of that year."

"That was the year my mother and grandfather were here."

Britches began a descent. Tall cholla cactus grew in thick stands and the horse had to weave in and around the thorny trees.

"I know there was something between my mother and your uncle," Charlotte stated with as little emotion as possible. "I didn't know that Barty was in such a difficult time of his life."

"Guess we all have them."

They had been angling southeast for a long while. Charlotte recognized landmarks in the country surrounding the Durham ranch north of the irrigation pond. The wall of cliffs west of the reservoir was glazed with the moon's soft light, and the crevasse that was the mouth of the canyon of the *Rito del Yeso* was a deep black wedge. An owl hooted. A second owl answered.

"I know where we are," Charlotte said. "The ravens' nest is right up there in that little cave. Amazing how such a huge, dark, wild place could feel so familiar!"

Jed's warm hand gently squeezed her arm.

"My mother said the camp out by the fossil quarry was the best home she ever knew."

"A good place to call home," Jed said.

They reached the muddy bank of the irrigation pond and Britches stepped in, dropped his head, and took a long drink. Charlotte and Jed gazed at the silvery walls of the cliffs.

"It was because of a raven that I'm here at all," Charlotte said softly, not wanting to disturb the silence around them.

"What?" Jed shifted sideways in the saddle and faced her.

"A raven landed on my car windshield when I was trying to turn around on the old road. I freaked out and drove over a boulder."

Jed was smiling. "Have you told Thea that story?"

"No. I'm kind of embarrassed about it."

"Why?"

"Because I yelled at the raven! I waved my arms and shouted at him to get away!"

Britches raised his head and stepped back from the water's edge. Jed turned forward again and gathered up the reins. Britches walked with a quicker gait now that they were on the road to the Durham barn.

"You probably don't have to tell Thea," Jed said. "She most likely knows anyway."

"Your grandmother?" Charlotte asked.

Jed laughed. "Yes."

The light on the barn door lit the cottonwoods that surrounded the ranch house.

"Why are you going into Santa Fe tomorrow?" Jed asked.

"To retrieve my other suitcase from the hotel."

"Who are you going in with?"

"No one. Francis said I could take Thea's sedan."

Britches's hooves made a hollow clopping sound as they crossed the little wood bridge over the *acequia*. The burros were lined up along the nearest railing of the corral watching Britches and his passengers approach. George was in the hen house, but Little Bit stood at the top of the porch stairs enthusiastically wagging his tail.

"Let me drive you in. I have some errands in town."

They reached the barn door and Britches stopped. Charlotte slid down and stood back while Jed dismounted.

"Aren't cars and engine fumes a problem for you?"

"Barty fixed up and overhauled an old Mustang convertible," Jed said as he wrapped the reins loosely around the corral fence. "We can put the top down."

"I'd like that," Charlotte said. "I'd like to go into Santa Fe with you."

The screen door opened and Thea emerged under the porch light. "Is that you, Bartholomew?"

"It's me, Nana, Jedidiah!" Jed called back. Jed looked at Charlotte and smiled. "Thea doesn't see well these days. She's always confusing me with my uncle."

{32}

The red Mustang was the only vehicle heading north on the county road at nine o'clock on Sunday morning the day after the Fourth of July. Jed drove the convertible like a man who had a need for speed. He hadn't been behind the wheel or in the cab of anything newer than the '47 Hudson in almost nine months. Last January Uncle Barty bought the '68 mustang from a car collector over in Sholow, Arizona. Barty spent the winter tinkering over the Mustang's engine, replacing anything that wasn't in mint condition, hoping to reduce the car's emissions. In April he took the Mustang into Santa Fe and had the exterior repainted a classic fire-engine red. Barty had refurbished the Mustang for Jed because it was a convertible. Everyone assumed Jed would be able to tolerate the car's fumes with the top down. But no one, not even Jed, knew for sure.

For the first time since he'd met her, Charlotte was wearing clothes that belonged to her urban world—khaki slacks, strappy, sexy city sandals, a silk shirt, and movie-star sunglasses. She looked terrific, even with the baseball cap pinning her wonderfully crazy-curly hair to her head.

Jed held his hand above the top of the windshield and let the oncoming air smack his palm backwards. Charlotte laughed.

"I love this car!" she said into the wind. "Have you driven it into Santa Fe before?"

"No. I haven't been in Santa Fe in five months. I've never driven this Mustang anywhere until today!"

"This morning I realized that I haven't been out of Agua Dulce in almost two weeks. I didn't think two weeks in the middle of nowhere could go so fast!"

"The Agua Dulce trance," Jed said. "There should be a sign at the turn-off for County Road 155: 'This road goes to south nowhere, drive at your own risk. Journey out not guaranteed.'"

Jed slowed the Mustang as the wheels gripped the hard curve around the island of rock known locally as *la Cuchilla*, the knife. Charlotte looked up at the narrow peninsula of sandstone as they passed below.

"What's that cross stuck into the pile of stones there?" She pointed behind Jed's shoulder.

Jed braked and pulled the Mustang to a quick but controlled stop on the edge of the asphalt.

"The memorial for Benjamin Bill." He looked across the road at the weathered wood cross. "This is where Kitty Bill had her accident. It's also where the school bus slid off the road last winter."

Charlotte studied the red mesa looming over the road. Jed reached an arm over the seat, retrieved a bottle of perfume-free sunscreen and gave it to Charlotte.

"Thanks." Charlotte rubbed lotion onto her arms that were already turning pink and gazed back at the stone pile and the wood cross. "The stone pile for Benjamin is like the memorial for the soldiers."

"This sort of memorial is called a *recuerdo* by the Spanish folks," Jed said. "You'll see these roadside all over New Mexico. Usually they're decorated with bright plastic flowers and pictures and mementos."

"Why doesn't anyone decorate Benjamin Bill's?"

"If you walk over there you'll find all sorts of things—feathers, strands of ribbons, pearl buttons, coral beads, sage, wild flowers if they're in season."

"Who leaves them?"

"Uncle Barty made the little cross, and my mother helped him pile stones around its base. Then, according to my mother, Uncle Barty asked that people leave the memorial to the elements. No anniversary wreaths or holiday bouquets. Everyone honored his wishes. Everyone except my grandmother. To this day, that piece of holy ground is maintained by Conchata Lonewolf Bill and her ravens." Jed looked at Charlotte. "Or so they say."

Charlotte was skeptical, but she nodded. "Okay."

"My mother told me," Jed said, smiling. "And Bernadette Morley, R.N., M.S., secretary treasurer of the Arizona Society of Medical Professionals, will tell you without hesitation or apology that whatever has been placed on Benjamin Bill's *campo santo* these past forty years has been placed there by the angels."

Charlotte rubbed the lotion into her skin and pondered this information. "So it wasn't a raven but a raven *angel* that caused me to drive over that boulder a few weeks back?"

"I wasn't there." Jed put the Mustang into first gear and drove onto the highway. "You tell me."

゠゠゠゠゠゠゠゠゠゠゠゠

The St. Francis Hotel lobby was busier today than two weeks ago. The summer tourist season was in full swing, and Charlotte and Jed waited several minutes at the front desk for an available clerk.

"I was here two weeks ago with the conference for teachers," Charlotte told the clerk, "and my roommate left my bags here."

"Your name?" The clerk dug around a shelf under the front desk.

"Charlotte Lambert."

The clerk stood up and smiled widely.

"Oh, you're *that* woman!" He raised his eyebrow. "You're the friend who disappeared into the outback!" The clerk leaned across the counter and said in a loud whisper that everyone standing near the front desk could hear: "I understand now why you vanished!"

The clerk glanced at Jed, who was studying tourist brochures at the far end of the counter. If looks could kill, Jed's expression would have slain the clerk and taken his coiffed scalp, too.

"Do you have my bag, sir?"

The clerk disappeared into a back room. Jed walked along the counter and stood by Charlotte. "So, you're kind of famous around these parts, miss?"

Charlotte chuckled and shook her head. "The circumstances surrounding my disappearance have been greatly exaggerated."

"Here you are, Ms. Lambert." The clerk swung the bag over the counter with a flourish. "There's a letter here that was left for you."

The clerk gave Jed a last glance before turning to a couple waiting to check in. Charlotte took the white envelope and studied the familiar handwriting: Maddie's. Jed wandered across the lobby to admire the paintings on the lobby wall. Charlotte opened the letter and pulled out a single sheet of St. Francis Hotel stationery.

Char—If you are not reading this whilst riding horseback into the sunset with Prince Charming then you still have much work to do. Lose the maps and get on with it! Love you—Maddie

Charlotte folded up the paper and slid it back into the envelope. She slung her leather carry-on over her shoulder and joined Jed by the front doors.

"Well?" Jed asked. "Everything okay?"

"Yes, although I apparently still have some work to do."

Thirty minutes later Jed and Charlotte sat caught in traffic a block from the Santa Fe plaza. Jed had made two stops—one at a sporting goods store where he bought four stakes to secure his kitchen tarp, and a second at a bookstore where he bought several magazines and half a dozen paperbacks. Charlotte had hoped to get into one of the art museums, but when they came out of the bookstore Jed seemed anxious to leave town.

"Where are we eating lunch?" Charlotte asked. They were stopped beside a sidewalk café with a blackboard boasting the special of the day: red chile enchiladas with chicken.

"We're going out into the hills, to a restaurant that's been serving native foods since the late 1800s." Jed held the back of his wrist to his nose, suppressing a sneeze. His nose was runny and he was sniffling. Charlotte couldn't see his eyes under his sunglasses, but he kept dabbing at them with a tissue, so she assumed they were irritated, too. "We'll be there in about twenty minutes, traffic permitting."

Tour groups clustered at every corner, and large buses choked the narrow made-for-horses-and-buggies streets. The tincture bottle kept in the glove box had made one appearance since Dos Rios. It made a second appearance at a traffic light by the Federal Building.

Charlotte found her attention shift away from the quaint and colorful street scenes to the rumble of revving engines, the squeaking of brakes, and cars without mufflers idling beside the Mustang. Maybe it was because they were in a convertible or maybe it was because she was with Jed, but she had never felt so assaulted by fumes and industrial-strength emissions.

"We could put the top up," Charlotte suggested. Jed eyed her as he considered her suggestion. "I'm getting pretty sunburned, even with all this lotion on."

Jed swung the car into a convenience store parking lot and stopped. Charlotte leapt from the car and unfastened the straps she had seen Jed secure before they left Agua Dulce.

They were back on the road minutes later. Jed seemed pensive, so Charlotte talked about Maddie—not about the note, not about riding into the sunset with Prince Charming, but about how Maddie had told her she needed to develop her sense of improvisation and adventure, lose her compulsive need for itineraries and lesson plans. Surely she had done that in the last few weeks? Jed nodded but said nothing. Charlotte told Jed about the private school in Scarsdale, about her home that was once a carriage house, about how she might visit Harvard later this summer and look through her grandfather's files. She wanted to ask Jed if he was feeling okay, but decided not to.

The congestion and traffic finally lessened and Jed drove very fast up Opera Hill onto the highway west out of the city. Charlotte was relieved when the road began the descent into the brown and red plateau that was the beginning of the clean, wide-open country. On the farthest horizon Charlotte recognized the shoulder at the north end of the Agustinas edging up onto the landscape, so faint you would miss the mountain range if you did not know what to look for. On June twentieth Charlotte had missed the emergence of those faraway mountains that marked the Lágrimas Valley. A few weeks ago the Triassic badlands of Grandpa Al's Coelophysis quarry, the kingdom of fossil bones, wild horses, and raven angels, were not part of her story. Today, Charlotte's story included all of these. And although she was still learning what to look for, she was looking.

{33}

Jed exited the highway onto a paved two-laner that took them north through several small villages that were no more than a gas station and a post office. Between these hamlets were irrigated fields of alfalfa and young corn and pastures with sheep and goats. The road rose up into a pine forest. After several sharp hairpin curves around a deep canyon the road dropped down to a valley and a cluster of adobe houses and shops.

"Cundíyo," Jed said. He had stopped sniffling and opened his window. Charlotte did the same, and a wonderful piney-sage fragrance filled the car. "This restaurant, Rancho de Cundíyo, is in the oldest adobe structure in this county."

Inside the restaurant Jed asked the waitress to seat them on the terrace. They waited a few minutes in a cozy, Old West-style bar before the waitress came and led them up stone steps to a table shaded by large catalpa trees.

"This is just wonderful!" Charlotte said after they were seated. There were several dozen diners on various terraces and in the patio below, but the giant leafy trees made natural screens, and each table was sequestered and private.

"I won't be drinking, but I highly recommend the Cundíiyo margarita." Jed removed his sunglasses. Although he had taken several droppersful of Thea's tincture in the last hour, his eyes had a reddish hue around the rims.

Charlotte sipped her margarita and dipped corn chips into mild salsa. Jed drank ice water with lemon and leaned back in his chair while they waited for their green-chile-and-chicken enchiladas, the house specialty. Jed was drained. Charlotte was tired too, from the whirl and bustle of town. After spending weeks away from city life, her senses felt positively bombarded by its sounds and sights and nervous, frenetic energy.

"My ears are ringing." Charlotte twizzled a straw around the ice cubes in her margarita.

Jed smiled and leaned forward onto his elbows on the white-clothed table. "Don't drink that too fast. Tequila's a potent drug!"

"My ears, my whole body, seem to be reverberating with the city. I never noticed it before; frenetic energy like that is tangible."

Jed rubbed his cheek across his sleeve and sat up straight again. "Silence can be so dense it becomes a sound."

Charlotte smiled. "I've heard that sound. The night I met the burros I thought it was my heart beating. But it was the sound of all that silence."

She wanted to tell Jed that her heart was beating pretty hard right now because she was so happy, because he was such a good man, because she admired how he handled challenges and never called attention to his suffering. Today Jed wore a light-blue chambray shirt that emphasized his tanned face and arms and his shiny black hair. When he strode onto the patio every woman in the restaurant between the ages of fifteen and fifty lifted her eyes and followed the tall, narrow, preppy cowboy as he strode past their table. Jed seemed oblivious to the attention he garnered, which only made him more attractive.

Charlotte became self-conscious of her own appearance and pressed her fingers into the curls surrounding her face. Jed watched her, amused.

"I need a haircut," she said. "Maybe Arthur has a razor I could borrow?"

"You look just fine," Jed said.

"Speaking of Arthur, did you find him last night?"

Jed stared off into space. Charlotte was sorry she had brought up Arthur Varela.

"He wasn't home, so I left a message on the door to his trailer," Jed said, fingering his glass of water. "I told him to take the day off."

"Well, that's good," Charlotte's body was feeling very relaxed and very warm. Maybe tequila was the reason New Mexicans took siestas at high noon. "We all needed a day off."

Jed slid his hand across the table and took her fingers in his. "You've been a real trouper at the ranch, with Arthur and the GED work at the library, with Thea and her plant gathering."

Charlotte stared at her fingers melting into Jed's hot, brown hand on the white tablecloth. The sun streaked in and out of the catalpa leaves and sparkled in the water glasses, and a very gentle breeze moved Jed's hair. Her blood pumped like warm syrup through her head, down along the walls of her belly, and around the insides of her thighs. Her bones and muscles were softening to gel inside her skin.

"Jed Morley?" A short, stocky man stood at the end of the terrace. "Is that you, Jed?"

Jed looked over his shoulder at the man now walking toward their table.

"Jaycee!" Jed stood up and the two men clasped hands. "What are you doing in New Mexico?"

The waiter brought plates of enchiladas and set them on the table. Jed motioned for Jaycee to take a seat at their table, but he declined.

"I'm here looking at a project in Santa Fe." Jaycee smiled at Charlotte. "You must be the famous Beverly McDermott, the woman who lassoed Phoenix's bachelor of the year!"

"No, actually, this is my friend Charlotte Lambert." Jed turned to Charlotte, embarrassed by Jaycee's mistake. "Charlotte, this is an old Scottsdale friend of mine, Jaycee Rowland."

"Hello." Charlotte knew she should be embarrassed, but the margarita buffered all sense of social *faux pas*. She did, however, feel a sharp, hard twist of disappointment as her brain began to reprocess the fact of Jed's fiancée. She smiled at Jaycee and took another sip of the margarita.

"Pleased to meet you, Charlotte." Jaycee nodded at Charlotte. "Anyway, I'm here with my partners. Jed, are you visiting your family? Aren't you from these parts?"

"I am." Jed remained standing beside Jaycee. "I'm not just visiting. I've been here since winter. I took a leave from—"

"—Oh, wow, I remember now!" Jaycee frowned and bit his lip. "You got sick at the Camelback Club job. Terrible thing! Some kind of chemical poisoning? How you doing now?"

"I'm much better." Jed squared his shoulders. "I'm doing much better."

"Ned Luchetti is about finished with the clubhouse you started. Had a terrible time with the drainage on the north side of the tennis courts. But he worked it out. When you coming back?"

"Not sure yet."

"There's a lot of work in Santa Fe. You're probably in on that already."

"Not really."

"Hey, I've got to go. We have a three o'clock with the surveyor at this new site south of Santa Fe, in Cerrillos. A new four-star spa and resort compound. They want to use rainwater and recycled gray water in a greenhouse for orchids or something. The owners want to try this new-fangled solar cell membrane that mounts onto the walls. Very high-tech-low-tech. I'm ambivalent. I'd love your opinion, Jed. What's your schedule like this next week?"

Jed looked at the patio of diners on the terrace directly below them. He was giving the question some serious thought.

"I might be able to come and see it." Jed said finally. "Where're you staying?"

Jaycee pulled out a business card from his rear pocket and handed it to Jed. "You can reach me there at night. During the day I'm hard to find. Leave a message and I'll call ya back."

"Okay. I'll call you on Monday."

"Great! That's just great! Your opinion about this design, especially these prefab solar cells they're making in California, would mean a lot to all of us. Charlotte, nice to meet you."

Jaycee walked off across the terrace and Jed sat down again.

"Nice guy," Charlotte said, picking up her fork. "Looks like you could have work here."

"Yes." Jed studied her. "Sorry about the fiancee remark. I'm not engaged to Beverly anymore. Most of my friends don't know that yet."

"Oh," Charlotte said, pausing while this information sank into her tequila-slowed brain. She looked up at Jed. "Why haven't you told people?"

"Because I haven't seen people." Jed fingered his water glass and rubbed his eyes.

"Maybe you're still getting used to it, not being engaged."

"Maybe. Let's eat."

⁕⁖⁘⁙⁛⁘⁙⁖⁛⁘⁙⁖⁘⁙⁛

The leisurely hour under the old trees on the restaurant terrace spent staring across the table at the beautiful face of Charlotte, plus the prospect of interacting with Jaycee and his partners, of actually working again, cleared Jed's head and injected his entire system with purposeful optimism. When they returned to the Mustang in the restaurant parking lot, he unlatched the top and folded it back down.

Charlotte watched but did not ask about Jed's decision to put down the top again. She smiled, climbed into the car, and pulled the Durham baseball cap back onto her curly head. Jed liked the way she looked in that cap—she had the body of a woman, a finely endowed woman, but her skin and hair were unselfconsciously lovely like a young girl's.

The clean, invigorating air of the mountain country of Cundíiyo was all too quickly replaced by the dense late-afternoon haze of Dos Rios. Jed's resuscitated sense of purpose dwindled, then vanished in the blinking of a few traffic signals on the east side of town. As he maneuvered around an eighteen-wheeler that was jake-braking into a truck stop, he felt his system change direction. The breakdown he had fought all day had begun.

Jed likened the onslaught of systemic collapse to old Ned Saunders's description of how a river changes direction: the current drops down into a hole, gathers more energy in the vortex, sucks itself into a whirlpool, surges into a fury of foamy confusion, and finally pushes through the only outlet, which is into, over, and under itself.

Charlotte was still a little numb from the margarita and stared out the open window at the passing cars and strip malls, gas stations and construction sites that were strung along every inch of Dos Rios's main drag. Jed prayed he could hold off the more serious symptoms until they were through town. Jed did not want to pull over here, to stop and linger, gulp up any more toxic fumes, so he drove the Mustang in and around cars like a race driver. He pulled his bandanna from his pocket and wiped his nose and dabbed at his eyes. Charlotte noticed his distress and sat up in the seat.

The poison began to leach from Jed's lung tissue into his blood. It trickled out through his capillaries and seeped through the pores of his skin. The invasion was going to be total: inside and out, Jed was losing ground, losing balance. He swerved behind a pickup truck and aimed for the wide entrance to a supermarket parking lot. Through the cloudy haze he saw Charlotte's hands on the steering wheel.

"Stop now!" he heard her shout. Jed pushed his foot down on the brake and the clutch. Charlotte put the car in neutral and turned off the engine. She pulled the bandanna from his hand and tied it across his face.

"Where's the epi-kit?"

Jed tried to respond but his tongue had become a thick sponge in his mouth. He heard the glove compartment drop open and switched his brain back to breathing: in and out, in and out. One more breath in, one more out. From far across the car Charlotte gripped his forearm and pushed the sleeve of his shirt up, up, up, tighter and tighter. In and out, in and out. He could not swallow. Or maybe he was swallowing but had nothing to swallow. Just a thin string of air, in and out. The fierce pierce of the needle ignited sparks at the base of his skull and his mind dropped down into the last fire and hunkered over in the ashes. Jed waited. In and out. Swimming in the darkness. In and out. The current folded over and over on itself. Tumbling, squeezing, the river bed was so narrow, the rocks hard and bruising. Then he broke away. The river widened, opened, and he was over the falls, free again, in and out, in and out.

Jed stepped back from the hot fire at the base of his skull. Charlotte's hands grasped him and pulled him onto the shore. Her hands were everywhere, or maybe it was just the wish for her hands to be everywhere, but Jed followed her cool palms on his forehead, his arms, his throat, his chest, his wrists, his stomach, his heart. She massaged and soothed. He wanted to thank her but his tongue was still a sponge. He managed to swallow and heard her speaking:

"I'm going to put up the top, okay?"

Okay, Jed wanted to respond. Good idea. When he opened his eyes the Mustang was sealed from the outer world. Charlotte was seated beside him, the opened epi-kit and wrapper on the floor beside her purse. She watched him, her face compressed with worry.

"I'll be okay in a minute," Jed mumbled through the bandanna. He pulled it away so he could get more oxygen. "Just give me another minute."

"I'm going to drive us from here. Is there a doctor we should be seeing here in town?"

"No, no, there's no doctor. I'm fine now."

"Well, you're going to be fine, but right now you're going to change places with me. Can you move yet?"

Jed sat up in the seat. He looked at his wrists. Hives. Not giant hives, but tiny lizard-skin hives that would spread up his arms and across his stomach. Jed Morley: the reptilian outlaw.

"I can move." He didn't mean to sound so dim-witted, but his tongue was still claiming three fourths of his mouth, and his head hurt like it was wedged between river boulders. He really just wanted to close his eyes and fall asleep for a few days.

⁂

Charlotte recognized the Quick Stop where she had asked for directions to the Lágrimas weeks ago, and merged the Mustang into the left lane in anticipation of the junction with County Road 155 two blocks ahead. At least this time she knew where she was going. She stole a look at Jed. He was propped against the door, his head leaning into the window. He had pulled the bandanna back up over his mouth, but he seemed to be breathing normally.

It had been the most terrifying five minutes of Charlotte's life. She had never felt so completely responsible for someone else's survival. What if she had failed? She gripped the steering wheel and waited at the last traffic light. The turn for the county road to Agua Dulce was fifty yards ahead. She glanced again at Jed. Even in a bandit mask, his shirt wet with perspiration, his body limp with exhaustion, Jed was someone she very much wanted not to fail.

Charlotte turned the Mustang onto CR 155 and sped past the last trailer park on the south side of Dos Rios into the blessedly empty desert beyond. They would be in Agua Dulce by six o'clock.

"Why don't you pull over by that *arroyo* and we'll put the top down?" Jed had removed the bandanna and was watching the landscape fly past his window.

Charlotte saw the pullout Jed was referring to and stopped the Mustang. Jed was out of the car before she could unbuckle her seatbelt. He walked away from the asphalt and stood on the sand with his hands on his hips staring off at the sand hills. Charlotte left the car and began to unfasten the canvas straps. Two ravens landed on one of the perfectly shaped little sand hills and began to fluff and groom themselves. She looked to see if Jed saw them but he had already turned and was walking back to the car. She wanted to say something light-hearted about his ancestors keeping an eye on them, about how the ravens were always nearby when you stopped your car out here on the desert. But Jed had dropped down into a deep interior place and would not make eye contact with her.

Fifty minutes later, with not a word or glance between them in the car, the trees above the B & B Service Station and Repair emerged into view. Two minutes and two miles more, Charlotte reached the station and was on the road to the High Lonesome. Barty's truck was parked in the shade near the station wall.

"Keep going," Jed mumbled. "I'll see him later."

"Okay." Charlotte glanced in the rearview mirror. Barty stood in the back door of the repair shop, wiping his hands with a rag, eyes on the Mustang.

The two elderly sister mares, Molly and Mandy, stood side by side on the front porch of the ranch house. The pinto was fifty feet from the old dwelling, and she turned and trotted away toward the windmill when the Mustang reached the barn. Charlotte drove around the house, past the water tank and windmill and onto the dirt tracks to Jed's camp. They reached the end of the road and Charlotte switched off the engine. Jed climbed out of the car and walked to the front of the Mustang. He had on his sunglasses. Charlotte couldn't read his eyes, or anything in his face. Jed was absolutely expressionless.

"I can walk from here," he said flatly. "Take the car back to the Durhams."

Charlotte's stomach knotted around Jed's words. He was sending her away.

"Are you sure?"

Jed nodded that he was sure. He removed his sunglasses and looked at Charlotte for the first time in an hour. "I think we need to call it a day."

{34}

In the last light of late afternoon the High Lonesome ranch house looked just like its name. Charlotte took her foot off the gas pedal and let the Mustang drift to a stop by the water tank. The two sister mares watched from the house porch. Charlotte turned off the car engine, climbed out and walked toward the metal tank. The pinto was standing in the shade made by the windmill. Her head jerked up and her nostrils flared with alarm when Charlotte left the car.

"You don't have to run," Charlotte said evenly. Through her sandals she felt the heat held in the sand. "I'm here to, well, I just wanted to . . . I don't know what I just wanted to. This wasn't part of the plan."

The pinto was at full alert now, poised to bolt.

"Jed collapsed today. It was pretty bad for him in the city. But you know, it didn't bother me at all. It really didn't. I was a little scared that I wouldn't get that shot in right, but I did. And he recovered."

Charlotte was standing on the far side of the tank from the pinto. She placed her hands in the sun-warmed water. The windmill was absolutely still in the late afternoon heat.

"I thought things were pretty good between us. But just now he sent me packing. Yup, pinto, he told me to go. Called it a day."

Charlotte cupped water in her hand and splashed it on her arm. She took off the baseball cap and threw water over her hair until it dripped off the ringlets around her forehead. The pinto watched wide-eyed and terrified, but held her ground.

"I'd call it a day all right. And what a day it was!"

The pinto shuffled her feet and stretched her head around to look at the pasture behind—her escape route to the river and the shelter of the *bosque* trees.

"I know you're getting ready to run. You aren't a fighter so you're a flight-er. Run to safety. Go ahead, it won't hurt my feelings. I've used that route out of a confounding situation a few times myself."

Charlotte looked back at the ranch house. The old mares were rubbing their necks on the porch railing. The sun had begun to slide down the sky into the mountains. Puffs of perfect pink clouds hung on the tips of the Agus-tina's indigo shoulders. Francis said those little woolly clouds would begin to build each afternoon from now until late July when the monsoon season would begin on the Colorado Plateau. Charlotte couldn't imagine a mon-soon, even a short, hard rain shower, ever reaching this rock and sand desert, but everyone, including Jed, assured her it would come.

Charlotte splashed more water from the tank onto her shirt.

"It must be ninety-five degrees out here. He could have at least invited me to take a swim in the river."

The pinto flicked her ears and tail and the muscles in her shoulders twitched. Flies buzzed around the water tank.

It was not very nice to send a woman you've spent the last twenty-four hours courting and sparking on horseback under the stars and in a 1968 Mus-tang convertible under the azure summer sky on her way without so much as a *sorry I'm not feeling so well, could we meet tomorrow for breakfast?* Or *perhaps you'd like to come back tonight when I'm feeling better and we could watch the moon rise from a lovely ledge above the river?*

"And he's not even engaged anymore!" Charlotte yelled out. The pinto leapt sideways, turned a half circle and cantered into the desert. The horse stopped when she reached the first trees and glowered over her shoulder at Charlotte.

"Sorry." Charlotte pulled the cap back onto her wet head and dried her hands on her pants.

She sat in the car. The sun burned her forearms and she thought about putting up the convertible top. The two sisters walked off the ranch-house porch and around to the east side of the renovated building. They stopped in the shade and looked at Charlotte doing nothing. It was six forty-five. Barty would be out in the next hour to feed the horses. She didn't want to be sitting here when he came. She didn't want to explain how Jed had collapsed. It was, after all, her fault that he went into town.

She scanned the sky around the ranch house and over the river to her right. No ravens offering divine interference this evening. Just two dowager mares sizing up her inadequacies and one panicky pony who wanted nothing more in life but to be set out to pasture and ignored by humans. What would Grandpa say? He'd say, what do you want, Charlotte? Do you want to take flight, or stay and fight?

There was still time to enjoy the sunset. She started the engine and carefully, slowly, turned the Mustang around and eased its tires back into the ruts of the road. In her rearview mirror she could see the mares against the wall of the ranch house. They would have plenty to talk about tonight. Charlotte hoped Barty's legendary rapport with horses didn't include speaking in some equine tongue that would grant him access to what the mares had seen and heard around the water tank this afternoon.

Britches nickered when Charlotte approached the stone corral. She stroked his soft muzzle and then walked on through the cedar trees to camp.

"Jed? Are you here?"

Jed's chambray shirt had been tossed over the canvas chair in the camp kitchen, and the bandanna that had served as a mask through the Dos Rios traffic lay on the table alongside his collection of black stones. Charlotte walked to the tent and pulled back the flap. He was not inside. She stood in the clearing. There was a faint smell of wood smoke but no evidence of a recent fire in the firepit. The only sound was the low hum of the river.

She began the long descent down the stone steps to the river one-hundred-plus feet below. The steepness of the path and the sheer distance between the top of the cliff and the bottom of the *bosque* caused her stomach to flutter. So Charlotte held her gaze to the step directly below her sandaled foot.

Down in the trees, she removed her sandals and set them on a large flat boulder. The river was pink, reflecting the early evening sky, and little birds skimmed its surface for flies and bugs. Charlotte walked through the grasses to the sandy bank and stood with her feet in the current. The steady sound of the river echoed off the cliff walls, making the whole *bosque* reverberate with the same chord: musical, moving water.

Jed was not in the river or along its bank. Charlotte walked upstream. Jed sat on a rock, stark naked, beside a small fire. He was bent over a steaming kettle, inhaling deeply. She stopped. She could leave now. Jed would never know she was here. She stepped back and turned. Her bare foot snagged on a dry stick, snapping it beneath her.

"Charlotte?" Jed called.

"I'm sorry, I . . . ." she stammered.

Jed reached for a towel and wrapped it around his waist as he stood up.

"I'm imposing on you. I shouldn't have come here. You need your space. I'm sorry to intrude..." Charlotte headed back toward the path up the cliff.

"Charlotte, wait!"

She stopped. Jed walked across the sand to her. His hair was damp and pressed back away from his face. "I came down here to detox."

Charlotte faced Jed. "We had such a nice day. And then you sent me away."

Jed frowned and shook his head. "I couldn't invite you back to this." He lifted his arms at the trees and the cliffs surrounding them. "I sent you away so you wouldn't have to run away. Later."

"What do you mean?" She looked out at the river and up at the sky. "I envy you having *this* to come home to!"

Jed and Charlotte stared at one another. A long moment passed. Jed began to shiver.

"You're getting cold," Charlotte said softly. "Go back to the fire."

Jed continued to hold her in his searing gaze. "I'm sorry I was abrupt. I thought it was best." Jed looked at the river sliding past them. "I'm going back into the river. I don't want you to leave, Charlotte. But I can't say as I have much to offer if you stay."

Jed walked to the river, dropped the towel from his hips, and stepped out into the dusky-blue water like a perfectly flawed bronze god. He pushed his arms into the current, leaned forward and slid under the river's surface. Jed re-emerged downstream in an eddy made by boulders that had fallen from the cliffs. He stood up in the waist-high water, splashing and rubbing his face and chest.

Before her head had time to direct her pounding heart, Charlotte stripped off her shirt and bra, khakis and panties, and walked into the river. The water was jolting cold and she gasped loudly as she sank down on bended knees. The Lágrimas swirled up and around her neck, and swept her through the dusky canyon directly into Jed's legs. He reached under her arms and pulled her from the current. Her feet found the bottom of the river as Jed's arms slid around her waist, pulling her into him. They kissed long and hard. Jed's skin was smooth and cool, like hers, and everywhere Charlotte's hands moved she found the same narrow, hard body reaching, moving, finding its way through the river to her body.

They explored the liquid landscape of one another's flesh and bones. Then Jed took Charlotte by the hand and led her out of the river. They lay down near the warmth of the camp fire and made love like it was the first time, the last time, the best time of their lives. They made love until the eye of the three-quarter moon rose into the sky above the stone cliffs and spilled lunar light onto the ledges and into the hollows of the river canyon. When the water of the Lágrimas River shimmered like glass, Jed and Charlotte drew apart long enough to remember that they were two separate bodies.

"Why did you send me away?" she said into Jed's ear as she pulled on the silky strands of his black hair.

Jed looked at Charlotte beneath him, propping his weight onto his elbows. "It's not very romantic, inviting someone to share cactus tea and a smudge-fest of *chamiso heidondo*. I was hoping my life was returning to normal."

Charlotte ran her hand up Jed's spine. "I was hoping my life will never return to normal."

Jed kissed her neck. Charlotte gazed up at the branches of a cottonwood tree rustling with the night breeze. Stars shimmered in and out of the leaves silvery with the moon.

"Charlotte, I—"

Charlotte held a finger to Jed's lips. "For tonight, let's believe that this is precisely where our lives were always returning, okay?"

His eyes caught the glimmering movement of the river. "Okay."

{35}

Barty watched the Mustang cruise past the gas station and onto the highway. Alicia's daughter was driving back to Agua Dulce. The clock mounted over the tire rack said 6:35. Well, at least they got up early. Probably sipped coffee and watched the sun rise. Nothing better. Jed made a darn good camp breakfast over his fire. It was time he shared it with someone his own age. Barty really ought to be thankful that Charlotte had come to Agua Dulce. These were good steps in Jed's life, forward steps after nine months of illness and stagnation. So why was Barty so agitated? Jed wasn't doing anything Barty himself hadn't done.

Barty popped the hood on Rusty Manzanares's Chevy Suburban and peered in at the colossal V-8 engine. Everyone in Agua Dulce seemed agitated. Even the dead. Usually the Fourth of July marked the start of easygoing midsummer, and everyone in the Lágrimas settled into the hot days, languid nights that would not end until later July when the monsoons began. These early dawns and long dusks were meant to be savored, to be shared with friends. But this year the Fourth of July had unleashed an epidemic of gritty emotions, interpersonal disturbances and ugly confrontations. Mabel Duran accused Sheila Stiles of stealing her best Corningware casserole dish, and had proceeded to unpack the trunk of Sheila's sedan until she found the missing bowl at the bottom of a cardboard box holding dirty pots and pans. Sheila had claimed it was an honest mistake, but Mabel told everyone in the cemetery parking lot that she was going to press charges.

All the boys but Jed had come and played their annual game of poker around the wobbly card table out under the flying horse. Even Gus Treadle and Grant Strickland had come and stayed a few hours. Gus hardly ever went out at night— he said all those years riding with the posse around the desert in the dark looking for something or someone in some kind of trouble had taken away his ability to enjoy himself after the sun went down. And Grant almost never socialized with the boys because his wife and six, or maybe it was seven, children couldn't spare him gone that many hours.

Barty hadn't expected Jed to show up—he could see there was just no stopping the tide of attraction pulling Jed and Charlotte together—but he had really hoped that Arthur would put his hurt feelings aside and join the guys at the B & B for a night of Independence Day penny poker. Dennis said Barty was an old fool if he believed a young man like Arthur wanted to spend a night with old farts like himself playing cards and sipping home-brewed root beer.

Barty grabbed the wrench from the work counter and unscrewed the bolts holding the battery in place. Rosa Tomé's public tongue lashing of Arthur cast a shadow over the whole holiday for Barty. Rosa had gone too far. Yes, Arthur had some habits he needed to outgrow; his drinking and carousing with Dos Rios dropouts every weekend worried Barty, too. And Arthur could drive a *lot* slower, and lose the Chicano gangster wardrobe of muscle shirts and obscenely baggy denims. But Arthur did not deserve to be called a *cabrón*. And Rosa had no right to insult Arthur and his brother Lucho in front of Lucho's five-year-old daughter. Arthur had come a long way with his reading over the past two weeks. Charlotte said he might be able to get his GED by Christmas. And the children who came to the library each afternoon absolutely worshipped the ground Arthur walked upon. Especially his niece, Violeta.

Barty would have disappeared into the night in a reckless display of screeching tires too, if Rosa Tomé had called his family an inbred bunch of oversexed, unemployed drunks. Maybe Arthur had actually made the better choice when he disappeared in a dramatic rage instead of punching Rosa in the face and going to jail for assault.

But more than twenty-four hours had come and gone, and Arthur had not reappeared. When Barty coached these boys and someone missed practice, he'd go right up to their houses and knock on the front door and find out where they had gone and what they were up to. But Arthur was not a boy anymore. And Barty was not his coach. So Barty kept an eye on the open garage door and watched the highway for Arthur's Honda, and said incomplete but heartfelt prayers in English, Spanish and broken Apache to his mother's

Angelic Spirit and his father's Presbyterian God that the boy and his car were not upside down in a ditch somewhere.

At least Jed was okay. Barty had obsessed most of yesterday about the kind of toxins Jed was getting bombarded by in Dos Rios and Santa Fe. When he came for the Mustang and started it up for the first time, Barty had pretended to hear something missing in the engine. Jed popped the hood, stood over the engine and listened to the idle of the California Special's V-8, and understood exactly what his uncle was trying to do: stall Jed's first prolonged interaction with a metropolitan environment. Jed closed the hood, told his uncle that the engine and the man were going to be just fine, and drove off.

Barty listened to Jed push the three hundred and twenty horses bundled under the Mustang's newly repainted hood through their paces with the touch of an experienced and appreciative driver, and wondered if Jed knew that his uncle was not nearly as worried about Jed's contact with the industrial poisons of urban New Mexico as he was about Jed's interaction with the sublime and radiant daughter of Alicia Rose.

Replacing the Suburban's battery took all of fifteen minutes. Barty knew because he counted every minute as it passed on the wall clock. Still no Arthur. The Suburban needed its fluids flushed, and the air-conditioning hose was fraying. But all of this could wait. Rusty said he would be back in Agua Dulce tomorrow, Tuesday, at the earliest—Rusty was a big collector of antique guns and had gone to a Civil War show over in Barstow this weekend.

Barty wiped his hands on a rag, walked into the office, and flipped the OPEN sign to CLOSED. He knew he was losing business and folks would be disgruntled with him, closing this early on a Monday morning. But Barty knew Jed would be trying to set the bond beam in the new room by himself. And Barty was curious as hell about Charlotte and Jed's Sunday in town. Better to get the facts than to let his imagination run away like some spooked horse. When Barty saw Jed, talked to him face to face, he would know that Jed was okay. He would know that this was 1998, not 1959, not 1976; today, July sixth, was a new day that did not and would not resemble any day of the past.

Barty parked his truck under the cottonwood tree closest to the High Lonesome barn. He could see his nephew straddling the top of the new adobe wall, hammer in hand. Barty waved to Jed and went into the barn to retrieve his tool belt and gloves. The two sister mares, Molly and Mandy, and Noches and Dolly were already at the corral feed trough—Jed had given them their oats and hay—but the five horses wandered to the barn door anyway to see what Barty was doing.

"Hey, ladies." He had several carrots tucked into his shirt pocket. He pulled them out and walked to the mares. "Here Dolly, Noches, Molly. A few manners, Mandy!"

The mares took their treats and walked into the open sun, flicking their tails at flies. Barty walked behind them across the sand toward the house where Jed was pounding nails into a two-by-twelve plank. The pinto watched them all from beyond the windmill. Barty had a carrot in his pocket for the pinto, too, but he'd have to leave it for her: it was an unspoken agreement between them—the pinto's apple or carrot was left on the east side of the stock tank, and the other mares did not go near the stock tank until the pinto had retrieved her treat.

"I'm coming up, Jed." Barty walked the circumference of the new eight-foot-high adobe walls. Jed had built the walls of this room higher than the others so it would have good ventilation. Until the tall adobe walls were secured by the planks that became the bond beam, they were wobbly. "Have you seen Arthur?"

Jed scooted two feet further along the plank and began to hammer another nail. "Haven't. I was hoping you had. Hand me the next board before you climb up."

Barty slid the twelve-footer up to Jed who pulled it onto the top of the adobe wall in front of him. Barty moved the ladder over to the next section, climbed up, and positioned himself. They talked between hammering.

"How was the Mustang? That timing belt okay?" Barty looked back at his nephew straddling the wall six feet behind him. "I still think it's running a bit fast, the idle."

Jed squinted off at the barn. Noches and Dolly were readying for a nap under the cottonwood tree. "The car was just great. What an engine! But I behaved myself."

"Good. Nana would have tanned my hide if I put you in a car that got a speeding ticket first time out."

"No laws were broken."

They each hammered another few nails and then scooted along their respective planks.

"I had an episode."

Barty swiveled his torso on his hips and faced Jed. "A bad one?"

"Yes, no—I'm fine." Jed went on hammering.

"Did you need the epi?"

"I did. Charlotte stuck me."

Barty banged his hammer down on the wood, missing the nail head entirely. "It was too soon, going into the city like that!"

"I had to find out. I got caught in some truck traffic and didn't get the top up fast enough. Next time I'll know."

"Next time! Jesus Christ, Jedidiah! How can you think about next time?" Barty threw his leg over the wall and turned completely around and faced Jed. "You don't want a total systemic collapse again like last November, do you? You're doing real well, but your body is still pretty sensitive, evidently. I know you want to—"

"—to live a life?" Jed hooked his hammer into his tool belt and stood up on the beam that was now secured onto the wall and would bond adobe to adobe, corner to corner, for a good century or more. "I thought I was past that kind of reaction. But I'll keep trying. I have to. How can I accept living in a cow camp for the rest of my life?"

Barty looked at Jed towering above him. "You can't think of it that way, for the rest of your life. Nothing is ever for the rest of your life. Even when you want it to be."

Jed walked across the wall to the top of the ladder. "Exactly, so I'll keep trying, keep testing the water, or the air. Because I know I can't forget about the rest of the world. You know, I saw an old partner of mine from Phoenix, Jaycee Rowland, and he asked me to consult on a project he's doing in Santa Fe. My first thought was, no, I'm not who I used to be. But then I thought I have to stop thinking of myself as sick, and start doing things that reinforce my idea of healthy. And hope my body will follow along. I'd rather collapse than not try to step back into the world."

Jed pushed two-by-twelve planks up to Barty and then moved the ladder around to the east wall. Back on top of the wall, he resumed hammering. After a few minutes Jed stopped and looked at Barty across the open space defined by the walls.

"Old Farley kind of spooked Charlotte out by the school on the Fourth."

"What?!" Barty held his hammer in midair. "Why didn't you tell me? Where? When?"

"It was probably just a coincidence, but she ran into him out there in the old playground when she went looking for me. Remember? Thea sent her with a bottle of tincture. I'd already left. Farley was lurking around and he scared Charlotte about out of her skin."

"Why didn't she file a complaint with the sheriff?" Barty set the hammer down on the board. "It's never a coincidence with Farley. The cops should know."

"She didn't want to make a big deal about it," Jed said. "I think she's embarrassed about what happened to her mother here. She'll just avoid Farley while she's here."

The image of Farley anywhere near Alicia's daughter made Barty's stomach fold over. He picked up the hammer and slapped it sideways into his palm.

"Gus Treadle told me that Farley went AWOL for close to eight hours last night. Mabel and everyone at the boardinghouse were hoping he'd met his maker in an alley somewhere. They were planning his post mortem—including a cake and ice cream—but then the ol' bastard came limping back into the house just after breakfast this morning. He offered no explanation. Said his business was nobody's business but God Almighty's."

"What can Farley possibly do for eight hours without a car?" Jed counted nails in his pouches. Barty slid an unopened box of nails down the plank to him.

"Farley still goes out to that disgusting Airstream parked by the old landfill. Bribes Earl for rides with cigarettes. You ever been out there?"

Jed shook his head no.

"Well, you imagine what the filthiest place to live would look like and then you double, no triple that, and then you add the fetid, foul stench of a smoldering heap of garbage. Put the devil in the dead center of that picture, surrounded by animal skins and carcasses collected like trophies over the years, and you have Farley's lair by the landfill."

"You told me he kept a string of horse ears—one from each of the mustangs he shot down. Is that true?"

"It is. I saw those ears myself when I was with the sheriff." Barty looked down the wall at his nephew. "Not Duende's ears. I only had a quick look at that string of coup, but I looked hard and the Thoroughbred's ears were not there."

"Why were you at Farley's with the sheriff? When was that?"

"1976. When they were looking for Alicia, before they—before I—found her body. A rancher from over past Ned's place said he'd seen Farley's truck at the end of the county road the same day Alicia arrived. But Farley had an alibi."

"What was it?"

The alibi: the big black wall that stopped any investigation into Farley's obsession with Alicia. The alibi that prevented the sheriff from getting a subpoena to search Farley's trailer.

"Virgil Lujan swore that Farley was playing dominoes with him at his *ranchito* on the river. Farley never plays dominoes. It's against his religion. And everyone from Dos Rios to Agua Dulce knew Virgil lived in terror of Farley because Farley had something on him."

"What did he have on Virgil?"

"Well, if we knew exactly, he wouldn't have it on him, but my best guess is it had to do with some land title papers and Virgil's sister's will. Supposedly back in 1961, Maria, Virgil's sister who lived in St. Louis, died and left her section of land to her cousin, Chancy, not to her younger brother, Virgil. It was just a theory, but people suspected foul play around the sister's will. It went lost. People had seen it, but couldn't find it. The judge gave Maria's land to her next of kin, Virgil. My guess is Farley found the missing will in the landfill—saw Virgil throwing it into the dump. Farley can't read but he recognized legal papers when he saw them. I'm bettin' Farley saved the papers and used them on Virgil for the rest of his life."

"So Virgil did whatever Farley wanted for years?" Jed asked.

"Yeah. You remember ol' Virgil Lujan: more stupid than mean. He died when you were at Stanford."

"So how'd you see the string of horse ears if the sheriff couldn't get into Farley's trailer?"

"He was wearing it around his neck the afternoon we went out there. Met us on the trailer steps. Kept fingering those shriveled appendages like talismans. Even Sheriff Davis, a fine lawman and a veteran of many a nasty crime scene, said later he'd never in all his days encountered such a dark and ugly human as Farley."

Jed looked off at the barn, his face knit with worry.

"Keep Charlotte away from him, Jed."

Jed looked at his uncle. "I will. You say Farley had a false alibi? Does that mean you think he had something to do with Charlotte's mother's death?"

Barty shrugged. "I don't know. Sometimes I just can't shake the idea. . . ."

Couldn't shake the image of Farley the day they brought out Alicia's body and placed it into the ambulance. Couldn't shake the way when Barty rode past Farley sitting in his truck he was positively gloating. Farley's face beaming with the satisfaction of a job well done. And the law could do nothing about it because of Virgil Lujan's lie.

"Charlotte should hear you talk about this. Your theories would mean a lot to her."

Barty shook his head. "I don't know. Maybe she's better off walking away from it all."

"Like you have?"

"She's young." Barty held Jed's gaze. "She can put this all behind her. Move on."

"You're thinking she can't move on with me, aren't you?" Jed asked. "I know you know that she stayed the night at the cow camp."

Barty dug into the leather pouch of the tool belt and pulled out four more nails. He held three in his teeth and began to hammer the fourth into the bond beam. He knew Jed was waiting for him to respond, but Barty really didn't know what to say. Two nails later he stopped hammering. "I saw her drive the Mustang into Agua Dulce this morning."

"It was a good thing. It is a good thing. We have a nice understanding."

Jed turned around on the beam and began to hammer. Barty did the same. After a few minutes of intense pounding, they both stopped and looked up at the landscape surrounding them: mountains to the southwest, river to the east, canyonlands of red hills, yellow rock chimneys, and burnt mesas to the north and west.

Jed smiled and looked back at Barty. "Good view?"

Barty smiled and wiped perspiration from under his hatband. "Good view."

"Seems changeless, but it isn't. In the months I've lived out here, I've seen things come and go I never knew existed on this desert. It might look the same, but this landscape reinvents itself every moment. It's all new."

"What are you getting at, Jed?" Barty spoke through a nail held between his lips.

"What I'm getting at is that *her* name was Alicia, and she was here in 1959. This *here* is in 1998, and *her* name is Charlotte."

Barty nodded. "Same families."

"It's just the circumstances of life that brought us all together." Jed dug in his pouch for nails and slipped two between his lips. "I'm sure Grandmother Conchata has something profound to say about now."

Barty looked off at the barn. "Can't say. All these years, whatever your grandmother's had to say she's said to Nana Thea. Sometimes to your mother, too. But I'm out of the loop. Always have been."

Jed swung his legs to the inside of the wall. "No, you've never been out of the loop. You've just been a skeptical recipient of Conchata's heavenly observations."

"Nana told you that, didn't she?" Barty smiled.

Jed laughed and nodded. "She did."

Barty's gaze moved past Jed to a cloud of dust on the road beyond. "We've got company."

{36}

Thea and Charlotte had walked into the barn by the time Jed and Barty reached them. Jed veered off to the corral where Charlotte was talking to the mares. Barty knew where he'd find Thea—in the storage room.

"Nana?" Barty called inside the barn.

"In your office!"

Barty stepped into the dusty, roughhewn room that served as the High Lonesome Ranch office. It was hardly an office, as there was a desk but no chair and the phone wasn't hooked up anymore. Thea, dressed in a floral printed dress that hung from her angular shoulders like a flouncy curtain, stood in the middle of the room. She held a Thomas J. Webb coffee tin triumphantly in the air.

"Where'd you find this?" Thea smiled at Barty.

"It was with the rest of the camping equipment up in the loft. I should have looked there first."

"Is Jed here too?" Thea leaned around and peered into the barn behind Barty.

"He is." Barty motioned out through the barn doors. Jed and Charlotte were talking out in the corral. "You know he had an episode yesterday."

"Charlotte told me." Thea took Barty's arm and with the coffee tin tucked against her body like a football, walked out of the office. "But they did just fine. Has Arthur come in?"

Barty led Thea through the doors and out to the corral railing. "No. Haven't seen hide nor hair of Arthur since Saturday at the picnic."

"Charlotte is supposed to meet him today at the library." Thea clung to the middle railing of the corral. "We saw Dennis before we came here. He told me that friend of Arthur's, what's his name, Chico? Chico was arrested on the Fourth. Drugs in his car. No one knows if Arthur was involved."

Barty pulled the baseball cap lower on his forehead. Jed and Charlotte stood beside the trough watching the water from the hose fill the tank.

"I hope to God he wasn't, Nana. Arthur was pretty upset with Rosa Tomé that night. That's when he does stupid things—when he's hurt and angry."

"That's when we all do stupid things, Bartholomew."

Jed turned off the hose, walked across the corral and climbed onto the fence. "Nana, good morning. What a fine dress you're wearing today."

Thea reached out her slender hand and grasped Jed's forearm. "You had an episode?"

"I did. But I recovered quickly."

Thea leaned into the corral and peered through the railing at Charlotte standing by the water trough. "Well, there's always more to healing than shots and tinctures. I'm going to take this coffee tin home with me."

"Is that all you came out here for, Nana?" Barty asked.

Thea tapped her fingernail on the lid of the coffee can. "I haven't seen the High Lonesome in months." Thea's opaque glassy eyes grazed the space between Jed and Charlotte. "Bartholomew, why don't you give me a tour of the new construction?"

Thea stood in the middle of the new room holding the coffee tin against her chest. Barty pulled two more boards over to the ladder preparing to slide them up onto the top of the wall, although he wasn't sure he and Jed would return to the work before lunch. Charlotte and Jed were walking out to the pasture with treats for the horses that had come up from the *bosque*. And Thea seemed in no hurry to leave.

"Never thought I'd stand in this old house with you again," Thea said. "Strange how life has a way of turning our beliefs around."

Barty said nothing. He knew what Nana was getting at and he wasn't going to bite into that topic.

"This is like a ruin in reverse," she said, pointing a finger at the sky framed by the new adobe walls. "Like the pueblo ruins we used to visit. But this ruin is lifting up out of the dust."

"How much can you see these days?" Barty liked this time during the building process, too, when a house had only sky for a ceiling.

"I can see color and light." Thea dropped her eyes to the coffee can held against her chest. "But I cannot see the gray anymore." She lifted her eyes to the space between her body and Barty's. "I see the beginning and the end. Conchata says that is enough now."

"I'm sure it is. I'm going to get back up and finish securing this beam before it gets much hotter. Let me walk you back to the barn."

"Wait another moment, Bartholomew." Thea stood in the doorway gazing into the hot sunshine. "Where are they?"

"They're out with the horses that have come up from the river."

"What are they doing?" Thea found Barty's sleeve and held onto it.

"Well, they're talking, standing with the horses,"

"Oh, Bartholomew. You've forgotten how it is with new lovers. They aren't standing with the horses, they are the horses! The horses, the sky, the grass, the sun. Don't you remember how when you're in love you're part of everything that is beautiful?"

"I haven't been in love in almost half a century. Come on, let's walk back to the barn."

"You're in love right now."

Barty frowned. "What are you talking about, Nana?"

"Whenever someone we love is in love, we share their delight." Thea closed her eyes and drew in a long breath as if love were a fine fragrance in the air around them.

"Well then, I reckon we have to share their sorrow, too. And we see it coming way before they do."

"Oh, you are a pessimistic grump! Come on, show me the camping gear."

Thea shuffled alongside Barty to the barn. She seemed very slow today, very frail. When they reached the office Barty unfolded an old lawn chair and made Thea sit down. "I'm going to go and ask Charlotte to take you home. Drink this water. I'll be right back."

"No, no, I'm fine." Thea took a long sip from the canteen. "Tell me how we used to get to Apache Ridge and the name of that high meadow where you and your father used to camp when you were a boy. Do you remember it?"

"I do." Barty realized that Thea was not going to let him leave, so he sat down on a wood crate. "That high meadow is set in a bowl surrounded by rocks and it is one of the most beautiful places on earth. High and green. The wildflowers should be in full bloom just about now."

"Tell me the name of that place."

"My father used to call it the summer camp."

"And that was where you set Iota free?"

"How did you know about that?"

"Conchata told me years ago." Thea held the coffee tin on her lap as she sipped from the canteen. "But she never gave the place a name."

Barty did a quick review of dates and timelines: Conchata died in December of 1952. He had taken Iota up to the meadow in the spring of 1953. Dennis was the only person who knew Barty had set Iota free in the mountains. Everyone else thought Barty had given the three-year-old mare to one of his cousins over on the reservation.

"Here's what I want to know, Nana: how is it that my mother gives you certain information that is absolutely right on the mark, and then other times she says nothing at all, and the slings, arrows, and catastrophes of men, horses, and weather broadside us without warning?"

"Because Conchata's not all here." Thea pursed her lips and squinted her eyes until they were almost closed. "And I'm not all there. Yet. Now show me the panniers you found." Thea's eyes were closed now and she tipped her head back until it touched the aluminum top of the chair. She was asleep.

Barty left the office and walked back to the unused stall closest to the rear door of the barn. The panniers and tarps were laid out on several worktables where Barty had begun to clean the ancient pack gear after he and Jed pulled it all down from the loft. Once the dust and dirt was removed, the leather and canvas panniers his father had ordered from a company in Kansas didn't look a day older than the first time Barty had watched his father assemble them in this very barn for their inaugural pack trip into the Agustinas some fifty-five years ago.

With a rag Barty began to rub saddle soap into the leather latigo strap of one of the panniers. He would do what Nana wanted and clean and restore the equipment. He would help Jed rebuild the ranch house and make it livable. He was not a pessimistic grump. He was a grumpy realist. A pessimist would not have restored the Mustang, would never have asked Charlotte to tutor Arthur, and would for certain have turned and walked away the first time he laid eyes on that starving, skittish, impossible pinto in Ike Finlay's corral. Barty was just a realist: he took life as it came, kept up with his end of a task, didn't burden his friends and family with the details of his aches and pains, and never looked back.

"Bartholomew!" A soft voice called. Barty went to the door of the stall and looked into the barn. No one. He walked to the office and leaned in the door, still carrying the leather strap and the rag with saddle soap. Thea was sound asleep on the chair. Maybe Conchata had called out to him; or perhaps it was Benjamin, hoping to have a talk with his grumpy father.

And he did remember being in love. Remembered how everything that was good and fine seemed suddenly to be part of his world. Everything was forgiven when you were in love, when someone loved you. But then love ended or was snuffed out: Kitty lost Benjamin and divorced Barty; Alicia left without saying goodbye and returned to Boston sick and confused. The same week that Ruth Rose arrived to visit the fossil camp, Alicia got the stomach flu. Barty and Alicia were never alone after Ruth came to Agua Dulce. Not a word was exchanged between them ever again, except in Barty's letters that Alicia never once acknowledged or answered.

Just like the summer of '59, the worry stabbing at Barty's stomach was Farley. Farley was just too close to Charlotte and his actions were never coincidental. They were premeditated, precise to the darkest detail. If Farley had his sights on Charlotte, then Barty needed to keep his sights on Farley.

Barty walked the length of the barn as he rubbed the saddle soap into the leather strap. He never did give Thea the directions to Apache Ridge. It wasn't hard to get there. He could ride that trail with his eyes closed. Why did she want to know? Barty set the oiled strap back down on the work table and stared into the dust drifting across the slice of sunlight angling in through the stall door. Was he expected to be the trail boss, take the reins, and push the family herd across the frontier to safety? What did he know? And why couldn't Conchata see how much everyone, including her son, was in need of a little clarity and guidance about now?

{37}

The Independence Day parade and picnic had left Farley dazed and confused. It was a challenge to keep his eyes on the prize while surrounded by so much foolish patriotism to a government that promoted sin and lawlessness. But he waited, watched, kept his focus. He'd almost corralled her in the school yard when the dead Apache witch thrust her poison between them and rescued her. Farley had hobbled back to the highway where God rescued his faithful servant and brought along some man and his fat wife who about ran down Farley standing in the middle of the road. They had to give him a ride.

When he reached the boardinghouse Mabel and the boarders were sipping fizzy lemonade on the front porch and talking about the fireworks like they were the stuff of miracles. Farley went right up to his room. With the army-issue binoculars hard against his eyeballs, he pressed his face close to the screen of the third-floor window and waited. An hour and more passed and then he saw them emerge from the shadows half a block from Mabel's. Cunning to come from the east, and so close Farley could hear the stallion's breath passing through his black nostrils, could hear the witch chanting her spell into the ear of her captive.

Farley followed their progress between the houses, in and out between the parked cars, until they slipped from sight up the side street. Farley stuck his head out into the night and listened: the cloven hoofs of the devil horse cut the night silence like gun blasts. Then silence. Farley collapsed onto his bed, wheezing, convulsing. The time had come.

Farley did not leave his room all of Sunday. Mabel knocked on the door but he did not speak to her. When she returned late afternoon and threatened to call the public health department, Farley hobbled to the door, opened it two inches, and told her to go away.

Sunday evening. Mabel and the boarders were watching a game show, eating popcorn, and drinking beer. Farley could hear them from the third-floor landing. It was the same every Sunday night, winter or summer.

Earl Turnball stepped out of his room one flight down and looked up at Farley. Earl said nothing, but Farley knew Earl was thinking it was time for a smoke. Farley fingered his tattered shirt pocket as if he had a pack of Marlboros tucked against his chest, then nodded at his room. Earl came up the stairs and stood in his doorway.

"What do ya want for 'em tonight?" Earl asked.

Farley shrugged. "The car." He pulled the crumpled pack of cigarettes from his trunk. "For a few hours."

Earl frowned and glanced down the stairs. Mabel was shouting at the television, telling the contestant not to take the money. "What are you going to do with my car for a few hours?"

"You want the smokes, you give me the car and don't ask questions!"

Earl idled the Falcon out of the alley behind Mabel's to where Farley waited on the curb.

"What ya tell 'em?" Farley asked Earl as he climbed out of the car.

"No one saw me leave." Earl made a grinding sound as he tried to clear the nasal drip that coated his throat and filled his ears.

"Good." Farley pushed Earl aside and fell forward into the car. It hurt like hell, but he managed to bend his knees and position himself under the steering wheel.

"Where are you going?" Earl leaned to the window but pulled back when he saw Farley's face. "You don't have a license. If you wreck my car you'll have to pay for it."

Farley's mistake had been staying out all night. It meant Earl was angry and Mabel was suspicious. But Farley had no choice and he'd done exactly what was needed: he had retrieved the old rifle he kept in his trailer—there was no way Farley could get the Winchester down the stairs and out to the Falcon without being seen—and he had buried the rifle under the blankets in the trunk of Earl's car. The rifle was cleaned and loaded. Earl never opened the trunk and if he did he would see nothing but his old wool Pendleton heaped like always under the jumper cables.

The spare car key was now Farley's, removed from the magnetic box under the front fender. He could never have crawled under the front end and pulled down that little box but for the great goodness of the all-knowing, all-providing Lord. Farley had driven north toward Dos Rios on the county road, and was heading back slowly to Agua Dulce, not ready to go back to Mabel's, when out of the darkness a hitchhiker had appeared, one arm outstretched like half a cross in the headlights. Farley pulled the car over. The boy was already a criminal. Farley saw it in his clothes and the dark of his eyes.

"My car broke down in Dos Rios," the boy said as he peered in at Farley in the dark car. "Isn't this Earl Turnball's Falcon?"

"None of your business." Farley snapped.

"Can I catch a lift into Agua Dulce?" The boy tapped his fingers on the rim of the window, nervous the way sinners are when they know they're being scrutinized.

"Climb in." Farley had seen this boy with Barty Bill in the hardware store. This sinner was connected. Farley drove very, very slowly down the highway because every nerve in his body was burning. Not just from the exertion of pushing the gas pedal with his swollen foot. No, it was the boy: be still and hear the Lord thy God speak through the lowliest criminals amongst you.

"You work at the gas station?" Farley asked.

"Sometimes. Mostly I work at the High Lonesome."

"With Barty?"

"Yeah." The boy looked at Farley. "But I'm studying to go to college."

"Studying?"

"At the library. With the teacher staying at the Durhams."

"Teacher at the Durhams?" Farley's heart jerked sideways.

"Visiting from New York."

"Curly hair, white skin . . . ." Farley's hands left the wheel.

The boy turned and stared hard at Farley. He did not answer.

Farley's hands had begun to perspire but he held the car on course. "Where do you meet?"

The boy's fingers had tapped the window ledge, nervous. He knew he was trapped and his only way out was to comply. "At the library."

"That the only place you see her?"

"She likes the horses at the High Lonesome." The boy shifted in his seat and cleared his throat. "You can leave me here at the corner."

Farley braked the car to a full stop at the red light at Main and Dos Hermanos. The boy pulled back the handle and opened the door. Farley reached across the seat and hooked the fabric of the boy's shirt between his gnarled knuckles. "She go looking for the horses every day?"

The boy pulled away and leaned his weight out of the car. As his hand pried Farley's fingers apart and he slid free, the boy gave Farley what the Lord intended him to have: "She loves the horses so she visits them every day."

The boy had slammed the door and jogged around behind the Falcon and down Dos Hermanos. Farley did not see the light change to green because he was seeing how and when he would *finally* finish this hell on earth. That's when Farley had remembered the key in the magnetic box over the right wheel. Farley swerved across the intersection and down Dos Hermanos. The boy was still jogging, was nearly to the end of the block. Farley almost ran him down he drove so close. The boy stopped and blinked into the headlights.

"Get the key under the car." Farley opened the door and toppled down onto the pavement. The boy stared down at him. "Right there! I can't git to it!"

The boy shuffled to the side of the car and stared at the wheel well.

"Reach under!" Farley barked. The boy groped about the metal over the tire. "Find it?"

The boy pulled the box free and stood up. Farley lurched at the boy's hand and took the box. The boy stepped away into the dark and Farley crawled into the Falcon, slammed the door and drove into the night with the key to the Kingdom in his hand.

{38}

This morning Charlotte had wanted to tell Thea about the dream she'd had last night. But it was awkward as Charlotte had woken up from the dream in Jed's sleeping bag. Everyone knew Charlotte had spent Sunday night out at the cow camp. But the details, well, they belonged to Jed and Charlotte.

It was such a vivid dream: the cliffs of stone rose several hundred feet into space, the space filled with stars, and the stars sparkled in the twilight between night and day. Some of the stars were not stars at all but were the eyes of the horses: four or five of them, maybe six, sleek and gleaming in the starlight, the dawn brushing their flanks and necks, catching the curve of their elegant heads as they bent down to Charlotte. The heavens were the home of the bone horses.

That's what Charlotte woke saying: the heavens are the home of the bone horses. Jed stirred and slid his arm back under the sleeping bag and around Charlotte's waist. The dawn pushed back the night's last shadows and the bodies of the horses faded until only their kind eyes remained a flickering memory in the pink sky. Jed nuzzled Charlotte's neck, and she said it again:

"The heavens are the home of the bone horses."

Jed lifted his head and opened his eyes. "I know."

Charlotte studied his face, the stubble of beard, his black hair pushed away from his high forehead, his tan neck. "How do you know? Did you dream about them, too?'

Jed turned his head and his eyes focused on her. He smiled, puzzled. "Dream about them? It's a story I've heard all my life. I mean, not about the bone horses, just the horses. The bone horses are your family's story, evidently."

Jed's hand ran down Charlotte's torso and past her hip to her thigh. She pressed her body into him and felt him hardening against her belly.

"No, this was a dream, not a story." She looked past Jed's shoulder at the clouds in the lightening sky. The dream was already fading. Only a feeling remained: a sense of having touched something that belonged to her mother.

Charlotte drew herself up against Jed. He slid his leg over her thigh and pushed his fingers into the curls over her ear. "We probably should get up and start a fire for breakfast."

"Yes, Thea has a big project for me and if Arthur calls . . . ." But Charlotte's thoughts about the day ahead were lost because Jed slid inside her and she was carried back into the formless euphoria on the other side of dawn all over again.

Monday afternoon and Arthur had not yet called Charlotte. She hoped he was out at the High Lonesome working with Jed and Barty. Safe. Reading his books. Still on track to the GED. She would call Arthur later today, before she went back out to the High Lonesome. They could meet tomorrow and make up for lost time.

Before Thea had retired for her nap she had placed the sixty-year-old notebook of Conchata Lonewolf Bill on the kitchen table.

"Use that book-binding tape Inez gave you," she told Charlotte. "Make this old book strong. And see if you can read the writing." Thea tapped the cardboard surface of the notebook held together with velvety soft leather laces. "I can't see these words anymore. You must tell me what is smudged or faded."

Alone in the kitchen Charlotte reassembled the torn and frayed pages of medicinal recipes, salves, tinctures, teas, and dressings. Using the archival tape from the library she reattached the yellow pages to the center spine and secured the front and back covers. After almost two hours of work, Conchata's notebook was in one piece. It would still need the extra security of the laces to keep the loose scraps of paper and bits and pieces of dried plants from slipping out. And the valuable notebook really needed a protective container. Charlotte would ask Inez if the library had an archival box she could buy.

Charlotte leafed through the pages covered with Conchata's lettering—childlike, but with an elegant swerve to the "t's, l's and b's." The ink on some pages was smudged by water or perspiration or by the pollen from some ancient flower. Thea said Bernadette could help decipher Conchata's notes and abbreviations, and would be in Agua Dulce in August.

August. Where would Charlotte be in August? And how would Jed's mother feel about Charlotte, the stranger who moved into her room, borrowed her clothes and bedded her son?

Maybe Conchata had a *remedio* for nervousness and doubt. Charlotte turned the fragile pages. One section was organized by disorders: stomach, liver, lungs, mouth, sinuses, joints. Charlotte was impressed at how detailed and clinical Conchata's knowledge of so-called folk medicine actually was. Some remedies had page-long summaries that included not only the pharmaceutical properties of a plant but also the local myth and history of its uses: a plant called *canutillo*, Mormon tea, was used to cure urinary infections and subdue venereal diseases. Conchata had drawn the plant, a leafless bush of small sticks. Several pages were devoted to *osha*, a root that could be chewed, boiled into tea, or powdered into a syrup. The old people of New Mexico believed that a piece of the root tied to an ankle or pinned inside a garment could ward off rattlesnakes, bad omens, and evil spirits.

And what would Conchata recommend for ambivalent lovers? Was there a root or dried flower that could be tucked into Charlotte's pocket, slipped into Jed's saddle bags that would make their passionate attraction to one another somehow fit into their lives? Jed told Charlotte in the wee hours of the morning about his very public liaison with society headliner Beverly McDermott. And Charlotte shared with Jed the train wreck she herself had instigated that had brought about her broken engagement to Michael Norton. They both agreed that the past and the future were not going to spoil the present—meaning the past was not discussed and the future was so vague it did not seem to be much of an option.

Charlotte leafed through the fragile pages looking for a tea or a salve for her nervous heart, for her reluctant but powerful passion for Jed. It was easy enough to find: passion flower.

A tea made of *pasionaria* was used as a tranquilizer. A tincture made from the same plant was recommended for insomniacs. Passion flower seemed to offer a good antidote to the agitation brought on by passion. The tea was also good for intestinal cramps. A note in the margin said if the stomach was tight and cramping, canela bark was a better choice.

Charlotte remembered her first morning in this kitchen and Thea's recounting of her last conversation with Grandpa, how she gave Grandpa a thermos filled with coffee that had been brewed with canela. For Alicia. Strange the details of our lives that remain precise and intact, the details that flit away and are lost. And what was the tea that Thea suddenly recalled as she left the kitchen that morning? Mari-something. For nausea. Mariola. Conchata told Thea the thermos was filled with cold mariola tea.

Charlotte scanned the pages until she found mariola listed with the Apache remedies. The fresh leaves were brewed by the Lonewolf clan to make a coffee-like beverage. Grandmother Lonewolf boiled those same leaves into a pain-relieving salve rubbed onto the abdomen of a pregnant woman. Conchata made a cold infusion of the aromatic mariola plant, and drank the tea for her own morning sickness.

Charlotte stared at the page. Thea couldn't remember if the thermos she had given Grandpa held hot coffee or cold tea. Conchata's memory could hardly be trusted: Conchata hadn't even been alive the morning Thea had said goodbye to Grandpa. What did it matter if the thermos had been filled with mariola tea, cold, for morning sickness; or coffee laced with canela bark, hot, for an upset stomach? And the Apaches drank mariola like coffee, so it seemed reasonable that Thea's memory had merged the canela-laced coffee with mariola tea.

Charlotte closed the notebook and slid it to the center of the kitchen table. Alicia had not been suffering from morning sickness. She'd been suffering from the flu. Alicia might have been love sick, heart sick, end-of-summer sick. But she had not been morning-sickness sick.

Charlotte pushed the chair away from the table, walked to the telephone, and dialed her home number in Scarsdale. There were five messages on her answering machine. The first was from a student's mother inviting Charlotte to Martha's Vineyard. The next message was from Maddie saying hello, hope you're having the time of your life, and send up a smoke signal when you have a moment. The last three messages were from the secretary of Richard Boudreaux, the attorney for Charlotte's father's estate. The estate was ready for distribution. She needed to come in and sign papers. If she was out of town for the summer she needed to give Boudreaux's office a mailing address where they could send documents via certified mail. But they needed Charlotte to give them directives ASAP.

She replaced the receiver in the phone cradle on the wall and peered down the hall. Thea would sleep another hour, until three o'clock. Charlotte went out onto the porch. In the summer afternoon heat all the ranch animals were snoozing. George was folded up under the hickory table. Little Bit was stretched out against the house. The burros were motionless in the shade of the cottonwood.

Charlotte had looked into a flight to New York on Thursday, July ninth, but had not made the reservation. Limbo. Her sense of time had drifted into limbo. In her canyon dream about Grandpa he held up a watch found in the dirt alongside fossil bones. What was Grandpa telling her? To keep track of time? Or was he saying watches and timekeeping were insignificant in the grander scheme? That limbo, like the bones in the dirt, was an acceptable, even inevitable, condition.

Charlotte reached out and pushed the rocking chair into motion. It didn't matter. It was so long ago it did not matter if that thermos was filled with hot coffee or cold tea.

Charlotte went back into the kitchen and picked up Conchata's notebook. She would copy what she could in whatever time she had here. Tonight with Thea, Charlotte would read aloud the entries that were smudged and disappearing, and Thea would fill in plant and place names, translate Spanish and Apache. Tomorrow Charlotte would reconnect with Arthur and help him through a few more sessions before the GED on Friday. And in and under and between it all, in limbo or not, Charlotte would enjoy every ticking moment she had with Jed.

{39}

Thea sat in the rocking chair bent over the notepad. The moon was nearly full and silver shadows fell on the porch floor around her slippered feet. Still, there was not enough light on the planet earth to enable Thea's old eyes to see the pad of paper on her lap. No matter. The crickets chirped in the garden and the pair of great horned owls was exchanging calls from the cliffs over the irrigation pond. She knew the burros were watching her because she heard the soft clomp of their hooves as they walked across the powdery sand of the corral to stand along the fence.

Earlier in the evening Charlotte had read aloud from Conchata's notebook, plant by plant, recipe by recipe, page by page. Slowly, slowly the wisdom of the past was anchoring itself in the present, securing a strong tether into the future. Thea reached down and touched Little Bit's wiry head. She could not see the road ahead, but she could hear very clearly the directions that revealed the destination.

Thea returned her attention to the paper on her lap. Her index finger remained at the top, and her thumb marked the middle of the page. Using these as a guide, Thea placed the pencil on the paper and began to write. She had to concentrate to avoid writing words on top of words; she had to be very clear so that Bartholomew and Francis would honor her last will and testament.

I leave you these instructions so that you, Bartholomew, will know exactly where you are going. And you, Francis, will know exactly when you have done enough. Francis, cremate this withered body of flesh and memories. Place my name on our marker at the cemetery, but place my ashes and bits of bone in that coffee tin from the High Lonesome.

Thea put the pencil onto her lap and lifted her face to the cool night of crickets, burros and moonlight. How could she be so weary and so awake? Perhaps she was dreaming. She had prepared for this task for weeks, lain in bed composing the words, seen herself here on the porch in her mind's eye. She pressed her left palm against her left cheek; her fingers followed the bones surrounding her eye. So many bones. The earth was riddled with bones. Where was Alicia's bone horse notebook and why was Conchata so insistent that they find it?

Thea found the pencil in the fold of her bathrobe and smoothed the paper of the notepad on her knee. How could she find her last sentence? She could not, so she turned the page:

Bartholomew, pack enough provisions for three riders to camp for two days. You say you have forgotten much, but not about packing the horses and riding into the high country. Conchata says you can do this journey with your eyes closed . . . .

The notepad was small and she filled several pages. When the specifics of her last will were written out, she placed the pad and pencil on the hickory table and leaned her head against the chair back. She closed her eyes to the silver sheen of the night world and fell asleep.

{40}

The telephone in the Durham kitchen was ringing. The phone rang about 6:30 every morning because Ralph called to ask if the Durhams needed him to bring anything from Agua Dulce. Francis answered the phone on the third ring.

"Why yes, good morning," Francis said. "I'm fine, thank you."

Charlotte listened from the pantry where she was scooping out dog food. Little Bit pranced at her feet, stiffly hopping up and down. George was running in a tiny circle on the porch in anticipation of his three morsels of Kennel Chow.

Charlotte walked through the kitchen with Bit's bowl. Francis lifted his hand to her. "Yes, she's right here."

Charlotte handed the bowl of dog food to Francis and took the phone. It was most likely Maddie calling to find out what in tarnation Charlotte was still doing in New Mexico. "Hello?"

"Teacher teacher!" It was Arthur. "How are you?"

Arthur's voice was tight. He was nervous.

"I'm fine, Arthur," Charlotte answered. "Where have you been since the Fourth?"

"Oh, *sí*, I was like stranded in Dos Rios. My car broke down and then my cousin had this problem with his girlfriend up in Santa Fe so I went over there and we. . . ." Arthur stopped his story midsentence. "I needed some time to chill out."

"Where are you now? Are we meeting today?"

"I'm at my trailer. I was thinking we could meet at the library."

"Remember, Inez told us last week the library would be closed today, Tuesday, while they installed the new windows in the front room."

"Maybe we could meet this morning downtown somewhere?"

"You're not going out to work with Jed and Barty?"

"I told them I needed to study."

Charlotte smiled. "How about I come and get you and bring you back here. It's quiet. We'll get a lot done."

"You'd come and get me?"

"When can you be ready?"

"I'll be ready to split in thirty minutes."

Charlotte replaced the receiver and turned around and faced Thea and Francis. "May I take the Hudson into Agua Dulce to get Arthur?"

Francis smiled and sat down at the table. "You can take whatever vehicle suits you."

Thea turned back to the stove and cracked five eggs into the frying pan.

"I'll make up some tea," she said over the sizzle of the eggs. "Do you remember, Charlotte, what Conchata recommended for hangovers?"

"Powdered pods and leaves of cat claw acacia as a tea." Had Charlotte read this aloud last night? She didn't recall a page devoted to hangovers in the notebook. "And bee sage, desert lavender, the kind that Bernadette brings from Arizona. But Thea, Arthur did not sound hungover."

Francis refolded the *Santa Fean* and placed it on the table beside his coffee cup. "I don't think Arthur Varela has been to visit us since he left high school. He and his brother, Lucho, were here from dawn to dusk when they were young. Back when Jed spent summers here."

Francis gazed out the screen door like he had a view of yesterday. "The ranch was a busy little place in those days, busy with cattle and horses. Remember, Thea? You'd make lunch for five, six or more. Me, Barty, and Dennis used to pack up the horses and head out with the boys—Jed, Lucho, Arthur when he was old enough—and Bernadette would come along too, when she came from Tempe in late August to retrieve Jedidiah."

Charlotte held the plates for Thea as she served the eggs and bacon. Thea listened to Francis with a sweet smile on her face.

"We must have had equipment enough for what, six riders and ten horses, what with all those panniers of Thomas Bill's, and the Matas' gear. Remember how they used to store their cooking pots here in our barn? My God, we packed a lot of food and supplies for those trips!"

"What were you doing on those expeditions?" Charlotte slid a plate on the table before Francis.

"We were rounding up someone's cattle, or looking for the mustangs." Francis fingered the rim of his plate. "We used to say if we rode any farther we'd be in another country. Gosh, those were just the best of times. You know, we were already in another country."

Thea sat down at the table. Charlotte did the same.

"The high country of the horses, the country where Bartholomew, and his uncles before him, set all those horses free."

"Where Duende and the wild horses lived?" Charlotte asked.

Francis looked at her across the table. "That's the place. The mustangs lived there until the drought of the 1950s forced them down. If they'd stayed up on the other side of the Agustinas, they might still be out there." Francis smiled at Charlotte. "Now my legs can't get around a horse anymore, and no one has time to go horse packing anyway."

"Jed's living on a horse." Thea moved her hand onto Charlotte's on the table. "And Charlotte is a fine rider."

"I sure do like riding again. Jed talked about going out for a ride today."

"You do that," Thea said quickly. "You need more time in the saddle."

"Arthur's going to be here until about noon—"

"There's rain in the forecast," Francis said, tapping the newspaper folded beside his plate. "Take a slicker."

{41}

Charlotte turned the Hudson into the Buena Vista Trailer Park where several dozen mobile homes were parked in two neat rows. Narrow elm trees grew between each unit. Charlotte scanned the trailers. Arthur waited on the metal steps of an older single-wide.

"Arthur, good morning!" Charlotte called through the open window. Arthur leapt from the metal step to the driveway and in two strides was at the Hudson. He climbed in and adjusted his baseball cap so it sat forward on his head.

Charlotte stared at him. "I don't think I've ever seen you in a baseball cap."

Arthur laughed. "Even we Chicanos can sunburn!"

Charlotte laughed as she reversed the truck and drove slowly down Borrego Lane. Children on bikes watched the ancient truck pass. Arthur waved at the children, but suddenly the smile dropped from his face. Charlotte glanced to her right to see what caused the change in his attitude.

"Violeta!" Charlotte stopped the truck. Violeta saw her Uncle Arthur beside Charlotte in the cab and ran across the small dirt yard to the road.

"¡Tío!" Violeta stood on tiptoes and reached for Arthur through the window. "Are you and teacher reading at the library?"

"No, mijita, the library is closed today." Arthur let Violeta climb up his arm and wrap her arms around his neck. "Tomorrow we'll read again, okay?"

"Violeta!" Rosa appeared on the porch of her mobile home dressed in a sheer nightgown that came to her knees. Her thick black hair was matted against her head. Charlotte realized how much effort it took for Rosa to look like the aged prom queen that was her preferred public persona. "I told you never run into the street! Don't you never listen to me?"

Rosa clomped down the metal steps in a pair of heeled mules and marched out to the Hudson. She headed around the truck to Violeta, who was still clinging to her uncle's shoulder, and violently jerked the child away from Arthur. "You've gone too far this time! I heard all about your *vato*, Chico! I'm getting a court order. Stay away from Violeta or you'll go to jail!"

Rosa marched around the Hudson dragging a crying Violeta by one arm. Rosa's nightie had pulled up to the bottom of her buttocks, and as she went up the porch steps her pink bikini underwear flashed the crowd gathered to watch the Tomé family circus. Rosa slammed the metal trailer door behind her. Everyone watching turned to look at Charlotte and Arthur in the Hudson.

"Good God!" Charlotte said as she put the truck in gear and drove out of the trailer park. Arthur stared straight ahead, his face flushed with humiliation. They reached the traffic light at Main Street, and Charlotte dared a glance at Arthur. He was looking out the window at the hardware store, chewing a fingernail.

"So what happened with your friend Chico that's got you in worse trouble than usual with Rosa?"

Arthur put his hands in his lap and looked at Charlotte. "I let Chico use my car on the fourth 'cause I was with Donacita, this girl I knew at school. Chico went and got busted with a trunk full of heroin. Shit!"

"But you had nothing to do with it?"

"¡*Nada*! I was with Donacita, I'm not accused of nothing, it was just he used my Honda. It's impounded in Santa Fe. Chico's in jail. Damn, he's a fool! Heroin!"

The light turned green and Charlotte swung the truck around the corner past the drugstore. Gus and the boys had their old eyes fixed like young hawks on the Hudson. Charlotte waved. They each raised a hand, but worry creased their faces. Did they know about Arthur's car, about the heroin?

"You must pass this test and get into college," Charlotte said as they passed the cemetery and the old school. "If you want to choose your destiny—if you want your niece to continue to adore and admire you—you must walk a very straight line."

"I know, Charlotte, I know."

She steered onto the sand of the shoulder, stopped the truck, and turned to Arthur. "We're all going to end up in some cemetery, sooner or later. But what we do between this moment now and that moment, whenever it is, is our choice."

"Oh, *sí*, teacher—"

"—No, I mean it! This is one of those crossroads, right here, right now! You make one choice, you go that way; you make another choice, you go this way."

Charlotte put the truck into first gear and drove back onto the road. She had driven this piece of highway enough to know precisely when it narrowed, precisely how to steer to avoid the ruts and bumps. She knew how the landscape exploded into space and heat and light again just here, knew like home territory this canyonland country where just two weeks ago—two weeks!— her own life had come to a crossroads. And what would she do next? Climb on a plane and flee her challenges? Here she was, lecturing Arthur to choose his fate, take control, and yet she was paralyzed with indecision, unable to take the reins of her own life.

"This is when you say, I'm this person, not that person, and everything I'm going to do is going to support this person I am now or am going to become."

Arthur stared at Charlotte, surprised by the vehemence in her voice. She was surprised, too. It made her very angry—Rosa yelling at Arthur. Rosa! Rosa was a lazy, immature, ignorant woman and a lousy role model for Violeta. But that wasn't why Charlotte was so angry. No, she was angry at herself and her continued half-commitment to her own happiness: she still couldn't take responsibility for being in Agua Dulce, couldn't bring herself to admit she wanted to stay here so she could be near Jed. Couldn't say 'I am this person who is falling in love with a place and a person in this place, and although I don't know what will happen I'm brave enough to stay and find out.'

"You have to declare what you want." Charlotte heard her loud voice through the noise of the wind in the truck cab. "I want this. *This* is what I want more of in my life. And then you hold that vision. You commit yourself to that."

"But what if people are against you?" Arthur removed his cap and ran his hand over his bristly scalp. "What if people keep pushing you down into the past, or into your family's past? Like they want you to stay back there and fail?"

"You don't have to apologize for your brother's mistakes. And if people want you to fail, you stand up to them, Arthur. Not with violence, just with your actions. You hold the course and get through this GED test, you enroll in the community college in Santa Fe, and Rosa and all of the Tomés will have to take you for who you are: a man with purpose. A man who Violeta is proud of."

Charlotte turned the truck into the Durham gate and stopped. The dusty red and brown road to the ranch wavered across the mesa and disappeared when it dropped down into the little valley to the house and barn. Charlotte loved this view: the Lágrimas desert was a different hue of red, gold and brown at each time of day. The mountains changed color and temperament too, and the sky, well, it was always enormous and imperious, but somehow comforting in that it was forever above it all. This was a timeless space, and the road to the Durhams' was the road into the timelessness. The road home.

Charlotte looked at Arthur leaning against the window, his hat in hand. "Your choices will define you, Arthur. Right now, you might choose to stay away from friends in Dos Rios."

Arthur whistled through his teeth. "I got to have some fun sometimes."

"Not with them, not if you want to be in Violeta's life."

Arthur pulled the cap back down onto his head. "Okay, okay! Let's get movin', teacher, cause this day, *como* me and you, ain't getting any younger."

{42}

An almost inaudible mumble of thunder rumbled across the early evening desert from the west. Charlotte stopped the Hudson on the road to the High Lonesome and listened. Sound was amplified by the thin air of the plateau. The clouds were a long ways away—over the Agustinas but not over the *llanos* or the canyonlands.

She gave the truck a little gas and drove on to the High Lonesome barn. Jed and Barty were leaning against the barn door, gazing off to the west at the gorgeous sunset over the mountains. The two sister mares and Britches and Dolly stood by the water trough. Jed and Barty waved at Charlotte as she parked the Hudson alongside Barty's truck.

"You worked a long day," Jed said when he reached her. His hand brushed her cheek and gently grasped her arm. "How's Arthur?"

"We spent the entire morning reading and reviewing trial tests at the kitchen table." Jed's hand was rough and warm, and the smell of his body sent a pleasurable current through Charlotte. "I thought we'd be done sooner. But he has so much to cover by Friday."

"How's he gonna do?" Barty walked up. He carried a jar of some kind of salve. "Should Arthur even be taking the test this summer?"

"Yes, he should take it," Charlotte said. "At the very least, it's good practice. But he struggles with his reading. I do worry about his getting discouraged."

"Are you going to the test with him?" Jed's hand slid down her arm and around her wrist.

"I thought you had a flight to New York Thursday?" Barty asked.

Jed dropped his head and squinted at Charlotte. This was news to him.

"I didn't book it." Charlotte held Jed's gaze. "I looked into flights last week but I wasn't sure how long I was needed."

Jed nodded. "I reckon Arthur could need you for a lot longer than you want."

"You do seem able to get his attention." Barty stood at the far end of the Hudson inspecting the taillight.

"Even with my working Arthur twenty-four hours a day he won't pass the GED this time around," Charlotte said again. "But I want him to have a good experience with it."

Barty turned and faced the west. "I see the pinto has come out to the edge of the trees. Think she'll let me near, Jed?"

"What's up with the pinto?" Charlotte joined Barty at the Hudson's tailgate and peered across the *llano* at the pinto standing alone beyond the water tank. The sky had lost its color and the desert was sliding into twilight. "What's that salve for?"

"The pinto." Barty held up the jar. It had one of Thea's handwritten labels across its side. "Wound salve."

"Chaparral?" Charlotte gestures at the jar. "Greasewood?"

Barty looked at the jar, frowning. "Greasewood. Yeah, that's what Conchata called it. Chaparral or greasewood, same difference."

"What happened to the pinto?"

"Don't know exactly. Maybe her old demons caught up with her. I brought some grain out this morning and she was all spooked about something. When I headed out on Dolly to the drip tank on the south pasture I could see the pinto had a cut on her right shoulder. As soon as Dolly and me headed her direction the pinto gets all worked up and takes off like she's been stung by bees. Dolly and I tailed her to Antelope Wash. The only thing that stopped that crazy pinto from running all the way to Mexico was the High Lonesome fence line. I thought she might try and jump the wire so I reined Dolly around and headed back. But I didn't like that cut."

"How'd you get her back here?" The pinto was watching through the oak branches where the twilight lit the white spots on her back.

"For all her crazy loco unsociableness the pinto likes to be in sight of other horses."

"She appeared about three o'clock," Jed said. "She hasn't left that oak thicket."

"How bad is the cut?" Charlotte asked.

"Could be deep. She may have snagged a sharp branch in the *bosque*, or crossed the river and tangled in the barbed wire on the far bank. There's not a chance I can get her into a trailer. And the vet wouldn't be able to get near her. I put all of the other mares in the corral and took some grain out to see if the pinto will come in. I need to get this salve on her shoulder. But she won't let me within thirty yards."

"I could try," Charlotte said. Jed and Barty both looked at her. "Let me try."

"Okay." Barty looked out at the windmill. "Yes, let's do this." Barty unscrewed the jar. "Scoop out a handful and walk up to her. The cut is on her right shoulder, low; just slather it across that wound best you can. If you get close, be prepared to move fast. Don't let her whirl into you. That horse is acting *real* loco."

"Okay." Charlotte took the jar and screwed the top back on.

Jed smiled at Charlotte and pointed at the southeastern horizon. "The moon is rising."

The white spots of the pinto reflected the light of the almost full moon lifting off the desert. As Charlotte approached the windmill she did not look directly at the pinto tucked into the shadowy scrub oak, but stared off at the dusk landscape glazed by the moon. At the water tank she opened the jar and scooped out the salve, set the jar on the ground, and turned to the horse standing in the shadows.

"Hey pinto, what scared you today?" Charlotte walked away from the tank and under the windmill. The canvas feed bag was hung on the windmill's lower support bar. She reached in and took a handful of grain. The pinto's eyes and ears were riveted on Charlotte. "There's supper here for you. You must be hungry after all that running."

Charlotte walked slowly and with as little extraneous movement as possible to the thicket of scrub oak. She stopped several yards from the pinto and held out the grain. "I know you see this strange-looking salve. And you know me. I won't hurt you."

The pinto was shivering, flicking her ears. She glanced into the shadows behind and stomped her front foot.

"There's a time to run and there's a time not to run." Charlotte held out the grain and moved closer to the trees. "This is the time not to run."

Charlotte stopped in a small clearing. Her hand with the grain extended across the open space between her and the pinto. The pinto sniffed and snorted. The moon's rays were just now striking the blades of the windmill, and the dusky desert glowed. The pinto dropped her head, took three steps and quickly mouthed the grain in Charlotte's open hand.

"Oh, that's very good. What a brave horse!" Charlotte tilted her head and saw the wound. It was three inches long and had begun to scab. "I'm going to put this on your cut."

Charlotte slowly raised her other hand and let the mare sniff the salve. The smell caused the horse to jerk her head up and away, but she remained in the clearing. "I know it smells, but here I come—"

With a fluid move of her arm Charlotte passed her left hand firmly across the pinto's lower shoulder and smeared the thick salve on the lumpy crust of the wound's scab. The mare stepped back. Her muscles trembled. But she did not run.

"Oh, good girl! Good girl!"

The pinto shivered and turned her head to the trees as if something or someone was watching, waiting in the shadows. The fear the horse felt was palpable, like a current. It made Charlotte's stomach tighten. She lifted her hand and pushed the sweaty bangs from her forehead. It was an innocuous gesture, but it triggered something in the pinto, and the mare plunged backward into the scrub oak as if she had been struck across the face with a whip.

Charlotte was alone in the clearing. She scanned the trees. Whatever had frightened the pinto was still here in the horse's imagination.

Charlotte walked quickly out of the shadowy oaks and into the moonlight flooding the ground around the windmill. Barty and Jed stood by the Hudson waiting for her. Charlotte drew in a deep breath to settle her nerves. There was nothing to fear. Even so, as she walked back to the barn she had to suppress the feeling she was being pursued by the same demon that haunted the pinto.

{43}

The current of air lifted the sleeves of her dress into a sail. Thea closed her eyes and pulled the scarf tightly around her head to keep it from soaring into the sky. Riding in the Mustang with the top down was like flying, like falling, like dissolving into wind, heat, sound and light. She could have spent the whole morning riding all over the Lágrimas in the open convertible, but Charlotte drove straight into Agua Dulce and parked before the drugstore.

"Gus is on the steps," Charlotte said.

Thea knew where they were even with her eyes closed. As they drove in from the ranch Thea knew when they were passing the old school, the church and the cemetery, the stone memorial, the tire shop, dry cleaner's and pool hall. She could outline the horizon to the north, south, east and west. These were the places of Thea's life; her body recognized each of them as they came and went, the markers on her journey's map. She did not need to see them again.

The Mustang's throaty engine was turned off, and Thea listened to Wednesday morning traffic on Main Street.

"Thea, give me your hand." Charlotte opened Thea's door. She lifted her arm into the air and Charlotte's strong hands deftly guided her out of the car. Without her cane, left on the porch beside the rocker, Thea was dependent upon Charlotte to navigate her through the morning errands. "I think I'll put the top up for the drive home. The sun is too hot. Your cheeks are flushed."

"Phiff! I don't sunburn!" Thea removed the scarf from her head and primped at her hair. It was still secured in a bun, but vagrant strands fluffed about her forehead.

"Gus is here." Charlotte tied Thea's scarf around her neck.

"Thea, will you and Charlotte have a malt with me?" Gus took Thea's elbow and led her up the steps. Gus's fingers were stiff around Thea's arm and she knew his other hand was gripping the railing for balance. Not quite the blind leading the blind, but close enough. "I saw Francis this morning. Had to get me a hinge for my shed door. Just fell apart, dropped the door onto the ground."

"The time has come," Thea said with a smile, "to find replacements."

Cool air moved about the drugstore under the ceiling fans. Thea's cheeks were flushed, she could feel them tingling, but it wasn't from the sun on her face.

"Thea, have a seat here." Charlotte guided her onto one of the soda-fountain stools. "Dennis, could we have some water?"

Thea heard Dennis filling a glass with water from the tap several yards down the counter to her right. The store was busy: the hum of voices mingled with the whirring swish of the fan blades.

"There you are, Thea." Dennis slid the cool glass into her hand. She took a long sip, then wiped her lips with the tip of her scarf. She sensed that everyone was watching her. Everyone was worried. Didn't they know that at her age dying was more natural than living?

"I'd like a double chocolate malt, Dennis," Thea said with as much vigor as she could muster. "And put some chocolate shavings on top. Today is a day for extra *extra* chocolate!"

"Every day is a day for extra chocolate," Dennis said lightly. She knew his eyes were crinkled up with a grin. Sweet, charming Dennis Mata. Where would Bartholomew have been without Dennis and his steady, reliable optimism all these years?

"I'll have the same," Charlotte said. "With chocolate shavings."

"Gus, what can I get you?" Dennis was standing directly before Thea. She smiled up at him and felt his loving gaze on her face.

"The same," Gus said. "But make mine only a half glass. I don't digest milk the way I used to."

Thea leaned into Gus and found his forearm. "You need to stay on the *manzanilla* tea. Are you out of the plants I dried for you? I'll have Charlotte harvest a fresh bag for you tonight from the garden." Thea turned to her right. "Charlotte, are you listening?"

"I am. Fresh *manzanilla* plants for Gus."

Thea released her grip on Gus and found Charlotte's elbow. "Why don't you go and see if the licorice lozenges Francis wanted are in the aisle closest to the pharmacy?" Thea tilted her head as if she were gazing over Charlotte's shoulder. "Do I see them there, perhaps?"

"I'll get them." Charlotte slid from the stool.

"She's just the prettiest young woman we've had visit these parts in a long time," Gus said. "Smart, too. I hear she's been out riding with Jedidiah. Maybe swimming with him, too."

"Charlotte Lambert fits into Agua Dulce like a smooth boot into an old stirrup." Thea took another drink of water and wiped her lips again with her scarf. "She's still learning to trust the good accidents of life, you know. Too many of the other sort have left her a bit gun-shy."

"Well, her family's had its accidents and the like right here in the Lágrimas. I reckon she's just being prudent, taking her time, you know, before forming an opinion."

"No, Charlotte came here with way too much of a formed opinion. Not hers, necessarily, but her Grandmother Ruth's, and her father's. Conchata says even you and I are blind to what is, what has been." Thea groped about the counter until she found Gus's thin arm. He was wearing a long-sleeved shirt with snaps at the cuffs. She could see it clear as day, a faded red plaid with pearl buttons. "You remember when we were young, Gustafson Treadle, when life didn't follow the road we believed lay directly ahead, how we worried we might be riding off course? And look at us! Journey's end we come to be exactly where we were always going!"

Dennis was frothing the first malt across the counter. Thea had to lean in close so Gus could hear her. "But we have to earn this view. Like a long ride up the Agustinas: you don't know how far you've come until you crest that last ridge. And then you discover how much you can't see from down here, can't even imagine is up there: trees, forests and lakes! Why, I've seen snow up there in July!"

The malt machine was turned off. Thea closed her eyes, and remained anchored to the room through her fingers gripping the fabric of Gus's shirt.

You can't go to sleep now, Conchata whispered into Thea's ear. *You must tell Gus about the lost child.*

Thea sat up straight on her stool. "Gus?"

"Here are your malts." Dennis set glasses on the counter.

Thea turned to Gus. "You were always the first one called, always the first deputy saddled up ready to head out." She heard Gus opening the wrapper of his straw. "I'm looking for a child, Gus."

"What child?" Gus sucked on his malt.

"A boy, I believe, but I'm too blind to see boy or girl! It makes me cross, these old eyes!"

"Is this the same child Francis was looking for in the newspaper a few weeks back?" Dennis asked. He slid Thea's malt glass and straw gently into her hand on the counter.

"Why, yes, I guess it is."

"Still missing?" Dennis asked. Thea knew Francis and Dennis had been talking, had shared their ambivalence about Thea's vision.

"Yes. The child is still missing. Francis says there was no newspaper story about such a child, and he called the sheriff's office in Dos Rios, and they had no such report of a missing child. But there *is* such a child and he or she is still missing." Thea sucked at her malt but it was so thick she could not get it to pass up through the straw to her mouth.

"Here's a spoon." Dennis placed a long-handled utensil against Thea's left hand. "There are customers at the pharmacy. Pardon me."

Thea spooned thick, delicious chocolate malt into her mouth. After the first ache of cold passed from her throat and chest, she turned to Gus again. "Gus, you were the one who noticed the turned stones, the compressed earth, the flattened grass. The trail. You must promise me this one thing: when the sheriff goes into the canyonlands looking for someone everyone has forgotten, you will go with him."

"Thea, I'm an old man. I haven't been part of a sheriff's posse in, oh, must be ten years! Why don't you ask Barty? He's as good a tracker as any."

"No, no, I have something else to ask Bartholomew. And your eyes are not clouded by those old opinions we were talking about a moment ago." Thea took Gus's arm and held it between both hands. She looked into what she remembered were the caramel-colored eyes of Gus Treadle. "Promise, Gus: when the sheriff goes into the canyonlands, you'll go with him."

"All right then. If it's so important to ya. I'll go with the sheriff."

{44}

Farley sat at the dormer window that faced Main Street and fingered the shriveled ears. The clock in Mabel's parlor two flights down chimed two times. It was close to a hundred degrees in the attic room, but Farley did not turn on the table fan. He did not want to fall asleep, and the rhythmic drone of the fan could lull him into a near-death snooze. No, Earl was down for a nap, and Mabel would close the door to her room any moment now and doze the rest of the afternoon like all boarders. Farley just had to stay awake another few minutes, and then the keys and the car and the road to salvation would be his.

The bald-headed Spanish boy had given Farley half-truths about Alicia's schedule. Early yesterday morning, after Farley had seen Barty Bill drive into Agua Dulce for his dawn chat with Dennis Mata, he had taken Earl's car and driven out to the High Lonesome. He had hidden in the trees for almost an hour, but only a skittish Indian pony appeared. That horse's crazy spots skewered Farley's aim and his shot missed the animal's mottled, lopsided head by yards. The horse bolted straight into the *bosque* and struck something, screamed in pain, and vanished before Farley could reload. Damnation. Maybe it would die anyway, bleed to death along the river. He had waited in the trees but the witch whore did not appear, and he had to leave before he was discovered.

Farley's eyes were folding up, closing down. He was about to give up and take a nap. He rested his forehead into the window frame. He could not last much longer. And then, by God, the devil's maiden appeared on Main Street in a red car with the top peeled back. With her hair, breasts, and shoulders exposed, she drove slowly past the boarding house. All sound ceased: Farley pressed his face into the screen and followed the witch's red tail as it disappeared up the road to the north.

"My God," Farley said aloud to the room, "the end is surely here."

He was burning up. Perspiration soaked his shirt and pants and he gasped for air in the stifling attic. He had prayed for this fire, for the immolation of everyone who opposed him. And the Lord had granted him a red-hot July afternoon that paralyzed the ravens and silenced the cicadas. Today, July eighth, 1998, the bones of the Apache-loving witch would burn to ashes.

{45}

Charlotte parked the Mustang under the cool cottonwood canopy on the east side of the High Lonesome barn. Bundles of clouds had tried to build over the Agustinas after lunch, but in such heat they seemed unlikely to become rainmakers. Even so, she put up the convertible top.

She was alone at the High Lonesome for the first time all summer. After Arthur's session with her at the library he'd gone with Barty to run errands around Agua Dulce. Jed said he'd meet Charlotte over at the ranch house later in the afternoon. He had some new solar-design material from Jaycee he wanted to read back at camp.

Charlotte studied the road of hard-boiled sand that led away from the ranch house, wove past the water tank, and dropped into the south to Jed's home on the bluffs. If she went out there now, unannounced, Jed would welcome her, stop what he was doing so they could walk down to the river for a swim. Or a nap. Or a roll in the grass. It was tempting. But Charlotte was here to find the pinto and to rub more salve on her wound.

The two old sister mares stood against the north wall of the ranch house. The heat made them listless, and they did not give Charlotte their usual nicker of acknowledgment. Charlotte paused in the open doorway of the barn and squinted across the thick atmosphere at the windmill. With no shade by the water tank, the pinto was either in the scrub oak or down the east pasture in the *bosque*.

Charlotte retrieved the wound salve from the barn office, secured the Durham cap on her head, put on her sunglasses, and headed out at a brisk stride across the hot pasture. It was a ten-minute walk to the refuge of green along the river. The pinto stood in a cool grove of cottonwoods midway between the edge of the pasture and the bank of the river. There was no easy path to the horse, and Charlotte had to push her way through the dense bushes to the pinto.

"Hey, pinto, how you doing this afternoon?" Charlotte ducked under a low branch and stepped into the clearing ten feet from the pinto. The horse's wound was drier than last evening, and had a thick scab. Barty said the salve would keep the scab flexible while the wound healed.

"I've got that salve again." Charlotte held up the jar. The pinto jerked her head. "I'm thinking we might try to get some more on your cut."

Although nervous about Charlotte's appearance, the mare held her ground, and did not seem so spooked and crazy like last night out by the windmill. Maybe all men, even the famous horse healer Barty Bill, frightened the pinto. Charlotte unscrewed the lid, scooped out a good-sized glob of the bittersweet-smelling ointment, and set the jar down in the grass. She had a carrot in her pocket and she pulled it out as she slowly stood up.

"This is what we're talking about." She slowly held up both hands, one with the carrot and the other with the salve. "I'm going to walk over to you and you can eat this carrot while I put this salve on your shoulder."

The pinto's nostrils flared as she caught a whiff of the salve.

"Okay, here we go." Charlotte kept her hands at waist level, lowered her eyes, and walked to the mare. Before either Charlotte or the mare could think too much about how close they were, Charlotte reached out and gave the pinto the carrot, and simultaneously swabbed the salve across the wound. The pinto shivered from her neck to her hindquarters, and stepped to the side. But the loco crazy horse did not run.

"That wasn't so bad." Charlotte stepped away as the pinto swung her head down to inspect the wound. The mare flicked her tail, shifted her weight onto all four legs, lifted her head and stared into middle space.

Charlotte and the pinto stood and soaked up the summer. The river murmured through the trees, and the cicadas buzzed. The *bosque* had its own fragrance: sharp, pungent sage, warm skin, moist sand, horse hair and dry earth. This was the world of the horse. This was the world of the high desert, of the Lágrimas River cutting its course through ancient stone, a world of days without names or numbers passing in a river current, life continuous and fluid for a hundred, a thousand, a million years. This was the world of Grandpa, of her mother, too. Charlotte's breath was carried by the pinto's inhalations, exhalations, rhythmic and deep, into the standing-sleep dream world of the horse.

Ravens called loudly from the cliffs. The pinto raised her head and looked into the trees behind Charlotte. More calls from the ravens, and the pinto did a quarter turn and lifted her head high, ears alert now. The tension of yesterday had returned. The pinto was preparing for flight. Charlotte looked down at her arms: the hair of her forearms was standing on end.

The sound of an engine and a loose muffler banging against the hard ground filtered down into the *bosque* from the pasture. Charlotte peered through the trees.

"That's Earl's car, he won't hurt you—" Charlotte turned as the pinto bolted in a powerful, crashing leap and vanished into the deeper thickness of the trees. Charlotte rubbed her arms. Cold. Perspiration soaked her shirt. The fear that had charged through the pinto was coursing through Charlotte's body.

The ravens flew into the trees above Charlotte and called and scolded a warning. Charlotte climbed back through the brush and trees the way she had walked in. When she reached the last stand of cottonwoods, she stopped. Why would Earl drive all the way down to the *bosque*? Didn't he see that Barty's truck was not at the ranch today? How did he know Charlotte was down in the trees? And what could be so important that Earl would risk driving his old maroon sedan across the bumpy, sandy pasture to find her?

Charlotte realized she had left the jar of salve in the grass of the clearing. She turned around and went back into the trees. She found the jar and could hear Earl opening his car door. He left the engine running. Maybe something had happened to Thea?

"Earl? I'm in here!"

The ravens were scuffling around in the tops of the cottonwood trees. There were four or five, six of them now leaping from branch to branch, wings wide. The pinto was long gone. Why was Charlotte so cold? Over the low drone of the idling engine she heard another door open. Who was with Earl? She walked quickly to the edge of the pasture and stopped. The blood drained from her head: Farley was limping across the sand dragging a rifle.

"Where's Earl?" Charlotte heard herself say loudly and with a bravado she did not feel. "What are you doing out here?"

A necklace of shriveled horse ears hung against Farley's chest. He was here to shoot the pinto, to add the mare's ears to his disgusting collection.

Charlotte prayed the pinto was halfway to Jed's by now, or had crossed the Lágrimas and scrambled up the steep bank on the far side.

"Witch whore, your time is done." Farley hoisted the rifle to his chest. The ravens were screeching like banshees in the trees. "Drop to your knees and pray for mercy, witch, because your time in hell is about to begin."

Charlotte's heart seized: the barrel of the rifle was aimed directly at her! How had she missed the signs? The pinto had run because she had seen Farley before. "You hurt the pinto, didn't you?"

"Apache whore, you die today." Farley wheezed, gagged and lost his balance. He pitched forward, catching himself with the nose of the rifle. "You knowd I'd find you again. You can't jump, can't escape, witch. Your kind is done. You and your harem of devil horses will be wiped from God's earth this day."

The pinto had tried to warn her, to tell her to run. Charlotte's panic turned to blind rage as she understood exactly what Farley had done to the pinto: he'd cornered her out by the water tank, had caused her to panic and lunge into the sharp branches of the scrub oak that ripped her flesh like a spear.

"You were here yesterday, weren't you?" Charlotte stepped into the sun. "You hurt the pinto!"

Farley, startled by Charlotte's aggressive posture, stumbled back, dragging the gun's nose through the sand. The ravens were in the lower branches now, their alarm calls continuous and shrill.

"That pinto didn't do anything to you!" Charlotte yelled through the ruckus. "What the hell are you doing out here anyway?!"

"It's done, witch whore!" Farley's stubby fingers clawed at the rifle and fumbled to balance the barrel between his hands. "Evidence! All the evidence! I kept it all these years! God's seen what you and the Apache done. God's seen your lust, Alicia Rose. No jumping, no bewitched horses to carry you away!"

As his hands struggled to grip and steady the gun, images of Charlotte's mother's last moments ripped into her heart: just like the pinto, just like Charlotte, Alicia cornered by the ugly, horrifying Farley. Her choices were no choices at all. Fight or flight. Her mother chose death by flight instead of death by Farley.

"You killed my mother!" Charlotte walked directly at him as he hoisted the rifle to his shoulder. "You killed my mother!" Anger boiled up from her belly, surged up her throat, poured down her arms and stung her eyes. "You *killed* my mother!"

Charlotte was ten feet from Farley. She pulled back her arm and pitched the jar of salve into his right eye. He collapsed to the ground, but managed to free the rifle and raise it. The ravens dropped from the trees ,and a swarm of black talons, beaks, eyes and wings descended on him. He was distracted by the ravens' fury, and as he lifted one hand to swat at them, Charlotte lunged. She grabbed the barrel of the rifle with both hands and felt it explode, heard the shell cut the air above her head like a train bound for the sky. As Charlotte fell with the rifle in her hands, the sun vanished. The ravens were everywhere, a frenzied tornado of black ash engulfing Farley.

Charlotte stood and stumbled back into the trees. The ravens regathered and ascended into the cottonwood branches. Farley lay folded on the ground like a dead animal. Tears streamed down Charlotte's face and dripped from her chin. She dropped the rifle on the sand and looked at her hands. Both palms and several fingers were burned where they had gripped the barrel, but miraculously she had not been shot.

{46}

Barty set the bag of groceries down on the kitchen counter. The house was too quiet. He walked to Thea's bedroom and leaned into the dim room. She lay fully clothed on top of the bed. Little Bit lay on the braided rug below and George was perched on the railing at the foot of Thea's bed.

"George, what the hell!" Barty whispered as he tiptoed across the floor. The rooster never came in the house. Never even wanted to come into the house. Ever. "How'd you get in here?"

George swung his head back and forth and made a murmuring, clucking sound. Barty stepped to the foot of the bed and reached for him. George puffed his feathers, flapped his stubby wings, and leapt noiselessly from the bed rail. In a burst of dove-like beauty the white rooster flew across the room to land gracefully on the blue ledge of the window.

Barty looked back at Nana on the bed, and realized what the rooster and the dog already knew: Dorothea Durham had departed.

~~~~~~~~~~~~~~~~~~~~~~~~~

The Lágrimas County coroner took Thea's body in an ambulance to the morgue in Dos Rios. After calling his sister Bernadette, Barty left Francis in the Durham kitchen in the care of Dennis and Earlene and headed out to the High Lonesome.

A police car was parked out front of Mabel Duran's boardinghouse, and everyone who lived within ten blocks was standing out front. Normally, Barty would have stopped to see what the commotion was about, but today, the eighth of July, 1998, was not and would never be remembered as normal: Nana Thea had died. Died peacefully in her sleep on her own bed. Died the death of a saint. Still, Nana's death had punched Barty in the abdomen, left him dazed and confused, a young boy who has twice lost his mother.

Vince Verger was peering into the office window of the B & B when Barty drove around back of the station and parked. Vince never did believe the station actually closed, day or night, winter, summer, spring or fall. Barty should just give Vince keys to the place and let him pump gas whenever he needed it.

"Barty Bill! You are here." Vince walked up to Barty parked near the storage shed. "Can I get some gas?"

Barty slid from the truck and stood with his hands on his hips, thinking. It was difficult to think, because his thoughts were drowning in emotion. Life as he knew it had stopped a few hours ago, and no one had told Vince.

"Vince, I'll give you the keys to the office and you can turn on the pump. You've seen me do it a thousand times." Barty reached into the truck's ashtray and retrieved keys to the station. "Here ya go."

"What? Aren't ya open?" Vince was a gentle soul who had worked for the state highway department all his life. He was a good customer, a person Barty had known for twenty years. Barty was afraid to tell Vince that he was not open because the world had stopped. Barty was afraid he might just break down and start crying like a child.

"No, actually, Vince, I'm not opening up. I'm headed out to the High Lonesome." Barty looked down at his boots and steadied his body like a plumb line over his feet. "Dorothea Durham died this afternoon and I need to get out and tell Jedidiah."

"Oh my gosh, my goodness!" Vince's hands grasped at his heart. They seemed to grasp at Barty's heart, too, although there was ten feet between them. "Why, I'm sorry, oh my, you go right ahead, I can wait till tomorrow. Goodness! How old was she?"

Thinking about something factual helped Barty realign himself with the physical earth. "I don't know exactly. Francis says she lied about her age to the Indian Service when she became a teacher, and her year of birth just became inconsequential after that."

"Imagine that."

"She used to say she was not as old as dirt, but she was old enough to become dirt one day soon."

"Imagine that."

Barty looked at the dirt by his boots. Could a life be worth as little as that? He turned on his heel and walked to his house. When he was inside the kitchen he sat down at the table and pulled out the envelope Francis had handed him back in the Durham kitchen. He studied his name written in Nana's shaky eighty-something-year-old hand, but he did not open the envelope. He needed to tell Jed first. He needed to drive out to the High Lonesome and find Jed. He needed to see Jed, to stand beside him, survey the renovations of the ranch house, talk construction, talk horses, talk cars, talk about what was to be done with Nana's body. Barty needed to find his nephew, find his sister's son, find a lifeline to tomorrow, to years of tomorrows that would not include Nana or Conchata, or his father, Thomas, his wife, Kitty, his soulmate Alicia, or his lost child, Benjamin Bill.

{47}

Farley was so mentally incapacitated and physically broken that Deputy Manuel Suazo did not bother with handcuffs. When Deputy Suazo asked Farley what he was doing, and why he had threatened Charlotte Lambert with a gun, Farley said she'd known it was coming for twenty years, and everyone who protected the witch whore would burn in hell alongside her. A confession, but not one admissible in any court in this world.

Jed stayed by Charlotte's side while the deputy radioed in to the sheriff's office for backup, and asked Charlotte question after question about what had gone on here. Finally, Deputy Suazo left the High Lonesome Ranch with Farley crumpled in the back seat of his cruiser, his raven-ravaged head bandaged with gauze. Jed and Charlotte returned to the barn. They stood in silence for a few minutes, staring out the open doors at the two sister mares, and at Noches and Britches standing in the corral.

"You told the deputy that Farley had threatened you several times." Jed turned to Charlotte, clearly distressed. "You never told me about the other time, your first day in Agua Dulce, when you were in the drugstore."

"No, I didn't." Charlotte swallowed a sob. "I just thought he was a crazy old man who swore at women. I didn't realize it was, well, personal."

"It wasn't personal, really. It was about your mother."

Charlotte looked quickly at Jed. "Haven't you noticed how everything my mother did here in the Lágrimas has attached itself personally to me?"

"Well, I think it's finally over now . . . ."

"Over? Jed, my family history was just completely rewritten! No, completely erased, wiped out! What I thought was fact is fiction! I've invested twenty years of emotions in a lie!"

"You don't have to digest this all at once." Jed stepped toward Charlotte but she walked out into the corral and took Noches by the halter.

"I think we should saddle up and see if we can find the pinto."

Charlotte, on Noches, and Jed, on Britches, rode through the *bosque*, weaving in and around the wide trunks of the cottonwoods. When they reached the sandy flats along the river they rode downstream until they found the pinto's prints in the mud of the riverbank. They followed them for a quarter of a mile, where the prints turned directly into the river.

"Can a horse swim that current?" Charlotte asked. The Lágrimas was narrow and deep here, and the far side of the river was a rock-strewn bank edged by sheer cliffs. "Why would the pinto choose to cross here? There's nowhere to go on the other side!"

Jed pulled Britches up alongside Noches. "Yeah, a horse can swim that current." Jed looked downriver. "But she'd probably come out down there where it widens, on that beach where the river bends. Let's go look."

Sure enough, the pinto's prints emerged from the water on the same side of the river.

Jed pointed at the prints leading back into the *bosque*. "The pinto wanted to lose whatever was after her."

Jed pulled up Britches at the edge of a cottonwood grove. The river made an unusually loud roar here because massive boulders dropped from the cliffs cut the swift current.

"I think she knows we're behind her," Jed said to Charlotte when she reached him. He gestured into the trees. The sun was low now, the golden strands of sundown grazing the tops of the cottonwoods and lighting on the highest stone ledges. "I say we continue downstream to my camp. The pinto can follow or not."

"She's okay out here?"

Jed's gaze was on Charlotte now. "That pinto is a survivor. She knows how to get back to the ranch. Or not."

They rode down the river canyon under a sky of pink and purple clouds. Dozens of swallows with mud homes in the crevices of the cliffs skimmed the river for insects, and larger birds, including five ravens, flew over the river and through the trees en route to their homes before dusk. Jed and Charlotte rode in silence. Charlotte was numbed by the chaotic collision of the old images of her mother with the new images, pictures still unformed, still distrusted, still without validity, or color, or depth. This new Alicia Rose Lambert was a stranger. But this Alicia, stranger or not, was Charlotte's mother.

Grandpa said it could take scientists years, even lifetimes, to prove their theories; it took the experts decades to accept a profound discovery, even with rock-solid data and irrefutable evidence. A long-held truth is not easily discarded. Human nature resists change and challenges radical alterations to familiar images. Proof. Everyone—paleontologists and biologists, astrophysicists and botanists, deputy sheriffs and daughters—demands proof.

Noches dropped her head down to the river, where a purple thread of dusk was reflected in a fluid, mercuric mirror, and took a long drink. Charlotte let go of the reins, leaned back in the saddle, and stared up into the sky. Grandpa said Alicia did not come to New Mexico to die. Did not return to the campsite on the desert near the Coelophysis quarry to end her life. He was absolutely certain of this. Even without evidence, he embraced this as a truth with his heart, mind and soul. Charlotte now knew that Grandpa's truth was accurate. But how did Grandpa know this and why didn't he share what he knew with her?

It was dusk when they rode the steep trail out of the river canyon onto the open ground of Jed's camp on the bluffs. After they unsaddled the horses, and put grain and alfalfa in the corral, Jed started the supper fire. Charlotte opened a can of beans, cut up sausage and cheese found in the cooler, and opened a bottle of red wine stored in the footlocker in the tent. While the fire settled down to a usable flame, Charlotte and Jed sat in the dark at the plank table and sipped wine from tin cups, and arranging and rearranging the smooth black stones.

"There'll be a full moon tonight, huh?" Charlotte asked Jed after a long silence.

"Yup."

The horses whinnied from the corral. Jed stood and peered in the direction of the corral. "Uncle Barty must be here. He probably heard about Farley."

Charlotte walked back to the fire and stirred the beans and sausage in the cook pot. Barty emerged from the juniper trees.

"Hello, Uncle." Jed greeted his uncle at the edge of the trees. "You heard about Farley."

Barty and Jed grasped hands. Barty did not let go. "Yeah, Dennis called me. And I saw the commotion at Mabel's. Jed, Nana died this afternoon."

ıılllıılllıılllıılllıılllıılllıılll

The flame of the kerosene lamp flickered on the black river stones on the table. Charlotte told Barty about Farley's horrifying attack in the *bosque*. Barty told Jed and Charlotte about finding Thea on her bed, her guardian angels, Little Bit and George, watching over her. All in one day. Barty's heart hurt so much he wondered if his valves were closing down.

The desert night became a desert wonderland as the full moon rose off the horizon. Jed, Barty, and Charlotte stood on the lip of the cliff and watched the luminous sphere lift into the eastern sky. It was the brightest moon Barty could remember seeing, and the light it cast was most certainly not of this world.

They returned to camp and sat down again around Jed's table. Barty took out the letter he had carried in his back pocket since leaving the Durham kitchen hours before.

"I found this letter on Nana Thea's bedside table." Barty turned the envelope over in his hand. "There was an envelope for Francis, too. Thea asked that Francis cremate her body and have the ashes returned to the ranch and placed in that coffee can she looked so hard to find."

In spite of the lump in his throat, Barty managed to smile. The moon was high enough to clear the trees and light Jed and Charlotte's faces. Their eyes glistened with tears.

"Francis was instructed to give me the coffee can. I assume this letter from Nana will tell me what to do with, well, with her ashes."

Barty opened the envelope and pulled out three small sheets of notepaper. He held them up above the table where he could easily read them in the moonlight.

"Now you must do these things I ask, Bartholomew. No arguing." Barty smiled and wiped his eyes. "As if we could argue now!"

Barty cleared his throat. "When my ashes are returned from Dos Rios, you will take me and Jed and Charlotte into the mountains on horseback.

296

Pack enough for two nights. Ride up the southern route, through the Puertocito, across Antelope Mesa to Apache Ridge. Camp on the meadow on the other side, at the summer camp where your father died."

Barty paused. Just two days ago Nana had asked him for these directions. But he never got around to giving them to her.

Jed reached a hand across the table and touched Barty's wrist. "The place where Farley shot Grandfather Thomas?"

"Yes." Barty looked back at the letter held up to catch the gleam of the moon. "At first light scatter my ashes from that precipice where we liked to eat oranges and apples. Conchata says it has the best view of Summerland, and is a fine place to begin a journey. . . ."

Barty's voice cracked. He read the rest of Thea's letter in silence, folded it up and slid it back into the envelope.

Barty stood and gazed out at the moonlit wonderland surrounding the camp. "We'll take Britches, Noches and Dolly. The two sisters are still good pack horses. Thea said we must take the pinto with us. With that horse missing and all, I just don't know how we'll do this."

Jed and Charlotte left the table and joined Barty beside the firepit where embers glowed.

"She said take the pinto to the mountains?" Charlotte asked. "Did Thea say to leave the pinto in the mountains?"

"Yes," Barty said. "I can't put a rope on her, so the pinto is going to have to want to follow. And given the events of the last few days . . ." Barty lost his thought. How could he have not been there for Charlotte?! All these years, how could he have let Farley walk free around the Lágrimas? Years ago Barty's intuition told him Farley was near Alicia when she died. Why hadn't he insisted the sheriff question more people, pry open more doors?

Barty looked at Charlotte. Her face was passive with exhaustion and shock. "Charlotte, I certainly understand if this whole mountain expedition is just too much for you to undertake."

"I want to go," Charlotte said quickly, looking up at Barty.

Barty held Charlotte's gaze. Her eyes shone. "Thea's instructions include spending the second night at the fossil quarry. We'll stop for an overnight at your grandfather's field camp."

Jed washed up cups and plates and put them away on the shelf in the camp kitchen. Charlotte put more wood into the fire and placed the cooking grill over the low flames.

"We'll talk details tomorrow," Barty said. "I think I'll head out now."

Jed reached for Barty and rested his hand on his shoulder. "Why don't you stay out here with us for a while longer?"

"Oh, no," Barty said. "I've got things waiting back at the station."

"I'll make a pot of chamomile tea," Charlotte said, as she opened a canvas bag hanging on a branch near the tent. She dug about the bag until she pulled out a glass bottle. "Just last Saturday, Thea and I made desert-anemone tincture. Five drops in our tea of this potent little *remedio* will make the passage of this night a tad less difficult."

The gear gathered from Dennis's garage behind the drugstore, from the storage shed at the hardware store, and from the tack room at the High Lonesome was spread out and meticulously organized on the work tables in the barn. Charlotte walked around the gear, fingering cinches, breast collars and latigos.

"Some of this looks like it belongs in a museum," Charlotte said, running her hand along the age-polished wood of one of the pack saddles Barty called a "tried and true sawbuck."

"Barty made a good decision about the bedrolls," Jed said. "To use them we'd have to take another pack horse because they're so heavy. The lightweight sleeping bags will be much easier. Nana Thea will understand."

Jed was attaching a leather strap with a buckle onto one of the panniers. There were six canvas panniers, three sets, on the work table, and all dated back to Jed's grandfather's time.

"We'll use only two sets of panniers for this trip." Jed set down the pannier with the new buckle, picked up a rope halter, and began to untie one of the knots. Charlotte marveled at the dexterity of Jed's fingers as he retied the rope into a complicated knot. "We'll put leather saddlebags on each of the horses we're riding. It will be a little tight; we won't take as much food, but we'll be fine."

Jed placed the halter on the table and walked to the barn doors. Barty was breaking open a bale of hay out by the windmill. Twenty-four hours had passed and the pinto had not returned.

"My mother would enjoy going on this pack trip," Jed said. "But she had knee surgery last winter. And Francis shouldn't be alone right now."

This morning's arrival of Bernadette Lonewolf Bill to the Durham ranch initiated a shift in the household atmosphere. Bernadette was energetic and energizing. She had the body of a teenage athlete—broad-shouldered and muscular—with black hair pulled into a ponytail that hung down her back. She moved into the Durham household like a whirlwind of organization and stability, insisting Charlotte remain in her room, and unpacking her bags in Barty's old bedroom. After greeting the burros and inspecting Thea's garden, Bernadette had gone into the kitchen and begun to cook and prepare food for the camping trip to the mountains.

"I was nervous about meeting your mother," Charlotte said. "What would she think of this stranger who walked in out of the dark a few weeks ago and was now living with the Durhams and sleeping with her son?"

Jed snorted. "And then you met her, and she probably said something friendly and blunt about you and me and the universe, right?"

Charlotte laughed. "Within ten minutes of her arrival your mother told me that your engagement had worried her for years, but she always knew you would come to your senses and remember who you are."

Charlotte walked to the far end of the work table where two pairs of leather chaps were laid out. "She didn't say anything about you and me."

"She hasn't been around you long enough," Jed said. "Give her time. But she already likes you, or the idea of you, because of how you came to be here."

Charlotte looked quizzically at Jed. "Because of my mother?"

"Well, that too, But I told her about the raven that landed on your windshield." Jed walked around the table and stood beside Charlotte. "*That's* a story that gets my mother's approval."

Charlotte smiled and picked up the smaller pair of chaps and held them against her legs. "Am I wearing these?"

"You are." Jed picked up the second, larger pair. "These are the real thing. They'll protect your legs."

"I'm a little nervous that I won't be able to keep up on such a long ride. You know, I'm *not* the real thing. I'm just pretending I'm a cowgirl."

Jed set the chaps down and reached over and took Charlotte by the shoulders. "You'll be able to keep up, you're a great rider. We're all pretending we know what we're doing. None of us has been horse camping in years. And to me, Charlotte, you're the first real thing I've known in a long, long time. Maybe ever."

Jed leaned down and kissed Charlotte on the mouth, pushing curls away from her forehead. "I'm going over to the ranch house to work with Arthur on the table saw. We've got to cut the tongue-and-groove for the ceiling before we go tomorrow morning."

Charlotte and Jed found Arthur unpacking a load of aspen tongue-and-groove that had been delivered from a lumber mill yesterday.

"Teacher!" Arthur tipped his baseball cap and smiled broadly.

Charlotte walked over to Arthur. He stopped moving boards and looked at her. "Arthur, you already know that because of this trail ride I won't be able to go with you to the test tomorrow. I'm sorry about that."

"I know. I heard. I'll be okay." Arthur pulled out another board and slid it onto the sawhorse where Jed measured it for cutting. "I'm okay, Charlotte. I'm, you know, making good decisions. *Como* this board: straight and narrow."

Jed pulled the tape measure down the board and marked the cutting line with a pencil. "We'll be needing at least forty pieces twenty-seven inches on center, *viga* to *viga*."

"Okay." Arthur nodded to Jed and turned back to Charlotte. "Did Inez tell you I'm reading to the children every afternoon now?"

"¿*Verdad*?" Charlotte shaded her eyes to see Arthur's face. He was smiling.

"*Verdad*." Arthur pulled the marked boards from the sawhorse and carried them to the table saw set up inside the unfinished room.

"Charlotte!" Arthur walked back out to Charlotte. "Wait. I want to apologize."

"For what?"

"For telling Farley about you being out at the High Lonesome. I was just so proud to be your student. My big mouth put you in danger. *Cristo*, I'm such a fool!"

Charlotte sighed and looked at Jed and then Arthur. "We were all fools about that man."

{49}

At seven a.m. on Friday the tenth of July Dennis brought the red and black coffee can of Thea's ashes out to the High Lonesome. He gave it to Barty, who placed it into one of Molly's panniers. Dennis stayed to help Barty, Jed, and Charlotte pack up the five horses.

If anyone besides Charlotte was aware of the date's importance, no one said so. At least not to her. It was better this way, she decided while she packed her saddle bags with a change of socks and underwear, a rain slicker, sweater, jacket, sunblock, plastic bags of nuts and dried fruit, apples, water bottles, a mess kit borrowed from Gus, and the grey stone she'd picked up from the stream weeks ago. Today might not even be the anniversary. Farley might have once known the exact day and time of Alicia's death in 1976, but he was no longer capable of sharing those details.

The sheriff's preliminary report about Farley's attack on Charlotte said that Farley was convinced that she was her mother. He repeatedly told the sheriff Alicia Rose was still alive. In Farley's sick brain no crime and no murder had ever been committed. Not now, and not back in 1976.

By nine a.m. the six horses were saddled and packed and waiting in the corral.

"How many miles?" Charlotte asked Jed as she climbed onto Noches. "To the mountains."

"Twelve." Jed climbed onto Britches.

"But the elevation gain will be more than three thousand feet," Dennis said as he led Mandy to Jed and handed him her reins. "Take it slow."

Barty on Dolly led Molly. Jed and Britches led Mandy, and Charlotte and Noches took up the rear. After a tearful goodbye to Dennis, they headed out past the windmill and the fresh, untouched hay for the pinto. Arthur would check the oat bag each day they were gone. But Barty thought the pinto would not return. She had run too far, been scarred too deep.

302

"I'm just real sorry I can't carry out Nana's wish," Barty said as the string of horses and riders passed the water tank. Four ravens, scrawny juveniles, preened themselves on the motionless blades of the windmill. The mares eyed the scrub oak but swung their heads back onto the road ahead. Their loco friend was gone.

"Not your fault," Jed said. He, like Charlotte, was scanning the *bosque* and the *llanos* along the river. "Not even Thea could see everything that was coming."

Two miles out from the ranch house they crossed the fenced boundary between the High Lonesome and federal land. Jed left the gate open in case the pinto followed them.

Midmorning they stopped by a lone cottonwood on one side of a beach-like expanse of finely grained white sand. There was patchy grass for the horses, and enough shade from the solitary tree for everyone to sit out of the sun and snack on fruit and water. Barty wanted to reach the first spring before noon and cut short their water break. They remounted and were back on the trail still munching snacks and gulping water from their canteens.

Charlotte slathered sunblock on her hands and forearms, and kept her bandanna over the skin between her collar and her hairline. Jed was right: the chaps, although unwieldy and awkward on foot, in the saddle gave Charlotte protection against branches and rocks.

The spring where they stopped for lunch was at the base of dark rock walls, craggy and jagged, not like the smooth forms of the canyonlands they had just crossed.

"This is the beginning of the Agustinas," Barty explained. "This water comes from deep in the mountains. The big trees begin at the top of this shelf."

"Cat Springs," Jed said. He ate his sandwich from a perch above the small pool. He'd been taking tincture all morning to manage seasonal allergies.

"Why Cat Springs?" Charlotte asked.

Barty had finished lunch and was stretched out flat on the shaded ground. "Because the mountain lions come and wait up there on those rocks."

"What are they waiting for?" Charlotte peered up at ledges where small trees grew from the stone. If a mountain lion was up there, he would be completely hidden from view.

"Lunch," Barty said, adjusting his hat over his face. Three breaths later, he was asleep.

The trail angled up and around the sides of two deep canyons, with sheer drops just a yard or so from the horses' feet. Noches was nonchalant about the trail's width and the gaping abyss to their right. Charlotte gave Noches plenty of rein, as Jed instructed, and kept her eyes on Mandy's rear or on the space defined by Noches' ears, until the trail left the cavernous canyons behind and they rode up into a dense ponderosa forest.

The trees gave off a heady summer fragrance of pine bark and sap. It was cool here and the deep carpet of pine needles muffled the horses' steps. Barty directed the string into a clearing of tall grass. Charlotte walked Noches into the small meadow, turned in the saddle and looked back: the slope they had just climbed dropped down and away to the red and brown Lágrimas desert that stretched into the eastern horizon.

"Wow," Charlotte said. "Did we ride across all of that?"

Jed rode up and stopped Britches and Mandy alongside Noches. "Follow that green vein, the river, and you'll see Agua Dulce. Just a few roofs glinting in the sun. The High Lonesome is there, left of the river, to the right of town. We've only ridden about a fourth of that expanse."

Barty dismounted and checked the straps on Molly's packs. "We'll stop for ten minutes."

The horses munched grass. Charlotte sipped water and ate raisins. Jed pointed out landmarks familiar to her so she could visually retrace their trail across the canyonlands. They were now nine thousand feet above sea level and the air was thin and clear. The meadow was blooming with wild irises and penstemon, favorites of Conchata's and Thea's, although the plants had no medicinal uses.

They remounted and walked back into the trees where Barty suddenly pulled up Dolly. He turned and looked behind them at the meadow.

"What is it?" Jed asked. Britches and Noches were also distracted by something.

Barty faced forward again and urged Dolly on into the timber. "We're being followed."

Charlotte looked back. In the shadows on the far side of the meadow was a horse. "The pinto!"

After seven hours in the saddle, Charlotte understood how a human in the wilderness came to depend completely on a horse. Charlotte hardly gave directives, and Noches established her own pace through the trees, around fallen trunks, and over tangled shrubs.

They left the forest for rocky scree where miniature flowers grew close to the earth between the stones. They were approaching the slender knife of gray rock called Apache Ridge, a narrow rim that crossed to the peaks of the Agustinas that were now the only horizon against the late-afternoon sky.

"This is the pass," Jed said, reading the tension in Charlotte's face. "We just ride to the shoulder, cross the ridge and drop down onto the other side. It's not as bad as it looks, Charlotte. Just trust Noches and give her her head."

Jed and Britches waited until Barty, Dolly, and Molly were fifteen feet ahead before following them onto the ridge. Jed instructed Charlotte to do the same behind Britches and Mandy. With her head high Noches stepped onto the grey surface of the narrow path and kept pace with the horses ahead. Charlotte watched Jed, mostly to keep her mind off the five-hundred foot drop to either side of the knife-wide trail. Jed was elegant and calm as he led Mandy over the dangerous ridge. Barty reached the wide wing of land on the other side and swung around to follow their progress over the ridge.

"That was gutsy riding," Barty said when everyone had crossed. "The Apaches knew a horse could cross that ridge. But the cavalry, looking at it from a distance, didn't believe it could be done."

"And the pinto?" Charlotte leaned into the saddle horn and gazed back at the trail.

Barty removed his hat and wiped his forehead with his shirt-sleeve. "If she wants whatever is up here enough, she'll cross." Barty reined Dolly around. "Let's go. We're almost to the summer camp."

The horses took long drinks before walking around the pebbly shore of a small lake filled with snowmelt. The earth to the south and west of this side of the Agustinas was brown and gold, more fractured with canyons and deep cuts than the Lágrimas side of the mountains.

"The Colorado Plateau," Jed said, pointing to the landscape below them. "Most of that is Navajo land. All that red, gold and brown reaches across New Mexico into Arizona."

"It really is another country up here, isn't it?"

"Who told you that?" Jed asked, smiling. He already knew.

"Francis."

{50}

Gus spent the morning seated at Inez's desk in the Agua Dulce Library staring at a computer screen as it flipped through the pages of the Dos Rios *Weekly Sentinel*. Inez had set up the computer for Gus. Prior to today Gus had never interacted with the internet, whatever that was. He really just wanted to thumb his way through old newspapers the way he did in the old days.

Gus had been awakened in the wee hours of pre-dawn by a voice nothing short of insistent that he get on with his work. Gus managed to go back to sleep, but at sunrise he woke up and knew that to get on with his work he had to go to the Agua Dulce Library.

The boys frowned when Gus walked past them on the drugstore bench.

"What's your hurry, Treadle?" Benny Madrid barked as Gus ambled past. "It's barely nine o'clock. You ain't had your cup of joe yet!"

"I've got work that can't wait," Gus told them.

"What work?" Alfredo asked, leaning forward on the bench and aiming his good ear at Gus to hear what he might say in response. "They already locked up our local criminal, Holoman Farley. You got some burro or cow needs tracking?"

The boys laughed, then became serious. Benny stood up. "Need our help?"

"I got to do some research first. I'll call ya if I need ya."

Just two days ago at the soda fountain Dorothea had told Gus to go along with the sheriff. Exactly what the sheriff might be doing that Gus could be going along with was a mystery to Gus then and now. But the insistent voice before dawn had instructed Gus to dig up the old papers. The only place that had old papers was the library.

At the library Inez kept asking Gus what he was looking for. Gus kept telling her he didn't know what he was looking for! He continued to press the 'page down' button on the keyboard as he squinted at the text and pictures going by on the screen. Nothing presented itself to be dug up: no unidentified remains, no unsolved murder, not even the lost child Thea had fretted about weeks ago. And now it was noon and Inez was closing up for her lunch hour.

Gus stood outside the library on the walkway that led to the alley wondering what in God's green earth had possessed him to waste a morning looking at a computer screen!

"I'll be back in an hour." Inez pulled the solid wood door closed behind her and stood beside Gus. "Do you need a ride anywhere, Mr. Treadle?"

A car rounded the corner from Dos Hermanos into the alley.

"Oh my," Inez said, walking away from Gus. "It's the sheriff."

Gus put on his cowboy hat and peered into the alley. Sure enough, the vehicle that had pulled alongside the adobe wall had the red roof-beacons of a Dos Rios County Sheriff's Department cruiser. Gus hobbled quickly down the walkway after Inez, who was already talking to the deputy through his car window.

"I'm headed out there now," the deputy told Inez. He greeted Gus with a nod of his head. His badge said Deputy Manuel Suazo. He was young, broad shouldered, and new to the Lágrimas. Deputy Suazo was telling Inez that he needed all the help he could get finding his way out to Mr. Holoman Farley's trailer. "Folks at the drugstore said Mr. Mata would go with me to the old landfill, but he's not there. I guess he's a close friend of the family that lost their grandma a few days ago."

"Dorothea Durham," Gus said, clearing his throat. "Yes, she passed away the same day you arrested Farley. Deputy, I can take you out to Holoman Farley's trailer."

Inez looked at Gus as if he had just suggested they enter a bull-riding contest. Gus ignored her and stepped in closer to the car window. "Why are you going out there, if I might ask?"

The deputy hesitated. "It's official business, sir."

Gus bent down to the window. "My name is Gustafson Treadle and I was a member of the Dos Rios sheriff's posse, was head of it, actually, for two decades before you could hold a spoon or drink from your own cup. I know this land like the back of this wrinkled but steady hand, and I am here to assist you with whatever business you have around Holoman Farley."

The deputy's face broke into a bright smile. "Well, Mr. Treadle! I've heard of you around the office! You're quite a legend, you are! I'd be honored to have your assistance."

The deputy cleared his throat and lowered his voice. "As you know, Mr. Farley was taken into custody Monday after he assaulted and threatened a young woman with a deadly weapon out at the High Lonesome Ranch. He's *almost* confessed to a manslaughter that happened twenty years ago, although Mr. Farley claims the woman didn't die, so there's nothing qualifying as manslaughter. I'm going out to his Airstream to see if there are any clues about the 1970s incident, or about this incident two days ago at the High Lonesome. Mr. Farley said the young woman he threatened was guilty of, and I quote, 'crimes against God and men, punishable by death.'"

"Goodness!" Inez exhaled and placed her hand against her neck.

Gus walked around the front end of the cruiser, climbed into the front seat and buckled up. "I'm guessing the deadly weapon he had out at the High Lonesome was a rifle, a Winchester 1894, not his older model."

Deputy Suazo was smiling as he put the cruiser in gear and said a polite good-bye to Inez still standing by the car. "We found a mint-condition model 1873 Winchester in a footlocker in Farley's attic room at Mabel's boardinghouse. Wonder what we'll find out at his trailer?"

{51}

Half a century of sun and stars had passed across the sky of this country since the last time Barty had set up for a night at summer camp. He knew where to find the stone ring of a long-ago firepit and dried wood for kindling. He knew the horses would have plenty of grass and that if a wind began in the hours before sunrise, the wall of granite that rose up to the peaks would block their camp from the high-mountain cold.

Jed was in charge of settling the horses for the night. He placed hobbles on Britches, Mandy, Molly and Noches but put a bell on Dolly, who had a disagreeable personality change if she was hobbled. Charlotte unpacked the pannier with the cooking gear and arranged a kitchen on the stone slabs near the firepit Barty resurrected. They placed sleeping bags on the flat ground in the southwest end of the meadow—Jed and Charlotte's to one side, Barty's far away on the other side—where they would get the first warmth of the sun tomorrow morning. Barty set the stakes for the tarp they would sleep under if it rained. Everyone was busy. They were all exhausted and withdrew into their own thoughts.

After supper, Barty wandered away from Jed and Charlotte sitting together beside the campfire. He walked far down through the meadow and out to a precipice of rock with a hundred-mile view to the southwest. This is where they would bring Thea's ashes tomorrow morning.

Barty had returned to this rock ledge above the plateau a hundred times in his imagination, had relived those last moments: Duende running at a full gallop between Barty's father and Farley, the explosion from Farley's rifle, his father's slow plunge from his horse, and the silence on the meadow after Duende leapt into open space and his father fell into death. Over supper Jed had told Charlotte about the great stallion's desperate leap from this very ledge, about how for years every rider from the Lágrimas who heard the story about

Farley, Thomas Bill, and the Duende, the Thoroughbred-gone-wild, searched the deep canyon below for Duende's remains. No one ever found them—not the stallion's bones or fur, prints or blood. Duende simply vanished.

All these years Barty had feared that a return to this ledge would crack open the door to an ugly, disturbing place in his soul. But here he was, looking directly into the vast space of myth and memory, and the only door opening was to the understanding that he was coming to the end of midlife. Soon Barty would move into his later years. His days on this earth, like his father's and mother's, like Thea's, like Alicia's and Duende's, were going to come to an end. How that end would come he could not say. But it would come. Alicia's end, like his father's, like Duende's, was hastened by the lunatic Farley. Barty ought to be feeling rage, but tonight all he felt was a numb understanding that he had no control over the people and events of this earth. The only part of this life he had ever had any control over was how he responded to loss and how he chose to acknowledge and to give love.

Rage, remorse, guilt, anger, regret—none of these would serve him. Never had.

A muffled thump echoed from the forest. Barty did not react but kept his eyes on the purple sundown sweeping the plateau below. When the purple burned itself to the silver of twilight, he turned his head slowly to the right. The ghost light of the mountain dusk was reflected in the glossy, wary eyes of the pinto who watched him from the shelter of a thousand trees.

ıllıllıllıllıllıllıllıllıllıllı

Their two sleeping bags were zipped together into one large bed that encased Charlotte and Jed in a cocoon of down. Even wearing silk long-underwear, a turtleneck, and thick cotton socks, and with Jed's long arms holding her body against his, before midnight Charlotte woke to feel the mountain's cold breath moving across the meadow.

The moon lit the meadow of summer camp. Across the grass was the sleeping form of Barty. The horses were beyond him near the trees, their heads low. Jed was in a deep sleep beside her. Charlotte looked straight up

311

into the moon and breathed in the mountain night. Barty told them he had seen the pinto before sundown. The horse wouldn't come near him, of course. But the pinto had made it to the mountains. Thea would be pleased.

"The heavens are the home of the bone horses," Charlotte whispered to the sky. And from the meadow of summer camp, their home in the heavens felt very close.

{52}

Charlotte woke before dawn. She had to pee but hated to leave the warmth of the down cocoon. She reluctantly opened one eye and peered over the top of the sleeping bag. A light so faint she could perceive it only by looking away edged the northeastern sky. First light. Charlotte tried to convince her bladder that it could wait another hour, but the need to relieve herself was painfully unavoidable.

She pulled her torso up through the top opening of the sleeping bag. Jed grunted and turned over, but did not wake. Her boots, jeans and jacket were beside the sleeping bag. Charlotte shivered as she stood and quickly put on her clothes, then walked across the meadow to the edge of the forest. At the first trees she dropped her pants, squatted on the ground, and urinated into the pine needles. She stood, pulled up her long johns and zipped up her jeans. The dawn was emerging in the east, but the moon still sailed in the western sky. Her eyes had adjusted to the soft light, and she made out the forms of the hobbled horses on the far side of the meadow. Charlotte turned around and peered into the forest behind. Something was standing in the trees.

"Pinto?" she whispered. The horse made a low sound. "Pinto!"

Charlotte took a step, but before her boot even found the ground, the pinto turned and walked into the forest. Charlotte glanced back at the meadow where the boys slept, then turned and broke into a jog after the pinto through the dim forest.

The pinto headed down a long, steep, heavily forested slope. Charlotte's boots slipped on the wet pine needles and moist earth. Twice she lost her footing and fell onto her knees. The thick cushion of pine and grass softened her falls, and Charlotte was up on her feet before the pinto vanished into the trees ahead. The sky turned pink, and through the tops of the trees that dropped down the mountain, Charlotte looked out at the sunrise on the desert plateau two thousand feet below.

The forest ended in a boulder field, and Charlotte slowed to a walk. Her heart was pounding from the fast descent. The pinto did not stop but trotted ahead and out of sight between enormous rocks. Charlotte followed the mare into a narrow slot between the boulders, then stepped out onto a meadow. She stopped to let her eyes adjust to the scene before her. The pinto stood knee-deep in grass and wildflowers that glistened with the sparkling sheen of the morning sky. The mountain ridge dropped to the south and the canyonlands.

Charlotte stepped back and refocused her gaze. There was more to this scene than the splendor of the high-country summer sunrise. Beyond the pinto, to the left and right, the near and far, were horses.

"Oh my God," Charlotte whispered.

The pinto seemed satisfied with Charlotte's response and walked into the meadow and began to graze. The herd—Charlotte counted twenty-five adults, with five youngsters—observed the pinto and Charlotte. Had these mustangs ever seen a human? Maybe from a distance, and even then their encounters with people must have been benign. These mustangs were not afraid of Charlotte, and within a few minutes of her arrival on the meadow, most of the horses dropped their heads and returned to their grazing.

Charlotte sat down on her haunches with her back against a boulder. The pinto grazed near a small chocolate-brown mustang with a thick mane and a tail so long it touched the ground. The pinto stood out in the herd because of her flamboyant markings. But appearances aside, she looked as if she had grazed with these mustangs all her life: she was not twitching or jerking her head, flicking her ears, or rolling her eyes. She submitted to the wild mares' inspections as they checked her over with outstretched heads, some with ears laid back, but otherwise without apparent animosity. The mountain mustangs seemed to intuit the pinto's character and story. She was home.

The sun struck the east side of the highest peaks and rolled over the tips of the ponderosas on the east flanks of the mountains to the south. Charlotte's stomach grumbled with hunger. She stood slowly. The herd stopped grazing, lifted their heads, and looked across the meadow at the human near the boulders. Would the mustangs still be here if Charlotte went for Jed and Barty? This magical encounter would not last forever. Charlotte did not want to leave. If she went back to the camp for the boys, brought them here and found the herd gone, could Charlotte convince herself that she had even seen them?

The mustangs dropped their heads again to graze. Only the pinto continued to watch Charlotte. She could see the wound on her right shoulder. It was dry and clean—healing. Another treatment with salve would help, but Charlotte knew she would never again get close enough to the pinto to dab ointment on the wound. The horse had crossed a boundary, stepped from the country of the tame into the country of the wild.

The heads of all of the mustangs lifted in unison as Jed emerged from the rocks.

"Charlotte? What, how did you, my God. Look at all those horses!"

"I'll be danged!" Barty walked through the rocks behind Jed.

They stood shoulder to shoulder and watched the horses in silence. After a few minutes, Jed and Barty began to speak softly about the beauty of a particular mare, the size of a filly or colt. Barty kept an eye on the forest and wondered where the harem's stallion might be. But the stallion did not show himself.

They watched the mustangs for close to half an hour. Then Barty placed his hand on Charlotte's shoulder. "Say your good-bye to the pinto. We have ashes to scatter."

Charlotte watched the pinto for a few more minutes. The mare had moved to the far side of the meadow. Barty and Jed vanished back into the boulders. Charlotte whispered a silent good-bye to the pinto and followed the boys off the meadow.

They walked single file through the forest that was now streaked with sunlight. When they were almost back to summer camp, Barty stopped.

"It was never about the ashes, this trail ride," he said. "It was about those horses. Thea always said the wild horses were safe in the high country. But she knew I had to see them for myself."

{53}

Jed and Charlotte followed Barty out onto the flat shelf of stone with the hundred-mile view of the canyon country. Barty set the can with Thea's ashes on the stone and unfolded the letter he'd carried for days in his pocket. Per Thea's instructions, he read aloud her last words:

"And so it is with great joy I am no longer of this body, and step into the realm of endless light and freedom. My children, you will soon return to the land below your feet. But now you know what of yours is up here. May the horses of the angels carry me, and one day each of you, to the summerland beyond the horizon. I love you and am with you always."

Barty pried the lid from the tin, held his arm out over the ledge and tilted the can. Thea's ashes fell into the sky below their feet, and what had been heavy particles of bone turned to fine dust and fluttered like feathers into the morning sunlight.

They talked about the mustangs as they packed up the panniers, sipped the last thick dregs of cowboy coffee, shoveled sand over the firepit, and saddled up. Barty said the six mustangs that came for the six fallen soldiers in 1942 were bays, all but one: the last mare was a palomino. They all agreed that there was a preponderance of stocky bays in the wild herd, and they had each counted three palominos with high white socks among the mustangs of the Agustinas.

Barty knew the stallion had seen them, was close by. As they broke camp he kept an eye on the tree line, looking for movement. Dolly and Noches were agitated when they returned to the meadow, and the two sister mares were distracted. Leather Britches, always a gentleman, was downright obnoxious, and nipped at the mares as if he had been shot up with testosterone.

They filed out of the summer camp meadow the same way they had filed in last evening. For Barty, everything had changed. The place was no longer only a place of death. It was still the place where his father died in the feathery grasses on the east side of the meadow, but it was a place of resurrection, too.

Barty turned in his saddle before they entered the first stand of dense trees and surveyed summer camp one more time. Even if he saw the stallion, and he was blue-black and racetrack fast, smart, sleek and had the perfect proportions of a registered Thoroughbred, Barty knew the stallion would not, could not be Duende. Even in the best children's stories, Duende would have been dead at least forty years now. Still, the little boy who saw the great black stallion leap into open space and vanish into legend, that little boy kept scanning the treeline for the improbable, miraculous ending.

{54}

Gus Treadle and Deputy Suazo stood side by side near the sheriff's cruiser and stared at the dilapidated hulk of aluminum that had housed Holoman Farley for thirty-some years. The ground surrounding the trailer was a charred color, the earth completely denuded of vegetation because Farley routinely burned off whatever desert plants attempted to grow here. Beyond the trailer was the trash-and-rubble-lined rim of the pit that was formerly the Lágrimas valley landfill. Ravens sat on the wire fence that surrounded the defunct dump, preening their black bodies while gurgling and chortling to one another. The large birds—Gus counted seven, all adults—were unimpressed by the appearance of the pistol-packing deputy and the retired chief of the Dos Rios sheriff's posse.

"I guess we'd best look inside." Suazo pulled a crowbar from the trunk of the cruiser and walked across the wasteland to the trailer. Gus shuffled behind him, wishing his legs didn't feel so wobbly and brittle. There was work to be done and Gus had no patience with the complaints and excuses of a geriatric lawman.

With the crowbar, the deputy popped the lock and latch on the Airstream's door. Like Gus, the deputy stepped back as the curved door swung outward on noisy hinges. A foul stench erupted from the interior. Gus stumbled back and covered his face with his arm. Suazo gagged and dropped the crowbar.

"Jesus Christ!" Suazo walked away from the trailer, pulled a bandanna from his rear pocket and held it over his mouth.

Gus's sense of smell didn't work so well anymore, but even he recoiled from the unmistakable reek of rotten, decomposing animal flesh emanating from Farley's trailer.

"Farley hasn't lived here for six months or so," Gus told the deputy. "There's something ripe in there. Probably an animal got caught in one of the ceiling vents."

"Foul." Suazo frowned at the open door. "I've got a face mask in the car. Why don't you look around outside."

Gus stood on the charred earth between the patrol car and the trailer. With hands on hips he did a slow 360-degree survey. People still brought truckloads of garbage out to the landfill—a crude gate had been cut into the wire fence—and they usually set fire to their trash before they left so that no one could trace the unsanctioned dumping back to them. Not that anyone from the county waste department ever ventured out here.

Suazo walked from the cruiser back toward the Airstream. "I'll call ya in if I think there's something needing your skilled eye."

"Okay." Gus watched the young deputy put on his mask and climb into the Airstream.

"I'm looking for a child, Gus," Thea said the very last time they spoke at the soda fountain. This was not a good place to look for a child. Gus's stomach dropped: the smell of decomposing flesh in the trailer! Oh, God, what if the lost child was in there?

Gus shuffled a half turn to look at the desert north of the trailer. He drew in a deep breath, as deep and long as his lungs would accommodate. Then he took another step and faced the west. Almost high noon. In the absence of shadows, the canyonlands were flat. It was time to do his job. Gus had to face whatever smelled in that trailer.

"Gus? You okay?" Suazo leaned out of the trailer door. He still wore his mask. "I found two dead pack rats caught in the old stove vent. You found anything?"

"Not yet, deputy," Gus called back.

Suazo disappeared into the Airstream again. Gus rebalanced himself.

"You were always the one who noticed the turned stones, the compressed earth, flattened grass. The trail." Gus looked at the ground. What trail could he find in this barren landscape? There were no stones left to turn, and the earth was so compressed it resembled concrete. But he had promised Thea he would go with the sheriff into the canyonlands and look for someone everyone else had forgotten. They weren't even in the canyonlands. And Gus was with the deputy, not the sheriff.

The ravens perched on the fence by the landfill spread their wings and hopped into the air. Gus squinted and followed as all seven flew directly overhead, then dropped from the air and landed in the scrawny, half-dead branches of a juniper growing against the western fence line. Gus studied the barbed wire that served as the boundary between the land poisoned by Farley and the pure, clean earth of the canyonlands.

The canyonlands. Gus walked across the blackened sandscape to the tree occupied by the ravens. He lowered his stiff torso down onto his bony old knees in the gritty dirt and crawled under the dry branches. And then he saw what he had been looking for: disturbed earth. Gus pushed his crooked fingers into the sandy soil. He needed a tool and reached up and snapped off the end of one of the dead branches. As Gus began to dig into the dirt, the ravens cawed and crackled, cheering him on until the stick struck metal. He dug his fingers around the sides of a lid and wedged the can free.

"Thomas J. Webb," Gus said to the ravens in the branches above him. "Thea could have just told me to find an old Webb coffee can."

Exhausted by the effort, Gus sat back against the trunk of the cedar tree. He placed the coffee can between his knees and pried at the top.

"Gus!" Suazo emerged from the trailer and removed his mask. He held up a weathered plank of wood. "I found this under the mattress. What the hell does it mean?"

Gus removed the can's lid and set it on the sand. He looked up and squinted at the narrow piece of grey wood the young deputy held high in the air: *No Fossils, No Jam.*

ᴧᴧᴧᴧᴧᴧᴧᴧᴧᴧᴧᴧᴧ

After recrossing precipitous Apache Ridge the three riders and five horses headed off the west end of the Agustinas by a different route than yesterday. This was all in precise accordance with Thea's last wishes described in the letter Barty carried in his rear pocket. Charlotte recognized the landscape below, identifying the spires and island mesas that were part of the vista from Jed's camp. The topography appeared in reverse. Instead of looking across the desert at the canyonlands, she was looking down at them.

The hot, dry air of the desert floor reached up the flank of the Agustinas and the cool, grass-carpeted ponderosa forests were replaced by old-growth juniper and piñon stands. Ground-hugging prickly pear and blooming yucca cactus replaced the wildflowers that were prolific a thousand feet up the mountain. Charlotte had pressed the stems and flowers of half a dozen plants into the notebook Thea had bought for her at Woolworth's. She would identify them when she could compare the plants to Conchata's specimen book back at the ranch. Barty knew the names of several of the plants but suggested she make notes about their exact location.

"You think you'll remember when and where you found those," he told her. "But you won't. Conchata used to say that a good *curandera* has to have the instincts of an Apache grandmother and the organization of a lab scientist."

"Just like a good fossil hunter," Charlotte said. "Grandpa used to say the marriage of science and technique with intuition and instinct makes a fertile union in the field."

By midafternoon the desert country was brutally hot. They had stopped for lunch in a cool thicket of junipers two hours ago and were now pushing on through the heat to a spring for their next break. Barty said they'd reach the fossil quarry and the old Harvard camp by supper.

Barty and Dolly, with Mandy, head slung low, veered off the sand flats and down to a wide arroyo. Jed, Britches and Molly followed. Charlotte and Noches did the same, sliding down a soft trail made by coyotes and deer.

"Just another few bends in this arroyo, and we'll stop." Barty pointed ahead at a wall of cliffs. "See there, the green tops of trees."

Seven cottonwood trees grew in a white sand basin where two arroyos merged into one. The ground was grassy, but there was no pool of water.

"The Spring of the Seven Trees." Barty frowned as he surveyed the dry white sand surrounding the trees. "Looks like the water is no longer reaching the surface."

"Did it used to have a pool?" Charlotte couldn't imagine that much water emerging from this arid ground.

"I saw it myself, even drank from it a time or two." Barty dismounted and led Dolly and Molly into the cottonwoods. "The summer your mother was here this place was a boneyard. The government shot down a dozen mustangs beside this spring. Easy pickings. The shooters waited behind those hills until the herd came in for water."

Barty glanced over Dolly's back at Charlotte still sitting in the saddle on Noches. "Alicia came here to draw. Spent whole days under these trees dangling her feet in the water. She loved the bone horses like they were alive. It was Alicia who named this the Spring of the Seven Trees."

Charlotte swung her leg over the saddle and dismounted. She looped Noches's reins over a low branch of one of the trees and thought how her family's Map of the World included the most beautiful places on earth.

With their backs against the cottonwood trunks Charlotte and Jed sipped water from canteens and munched on nuts. Barty stretched out on the fine white sand with his hat over his face.

"Uncle," Jed said, ignoring his uncle's obvious desire to nap, "what will become of the pinto?"

"Mmm," Barty grunted, "the pinto will live out her days with the family she never had."

"She has a good chance of surviving up there? With the mustangs?"

"As good a chance as any of 'em." Barty adjusted his hat and rested his bent arm on the sand over his head. "They'll die of natural causes, of course. But if men don't find 'em, that herd of mustangs will thrive forever."

"I won't tell anyone," Charlotte blurted out. Jed nodded in agreement. His face was so tanned now that the whites of his eyes and teeth had a bleached brightness.

"The way I remember it," Jed said, removing his sunglasses and looking at Charlotte, "I saw those horses in a dream."

Barty shifted his weight in the sand and exhaled a long sigh. Sixty seconds later, he began to snore. Charlotte looked at Jed propped on his elbow, as native to this time and place as stone and cactus.

"What?" Jed smiled at Charlotte.

"*Nada.*" Charlotte removed Jed's hat, pressed him back against the trunk of the cottonwood, and kissed him. He tasted like summer, like sage, like lips parched and fire-roasted by the July sun. Kissing Jed was kissing a love rooted to the earth beneath them, between them, a love that had waited here, dormant, for decades. A love between lovers, a love between uncles and nephews, between fathers and sons, grandfathers and granddaughters, mothers and daughters. Love endless and timeless, love lost, forgotten, and found again. Love.

{55}

The horses crested a ridgeline and Charlotte fixed her eyes on the polished wall of gold-and-red-banded cliffs that marked the fossil quarry.

"Two miles to go," Barty said.

Charlotte had never been so physically tired, not even the night she walked with the burros into the Durhams' from her stranded car. The desert had cooled considerably over the past hour because of immense clouds that had built high into the sky over the Agustinas. The thunderstorm that had begun as a faraway rumble was now on their heels, and the horses had become agitated as the power of the approaching storm intensified. The riders pushed to reach the site of Grandpa's field camp before the rain began.

"Let's set up camp pronto," Barty said as he dismounted Dolly. "We want to have the tarps up and find dry wood before this rain cuts loose!"

The rain came across the canyons in a dark curtain hung from the base of a mammoth black thundercloud that moved west to east. As the rain reached each butte and engulfed each mesa and canyon, the veil swallowed the landscape. Charlotte watched the storm's progress from a knob of rock at the edge of camp. She had never seen rain arrive with such precision, with such a definable line between wet and dry.

Jed and Barty anchored one of the large canvas tarps to three junipers and then to stakes driven deep into the ground, making a lean-to that protected the gear from the wind and rain coming from the southwest. The horses were hobbled in a grove of low trees on a small plateau below the camp. Barty wanted the animals to wait out the storm in a protected place.

"I've lost more than one horse standing out in the open during a thunderstorm," he told Charlotte. "They don't know to lie down flat on the ground. They just become lightning rods."

The sky was black. Each crack of thunder was instantly followed by lightning that splintered from the clouds and stabbed at the ground with terrifying intensity. Charlotte wore her slicker over her jacket and stood under the tarp between the boys and watched the deluge. Visibility was less than a mile in any direction and wind came in gusts that swept sheets of rain into the lean-to. Jed and Charlotte moved to the rear of the shelter, but Barty remained near the opening where the rain ran off his Stetson and dripped down his shoulders. The storm was directly over them and rain pounded the tarp until it sagged under the weight. The surface of the ground beyond the shelter and the firepit began to move as the sand became a red current of mud. And then it was over.

The storm moved swiftly to the northeast. In the western sky slivers of sun broke between the clouds and pierced the canyonlands. In the east, a double rainbow arched from the cliffs along the Lágrimas River to the high *llanos* on the far side of Agua Dulce.

"It's so beautiful!" Charlotte said. Jed squeezed her around the waist, then released her and walked to the open end of the shelter.

"Listen." Barty held up his hand. "Hear that? The arroyos are running."

A low roar accompanied by thumps and clunks that resembled bowling balls striking into one another reverberated from all sides of the camp. Barty made his way across the slick, muddy ground to the western side of camp. Charlotte and Jed followed. From a rock perch they watched previously dry arroyos become gushing, foaming red streams. As the sun returned to the western desert, Charlotte could see the reflection of a dozen little rivers flowing across the country they had ridden just a few hours ago.

The sun's last light grazed the wet desert and then vanished into the Agustinas. The evening air was cool and crisp. Clouds lingered to the northeast, caught the sun, and became spectacular mountains of pink and purple. The wet desert took on a deeper color palette, and the piñon and junipers, sage bushes and cactus seemed greener and fatter with the moisture.

The campfire was especially appreciated after the storm. Charlotte's jeans were wet, but her torso was dry under the slicker. Still, there was a damp chill tonight that penetrated clothing. While Jed went to check on the horses, Barty and Charlotte pulled out tarps to put over their sleeping bags.

Jed and Charlotte sat near the fire. Barty sat back and looked up at the sky. Stars twinkled in and out of the clouds that came and went in fleeting strands. The horses made muffled sounds from the piñon grove, and the arroyos gurgled with the last of the storm runoff. Jed stood and said he had to see a man about a horse, and disappeared into the desert.

"Did you want more tea?" Barty held up the kettle of hot water.

"No, I'm fine." Charlotte threw a small twig into the fire. "Barty?"

"Hmm." Barty placed the kettle on the sand near his boot and looked across the low flames at her. He looked so kind and benign in the firelight she thought she was the greatest fool to have ever been afraid of him.

"Did you always suspect Farley?"

"I did."

Charlotte nodded. Of course he had suspected Farley. "I've never felt such rage as what I felt toward Farley out at the High Lonesome. Never. I wanted to kill him. When I realized he had hurt the pinto, and had stalked my mother and was somehow responsible for her death, this ugly, dark rage took over my whole body. Every thought, feeling, all of me was just gritty hard hate!"

Charlotte choked on a sob. Barty reached around the side of the fire and grasped her forearm with strong, warm fingers. "I know that rage. It's about survival. You have a right to it, a right to survive. But don't let it run you, Charlotte. Rage ran me for decades and I didn't even know it. Now I'm becoming an old man. And old men who are still in a rage about something are just old fools."

"You're not an old man. And you're nobody's fool."

Barty squeezed Charlotte's arm again before pulling his hand back onto his knee. "I was a fool for your mother. Still am. And I can't say I ever minded that at all."

Swift but harmless bursts of lightning flashed in the sky over the Agustinas. Jed returned from the desert blackness and sat down beside Charlotte. She felt fatigued in a satisfying, peaceful way. Every muscle and bone in her body was ready to sleep.

"We'll never really understand everything that happened to her, will we?" Charlotte looked up from the fire and into Barty's eyes.

"No, I suppose not."

She looked back into the fire. He was watching her, but she didn't mind anymore.

"The place where I found your mother's body is a ten-minute walk from here," Barty said quietly. "I can take you there in the morning."

Sunrise was fragrant with a musky, moist scent. Charlotte was up and out of the sleeping bag and into her clothes and boots before Jed and Barty even stirred. She wanted to build the breakfast fire and set the kettle to boil before the boys opened their eyes.

After relieving herself behind a wide juniper, Charlotte walked the long way back across the quarry to camp. The sun lit the top peaks of the mountains and swept down the eastern sides of the buttes and spires of the canyonlands.

"Good morning." Jed blew on the kindling in the firepit, making the first red flames jump into the air. "Barty went to check on the horses."

"I think I'll go find him," Charlotte said.

Jed nodded. "Breakfast'll be ready when you return."

Charlotte followed Barty's boot prints in the wet sand. They wound through the trees, then out to the open desert. She found Barty with his back to the sun watching her approach.

"Jed said you'd gone after the horses." She gestured back at the ground they had just crossed.

"The horses are over there." Barty turned his head toward the north.

Charlotte stood beside Barty and looked out at the five horses leisurely pulling at tall grass in the small draw below them.

"This is where your mother's car was parked," Barty said, turning to his right. "Beside that juniper. She had the Volkswagen's nose pushed under the branches in the shade."

Charlotte walked over to the juniper and stared at the ground.

"Dr. Al used to park the two Willys Jeeps right up against that tree. It's a challenge to keep a vehicle shaded out here in July."

Charlotte remembered how Grandpa couldn't pass a Jeep, not that they saw many in Cambridge, without pointing it out and reminiscing about the Willys they used to drive around the Lágrimas.

"The Volkswagen was not locked, and Alicia's purse and wallet were on the floor. The purse had been partially emptied, but the wallet was untouched. Her rain slicker was on the seat with her hat. She hadn't unpacked her gear. Five gallons of water, cook pans, and a box of canned foods were still in the front trunk. I've marveled all these years that she even undertook driving that car out here. She learned a lot from her father about negotiating the terrain. The rain washed away her tire tracks, but I guessed she had followed the route of the old quarry road. Alicia had a fabulous sense of direction."

"I remember reading about these details in the sheriff's report," Charlotte said. "But they had no context. No meaning in my world."

"The sheriff's report doesn't list the things that were missing," Barty said. "Those things that anyone who knew Alicia at all knew she would've brought. Her field bag. Her notebooks. Her drawing pencils."

"I never saw those things at home," Charlotte said. "A lot of years had passed since the summer she drew bones and horses. She never drew at all that I remember."

Barty stared at Charlotte, incredulous. "She had such a gift. How could she let go of such a gift?"

Charlotte looked away from Barty's sad face. "I don't know."

"I'm sorry. That's not a question for you to have to answer." Barty turned to the north. "We can walk to where I found her body."

They walked up and down the moist sand hills. The sun warmed the damp earth and for the first time in her three weeks in New Mexico, Charlotte's skin slicked with sweat. The desert air was actually humid.

"We'll have thunderclouds by noon," Barty said eyeing the horizon. "This is how the monsoons begin: one good rain soaks the ground, evaporates the next morning, forms clouds by early afternoon, and it rains again. In a good year, it can go on for weeks."

They headed northwest across a plateau where last night's storm had left shallow pools of water. The red desert ended at the foot of a shelf of gold cliffs that extended for a mile in either direction. At the base of the cliffs were giant slabs of rock that had broken into angular chunks. Some one hundred and fifty feet above the desert floor were similar rock blocks still attached to the cliffs.

Barty climbed up onto the stone slabs. He reached back and pulled Charlotte up on top of the boulder field. Her eyes moved across the giant rocks. She knew before Barty told her where Alicia had fallen.

"You built a stone memorial for her."

"I did." Barty seemed embarrassed. "It seemed the thing to do."

Charlotte climbed across the fractured rocks and knelt down beside the stack of ten or twelve stones. "I'm so glad you did this."

"Alicia was here." Barty pointed to a crevasse between two stone slabs. "Her body was between these two rocks. Only her hand was on the surface."

Charlotte stood above the slender opening between two yellow boulders. The space that had caught her mother, killed her, the place that became her final resting place was no more than three feet wide and four feet deep. Charlotte knelt down on one knee, pressing her palm and fingers against the interior side of one of the giant stones. It was still cool and moist from last night's rain. She looked straight up at the wall of stone. Ravens soared out over the rim and circled slowly high in the sky. The upper lip of the cliff was not visible because a ledge of gold sandstone jutted out from the wall. The edge of the cliff had been eroded into a smooth channel where rainwater plummeted from the precipice down onto the desert. Last night's storm had left numerous pools of water glistening in the bowls and pockets carved into the rock shelf near Alicia's memorial.

"But how did she get up there? And why would she *be* up there?" Charlotte stood and faced Barty. "How do you know she didn't just stumble while walking on these boulders, fall down in between these rocks and break a leg or—"

Charlotte's heart was stampeding around her chest. The formerly vague pictures of her mother's death on the desert in a rainstorm now included the repugnant and horrifying Farley hell-bent on killing her, included his raspy voice calling her an Apache-loving witch whore. Her mother's last moments here were taking on flesh and blood. Mostly blood.

"Remember it was pouring rain," Barty said stepping closer to Charlotte. "And the coroner's report concluded that the number of broken bones in Alicia's body could be caused only by a long fall."

"Of course." Charlotte knew the coroner's conclusion. She was just attempting, once again, to rewrite her mother's last moments, trying to design a storyline in which her mother didn't actually suffer a lonely, painful and terrifying death. Charlotte looked up at the ledge again. "Farley went up there?"

"There's an old trail along that cliff used long ago by the Apaches. I showed that trail to Alicia in 1959." Barty directed Charlotte to follow him along the base of the cliff wall. "Around this corner, see the slot canyon? Using the walls for hand and foot grips, you can climb to the top of the cliff. But before you reach the top, the path turns and uses that ledge. See where the stone changes from pink to gold? It's a very narrow slice of land to try and step across. It was raining and dark when Alicia tried to cross."

Looking over his shoulder at Charlotte, Barty pointed again at that slot used to ascend the steep cliff. "Farley has a bum foot and wouldn't climb this, even in dry weather. Alicia knew she could get away from him up here. She just didn't realize how slick that stone had become in the rain."

Charlotte walked back to the stone memorial. "I have this grey stone back in my saddlebag. . . ."

She sat down, set her chin on her knees, and sobbed—great gulping sobs from deep in her belly. Barty sat down and wrapped his arm around her shoulders. When Charlotte's belly emptied, she wiped her face and looked out at the canyonlands bright with morning. Barty squeezed her shoulder and removed his arm.

"I still have so many questions to ask her," Charlotte said. "Even knowing more about what happened, I still have questions."

"I have something of yours." Barty dug his hand into the right front pocket of his Levi's. "This belongs to you."

The Swiss field watch with the leather band lay in Barty's open hand.

"Your mother was wearing this when I found her." Barty placed the watch into Charlotte's palm. "It was left at the sheriff's office. I believe the watch was your grandfather's."

The Dos Rios sheriff had told Grandpa how the rider had located Alicia's body because the sun had glanced off the face of her wrist watch. The rider was Barty. The watch was Grandpa's. He had given it to his daughter, Alicia, before she left for her camping trip in their beloved New Mexico.

Barty tapped the watch in Charlotte's hand. "Dr. Al always wore this field watch."

"He did." Charlotte stood up. Tears stung her eyes as she struggled to fasten the watch's brown strap around her wrist. "Grandpa gave me this watch in a dream I had when I fell asleep by the stream in the box canyon."

Charlotte wiped her sticky cheeks with her shirt-sleeve, and climbed back down the boulders to the desert. In the next half hour she carried twenty-two stones from the desert up across the rocky ledge to her mother's memorial. Barty offered to help, but Charlotte told him she had to do this alone.

"Why twenty-two?" Barty asked when she was done stacking the stones.

"One for every year I have not come." Charlotte straightened up. "For every year I doubted what my grandfather told me."

"What did he tell you?"

"That my mother did not come to New Mexico to die."

A pair of ravens soared out over the cliffs. Their flight was a dance of lovers, of partners, of old souls that never tire of the simple joys found in the morning sky.

"Ravens." Charlotte gestured at the pair overhead. "Always ravens. Why ravens?"

"I don't know." Barty watched the pair, too. "My father was a good Christian. And my mother became a Christian. But that didn't change the form of the resident guardian angels, I guess, watching over the Lágrimas."

Charlotte leaned into Barty and hugged him. "Emily Dickinson said that hope is the thing with feathers that perches in the soul," she said, as they both shaded their eyes and followed the ravens' flight over the red hills into the sun. "I think hope is the thing with feathers that flies just ahead and shows our souls where we're going."

{56}

Dennis met the riders at the High Lonesome barn and helped them unpack the equipment and unsaddle, water and feed the horses. Charlotte
was bone tired, as were Jed and Barty. They had ridden the last few miles in
silence, the horses walking with heavy feet and lowered heads. When they
rode past the windmill and water tank, Charlotte glanced back at the Agustinas. Sundown. Early evening would be cool on that high meadow on the
far side of the mountains. Barty assured Charlotte that the pinto was in good
company now, was part of a family of horses that would most likely never encounter humans. The fears in the pinto's memory would slowly dissolve into
an uneventful life of days spent in a world inhabited only by horses.

Jed and Charlotte carried saddles into the barn. When most of the gear
was put away or hung out to dry, Charlotte and Jed walked out to Dennis's
truck. Although Jed and Charlotte did not say so in words, they both needed
a night alone.

"Charlotte." Jed opened his palm as he extended his hand to her. "You
left this stone in your saddle bag."

"Oh, gosh!" Charlotte took the smooth silver-grey stone and turned it
over in her hand. "I really meant to leave it out there."

"It's a good stone," Jed said. "Put it somewhere special." Jed kissed Charlotte tenderly and stepped away. "I'll see you tomorrow."

It was dark when Charlotte and Dennis drove away from the High Lonesome. Dennis told her that Arthur had spent yesterday afternoon at the library reading to a room full of children.

"How did the test go for Arthur?" Charlotte asked. "Did he say anything
about it?"

"He came into the soda fountain this afternoon and said, 'Dennis, I don't
know if I passed or failed, but I took that test and finished it!'" Dennis smiled

across the dark cab at Charlotte. "He was just so damned proud to have gotten through it!"

Charlotte smiled. "Aren't we all."

They drove past Barty's house and the service station. Dennis honked as they pulled onto the county road. Barty waved from inside the garage. The flying horse was lit. Dennis leaned forward and looked up at the red horse. "I suppose it's for Thea."

"For all the departed mothers," Charlotte heard herself say.

It was a little past nine o'clock. Main Street on a Sunday night was deserted. Charlotte hung her head out the truck window, letting the wind ruffle her tangled curls. The warm night air smelled like rain, although the clouds remained near the mountains. Earl Turnball sat on the rocking chair under the porch light of Mabel's boardinghouse. Charlotte lifted her hand and waved, but Earl was lost in his own thoughts and did not see them pass. Dennis stopped at the traffic light in front of the hardware store. There was not another vehicle coming or going from any direction.

"I need to get the neon lady from Dos Rios to come out and fix the 's' on the Soda Fountain sign." Dennis pointed over the steering wheel at the drugstore window across the street. "I forget it has that flickering tail because I never see it at night!"

Bernadette's sedan was parked near the barn. The burros stood along the corral fence, the single bulb over the door lighting the tips of their ears. Charlotte walked along the corral with her palm open to their soft muzzled greetings. Little Bit sat on the porch and vigorously wagged his tail as she and Dennis approached the house.

"Hey, Bit," Charlotte bent down to pet his tiny head. "Are you doing okay?"

Inside the kitchen Bernadette and Francis were sitting at the table having a cup of tea. Dennis went down the hall to use the bathroom before he headed back into Agua Dulce.

"Welcome home!" Bernadette stood and wrapped her arms around Charlotte. "I know you have a story to tell! But you must be exhausted. I've brewed some peppermint tea."

"It's good to have you back," Francis said. He looked very fatigued, but he stood up and hugged Charlotte. "You have seen some grand country."

Bernadette handed Charlotte one of the Blue Willow teacups steaming with the fragrant tea. Charlotte leaned against the counter by the sink and sipped the warm brew.

"Barty called already," Bernadette said. "He told us about what you found in the mountains."

"My God!" Dennis stood in the kitchen doorway holding a long piece of worn wood. "Where did you find this?!"

Dennis turned the plank toward Charlotte. On it was inscribed *No Fossils, No Jam.*

"This was your grandfather's."

Dennis looked at Bernadette. "How did you get this?"

"One of the sheriff's deputies went out to Farley's old trailer by the land-fill yesterday," Bernadette said. She looked at Francis.

Francis placed his hand lightly on Charlotte's shoulder. "Gus went with the deputy out to Farley's. They found some things that belonged to your family. Personal things. I've left them in your room."

Charlotte stared into the brew held in the lovely old teacup. The handle was chipped and the blue vine on the left side was faded. This was the same cup Thea had handed to Charlotte the night she walked in off the desert with the burros.

"Okay." Charlotte set the teacup on the counter and walked out of the kitchen and down the unlit hall to her room. The lamp on the bureau lit her face in the mirror. The image startled her: a woman with tanned skin and wildly curly hair dressed in a trail-weary shirt and grubby jeans. She liked this woman.

There was a familiar container on the bedside table. The label was chipped and faded but otherwise it was exactly like the Webb coffee can that had carried Thea's ashes up to the mountains. Charlotte sat down on the bed with the can on her lap and removed the lid. Inside was a tightly rolled notebook. She pulled it out and gently pressed the notebook flat on her lap. On the blue cover in her mother's handwriting was *Summer 1959*. Charlotte opened to the first page: *Notes and Drawings, Harvard Field Camp, Agua Dulce, New Mexico 1959.* Below this in a rounder script and a different ink was, *The Bone Horses: A Pictorial Memoir of Mustangs, Dinosaurs and Star-Crossed Lovers,* by *Alicia Rose.*

The pages of the notebook were yellowed and gritty with sand and age. The first twenty pages were Alicia's sketches and drawings of the fossil quarry—of Grandpa and his students working under the shade tarps on the sandy ledge where they excavated the Coelophysis bones. Alicia's expert hand provided detailed depictions of the fossils as they emerged from the hillside, with labeled illustrations of the size and extent of the splints and plaster jackets built around and under the skeletons. The bones were thus safely moved out of the quarry in their plaster blocks. Alicia had several sketches of Dennis on his tractor moving fossil blocks across the sandland to the flatbed trailer on the highway.

Alicia's drawings of the Coelophysis dinosaur in what would have been its home territory two hundred and thirty million years ago—not the Colorado Plateau of sand and stone, but a tropical swampland—were as skillful as the murals Charlotte had seen at the Harvard Museum in Cambridge or at the Museum of Natural History in New York. Grandma Ruth was right: Alicia could have been a fine restoration artist. With just bare bones to guide her, Alicia's hand, eye and imagination blended science and art together. Her skillful images provided accurate, lively renderings of the Coelophysis and the world they lived in.

In the notebook Alicia also drew the field school's summer campsite, their tents and canvas chairs, plank lab tables, kitchen tree, clothesline, firepit, even the two Willys Jeeps Grandpa loved. One drawing placed the field camp in the greater landscape of the canyonlands, the same wide and wonderful country Charlotte had just crossed on horseback. The last drawing of the field camp was a sketch of six smiling students, each holding a bleached cow bone. Over their heads in the juniper that shaded the camp kitchen was the exact same sign Dennis held up in the Durham kitchen: *No Fossils, No Jam.*

On July thirteenth, 1959 the pages of the notebook departed the Harvard field camp and the Coelophysis quarry and leapt into the story of the bone horses of the Lágrimas. The next twenty or more pages of pencil drawings were extraordinary, more sophisticated in detail and shading than the previous illustrations, filling the notebook pages top to bottom, side to side. Alicia must have spent hours on these perfectly rendered drawings of individual horse skeletons.

The skeletons were labeled bone by bone, and the sketches provided the precise configuration of each horse's death-pose—some with legs folded under their spines, others with necks thrown back and arching over shoulder blades, skulls placed at impossible angles at the end of broken vertebrae. For some of the skeletons, Alicia had recreated the three-dimensional bodies of the horses, brought them back to life with muscles and fur, eyes, ears, manes and tails, color. She had marked the location of each skeleton on a field grid like those Grandpa used for the fossils; several were marked on small hand-drawn maps. And she had named each of the horses.

The drawings, the story, the magnitude of the slaughter took Charlotte's breath away. The story of the bone horses needed no supplemental words, no additional narrative.

She looked up from the notebook and listened to the sounds of the house. Bernadette washed teacups in the kitchen sink and Dennis talked softly to Francis. Charlotte looked back down at the book opened across her knees. She flipped through the last section of drawings: these were not bones and skeletons. These drawings were of lovers, of lusty young bodies entwined in all-too-familiar positions. On sand along the river, under the *bosque* cotton-woods on fire with sunset. This story belonged to Alicia and Bartholomew, not to Charlotte.

Inside the back cover she found several loose items. One was a slip of yellow lined paper, folded in half. The other was an envelope addressed to Alicia Rose Lambert of Briarcliff, New York from Albert Rose of Cambridge, Massachusetts. It was postmarked April fifteenth, 1976. Charlotte turned the envelope over and over in her hands, then removed the letter from the envelope and unfolded the ivory stationery. Grandpa usually typed his correspondence, but this letter was written in his own hand:

"My very dearest Alicia: Because you have asked, and because you have always deserved to know, I am going to tell you about your son, Benjamin, and the family that adopted him. . . ."

{57}

Except for the fiery red blaze cast by the horse flying over the gasoline pumps, the B & B service station was dark. Easing the Hudson down the sandy corridor between the rear of the garage and the shed, Charlotte parked beside Barty's pickup truck. His house was dark. It was just after eleven. He had probably fallen asleep an hour ago.

Charlotte took a quick breath, picked up the coffee can, and left the truck. As she approached the front door, a light went on inside the house. The front door swung open and Barty stood in the doorway in jeans and a denim shirt, his hair wet from a shower.

"Charlotte? Is something the matter?"

Charlotte stepped onto the flagstone front step and held up the red and black can. "Gus found this." Charlotte was shivering, although she was not cold. "Gus Treadle found this at Farley's."

"Come in." Barty stepped aside. Charlotte walked past him and through the dark living room to the lit kitchen. She set the coffee can on the dinette table, sat down, and popped the lid off. Barty dropped into the chair next to her.

"It's my mother's notebook." Charlotte pulled out the rolled notebook and looked at Barty. His face was completely blank.

"Oh my God," he said slowly, flatly. "The notebook from 1959."

Barty took the notebook from Charlotte, flattened it on the table, but did not open it. "Have you looked through this?"

"I have. Most of it." Charlotte reached for the notebook, opened it to the back, and pulled out the folded yellow note and the letter from Grandpa. "This note is from my mother—it's to the Durhams and you. It must be the note she left at the hardware store, remember? The one Earl said she left under the register, but no one ever found."

Barty took the folded yellow note. Charlotte grabbed his arm. "Wait. This letter—I think you should read this first."

Charlotte placed the envelope into his hand. He read the address and studied the return address before turning the envelope over and pulling out Grandpa's letter. Before he unfolded it, he looked at Charlotte for some kind of explanation.

"Just read." Charlotte stood up and walked over to the open door. The moon was beginning its climb into the sky, smaller than last night, but still bright and brilliant.

Barty gasped. And gasped again. When he finished reading the letter he set it down and smoothed it on the table with his hands.

"Benjamin." Barty looked up and stared blankly across the kitchen. "She had a baby named Benjamin."

"Yes! My mother had a baby in May of 1960." Charlotte walked over to Barty at the table. "A baby she named Benjamin."

"My God." Barty stood up, clutching the letter.

"They named him Benjamin because that's what my mother asked for before the adoption was finalized—that her son, and *your* son, be named *Benjamin.*"

Tears rolled like marbles down Barty's creased and weathered face. Charlotte wrapped her arms around his broad torso and cried with him.

٭٭٭٭٭٭٭٭٭٭٭٭

Barty and Charlotte dragged chairs out of the station office, opened two bottles of root beer, and sat in the red glow of the flying red horse listening to crickets. One lone car passed on the county road, but the world of the Lágrimas fell silent as midnight turned today into yesterday and tomorrow into now.

"She never contacted him." Charlotte broke the silence. "She was going to tell you first."

"It seems like that was her intention, from what your grandfather wrote." Barty still held the letter in his hands. Charlotte figured he had read it ten times in the past hour.

"I understand why she wanted to tell you first," Charlotte said. "But I don't understand why Grandpa didn't tell me about Benjamin after Alicia died."

"Your grandfather and this Neil Summers that arranged the adoption with the Ryan family had an agreement. Only Dr. Summers knew the identity of both families."

"I know. But in 1976 Grandpa asked Dr. Summers for Benjamin's family's name. And then Grandpa told my mother. They had already broken the agreement."

"But Alicia was the mother. And she asked. Your grandfather believed as a mother she had the right to know what had happened to her son."

"But a sister should know, too!" Charlotte stifled a sob. "And a father!"

Barty took Charlotte's forearm and leaned out of his chair so he could make eye contact. "A sister and father should have known long ago. And we can do nothing about the long ago. But tonight, from this time forward, you know you have a brother. And I know I have a son."

Charlotte wiped her eyes and nodded. "Thea knew."

"What do you mean?" Barty sat back. "No, Thea would have told me."

"You're right," Charlotte said. "Thea didn't know that she knew. Conchata tried to tell her my first morning here."

Barty looked at Charlotte. "Conchata?"

"Thea was trying to recall what she put in a thermos and gave to Grandpa the morning he and my mother left New Mexico in 1959. Thea said it was coffee brewed with canela, but Conchata said it was mariola tea. And mariola tea is—"

"—used for morning sickness." Barty stood and walked out under the flying horse. "Alicia wasn't sick with the stomach flu that last week, she was pregnant." Barty looked back at Charlotte, frowning, sad. "No wonder your grandmother was so anxious to get Alicia out of Agua Dulce. Jesus. I was such a blind fool."

"No more so than everyone else," Charlotte said. "Everyone but Grandma Rose."

Barty sat down again in the chair beside Charlotte. "Well, we're not blind anymore. Remember how Thea had that obsession with a lost child? Benjamin's the lost child Thea was trying to locate."

"And we can find him, right?"

Barty sat back and gazed up at the flying horse. "I'm thinking first thing tomorrow morning we're going to find Benjamin Ryan."

{58}

Charlotte and Bernadette tied long stalks of yarrow into bunches that would be hung and dried for use this fall in tonics and salves. *Achillea millefolium*, Bernadette called it.

"Yarrow was in Civil War medical kits. It stops the bleeding when applied to a wound. It can also lower blood pressure."

Charlotte remembered Conchata's notes about yarrow. "It makes you a little sun sensitive, right?"

Bernadette smiled. "Yes, it certainly does."

Francis sat on the porch in the rocking chair reading the paper. Although it was a Monday morning, Francis was not going to work today. He told Ralph he'd come into the store later in the week. Francis was not sleeping very well and was taking a lot of naps. Bernadette never left his side. A good nurse and a devoted daughter, she monitored his food, moods and sleep. She had taken a month's leave from Phoenix Presbyterian Hospital so she could put Thea's things in order. That really meant helping Francis to reconfigure daily life without his partner of fifty-eight years.

Barty had gone out to Jed's camp at dawn and told him the news about the notebook and the revelations held in the letter. Jed had ridden over to the Durhams and joined everyone for breakfast, and gone out to do the chores in the barn.

Charlotte, Bernadette and Francis talked about plants and herbs, about the monsoon season, about the high water level in the irrigation pond, and the alfalfa in the west pasture Dennis would harvest later this week. All good conversation for a Monday morning, but everyone was really just making small talk until Barty completed his phone calls in the kitchen.

Barty called directory assistance and found that only one Dr. Chad Ryan lived in all of Massachusetts. There was not, however, any listing for a Benjamin

Ryan. Although it was two hours later eastern time, at eight a.m. mountain time, Barty had still not dialed the Ryan's Amherst home number.

"Oh, for heaven's sake," Bernadette said suddenly. She set down her clippers and bundle of plants and walked into the kitchen. Charlotte and Francis exchanged glances. "Bartholomew!" Bernadette called inside the house. "Where are you?!"

A few minutes later Bernadette returned to the porch. "Sometimes he just needs a nudge," she said, picking up her bundle of unclipped plants. "Too much thinking can send my brother into emotional paralysis."

They could hear Barty dialing the rotary phone in the kitchen. Everyone on the porch seemed to have stopped breathing.

"Hello, is this Dr. Chad Ryan?"

Bernadette stood up, walked to the kitchen door, and pulled it closed. "We'll know everything in a few minutes."

It was another half hour before Barty emerged knowing everything. It felt like half a lifetime to Charlotte.

"He lives in Vermont." Barty stood on the porch and talked directly to Charlotte and her lapful of yarrow flowers. Charlotte had never seen Barty smile the way he was smiling now. He looked like a young man—like a young father. "Benjamin Ryan is a thirty-eight-year-old veterinarian with a wife and two children in Brattleboro, Vermont. His father, his adopted father, said that Benjamin has waited twenty years for me to call."

Benjamin's adoptive father, Chad Ryan, had been a student at Harvard in the early 1950s. Chad Ryan had never been one of Dr. Al's students—he was a doctoral candidate in biology—but he had come to know Albert Rose through his advisor, Neil Summer, a close friend of the Rose family. Chad Ryan and his wife, Betty, had been trying to have a baby for five years when they learned about Benjamin through Dr. Summer. They knew that Benjamin's mother was the teenage daughter of one of Dr. Summer's colleagues, but did not know until Barty told them that Benjamin was the grandson of Albert Rose.

Benjamin Ryan had begun asking about his birth parents when he was a teenager. He was told by the Summers' attorney that, per legal stipulations in the private adoption arrangement, unless the birth parents chose to contact Benjamin, there would be no communication.

"Chad Ryan said that Benjamin has known all his life that his father was a Native American from the southwestern United States, and that his mother was white." Barty studied his notes scribbled on a piece of scrap paper. "But that was all. It was clearly stated in the adoption agreement: the name of the birth mother was not to be divulged, and the baby was to be named Benjamin."

"Have you called Benjamin?" Bernadette asked. Francis was standing beside Barty. Jed listened at the bottom of the porch steps. Charlotte could not seem to move from her chair at the flower-bundling table.

"I have his home phone number." Barty held up the scrap paper. "But I don't want to shock him, or make him feel uncomfortable, or obligated—"

"—Oh, pooh!" Bernadette secured the twine around another bunch of yarrow, set it on the table already piled with bundles, and walked across the porch to her brother. "You've waited all your life to have a son! Give me the number, and we'll ring up this miracle!"

{59}

It was Barty's idea to hang the *No Fossils, No Jam* sign in the juniper over Jed's kitchen at the High Lonesome cow camp. The sign had enjoyed a brief residency in the Durham house propped up against the window over the sink. Then it was exhibited in the B & B office for a week where folks around the Lágrimas could come in and hear the story about Dr. Al and the fossil quarry, about how Gus Treadle and Deputy Manuel Suazo went out to Farley's and unearthed the sign and a whole branch of the Rose-Bill family tree that no one knew existed.

Every time Charlotte looked up at the *No Fossils, No Jam* sign she smiled. Today, she gazed upon it from a folding camp chair at the breakfast table where she was rearranging Jed's black stones into a wavering line across the white cotton tablecloth. It was a fine late-July morning. A cactus wren whistled from the trees at the trail head to the river. In the warm dawn, Charlotte and Jed had gone to the river for a swim. When they returned to camp, Barty was fixing them scrambled eggs and toast.

Thunderheads were already building over the Agustinas. Ever since their trail ride to the high country Charlotte closely followed the weather patterns over the mountains. It was like her parallel universe, the world of the wild horses. She could shift her focus and see the mustang herd grazing on some lush high meadow, running across the fields and scrambling up the rocky ledges of summerland. Mostly Charlotte saw the pinto. Charlotte's heart followed the mare as she stepped into her new life a day at a time.

Maddie also said Charlotte was stepping into her new life a day at a time. "Sounds like you found Prince freaking Charming," Maddie said when they spoke on the telephone last week. "Tell me again why you're leaving?"

"Actually I found five or six Prince Charmings," Charlotte said. "Jed, Barty, Francis, Dennis, Gus, Arthur, Earl. Oh, and George, and Bit and—"

"—and your brother! That's ten, Char."

"And I'm leaving so that I can return. And maybe even stay." Charlotte was going back to Scarsdale to put her house on the market and settle her father's estate. And as of two days ago, she had officially resigned her position at the Scarsdale Academy.

"Okay, so you put the house on the market and then go to Harvard?"

"I'm going to go through my grandfather's papers," Charlotte explained. "I want to find out if there is an unfinished manuscript about the Coelophysis quarry. If there is, I'm going to see what it would take to finish and publish it."

"Charlotte, when do you meet your brother?" Maddie was the first person Charlotte called the day Barty made contact with Benjamin.

"My brother's coming next Tuesday." Charlotte could hardly believe she was saying the words. "Benjamin is coming to spend a week in Agua Dulce. He decided to come alone, although he's anxious for Barty, for everyone, to meet his wife and sons."

"Char, I am so happy for you."

"I think sometimes that I owe it all to you, Maddie."

"Me?"

"If you hadn't prodded me to take that rental car and drive out to the Lágrimas . . ." Charlotte stopped talking while the full weight of what she was saying sinking in.

"Well, there was that raven too," Maddie said after an appreciative pause.

"Yes, where would we be without the resident angels?"

"So, listen Char, I'll help you pack up your house, okay? I'm gonna miss you like crazy at school this fall, but you bring a whole new meaning to happy endings—or do we call this a happy beginning?"

"Both."

And now next Tuesday was here. Benjamin was flying into Albuquerque this morning. He would drive up to Agua Dulce by early afternoon.

"Charlotte?" Jed emerged from the tent in a white shirt and his best faded jeans. He looked elegant and comfortable at once. "You can ride with Barty in his truck or with me in the Mustang over to the Durhams."

Barty was admiring the *No Fossil* sign. He stared into space a lot these days, lost in thought, or feeling, usually with a perplexed expression that was part surprise, part joy. He turned around and looked at Jed. "Are you sure you want to risk getting into a car this morning?"

"I'll be okay." Jed smiled at Charlotte, who was thinking the same thing as Barty. "I did just fine last Thursday when I had lunch with Jaycee and his partners in Dos Rios."

"Yeah, but that was at an outdoor café on the far edge of town," Barty said frowning. "You stayed out of traffic and still you were itching your eyes and—"

"—and I survived." Jed held up one of Thea's tincture bottles. "And Charlotte and mom made a batch of calendula tincture. I'm in good if not overbearing hands."

Jed winked at Charlotte. She knew her hands were not the overbearing ones.

"Okay, you're right. I'm being an old worrywart." Barty adjusted his Stetson. "I guess I'll get going. I've got to stop at the station and look at Andy Dominguez's Chevy. He says the choke won't turn off."

"Forget about Andy's Chevy. Go take a shower, change your clothes, shave, comb your hair, do whatever you have to do, Uncle. Your *son* arrives at the Durhams' at two o'clock."

Barty stood with his hands in the rear pockets of his jeans and looked again at the *No Fossils* sign as if he had never noticed it before. "Dr. Al had a fine sense of humor. His students loved it. You know, they were city kids, and they worked hard all summer long under the hottest sun, the worst rain. But Dr. Al made sure they had the best summer of their lives."

Barty looked across the outdoor kitchen at Charlotte, who was still arranging the black stones on the tabletop. "I wish I had known your grandfather better."

Charlotte swallowed back the lump of love and loss that seemed to be permanently lodged in her throat these days. "They say people live on in their children and grandchildren. You're the father of Albert Rose's only grandson, so I believe you will get to know Dr. Al better."

Barty bit his lip and nodded. "Hadn't thought of it that way. Well. I'll be going now. I'll see you both back at the ranch."

Jed and Charlotte did the breakfast dishes in the tub of soapy water. It was a morning to be savored and they both knew it.

"Arthur took the news about not passing the GED pretty well, I thought," Jed said. "He has you to thank for that. You gave him back his self-esteem."

"No, Arthur did that for himself, reading to all those children every day. They adore him, worship him. And he aced the math test. He'll pass the other sections later this fall."

Charlotte dried the three tin plates and stacked them on the shelf in the outdoor kitchen.

"He said he'll enroll at the community college." Jed passed rinsed cups to Charlotte. "You know Arthur might really become a teacher."

"He would be a great teacher! Children around Agua Dulce need a role model like Arthur—tattoos, shaved head, and all!"

Jed laughed as he sat down at the table. "And what of your students?"

"What do you mean?" Charlotte hung the wet dishtowel over a branch of the juniper and sat down across from Jed.

"What I mean is, what have you decided to do, Charlotte Lambert? After you sell your house, and spend time at Harvard, and go up to Vermont and visit your brother's family?" Jed wasn't wearing his hat or sunglasses and his green eyes shone like emeralds in the morning sun. "I've heard a couple of parents—Susannah, Grant Strickland's wife, Sally, others—talk about how you're going to run a home school here. But I think that was Thea's dream, not yours."

"Have you noticed how Thea's dreams have a way of becoming your dreams?" Charlotte laced her fingers through Jed's on the tabletop. "Of course I still have to take responsibility for my own dreams, and nightmares." Charlotte squeezed Jed's hand, then removed hers and picked up one of the black stones. "That folded-up note, the one in the notebook in which my mother told the Durhams that she was here for the summer, camping out at the old quarry? That little scrap of yellow paper changed everything. Everything. My mother did not come here to die. What I thought was up is down, and what I believed to be a bottomless pit of bad is this magnificent mountain of good. It goes on and on in my mind. Even about myself. Decades of wasted emotion, of blame and fear. And doubt. I've got a whole lifetime of decisions and assumptions anchored to an event that never happened. How do I sort myself out of this mess? Who am I now?

"I'll be thirty-three in September. A few weeks ago, I was feeling pretty darn old. My mother was thirty-three when her life ended. I think now about how young she was, how much more life she could have lived if Farley hadn't been obsessed with her. I'm reexamining my self-limiting pronouncements like, I'm too old to move, to change careers, to, well, *start over*. Because that is exactly what I'm doing."

Charlotte's cheeks were flushed. She glanced up at Jed. "As if you don't know all about starting over."

"And today you're going to meet your brother!"

"Oh God, Jed, I'm so nervous! What if he doesn't like me?"

Jed snorted. "He won't just like you, Charlotte, he'll love you. And like you, Benjamin has just found out that he's part of a whole story, a place, a family." Jed lifted Charlotte's chin so that her eyes met his. "Benjamin's learning about his birthright. So are you, Charlotte. Starting over in a story that was always yours. You don't have to know up from down with your family. Or with me."

Jed leaned across the table and kissed Charlotte on the nose. Charlotte wiped a tear from her cheek and flipped over one of the black stones on the table.

"Where's that gray stone you carried up into the mountains?" Jed asked. "The one you found in the box canyon stream?"

"Oh, it's on the bureau in my room. It doesn't seem to belong anywhere yet."

"Why don't you put it here?" Jed's finger tapped the white cotton surface. "Bring it out and leave it right here."

"Well, but it's grey, and not nearly as shiny as your black river stones."

"It's silver-grey. And I think your stone would bring some texture and contrast to the camp, don't you?" Jed pushed the stones before him into a pile on the table. "You know, I'm moving away from black and white. I'm liking contrast, texture. You give my life texture, Charlotte."

Charlotte smiled and pushed more of the black stones into the disorganized heap in the center of the table. "Okay, Jed Morley, I'll bring you my silver-grey."

{60}

The crockpot on the porch bubbled with a chaparral-and-yucca-root concoction Bernadette and Charlotte had mixed up yesterday morning. It
would cook on low for four more days. Then they would pour the thick,
gooey, smelly liquid into tinted storage jars and distribute them to Gus Treadle, May Culbert, and a dozen other Lágrimas geriatrics who would use the
remedio to assuage their arthritis.

Charlotte swept the porch and the steps because she could not sit still.
Since she and Jed had arrived at the Durhams she had made two pots of cowboy coffee, weeded the east half of the garden, picked nasturtiums and mint,
brushed down the burros, and taken a walk with Little Bit and George to the
irrigation reservoir.

Little Bit stood in the middle of the yard while an agitated George paced
a wide circle around him. George could not seem to grasp what was expected
of him: the ranch was busy with people waiting for someone to arrive, something to happen that had never happened before. The people seemed happy,
but there was a very tangible apprehension in the hot air of early afternoon.
Even the ravens had skipped their midday siesta in the cliffs above the reservoir and were gathered in the branches of the old cottonwood beside the
ranch house.

Done sweeping, Charlotte stood with the broom handle wedged under
her chin. She watched Barty top off the water trough in the corral, although
Jed had filled the same trough an hour ago. Barty had never looked so handsome. Hatless, he had combed his black shiny hair away from his forehead
and changed into a blue chambray shirt Bernadette said was his Sunday best,
although she couldn't remember her brother actually wearing the shirt on a
Sunday. He was also wearing a bolo tie with a triangular chunk of turquoise
that had belonged to his father. When Charlotte commented on how nice
Barty looked, he blushed like a young man.

Charlotte put the broom into the corner of the porch and sat down on the porch railing. It was one thirty-three. They had all done the math: Benjamin Ryan's plane landed at the Albuquerque airport at ten after ten this morning. Even if he walked very quickly from the plane to the luggage carousel, and was first in line at the car-rental counter, and jogged out to the parking lot to retrieve his car, Benjamin could not begin his drive north to Santa Fe much before ten-thirty. If he skipped lunch in Santa Fe and drove straight on to Dos Rios, then south to Agua Dulce, the absolute earliest that Benjamin could reach the Durham ranch was two o'clock.

"Do you want the last of the coffee?" Jed leaned out the door and held up the coffee pot.

"No, I'm fine." Charlotte's eyes moved to the rocking chair on the porch. It was not moving, of course. But something moved in Charlotte, and she stood and went into the kitchen. "Wait, Jed, I've changed my mind."

Charlotte returned to the porch with two of the old Blue Willow teacups filled with coffee. She set them on either side of the hickory table and sat back down on the porch railing. Thea said Charlotte would see Alicia again when she opened her heart to her mother. Since that evening nine days ago when Charlotte had seen her mother's notebook, read the note Alicia left in the hardware store and the letter from Grandpa, Charlotte's heart had broken apart with love for her mother. But although she looked high and low in the cliffs and mountains and skies of her waking and dreaming world, Charlotte had not seen her mother. And except for the chatter and clatter of the ravens, she hadn't heard a word from Alicia, or Thea, or Grandpa, anyone at all who might be watching from the other side.

Maybe the aroma of good strong cowboy coffee would get their attention, bring those beloved winged souls back down to earth for a sip and a sit on the porch.

All clocks, including the Swiss field watch with the new battery on Charlotte's wrist, said forty minutes after one. Jed and his mother were sharing a moment in the kitchen and Francis was reading the paper at the table. Although there had been rain, Barty was dragging the water hose from the barn out to the elm tree near the road.

Charlotte leaned into the porch post and closed her eyes.

Preguntas: Grandpa, did Grandma Ruth know that you told Alicia about Benjamin? Probably not. And Leonard? Did Leonard know about Benjamin? Charlotte decided that her father did not know. Leonard was angry with Alicia before she left for New Mexico and confused and hurt after she died, but not like a betrayed husband. Leonard was angry because he felt abandoned.

Alicia did not go to New Mexico to die. Why didn't Grandpa tell Charlotte *your mother went to New Mexico to tell the father about their son?* Grandpa could not. Or would not.

Charlotte opened her eyes and looked at the coffee cups on the hickory table. Maybe that was Grandpa's one Big Mistake? Not telling Charlotte about Benjamin may have been Dr. Albert Rose's singular major error in judgment? He could have told Charlotte about the bones waiting in the Lágrimas sand, but he did not. Maybe Grandma Ruth was in the hospital room during that last phone call? Or maybe Grandpa did not realize how close to death he was and wanted to tell Charlotte person to person about her mother, about her brother.

"It's okay, Grandpa," Charlotte said over the teacups on the table. "You couldn't see everything that was coming." Charlotte stifled a sob and grasped the arm of the rocking chair. The chair began to rock to and fro—or Charlotte began to rock the chair. She couldn't say which, but it didn't matter. All was forgiven. She knew Grandpa loved her. And Grandpa knew Charlotte loved him.

In the yard beyond the house George stopped his maniacal circling of Little Bit. The five burros stood with their heads over the top rail of the corral and eyed the mesa to the east. Charlotte stood up. Barty turned off the hose and gazed up as the ravens flew en mass from the cottonwood tree onto the tin roof of the barn. Bernadette, Francis, and Jed came out of the kitchen, and joined Charlotte on the porch. Finally, a car engine was audible on the ranch road.

George scurried across the yard to announce the arrival to the burros in the corral and the chickens in the hen house. Little Bit ambled after George, his tail wagging faster and faster. Charlotte's heart bumped up against her chest as she clumsily descended the porch stairs. When she reached the bottom step she stopped: this was Barty's moment. This moment unfurling out in the yard was Bartholomew's child being born into his life.

Barty placed the hose on the ground and walked to the car circling to park in front of the house. But then Barty stopped and faced Charlotte standing on the bottom step. He grinned and cut sideways behind the car and ran to her. When he reached her Barty slid his arm around her waist, and together they walked over to the beige sedan.

The driver's door opened and Charlotte watched the impossibly curly black-haired head of her handsome, smiling brother emerge into the New Mexican sunlight. Benjamin Ryan opened his long arms and embraced his father and his sister. For just that moment, there were no words. But as the ravens chattered on the roof of the barn above them, and George and Little Bit danced a circle around them, Charlotte remembered how much her mother loved her, because she felt that love as it swept down, a joyous song from the high country that secured itself deep into the hearts of her children.

Lesley Poling-Kempes is the award-winning author of five books about the American Southwest, including *The Harvey Girls: Women Who Opened the West; Valley of Shining Stone: The Story of Abiquiu;* and *Ghost Ranch.* Her work has won the Zia Award for Excellence, and her first novel, *Canyon of Remembering,* was a Western Writers of America Spur Award finalist. She lives in Abiquiu, New Mexico.

www.lesleypoling-kempes.net

Photograph of the author: Kent Bowser

COLOPHON

Set in Adobe Garamond, a revival created by Robert Slimbach in 1989 based on the type cut by Claude Garamond in the late 16th century. There are many "Garamonds" and some are actually the work of Jeanne Jannon from the early 17th century. With similarities as well as differences, all have a balanced refinement which has held up definitively over the years. Slimbach visited the Plantin-Moretus Museum in Antwerp, Belgium to study their collection of Garamond's metal punches and existing specimens. His interpretation retains the elegant beauty of the originals with subtle optical adjustments which further enhance a contemporary reader's pleasure.

•

Book design: JB Bryan